Advance Praise for *The Silence of Bonaventure Arrow*

"This mystical fairy tale set in a 1950s-era Louisiana rife
with religion, superstition, and tradition draws you in
from the wondrous first page. Silence has never been so
boundlessly eloquent."

— *Booklist*

"An imaginative and touching story of the surprising
ways that we heal. Rita Leganksi has created a gem in
Bonaventure, a young boy who cannot speak but whose
silence rings with truth and humanity. If I could hear a
fraction of what he does, my heart would explode with joy."
— Todd Johnson, author of *The Sweet By and By*

"I'm very grateful for opening to this book's first page.
Everything else I had to do fell away as I was transported
by this special little boy and his remarkable gift. I happily
ignored my real-life commitments for the magical,
mysterious world of this novel about secrets, forgiveness,
and healing of all kinds, and my 'real life' has been better
for it ever since."
— Katrina Kittle, author of *The Kindness of Strangers* and
The Blessings of the Animals

THE SILENCE OF BONAVENTURE ARROW

A Novel

RITA LEGANSKI

HARPER

NEW YORK • LONDON • TORONTO • SYDNEY

HARPER

P.S.™ is a trademark of HarperCollins Publishers.

HarperCollins books may be purchased for educational, business, or sales promotional use. For information please write: Special Markets Department, HarperCollins Publishers, 10 East 53rd Street, New York, NY 10022.

FIRST EDITION

Designed by Lisa Stokes

Library of Congress Cataloging-in-Publication Data is available upon request.

ISBN 978-0-06-211376-4

13 14 15 16   OV/RRD   10 9 8 7 6 5 4 3 2 1

*For Paul
and for
The Pelican*

SILENCE IS THE PERFECTEST HERALD OF JOY.

—*William Shakespeare*

PART I

Bellwether
1949–1956

GIFTED

BONAVENTURE Arrow didn't make a peep when he was born, and the doctor nearly took him for dead. But the child was only listening, placing sound inside quiet and gaining his bearings because everything had suddenly changed. The water chant was gone, as was the oxygen whisper and the comforting beat of his mother's steady heart. Where were the voices? Where were the dream tones? Where was the hum of the ever-present night? Bonaventure didn't know what to do with all that loss. The world he'd known had vanished. Been swallowed up whole by harsh light and shocking coldness and a terrible, hurtful, clamoring dissonance. He shivered when the doctor handed him over, but he gave no hearty newborn cry. Instead, Bonaventure listened hard as he could for that missing steady heart.

Bup-bup, bup-bup.

The heartbeat was lost in a lot of other sounds now, but was strong enough to bring forth a calmness that allowed him to be wide-eyed and hopeful. His mother, Dancy Arrow, thought she heard him cry from a long way off, but that was nothing more than a trick of the anesthesia.

Bonaventure stayed like that, all wide-eyed and hopeful, and continued to keep his silence. People worried about it right away. Except for Dancy. She was too taken up with what else was missing to grasp that her baby was quiet all the time.

Bonaventure settled into the hospital nursery, finding comfort in his swaddling blankets and coziness in the confines of his bassinet cocoon. He matched voices to touches, and footsteps to nurses, and formed a great fondness for the ticking of clocks. His silence gave pause to the experts who examined him; here was a curiosity beyond their expertise. (They could never have explained Bonaventure anyway because there is no scientific word for *miraculous*.) They knew nothing of Bonaventure's rarefied hearing, the acuity of which was an extraordinary grace and an unearthly symptom of the mystery behind his silence. They didn't know that through his remarkable hearing he would bring salvation to the souls of those who loved him. Nor did they know that Bonaventure's silence was full of sound that came to him in the same way it had come to the universe when space expanded to form nebulae and novas and all things celestial out of a divine and loving pulse.

Bup-bup, bup-bup.

All told, Dancy and Bonaventure spent a week in the hospital, as mothers and babies did in 1950, and then they were discharged. It had been determined that they were hale and hearty and that this silent situation was not the end of the world.

"Mrs. Arrow," the doctor said, "you have a fine healthy boy, though we are greatly concerned that he has yet to make a sound. You must pay special attention to the matter and come back to see me in six weeks or so."

To which Dancy smiled and said, "Thank you. I will," and though her heartbeat stumbled, she said no more than that. In the deepest places inside herself she was joyful and jubilant and over-the-moon about her quiet baby boy. It was just the numbness that kept her subdued, like a sleepwalker who puts one foot in front of the other on a journey she won't even remember.

Luckily, Bonaventure heard one small sound of his mother's dormant joy, and that small sound was enough.

The nursery at home on Christopher Street in Bayou Cymbaline held all the receiving blankets, diaper pins, and talcum powder anyone could want, as well as a rocking chair right next to the window. It was an altogether fitting place for twinkling stars and lullabies and dishes that ran off with spoons—there was no hint of unusual circumstance, no visible trace of tragedy.

Bonaventure managed the breathing sounds that all infants make, but they had nothing to do with larynx or vocal cords or deliberate intentions. Nevertheless, his mother was in love with those unintended noises and with everything else about him: the translucency of his eyelids and the lilting look of his brows, his tiny feet and toes, each perfect little nail, the plumpness of his sweet bottom lip. Sometimes a look passed over Bonaventure's face while he slept, as if he'd seen something spectacular in his dreams, and Dancy would try to imagine what it could possibly have been.

Six weeks went by and Bonaventure maintained his silence. Without even realizing it, Dancy gave up listening in favor of watching and did the best she could.

"Has he made any sound at all?" the doctor asked. "Any crying, any fussing?"

"Well, no crying, but he does fuss some," Dancy told him.

"How do you mean?"

"I mean if he's hungry he scrunches up his face and kicks

his legs and stretches his arms up over his head. And if he's wet or he's messed in his diaper, he squirms around until he gets cleaned up."

The doctor lowered his head and smiled the kind of smile one puts on pity. Then he gave that smile to Dancy and said, "We need to do some tests."

"Maybe he just needs a little more time. After all, he was born two weeks early."

"I'd like to do them soon, Mrs. Arrow."

Dancy nodded and held Bonaventure closer, kissing the soft spot on the top of his head.

A physical examination showed no irregularities, and auditory tests established that Bonaventure could definitely hear. In fact, it was obvious that he responded strongly to even the faintest sounds. This was believed to be connected to his muteness in some way, but no one could quite say how. It became a matter of much speculation. There were those who were certain his condition was a blessing, and those who feared it might be a curse. Dancy Arrow wondered fearfully which one it was. She was wondering about it on a Wednesday afternoon when Bonaventure was five months old. She was rocking him to sleep in the chair by the window when the suggestion of blame smoked in through the keyhole, for even a shut door won't keep blame away. Dancy continued her to and fro rocking, an unspoken apology sitting on her lips. Had she abandoned her child for the sake of her loss? Had she failed to pay attention when she held him in her womb? Was Bonaventure's absent voice her fault, too?

She sang a song to him then and put a kiss on his forehead; he lay in her arms looking up and directly into her eyes. Then he knitted his brow in a serious way, which gave him the look of a very old soul. He slowly breathed in and breathed out three times, then smiled up at her with all the strength he had.

Dancy had been wandering ever deeper into mourning, and Bonaventure had beckoned her back. And that became the moment in which Dancy Arrow knew there was something more to her little one's silence; knew it as surely as if some talkative angel had come into the room and told her so. She wasn't sure what to do with this realization, so she set it down in the back of her mind and turned her thoughts away. She moved to the daybed, lay down on her side, and wrapped her arm around her baby as if to put him back inside her.

Dancy had missed the other side of Bonaventure's silence. She did not realize he could hear her heartbeat whenever he wanted to. She was unaware he could find the sound of her blood flowing and of the inflation and deflation of her lungs no matter how far away she was. She had no idea he could hear a bluesy trumpet in a French Quarter alley, or the shuffling of tarot cards in a Bogalusa sanctum, or the echoes of footsteps made by the Acolapissa more than three hundred years before, or the fog rolling over Saint Anthony's Garden some fourteen miles away.

Bonaventure Arrow could hear conjured charms and sanctified spirits deep in the marrow of New Orleans. He could hear the movements of voodoo queens and the prayers of long dead saints. He could hear the past and the present.

But even had she known all that, Dancy would not have imagined that such hearing was only a bellwether of what was to come. She could not understand that Bonaventure's muteness was not a handicap at all but a gift—an extraordinary, inexplicable, immeasurable gift that allowed him to hear what no one else could. The silence that had taken the place of Bonaventure's voice was the very same silence in which exists the Universe of Every Single Sound, a place that reverberates with perfect peace and mirthful bliss, but also with despair's deep moaning and the whispers of secrets.

Two such secrets lived right there in the house on Christopher Street in Bayou Cymbaline, while yet another was scattered over miles and miles and miles. Those secrets were waiting for Bonaventure to hear them and find them and take them out for healing. They would have to wait seven more years, for Bonaventure Arrow needed to grow into his gift; after all, he was only a baby. And he needed to join with a kindred spirit, one Trinidad Prefontaine—a female Creole servant, childless and widowed, who lived in Pascagoula, Mississippi, at this time.

As for Dancy, Bonaventure was the child she loved with all her heart, and a tether to the time she simply thought of as Before.

THE TIME SHE SIMPLY
THOUGHT OF AS BEFORE

BONAVENTURE Arrow was conceived during an evening twilight, the fruit of a casual Catholic and a fallen-away Baptist who'd made unwed, unrepentant, consummated love on a Sunday in May of 1949, with a tenderness and a passion uncommon in two so young.

Bonaventure's parents, William Arrow and Dancy Roman, had met at a place called Papa Jambalaya's, a gumbo joint out on Atchafalaya Road, where food bit the tongue and liquor stung the eyes and some Creoles from Opelousas played hot zydeco. Cigarette smoke and drugstore cologne twirled the room on the heels of the two-step, while trills of laughter, hum, and sizzle accompanied the band. And every now and then, off to the side, came the cracking sound of a break shot in a game of crazy eight.

The first time William saw Dancy he lost his breath completely. By the time she reached his table, he barely had it back. There was nothing but the sight of her—no smell of Creole cooking, no beat of stomping feet, no sound of strummed-on washboard or of button accordion song. Never in his life had he been so enthralled. The curve of her cheekbone transfixed him; the sweep of her jaw threw him down; and the delicacy of her ear lobe ran off with his heart.

It took everything he had not to put his hand on her face, just to know for an instant what that would be like.

Dancy touched the nib of her pencil to the tip of her tongue, placed it on her order pad, and asked if he'd decided. He couldn't stop staring long enough to reply. The tip of her tongue might as well have been a lightning bolt that struck him in the chest.

She smiled while he fumbled to find his voice and recommended the chicken étouffée. He nodded and said that would be just fine.

"What's your name?" he blurted out, as she turned to walk away.

She hesitated a bit, he was a stranger after all, but he had such an innocent face. "Dancy," she replied. "What's yours?"

"William."

He ate dinner at Papa's for several nights running, taking four hours to drink three beers. He wanted to be wherever she was. Every night, they talked to each other and joked around. William tried to get up the nerve to ask if he might take her home; he'd rehearsed it at least five hundred times but couldn't get any further than asking about the special. And then on the seventh night, ignoring the oceans of blood that roared in his ears and the winds of anxiety that blew his mouth dry, William Arrow's last nerve finally came through.

Papa's was noisy as usual while he waited for a table in Dancy's section. But he was patient and determined.

"Hey there, William, need some time to decide?"

"Not tonight, Dancy. I know exactly what I want."

"Well, good. The food gets here quicker if you tell me what to bring." She winked at him and did that pencil-to-tongue thing. After a good ten seconds went by, Dancy started to say he would have to speak up some, but the look on his face made her words turn back.

Her blue eyes found his brown ones and their gazes locked in tight. There was no one and nothing else in that time and place for as long as it took life to turn inside out.

"I don't want any food," William said. "I just want to know if I can see you home tonight. That is, unless you've already got a ride."

She didn't say anything right away; she was lost in the brown of his eyes. Several seconds ticked by before she managed to tell him that she got off at eleven, and no, she didn't have a ride. She said she walked because home wasn't that far, just under a mile she supposed. She explained that she liked walking because the noise and the smoke and the grease of Papa's always stuck to her, and the night air made everything fall clean away. William didn't mention that he had a car; a ride would be over too quickly.

The pulse of the earth thrummed through the moonlight, mixing its heartbeats amongst theirs and offering them a promise. William and Dancy had never even seen each other outside of Papa's, so there was awkwardness between them at first, the sort that will put a notch in a breath. But then they fell into step as they walked side by side, and they swallowed and blinked in a comforting synchrony. Their hands never touched, not even in an accidental brushing, and that was a good thing, for real intimacy has a dawn. They stuck to the shoulder of the backcountry road until Dancy turned onto a shortcut that took them through a forest of loblolly pine. Fallen needles covered the ground, giving hush to their shoes and a spring to their step, though the bounce was more to do with them walking together along the edge of possibility.

That evening's walk turned into an every-evening ritual that allowed them time to become better acquainted, not to mention familiar with nuances of voice and speech—

William was just as fond of "in my opinion" as Dancy was of "that's how I see it, anyway." They watched for a smile to go from mouth to eyes, which usually happened in unison on both of their faces. And so they slipped into courtship. He taught her to drive his '47 Chevrolet, and she taught him to whistle real loud through his teeth.

The driving lessons were quite the experience for William. They practiced in the lumberyard parking lot when she got off work, and later graduated to some back roads that were mainly used by farmers. Then one Saturday afternoon, she just up and drove out onto the highway without even saying she was going to do it. Dancy declared she'd never felt so free and promised to teach him to whistle like a longshoreman in return for his patient instruction.

William and Dancy were opposites, different by nature yet equally smitten. She was rather fair-skinned and fine-boned, while he was quite tall, with a suntanned face he'd earned on his college rowing team. He had a sweet tooth, while she preferred salt, so when it came to agreeing on food they were beat before they started. There were, however, two things they had in common: their fathers were dead, and their mothers were fixed on religion.

Likenesses and differences set to the side, it could never be said that one had fallen harder in love than the other. Before long they had formed into a circle, and neither of them could imagine being a straight line again, caught in the loneliness of blunt, severed ends.

When he said he wanted to introduce her to his mother and would like to be introduced to hers, she told him she wasn't ready for all that and didn't care to discuss the matter further. And so they continued to live in a world that fit inside a few hours. That is until he drove her to the small house he was renting on Washington Avenue in New Orleans, where they spent an entire afternoon kissing and caressing and moving against each other. There were several such occasions after that one; occasions in which they managed to find fulfillment within the confines of risk-free touch.

And then came that Sunday in May.

William had picked Dancy up precisely at noon; they planned to spend the entire day in New Orleans. She was wearing a green-and-blue-striped sun blouse and a light green skirt, and she'd let her hair fall loose, the way he liked it best. When she hopped into the car and leaned over toward him, he knew just how to touch her chin and tip it slightly, and how to move his own head to catch the lightness of her kiss. Their first kiss of the day was always sweet like that, soft and a little bit breathy.

While William and Dancy were driving to New Orleans, Dancy's mother was still attending services over at the International Church of the Elevated Forthright Gospel, to which she'd converted—the one she'd left the Southern Baptists for. The Forthright Gospelers didn't have an actual house of worship made of bricks or stones or Louisiana lumber but met down by the river under what they called the Resurrection Tent, a structure that was really nothing more than some canvas tarpaulins from a surplus store over in Gretna. Dancy had gone to the tent service just once and refused to ever go again. The preacher was a fearmonger in her eyes, a man who could only threaten. His face became grotesque and spittle gathered in the corners of his mouth as he beseeched God Almighty in a doom-laden voice.

But the ranting didn't work on Dancy. She wasn't afraid of her mother's odious preacher, or of that preacher's gruesome God. When she came right out and said as much, her mother told her she was taking the shortest road to damnation there was. Dancy said she didn't care. After that, she proceeded to excuse herself from organized religion alto-gether, which is how she came to have Sundays free to do whatever she liked.

William parked near his house, and they took the St. Charles streetcar to Canal Street, getting off at the French Quarter. The day was beautiful, pure-aired and velvet. William took Dancy for brunch at Antoine's, and then they strolled the Vieux Carré, ducking into shops, trying on hats, and sizing up antiques for imaginary purchase, though the only thing they really bought was a box of pralines. They listened to a street band play some good jazz. They went for a ride in a surrey. They savored the stirrings that would lead to Wil-liam's bed.

When they returned to the house on Washington Avenue, some essence of pent-up passion that always haunts the Quarter returned along with them. They'd felt arousal before, but this time was different. They wound around each other with a languid tension and a wild thirst for more. They went to the edge and back, and then they took the jump. They had never felt anything like it.

Afterwards, as they lay together on William's soft sheets, coolness crept over their skin like dry dew. He tightened his arms around her and pulled her close as he could. She nes-tled her head beneath his chin and tangled her legs up with his. Neither one spoke for a while, and when they did, it was in whispers.

"I love you, Dancy."

"I love you, too."

And so William and Dancy became a destiny fulfilled, two halves of the same whole, a sun and a moon in their own private galaxy. They lay entwined and thought them-selves alone. But that is one thing they most definitely were not, for Bonaventure had begun. The cells of his body were doubling again and again, dividing in two, then four, then eight, becoming many thousands.

A few days after their incautious passion, tiny embryonic Bonaventure floated down a fallopian tube and settled in to grow. About five weeks later, his arms and legs began to bud, his heart had started to beat its own drum, and blood swirled through him at four miles an hour. Bonaventure would keep on growing and changing and changing again and soon would weigh as much as a three-page letter.

Trinidad Prefontaine detected a change in the night sky. She ascribed it to a new presence, one that needed some time to reach her, for starlight does not hurry.

One missed period and two sore breasts later Dancy said she had something to tell William as he walked her home through the loblolly pines. She didn't say anything for a pained eternity, and then she stopped walking and looked him straight in the eye. Her tears welled up and spilled over before she even said a word, and William was certain she was about to break his heart.

THIS TURN OF EVENTS

WILLIAM Everest Arrow and Danita Celine Roman stood before the justice of the peace upstairs in the courthouse on Lafayette Street in Bayou Cymbaline, on a Wednesday in July of 1949, promising to have and to hold from that day forward. He was twenty-two and she was just nineteen. Both of them were excited-nervous. The bride wore a powder blue, short-sleeved dress with eleven buttons down the front and a cinched waist that would be too tight in a week. She'd fashioned her long blond hair into a chignon that she felt was in keeping with the feather and rhinestones on the netted felt hat she had borrowed from a friend. The groom was dashing in dark gray serge and a white bespoke shirt, with twenty-four-karat gold cuff links at his wrists. The scents of Evening in Paris and Old Spice puffed into the air from the pulse points on the sides of their necks, near the veins that carried blood from their heads to their hearts.

The county clerk acted as witness, and the certificate of marriage was signed and recorded.

The young man's background was full of pedigreed ancestors, a businessman and bankers among the paternal Arrows, and landed gentry among his mother's people on the old-moneyed Molyneaux side.

Not so the young lady's. Her father's family, the Romans,

owed their living to the various crustaceans of the Louisiana delta; anything that crawled, swam, or burrowed in the
muck around Shoats Creek. Her mother's stock, the Cormiers by name, were good-natured, hard-scrabble bayou folk
who dwelled amidst the palmetto jungles of Beauregard
Parish along with lizards and spiders and dark-loving bats.
They were steeped in all things Cajun and Creole and wore
the pungent, musky taint of the swamp like a badge. Dancy's
mother had never fit in with her folk.

Though the lovers paid no mind to their dissimilar
social standing, it was evidenced by more than the quality
of their clothes and ancestral pedigrees or lack thereof. He
had recently graduated from the law school at Tulane, and
she from a third-rate beauty school above Slocum Brothers
Furniture in Bayou Cymbaline, an education she'd paid for
with waitressing wages.

But such trivial things mattered not.

There'd been no talk of conversion on either side. Their
mothers, Letice Arrow and Adelaide Roman, being a couple
of churchgoing women, were greatly affected by this turn
of events. Each had a grievance with the very sudden wedding, one regarding it as socially improper, and the other
as inconsiderate (Just imagine what people will say!). In the
aftermath of the bare-bones nuptials, unease and embarrass-
ment tried to choke those mothers to death. The shock of a
courthouse wedding attended by a premarital baby would
certainly not wear off quickly. Letice Arrow hadn't liked the
idea of a civil ceremony, but it was the fact of the baby that
distressed her more, though not for the obvious reason but
for one that would be revealed much later.

Familial relations were strained at best—a situation
helped along by private demons, not the least of which was
envy: Letice Arrow would spend more on a hat than Adelaide Roman could spend on a sofa.

THE WANDERER,
AS YET UNKNOWN

THERE was another who knew private demons, a solitary wandering man. He'd spent more than half his life moving from place to place, laboring as only an angry man can, pounding harder and cutting deeper and wielding an axe with an arm full of rage in attempts at substitute vengeance.

There'd been stints as a farmhand and a ranch hand in the twenties, when he was very young. The Wanderer had experience with animals. But then the Great Depression came and those jobs disappeared. In the thirties he found his meals and a place to lay his head in work camps run by the WPA. He helped build roads and bridges—sturdy, useful things. He was left alone. There was the occasional woman, the type who was thrilled by his looks and never cared that he didn't want her to talk, the type who didn't wonder why he wanted her to wear a pearl necklace, the type who didn't mind being a stand-in.

The Wanderer had been too young to fight in the First World War but had volunteered to fight in the Second, though by then he was older than the average soldier. He was sick of the loneliness of his angry life, and so used the war to court death. In the thick of the action, he swallowed his fear and vomited it back up. By the time the war was over, he knew a two-part suffering: one part injury and one part survivor's guilt, and that two-part misery curdled his bitterness.

He came back home in general good health, that is, except for his face. He'd lost a part of his jaw near Mézières in the Champagne-Ardenne. The medics did the best they could on his once handsome, shot-up jaw. The doctors worked on the leftovers, wiring and grafting and stitching together. What remained of his chin no longer sagged open and he could chew his food enough, but his eyelid drooped and he'd lost half his hearing. The Wanderer no longer resembled himself.

The doctors told him he was lucky. They were quite proud of their work. But no one had done a thing about the piece of his mind that had stayed in the Champagne-Ardenne with scraps of his bone and teeth and sinew. The Wanderer became permanently troubled.

The only women who would have sex with him now were the ones who did it for pay, and even some of those refused. He took to drink because he could count on Jack Daniel's to offer him cold comfort.

"She's just another damned old whore," his whiskey friend would say.

THE NEWLYWEDS

WILLIAM and Dancy honeymooned at the Hotel Monteleone on Royal Street in New Orleans. Dancy had never seen so much marble, had never even imagined that a ceiling could look like a painting, had never checked the time on a tall and hand-carved grandfather clock until she walked into the Monteleone. This was William's world.

"Have you bags, sir?"

"My wife has one," William replied, and turned to wink at Dancy.

The porter took her overnight bag and with a gracious nod escorted them to their room.

"It's nice and cool in here," Dancy said when the porter had gone, "even without the ceiling fan on."

"Air-conditioning," William said.

"Oh."

"Are you thirsty?" William asked. "There's ice water."

Dancy didn't reply. She'd picked up a card on the writing desk and saw that they could get a cup of coffee until one o'clock in the morning if they wanted to, and that the Monteleone would do their laundry.

"Dancy?"

She turned to him and with a serious look asked, "Are you sure about this, William?"

"What? The cost? Of course I'm sure," he said. "It's our honeymoon."

But that wasn't what she'd meant.

Dancy looked at him without saying a word. She was afraid she'd start to cry.

"Are you feeling okay? Do you want to lie down?" William asked.

Dancy nodded.

She didn't want to wrinkle her wedding dress—it was the only really good thing she'd brought—so she took it off and lay down in her slip.

William took off his jacket and necktie, lay down beside her, and took her in his arms.

That's when the tears came.

William thought it was a sudden bout of pregnancy emotion, and so he cradled her and smoothed her hair and told her everything would be okay. After a while, he got a cool cloth for her face.

"Feel better?" he asked.

Dancy nodded.

"Are you hungry?"

She nodded again.

"Well, then, let's get dressed again and go downstairs for some dinner."

As they were looking at the Hunt Room's menu, it struck William that Dancy seemed anxious. He thought she was worried about the money again but then noticed how her brow knit and her lips moved as she read, *pressed pompano moutardine*.

"I have to chuckle a little bit at these places," he said. "They say pressed pompano when all they really mean is jack fish."

Her face lit up when he said it—they served jack fish for

dinner in William's world! Maybe everything really would be okay.

They went to the Carousel Bar after dinner, where Dancy had some sparkling water, what with the baby and all. Dancy loved the Carousel—fancy as it was, they served gumbo and crackers.

They made love that night as a married couple and, oddly enough, were kind of shy.

Mr. and Mrs. William Arrow remained at the Monteleone for two nights. They couldn't stay any longer because William had recently secured a position at the law firm of Robillard & Broome and he had a family to think of now. They checked out and went straight to the Café Du Monde because Dancy was craving beignets. Then they returned to the rented house, where over the next few weeks, Dancy put up curtains and gave the place some color with rag rugs and plants and a picture of Paris.

Almost immediately they fell into ritual: She put on his robe like a child playing dress-up and sat on the tub's edge to watch him shave, getting so absorbed in the act that she stretched her own lip over her teeth as he scraped the razor under his nose. They learned the things that couples come to know: how he put his socks on, or how she put away the dishes, or that she slept on her side and he slept on his back, or exactly how they brushed their teeth and swished to rinse their mouths. Upon waking in the morning she had the habit of bunching her hands up and rubbing her eyes, which always made him smile. William loved everything about Dancy in the morning, but most of all he loved the way she walked when she was barefoot—soft and quiet like a puffy little cat.

Dancy cooked and cleaned and read library books, and

Monday through Friday at 5:25 in the afternoon she dabbed perfume behind her ears and waited for William to come home. He always nuzzled her neck when she met him at the door, and each settled into the warmth of the other and into a love that was stronger than it had been just hours before.

During the early weeks of her pregnancy Dancy slept a lot, which was just as well considering the nausea that could come over her like motion sickness even when she was sitting stock still and nowhere near an automobile or a spinning carnival ride. Mostly it was smells that bothered her, smells she used to love: bacon or coffee or Borax detergent. The nurse at her doctor's office said it was a good sign because being sick meant the baby was healthy, which brought some much-needed consolation but absolutely no relief.

Bonaventure could move his eyes and wrinkle his nose and pull his mouth into smiles or frowns. Nine weeks after he'd been conceived, his arms had hands, his hands had fingers, and his fingers had fingerprints unique just to him. In no time at all his eyes were brown, and sometimes he got the hiccups.

After four months of intermittent sickness, Dancy began to have more good days than bad. Eventually, she was sleeping less and spending hours and hours reading cookbooks and practicing recipes. She enjoyed the cooking, but she enjoyed eating more: pancakes or liverwurst or sausage and grits, most of it smothered in blackstrap molasses. She gained enough weight to look more pregnant than she was. Her skin glowed, her hair shone, and her eyes had taken on a sparkle. Both William and Dancy marveled at the rounding of her belly, at the perfect dark line that ran from her navel to her pelvis, and at the amazing thing that had happened to her breasts.

Both of them had an overwhelming feeling that their

baby was a boy, and they tried to imagine what he would be like. Dancy envisioned an active child with a face full of freckles and hair that was brown and very, very straight. William saw a slender fellow with an interest in bridges and a fondness for fishing. It would turn out that they both were a little bit right.

"Do you think he can hear us from inside my belly?" Dancy wondered aloud over orange juice and toast when she was about four-and-a-half months along. William assured her that he absolutely did. Having come to an agreement on their baby's ability to hear them, they sang a pretty good rendition of "Shoo-fly Pie and Apple Pan Dowdy" and laughed when they had finished.

Unborn Bonaventure listened to the song and the laughter. It thrilled him so much he did a little dance and reveled in the constancy of his mother's beating heart.

"William!" said Dancy. "I felt him! He moved!" And Dancy put William's hand right there. He felt nothing at first, and then came a flutter, and William Arrow's breath got caught in his throat when Bonaventure brushed his fingers beneath the place where his father's hand rested.

Once the pregnancy sickness stopped altogether, William and Dancy made love with the abandon of those who haven't a care in the world. He would hold her against his chest in the afterglow and brush his fingertips up and down her arm, and she would curl into him, feeling safer than she'd ever felt in her life. But there was even more to their happiness. They sang with the radio and danced in the daytime. They made lemonade and iced tea and drank it on the porch, while crickets sang in the grass. They furnished the nursery, painting it yellow and hanging a mobile over the crib. They breathed in unison through the sleeping hours, never once sensing the nearing hand of fate.

When Bonaventure heard their harmonized breathing, he would close his fingers and make a little fist, and it wasn't but a minute until he was sucking his thumb, which always brought him comfort. The memory of their singing flowed from his ears to his knees and down to his feet, where it caused him to wiggle his toes in his sleep.

THE VOICES WERE
VERY ENCOURAGING

AFTER the war, The Wanderer got a job at the Rouge, Henry Ford's most famous factory, located upstream from the convergence of the Detroit River at Zug Island. He had to clench what was left of his jaw against the rat-tat-tat of mass production that sounded so much like machine guns. His rented room in the basement of a Melvindale house felt just like a foxhole with the booming that came from the underground blasting in the salt mines located nearby. His days were filled with steel and sweat, his nights with edgy bitterness; he could not escape the smells and the dust. Sometimes his head ached as if it were caught between an anvil and a white-hot hammer. The headaches became more frequent. They grew talons that stabbed into his memory, causing wounds that oozed resentment.

And those headaches brought voices with them, and then the voices came on their own, constant and buzzing, speaking to him of all that he'd lost: his family, his roots, his young man's hopes. He'd been lonely for over twenty-five years. He felt empty, cold, and gray all the time. He mended his own clothes and took his meals in isolation; he knew no friendship or comfort. He'd never married or beheld his own child or slept with a woman all through the night.

Now the voices spoke to him of home. They reminded him of the hurt on his father's face; they echoed his mother's pleading—his parents had not known his real reason for leaving. Mostly those voices whispered to him about the one who had taken from him and broken his spirit; of late they'd been speaking of settling the score.

Reading was the only thing that could quiet those constant voices, and so the library became The Wanderer's haven. He'd always been an avid reader; his personal tastes favored the classics, and it was in that section that he rediscovered *The Count of Monte Cristo*, a book he'd read when he was young. He remembered being inspired by the better nature of the character Edmond Dantès: loving, kind, and good. This time he was inspired by the man's need for vengeance.

The voices began to steal from the book. In the predawn hours of The Wanderer's insomnia they whispered Dantès's words: *I wish to be Providence myself, for I feel that the most beautiful, noblest, most sublime thing in the world, is to recompense and punish.*

The Wanderer became the Count of Monte Cristo. He had been wronged. He had been exiled. Now he would take justice into his own hands, for God had failed to dispense it.

He didn't go to work on the last day of November in 1949. He would need money for the business he had in mind, so he went to the bank instead. He closed out his account and put the cash in an unmarked envelope in his pocket. Just after sunrise on December 1, he was at the bus station in Detroit.

He could tell the ticket seller was nervous. The Wanderer's corrupted face did that to people.

"Where to, fella?" the ticket man said.

"Cahgo," The Wanderer answered.

"Did you say Chicago?"

The Wanderer gave him a nod and a grunt and paid the man his due. There was time before departure, so The Wanderer bought a cup of coffee and sat in a back booth to drink it in his crippled-face way. He left a twenty-cent tip on the table when he got up to go. Dimes were his favorite coins. The one that had come out just after the war had Franklin Roosevelt on one side and showed only half his face. The Wanderer liked that about the dime.

He was restless on the trip, spinning within his own head. His guts churned inside him and he breathed like a jacked-up soldier relishing the thought of carnage. The Wanderer closed his eyes as he listened to the tires pass over the road, and he prayed just like a sniper.

He left the bus depot in Chicago and walked to Union Station, his collar pulled up against the wind. He consulted a schedule and approached the window. The ticket master stared, but not for long. The Wanderer supposed he'd sold a lot of tickets to mutilated men who were headed for home and a town full of sympathy.

"Where to?" the man said.

"Na Orrrn," The Wanderer managed.

"New Orleans, is it?"

Nod. Grunt.

"That'll be the Panama Limited," the ticket man said, "Southbound number five. You're just in time; train leaves at five o'clock. You'll be in New Orleans by nine-thirty tomorrow morning."

The Wanderer paid for his ticket, bought himself a *Tribune* newspaper, and waited.

The train stopped in Carbondale and then went on to Memphis, where The Wanderer got off to stretch his legs and buy himself a sweet roll at an all-night diner in the depot. He decided to keep the paper napkin because of the slogan printed on it: *Memphis—Home of the Blues*.

Fields and forests were punctuated by small towns. The Wanderer didn't even try to get comfortable on the Pullman sleeper; he just stared out the window into darkness. He refused the on-train breakfast; he was much too wound up to eat. By the time the train rolled into Jackson, Mississippi, The Wanderer could smell the past and feel it crawl over his skin. When he arrived in New Orleans, he'd been staring for 939 miles and listening to the voices all the while.

He felt in his pocket for the button he'd taken off his army uniform; it was the closest thing he had to a good luck charm. There was a book of matches in his pocket too, from his favorite tavern in Melvindale. The Wanderer liked to think he could burn something down if he wanted to.

He ended up in a hotel in the seediest part of New Orleans, where he registered under the name Edmond Dantès. Coming through the thin walls of The Wanderer's psyche, the voices were very encouraging.

He was afraid to sleep.

He got hold of some Benzedrine and washed the pills down with liquor.

He couldn't eat.

The headaches got worse.

He went on like this for days.

He bought a gun from a fidgety junkie, the one who'd sold him the uppers.

The Wanderer spent hours in the public library; he knew the librarians felt sorry for him. One in particular, plain looking and awkward, was all too happy to help. Her name was Eugenia Babbitt and she let him into storage vaults that contained back stacks of local newspapers. She let him into the closed stacks too, even though she wasn't supposed to do that.

Eugenia Babbitt had never married. She spent most of her time lost in fiction, favoring it over reality. Eugenia wanted to find the tragic and mend the flawed. The day The Wanderer walked into the library, she could see how lost and lonely he was, and Eugenia fell in love. One night at closing time, she reached for his hand and took him home with her. He only agreed to go because she wore a pearl necklace.

The Wanderer never returned to the library. He didn't want her kindness and he didn't need her anymore.

LEFT, RIGHT
CLOSER, CLOSER

WILLIAM tapped on Dancy's stomach and said, "Rise and shine, little man, Daddy has to go to work; we need money for a Christmas tree." When Bonaventure tapped back, William grinned at Dancy and said, "My son just told me to have a good day."

"We could be wrong, you know. We might have a girl."

"Nah," was William's reply. "It's my birthday, and today I'm right about everything."

"Is that a fact?" Dancy said. "I'll have to remember that on mine." She was seven months pregnant and getting fairly round. She rose up on her tiptoes to kiss William goodbye. "Don't be late," she said, as she tucked a note in his pocket and told him he could read it later.

William had taken to leaving the car for Dancy, just in case she might need it. He ignored his wife's instructions and read her note as he walked the two blocks to the St. Charles streetcar, and he couldn't help but smile. He was still smiling when he got off at Gravier and walked to his office on Magazine Street.

At five, the receptionist ducked her head in his door and said, "Good night, Mr. Arrow. Doing anything special for your birthday?"

"Something tells me Dancy has a surprise planned; it would be just like her," William answered.

"Well, y'all have fun, now."

"Thanks, Beverly Ann. Have a good weekend," William said. Ten minutes later, he turned off the lights and set off on his journey home.

Christmas decorations hung from lampposts, filled store windows, and decorated doorways. The lights brought The Wanderer clusters of headaches. He knew every inch of these certain few blocks. He'd been pacing them for nearly two weeks because he was following a certain person, waiting for a chance to return the hurt. Today was to be the day.

He walked toward William, admiring the cut of his suit and the shine on his shoes. The Wanderer thought he detected a lightness in the young man's step; probably an excess of Christmas cheer. No, it was because it was his birthday! Of course! The Wanderer had read it in the Social Register, hadn't he? People would marvel at the coincidence.

Left, right. Closer, closer.

A headache pounded spikes into The Wanderer's skull. He could hear William whistling a Christmas song. On impulse, The Wanderer moved slightly left, enough to bump William's arm with his own as they passed each other near the corner of Magazine and Gravier.

"Sorr," he apologized in his manner of speech.

"That's okay," William said. And then added, "Merry Christmas!"

What passed for a grin crossed The Wanderer's face. He wasn't really sorry.

He took six more steps before turning around so that he was behind William. It surprised The Wanderer when William turned right on Gravier instead of left toward the streetcar; it wasn't the usual pattern. But he liked the unexpected suspense and followed without missing a beat. William went into the A&P at the corner of Gravier and Tchoupitoulas. The Wanderer went in after and moved up and down the aisles, past the soup and cornstarch, the olive oil and Crisco. The shelves were low; he could keep William in sight. Eventually, The Wanderer made his way to the produce section and hovered there like a heat mirage, close enough to William to see where the younger man had nicked himself shaving.

The Wanderer felt sick from the headache.

As William stood at the checkout, The Wanderer moved toward the door. But then he turned back around. This would be the place. His movement caught William's attention. The Wanderer saw the recognition on William's face, as if he was about to say, "Hey, aren't you the guy . . . ?"

There was nothing but coldness in The Wanderer's gut.

He couldn't swallow.

His arms tightened up.

He detected the smell of apples.

He lifted his gun and fired four times.

The Wanderer knew elation as never before. At last, he'd settled the score. At last, they were even. His euphoria lived but three short seconds before horror exploded around him, blowing him far away from reality. All he could see was red. The Wanderer was sure bits of flesh and blood had splattered onto him. He became aware once again of the gun in his hand. Had he done this? Had he shot a man at close range? Someone he knew? A fellow soldier? The Wanderer could smell the foxhole. He thought he had called for a medic, but of course the word remained trapped in his mind. There had to be a medic somewhere! What was taking so long? The

Wanderer sank to his belly and tried to crawl. He would keep the kid warm until the medic arrived. If he could keep him warm, the kid might stand a chance. Oh, God! How could he have shot his own man? Then everything went black.

William escaped through his mortal wounds and stood apart from his fallen body. He didn't quite get it at first; it took a moment for him to realize he was dead. He recognized the shooter as the guy who'd bumped into him out in the street. When he took a closer look, he knew with suddenness and with certainty that he and his killer were tied to one another, that this was their link in some chain-of-life sequence. But what that link was William did not know. He couldn't look away from the commotion. He hoped they would be able to clean up his body before Dancy saw it. He didn't want her to remember him this way.

There was no point in interrogating the perpetrator. A man with half a jaw is not easily understood. It wouldn't have mattered anyway; The Wanderer no longer knew his own name or any reason for what he had done. He had stayed sunk to the floor in the A&P until the police came to take him away. He ended up in an asylum for the criminally insane, where he kept to himself, speechless and bewildered.

The voices were finally silenced.

Dancy wondered how long she could keep supper warm. She'd prepared a birthday dinner, but the candles had burned down and the filé gumbo had simmered all it could. She kept looking at the phone, wishing it would ring. At quarter past seven, two policemen came to the door and asked if she was Mrs. William Arrow.

"There's been an accident," they said, and put her in the police car, where the smell of sweat and leather and cigarette smoke set her to wretched gagging. Hysteria nipped at Dancy's neck and fear got a grip on her insides. Her teeth chattered and her throat became tight and she felt she was being strangled.

"What's happened to William?" came the words of her panic. "Where is he? Where is he? Oh, please, please tell me. Why won't you tell me? I'm begging you! Please!"

Alarm hammered its way into Dancy's womb and terrorized Bonaventure; he did not recognize the sound of shattering frenzy. His mother's screams took the form of an enraged demon that squeezed his chest and banged on his head. He sucked his thumb in full-blown panic. He pulled on his ears. He struggled to breathe.

In her bed one hundred ten miles away, Trinidad Prefontaine was awakened by chills caused by the coldness of an unknown terror.

Dancy's screams were enough to make those officers get all choked up with the sad, sad pity of it all. They took her to the hospital, where they said they were sorry to tell her . . . and then, though their lips moved, she couldn't seem to follow what they were saying. They had to repeat over and over that William had been killed while standing in line at the A&P, shot dead by a crazy man who'd gotten hold of a gun, a vagabond sort that nobody knew. There was heartbreak from the start, and now with the telling of things to the young widow that heartbreak split and multiplied, filling every inch of the room.

A merciless pounding caused a great tide within Dancy sending thundering waves to crash against her skull—a precursor of the earthquake that would rip her life open and take her into its slavering maw. The sharp edges of distress scraped her mind and her heart as she fell into the bottomless blackness of pain.

One of the policemen ran out, shouting, "Doctor! Doctor! We need a doctor right now!" But by the time one got there the newly widowed Dancy was asleep on the floor, knocked flat-out unconscious by the fist of shock. The doctor ordered her admitted, and an orderly laid her down on a bed. One floor below in the hospital morgue the remains of her husband lay still and stone cold.

William and Dancy did not breathe in unison, nor did his fingertips caress the skin of her arm. But fate did make one very kind adjustment. As they lay in the hospital, one above the other and fallen into different sleeps, some corner of the whole ragged tragedy turned back and gave them a chance to come closer. From behind closed lids each could see the other and could speak in a way that was utterly soundless. Love transcended loss long enough for them to find that the depth of feeling is best known in silence, because in the presence of such love words are never quite enough. William and Dancy faced each other across a misty divide, outside of their bodies and stripped down to their souls. Then the distance between them slowly melted away, and they reached out and touched in the softest embrace. So light were their souls that they rose up and floated out into the night amidst sparkling stars. They stayed in their floating embrace until morning, when Dancy woke up and William did not.

Dancy cried solid for six days and nights and then, in an unintentional mimicking of God, on the seventh day, she rested. She was convinced she would never be able to love that deep or cry that hard at any time ever again. Sorrow filled her completely, flowing through her veins like a second blood and making its way through the umbilical cord that attached her to her baby.

Bonaventure fell into a profoundly deep sleep. A tug came into his throat while he slept and the slightest touch visited his lips, tongue, and ears. Something stopped happening at the top of his trachea: the vocal cords inside his larynx were no longer meant to chop air into sound. It wasn't that they were paralyzed. It was simply that a farewell had taken place between those cords and their purpose. However, it is important to note that their purpose had not been removed but was altered and transferred to another of his senses. Bonaventure would now hear as no other human could.

Bonaventure Arrow had been chosen to bring peace. There was guilt to be dealt with, and poor broken hearts, and atonement gone terribly wrong. And too there were family secrets to be heard: some of them old and all of them harmful.

A PRIVILEGE ALLOWED
RESTLESS SOULS

NEW Orleans is a place of cemeteries in which dignified sepulchers stand aboveground, guardians of love and remembrance. In those cities of the dead, statues and etchings mark resting places, and a populace of angels stands in constant pose directing the departed toward heaven. Broken flowers and weeping willows pay reverent homage, while poppies bestow eternal sleep. Doves bequeath peace, Christ's bleeding heart wears a crown of thorns, and lambs mark the graves of children. Every statue and every design keeps vigil over the dead. Some say they drive evil spirits away—a task well noted in New Orleans.

It has long been known that bodies decompose rapidly inside their tombs in the heat of Louisiana summers. The locals call them bone ovens because year after year there is nothing left but skeleton, the rest of the corpse having all but baked away. Lying at peace and rid of their flesh, the newly baked bones are politely placed into an opening in the crypt's floor, down into a hollowed-out space beneath, in a macabre and gracious gesture of making room for more—a natural thing in a place like New Orleans.

Such was not the case with the Arrows. They were a well-to-do family that had long ago commissioned a mausoleum in Cimetière du Père Anastase large enough to hold twelve bodies at rest, never to be disturbed. William's remains would be placed near those of his father, Remington, who rested near his own parents and grandparents. That was the way of the Arrow family.

William attended his own funeral; it is a privilege allowed restless souls. The transcendence of the requiem mass offered to take him into the sky above, but he resisted and sat next to his coffin in the hearse on the way to the cemetery. He took note of the freshly engraved letters on the tomb—"WILLIAM EVEREST ARROW ~ BORN DECEMBER 16, 1926 ~ DIED DECEMBER 16, 1949"—and of the graceful script that flowed into the shadow of the Valley of Death spoken of so poetically in the Twenty-third Psalm.

There was, however, no psalm to describe the irony of William dying on his twenty-third birthday, or of the fatal bullet having traveled a notable distance, around corners, through tree trunks and solid red brick to lodge in the life of his pregnant young widow.

William Arrow did not rest in peace.

In the weeks following the funeral, Dancy couldn't manage much in the way of sleeping or eating. Her skin grew ashen, her hair hung limp, and her eyes became dull as gray slate. In this regard she was not unlike The Wanderer—lost in an emotional catalepsy, her consciousness made ethereal, her heart made paralyzed.

Wanting the best for her daughter-in-law and soon-to-be-born grandchild, Letice Arrow insisted that Dancy come live with her in William's childhood home. It would be hard enough to care for a newborn, she said, never mind trying to do so while mired in the throes of grief. But there was more to Letice's kind offer than that. She wanted to hold a living baby, to show God once more that she could be a good mother.

Dancy acquiesced because she didn't have the will for much else, and she didn't like being alone in the house in New Orleans, to which William would never come home.

Letice's house faced a park and was a lovely reminder of the antebellum South. Like so many others in that part of the country, it was an Italianate, with pronounced eaves atop decorated corbels and, set off with ornate wrought iron, an upper belvedere from which to view cypress trees and live oaks all draped in Spanish moss. There was a smooth-as-glass pond across the way where geese and swans floated gracefully in imitation of their brethren in New Orleans. It was the perfect place for dragonflies to skim above the surface, glimmering green and purple between the water and the sun.

The house had been built by a seafaring man who'd furnished it with the exotica of his travels. The interior was full of ebony, teak, and thick Turkish carpets. The banister of the front stair had been carved in Africa, while every hinge and hasp was made of brass and bore the likeness of a heron, etched by a Viennese craftsman who'd had the steady hand and eye to accomplish such a thing.

The desk drawers in William's old room still held his stamp collection and baseball scrapbooks, as well as a cigar box containing three Indian-head pennies, a rabbit's foot on a chain, and no less than a dozen number-two pencils, every one of them with teeth marks set in its wood.

Vestiges of William's boyhood shouts hovered somewhere near the ceilings, while memories of his trampling feet pattered over all the floors, and echoes of his singing voice inhabited the walls. Ghostly William did what he could to let those sounds find their way into Dancy's head, but things didn't work out in the way he'd intended. Those shouts and footsteps and echoes of songs could not chisel their way into Dancy's grief-stricken mind and so went to her womb instead.

Even though Bonaventure didn't always understand the sounds he was hearing, he did know how they made him feel, and the carefree noises of William's childhood made him feel much better than the constant forlorn sounds of mourning.

William had been admitted to Almost Heaven, but he found it a lonely place and so made visits to Christopher Street, where he stayed for days on end. During one of those visits, he wondered if his unborn baby could still hear him, and so he spoke a question: "Hey, little man, how's it going in there?"

Bonaventure turned in a circle when he heard that familiar voice. His movement caused a stir inside William's dead man's heart.

AS IF TO KEEP
FROM BREAKING

SORROW has a nature of its own, and of course it always does change things. In the case of Bonaventure Arrow, Sorrow moved in with his family and enjoyed the status of uninvited guest.

For all intents and purposes, Dancy and Letice were strangers who stood at the edge of reality. Dancy occupied the fringes of each day avoiding people and conversation, while her mother-in-law walked ever deeper into prayer. They dressed; they ate; they went through the motions. They held themselves stiffly as if to keep from breaking. Though they had come together to mourning's abyss, each looked into the gorge alone.

This familiar estrangement was due to a couple of characteristics the two women held in common: The first of these was the practice of keeping emotion at bay; while Dancy was new to it, her mother-in-law had long been a master. Letice was a disciplined woman, albeit quite kind, and commanded respect without saying a word. The second shared characteristic was that both of them had made a deliberate choice to lock down heartbreak. To set their sadness free would be to let William go, and neither of them could do that.

Although they grieved in company, there was one major difference in their thinking: Letice wanted to know the killer's name and where he had come from; Dancy, however, did not. Letice had a private theory, one she'd woven from the threads of a secret that had been haunting her for years. This theory laid the blame for William's death directly at her door.

Ironically, Dancy believed that she was the one at fault, and that being left to wonder was part of her punishment. Neither woman came right out and blamed God. Letice could not tolerate the thought, and Dancy felt that if there was a God—and she had started to doubt his existence—he was the monstrous one her mother worshipped, and she refused to recognize any such being.

Adelaide Roman also believed that her daughter was being punished, but she felt it was for sneaking off to have sex before marriage, bringing shame on their family like the worst kind of sinner, and making Adelaide a grandmother at the age of forty-one. Well, Dancy would have to pay for that: *Vengeance is mine; I will repay, saith the Lord.* Adelaide always cherry-picked verses from her King James Bible and applied them any which way she liked.

Letice Arrow contacted Sergeant Turcotte, the New Orleans police sergeant in charge of the investigation, to see what, if anything, he had been able to ascertain. She was told the perpetrator, referred to as John Doe, was uncommunicative.

"The doc up to the asylum thinks he doesn't even know his own name, Mrs. Arrow," were the policeman's exact words.

"Was there no wallet, nothing at all?"

"No, ma'am, I'm sorry to say. He didn't have much on him. He kept his money in an unmarked envelope and a few whatnots in his pockets, but nothing that points to who he is or why he did it. We fingerprinted him, and nothing turned up."

"Are you saying that there is no clue whatsoever?"

"We're asking around town. He was kind of an eyesore, if you know what I mean. I believe that eventually somebody will come forward, someone who noticed him, who can give us an idea of where he was staying or where he came from. In addition to the cash, I remember he had a Chicago newspaper with him dated December 1, 1949, and a paper napkin. The napkin was from a coffee shop in Memphis, so put all that together and it looks like he was a drifter. That's about all I can tell you right now, Mrs. Arrow."

"How much cash was he carrying?" Letice asked.

"A pretty good amount, over $700 I think it was."

"Do drifters usually carry that much money?"

"Maybe he was a gambling man," the sergeant said.

"Maybe? Is that the best you can do, Sergeant?"

Turcotte let a few seconds of silence come between them. "Mrs. Arrow, I am not your enemy here. We're doing the best we can."

"I don't think you are, Sergeant. I don't think you realize how important this is."

"I assure you, ma'am, I do."

Subsequent conversations took place every week. Letice was obsessed with the notion that William's life had been payment for a terrible sin she'd committed, and for tricking Remington Arrow into marrying her by letting him believe she was something she was not. She'd been living a lie, and William had paid the wage of her sins.

She didn't tell Dancy about her talks with the sergeant; the girl might wonder why she wanted so badly to know the killer's name. Letice was afraid that if she tried to explain, she would have to go back years, all the way to the passion and the potion and the innocent blood, and the prediction that *seven times seven gwine come to you.* She hadn't known what it meant at the time, but now she knew: William had been murdered in 1949, and forty-nine is the same thing as seven times seven. Letice had fallen into the trap of finding sense inside the rant of a superstitious woman. Such traps are not uncommon in a place like New Orleans, spongy as it is with tales and magic.

The funereal scent of magnolia and white lilies hung heavy in the air of the house on Christopher Street, settling on the black crepe de Chine that covered its mirrors and clinging to the women who lived within its walls. Dancy moved through the rooms of William's brief life, touching door knobs and newel posts she knew he had touched, collecting his fingerprints in the palm of her hand. Sometimes she felt that she was drowning in the very air she breathed, and just when it seemed her lungs had filled with combustible anguish and were about to burst into flame, she would feel a pulling such as that which comes to a body in water, lifting it up and taking it to the surface. She welcomed the sensation but never told anyone about it, or of how it would take her all the way to the crypt at Père Anastase, where her sweet murdered husband lay.

Dancy loved those visits. They were a surviving intimacy, the only intimacy she had left. She talked to William when she was there, told him how much she missed him and that she would love him and only him forever and ever and ever. She went to the cemetery on Christmas Eve but didn't leave her room on Christmas Day.

William didn't leave it either; he watched Dancy pace the floor or stare out the window hour after long empty hour.

. . . .

Dancy visited William's crypt on the third day of January in 1950. She was seven-and-a-half months along, and unborn Bonaventure could push pretty hard. He pressed so hard against her insides that day that she could see the outline of his tiny baby knuckles right through her clothes, and she sang "Shoo-Fly Pie and Apple Pan Dowdy" in an attempt to calm him down.

The music worked. From inside Dancy's warm, safe womb Bonaventure heard two voices singing, and his little heart beat out a raining tattoo as if to keep time with the song. He had no suspicion that anything had changed, because for him they had not; he'd always known those two voices, one soft, one deep, and had always found them soothing.

Hap Wilkens, the head groundskeeper at Père Anastase, was tending to a fallen urn at a crypt two rows behind when he saw Dancy and heard her singing. That night while playing double solitaire at the kitchen table, Hap told his wife about what he had witnessed. The two of them speculated that the poor girl had lost her mind, standing in the cemetery like that singing "Shoo-Fly Pie and Apply Pan Dowdy." And didn't she have a right to go crazy, what with her husband being killed at the A&P and all? They shook their heads and tsk-tsked, and said it truly was a pitiful situation. Purely pitiful.

Rather than diminishing with time, the pulling sensation became stronger. It would come to Dancy from nowhere, on the wings of thoughts she did not consciously have. And then a sort of relationship formed between Dancy and the pulling, as if it were her only real friend, the only one that understood. She began to wonder if she should give the sensation a name, companion that it had become. But the pulling already had a name; it was William Everest Arrow.

. . . .

Letice was at all times gracious, and Mr. and Mrs. Silvey, the live-in help, tried to show that they cared very deeply and felt terrible about the whole situation. Forrest and Martha Silvey were ideally suited to dealing with loss, having met as hospital volunteers in the First World War when both were very young. Their wartime romance had been an effort in tenderness, touched by the leavings of war that were so visible in the dead eyes of living soldiers (the memory of which came back to them whenever they looked into Dancy's). Both of them were from the South— she from Mobile and he from Baton Rouge—a trait that endowed them with a love of home and an appreciation for etiquette, both of which had greatly appealed to the Arrow family when they'd hired them back in 1926 right before William was born.

The Silveys were a childless couple, patient and kind and devoted to each other. They were a living example of the axiom that people who live together for a long time begin to look alike; Mr. and Mrs. Silvey even got taken for brother and sister by those who didn't know better. They were both rather shapeless, with stooped shoulders like melted-down candle wax. They had no waistlines to speak of, and their faces sagged from cheekbones to chins.

They hadn't always been childless; there'd been a baby once, a little girl, when they were first married all those years ago. They'd named her Caroline, and she'd died a sudden naptime death. That's when their sagging faces started, and also when their hair gave up all color and turned a bright snowy white. The loss of William deeply hurt the Silveys, for he had been precious to them, as precious as the child they'd lost.

. . . .

Bonaventure loved Mr. and Mrs. Silvey's voices; they had a way of cooling the scalding, unshed tears that boiled around his mother's heart, burning holes in its tender tissue; he could clearly hear it happen. Far in the future he would hear the same thing in the lovely cooing of a pair of doves. But for now he listened from where he lay, curled inside his mother like a flesh-and-blood rosebud preparing to bloom.

FROM WHENCE SHE'D COME

WHILE unborn Bonaventure was doing all that listening, his kindred spirit was going about her business. Trinidad Prefontaine was descended from the beautiful Consette, a mulatto girl who'd been born in Haiti, sired by a white man on a girl off a slave ship. Consette had been traded by that white man to a thieving midshipman on the cargo ship *Andanza* for a dozen cases of bumbo rum. It happened in 1820 when she was just sixteen years old. The midshipman sold her to the captain, who gave her as a gift to one Augustin Tulac, a white Creole plantation owner who lived with his lawful wife and legitimate children outside the city of New Orleans.

Consette had eyes the color of lapis lazuli, a blend of azure with glimmering turquoise that put the skies of the heavens to shame. Her skin had the feel of an orchid petal. She was structured delicately like a hummingbird, with luxuriant hair that was two shadows blacker than midnight. Consette was altogether enchanting.

Augustin Tulac kept Consette in a stately home on Esplanade Avenue in Faubourg Marigny, a neighborhood famous for *marriages de la main gauche*, "left-handed marriages" in English. Her patron was generous, and her bank account grew monthly; even her servants possessed a veneer of sophistication. But all that aside, Consette harbored a deep hatred for Tulac. On nights she lay beneath him, she lost herself in memories of the Quarter: the dancing flames and the beating drums and the half-closed eyes of the *Mambo sur point*, priestess to the *Asogwe* Eulalie Bibienne. When she thought of these things, a fever would start deep inside Consette's body, causing her to arch her back and move her hips in a pulsing, pumping rhythm.

When her loathing of Tulac grew enough, Consette paid a visit to Eulalie Bibienne, seeking her advice. On a hot steamy night, she did as the *Asogwe* bade her do and took her hatred to the Quarter, where she let the *Caplatas* do with it as they would. In two short weeks Tulac was dead, a look of terror on his frozen face. No investigation was made; a death like Tulac's was left alone at that time in New Orleans.

Consette shed herself of her home and her servants and chose a husband after Tulac's demise, a freed man named Isaac who was a sharecropper and the grandson of a slave called Zimba. She moved to his farm and gave birth to four dark daughters, whom she endowed with her fascination for the occult. Consette's fixation passed down her line through all generations to follow.

In 1913, one of Consette's descendants gave birth to Trinidad and nurtured the child with superstition and the demon side of plants. Trinidad learned that the bulb of a hyacinth could cause vomiting and diarrhea so severe it could be fatal; that oleander leaves are poisonous and harmful to the heart; that all parts of the dieffenbachia will burn the mouth and can swell a tongue enough to cut off air; and that one or two castor beans are deadly things to eat. Trinidad was given all that knowledge, but not a solitary ounce of healthy love.

She took it all in, but unlike her mother, Trinidad was

not interested in the poisonous, the harmful, the burning, or the deadly. Instead, she looked for healing.

Oddly enough, Trinidad had been born with a condition for which there is no herbal remedy. In Latin it is called *dextrocardia situs inversus*—spoken plainly, her heart was positioned in the right of her chest, a mirror image, completely transposed. But this was not her only distinction, for Trinidad was a Knower and also a receiver of visions. For most of her life, unbidden knowledge had floated itself to the anterior of her body cavity, above and just to the right of her gut, before settling on the surface of her turned-around heart. She'd first found out about the Knowing back in 1922, on the day she turned nine years old.

The memory of the discovery was this:

She'd worked alongside her mother in the fields that day, and they had snap beans and boiled potatoes for dinner. It happened to be a Monday, the only day of the week that the hoodoo woman would read your tea leaves if you gave her two copper pennies. The woman was called Mam Judith, and she'd been the bringer of hopes and omens to the colored part of Bayou Cane for coming up on fifty years.

Trinidad didn't say a word during supper, and she chewed as fast as she could. It was the first time she was being allowed to visit Mam Judith, and the girl was in a rush to get there. She tried to plant a hurry-up thought in her mother's head just by staring at her when she wasn't looking. Finally, after a dozen forevers came and went, her mother took one last bite of beans, picked her teeth with the fingernail of her right pinky finger, gulped down the dregs of her chicory root coffee, and let out a very deep, very long belch before she finally spoke.

"Whatchew looking at, girl? Get up off your behine and

clean up here. We gots somewhere to go." This was as near to an expression of affection as Trinidad was ever likely to hear from her mother.

The child did as she was told, taking extra care so as not to have to do anything twice. When she'd hung the kitchen rag over the washtub's edge and stood still waiting for approval, her mother spoke again.

"All right then. Go getchew a clean head cloth. I won't have my chile stand before Mam Judith looking all nappy." As Trinidad ran to do it, her mother's voice pinched at her back: "Didjew hear me? I said make it a clean one. Make it your best clean one. You ain't a sharecropper's chile, and you ain't no white trash neither. You be a Fontenaise."

This was something her mother often said, this "You be a Fontenaise," and her mother was fond of calling herself Missuz Fontenaise as if it were a claim to something fine and proud. It seemed to Trinidad that her mother's voice was filled with haughtiness when she said it, though she never explained her claim to such arrogance. The truth of the matter was that Trinidad was the child of a rapist who'd used her mother five times in one night, taking off and leaving her half-dead and bleeding something more than three-and-a-half miles from home. She was never part of any marriage, and Fontenaise was a name she'd heard only once and bestowed upon herself.

The mother and daughter set off down the red clay road that never seemed to dry out completely, even if there hadn't been rain for a month. They walked until they came to a weather-beaten tombstone that jutted up out of the ground like a moss-covered, ancient stone drunkard askew. That tombstone was how they knew to turn left and follow a smaller footpath that was mostly overgrown with swampish vegetation, until they came to two rotten fence posts held together with rusted barbed wire upon which hung a handmade cast-iron bell—the tea reader's attempt at dignified formalities, as if to say, "Mam Judith is receiving today."

Trinidad's mother rang that bell three times and turned in a circle once; then they proceeded on. That's how this business was done if done proper, according to local lore.

Mam Judith was as close to majestic as anyone from those parts ever got. No one knew how old she was, though it was said she was two days older than dirt. Her skin was the color of tree bark—mostly gray, save for the brown of the wrinkles that ran down her face like the graves of gone-away roots—and her eyes were green, like emeralds. Huge golden hoops always hung from her earlobes, and one tiny gold stud pierced the right side of her nose. And Mam Judith was diminutive; she looked like a wizened child sitting there on a cushion in the big rattan chair that flared up behind her and made her seem queenly.

Naturally, it was the silks that grabbed one's eye in Mam Judith's place, silks not being common in a part of the bayou where the general population had to look up to see bottom. And all those colors of all those silks were reflected in the small silver tea kettle that simmered on the cook stove.

Trinidad and her mother stepped inside the door and stood still as statues. Mam Judith moved her head in an almost imperceptible nod, and Trinidad felt her mother push her forward. The reader of tea leaves looked straight into the young girl's eyes and said in a voice deep as a well and cold as a river bottom, "Pour some of that water into this cup and then drink it down, girl. I got business witchew." She didn't take her eyes away from Trinidad's even for a second.

Trinidad did as she was told and set the cup between them when she finished. Mam Judith's hand, a gnarled and brittle and broken-off branch, reached out to slide the cup closer to her own self. She perused the tea leaves in its bottom, squinting and harrumphing every now and again and sometimes seeming to growl.

When Trinidad swallowed, the sound of it rolled and crackled off the walls and the floor.

"You gots the gift, girl," Mam Judith said, and then stopped in order to let the drama settle in. She shut her lips tight and stared into Trinidad's face and finally said in a snake-hissy whisper, "You don't be all the way of this world. There something in you can't be from this world. You gots the Knowing. You mark what I say: when the time be right, things gwine come to you by thoughts and by visions. And you gots a Purpose too. Your Purpose gonna show itself when the time be right."

There was no further explanation, and no one spoke of it ever again.

Trinidad's life took tumbles and turns after her mother died. She married a man named Jackson Prefontaine but was widowed while still quite young. She ended up as housekeeper for the Virgil B. Hortons, a wealthy white family in Pascagoula, Mississippi, but she was not meant to stay there forever. Trinidad was meant to go to Bayou Cymbaline at a time in the future and join with Bonaventure Arrow, who, like her, would have a touch of the divine.

THE OTHER GRANDMA

THE voice of Adelaide Roman came around sometimes, although only once in a while. Whenever unborn Bonaventure heard it, he would climb up behind his mother's ribs and form himself into a tight little ball, because Adelaide's voice was sharp and scraping. Sometimes its sound waves beat viciously on his eardrums, nearly shattering his tiny hammer and anvil bones. These instances provided first evidence that the gift of peculiar hearing could sometimes be unkind.

Adelaide had been born and raised on Bayou Deception Island, the only child of Etienne Cormier and the former Reevy Simonette, two full-blooded Cajuns, neither of whom was very much to look at. But they were good people and well thought of, which is why no one could ever figure out how Adelaide fit into the picture. Not only was she pretty, but she had a tendency to act like she'd wound up with her parents by mistake, like she was never meant to be a Cormier at all. She'd been a colicky baby who grew into a prissy kind of child, never wanting to play outside, never wanting dirt on her clothes, and never wanting people to touch her. She narrowed her eyes at her parents, and slapped their hands away. It wasn't because she was scared; it was because she thought herself better. As she grew up, it became apparent that Adelaide was ashamed of her family.

Her good looks only added to Adelaide's conceit. Once she matured and became aware of how pretty she was she removed herself mentally and emotionally from Bayou Deception Island. She turned eighteen in 1927 and left the place physically once and for all. She got herself to a town called Cooksville, where she found a waitressing job at a rundown restaurant called the Last Stop Diner. The following year she met Theodore Roman, a man twelve years her senior.

Theodore Roman was a tall, good-natured fellow with a strong chin, a receding hairline, and a voice as smooth as butterscotch pudding. Theo wasn't from Cooksville; he'd only been on the back side of a fishing trip he'd taken to Big Eddy Lake out near Shoats Creek, where he'd spent his formative years. Theodore lived and worked in Bayou Cymbaline and had only gone into the Last Stop Diner for a cup of coffee and some poppy-seed cake.

Adelaide knew a hardworking man when she saw one, and once she confirmed Theodore Roman had a good-paying job at a cannery, she flirted enough to make him want to come back. It worked. By his second visit she was making sure he knew that she'd cut him an extra large slice of poppy-seed cake, and she made a little show of running her finger along the cake knife and licking the frosting off slowly. By his third visit she was batting her eyes and bending over to pick up things she'd accidentally-on-purpose dropped, because she'd been told one time that she had a nice backside.

After two months of coming all the way from Bayou Cymbaline for a cup of so-so coffee, and without having received so much as a kiss, Theodore Roman produced a dia-

mond ring from his left shirt pocket, and Adelaide Cormier
judged it good enough for now. Theo was a nice man; he
really did deserve better. But all things happen for a reason.

The wedding was a low-key ceremony that took place
at the Cornerstone Southern Baptist Church in Bayou Cymbaline, which was two blocks west of the VFW Hall, where
a small reception was held. The day's events were attended
by Theo's coworkers and all of the Shoats Creek Romans
who could make it. It seems the Cormiers' invitations went
out late. Theo wouldn't meet his in-laws until a few years
later, when he took Dancy out for a visit. But Adelaide never
went back.

The low-budget wedding was intentional on Adelaide's
part. The big money was reserved for the honeymoon and
her trousseau. Theo scratched his head and questioned the
need for six pairs of new shoes, to which Adelaide responded
that if he couldn't afford for his wife to have shoes maybe he
should have said something before she gave up everything
to marry him and move to a place where she didn't know a
single soul. Theo never questioned her spending habits again.
He learned that if he just let her buy what she wanted for herself or the house, she could be pleasant enough. By the same
token, Adelaide had figured out that it was best to have mari-
tal relations before she spent more than ten dollars on anything, which is how it was that Dancy came to be conceived
the night before the purchase of a dining room set complete
with a sideboard, a hutch, and two leaves for the table.

Adelaide didn't dislike pregnancy; she despised it. It
wasn't that she was sick in the mornings, or at any other time
for that matter; it was how heavy and painful her breasts
became, and how stretch marks ran all over her abdomen
like silvery mucous trails left by snails, and especially how
her belly button stuck out. Adelaide seethed through the

whole nine months and vowed she would never be pregnant again.

She'd labored for less than two hours when Dancy glided out of her body as if she were covered in Vaseline. Adelaide could have filed her nails through the whole thing with very little disruption. The doctor said that in all his years of practice he'd never seen a woman have such an easy time of it.

Theo came to her hospital room afterwards, a dozen red roses in one hand and a jeweler's box in the other. Adelaide said that the roses were pretty, but for future reference she preferred pink or yellow, and that she would exchange the opal necklace as soon as she was able. He had the receipt, didn't he? Then she told him there would be no more sex in their future because the doctor said she'd almost died while giving birth and would most likely be in pain the rest of her life.

As for forming a bond with her daughter, well, that would have to come about all by itself and would definitely not happen through nursing. Nursing was for broodmares and barn cats, she said, and that's why God made bottles.

Theo was another story. Dancy took over his heart from day one. It was Theo who stayed up nights when she was sick with a stomachache, a cough, or a fever; Theo who taught her to tie her shoes; Theo who taught her to ride a bike; and Theo who did just about everything else a parent could and should and ought to want to do. This included taking her to visit her grandparents, which meant going to see the Cormiers, since his own parents were deceased by then. Adelaide was all too happy to stay behind in Bayou Cymbaline with her indoor toilet and her linoleum floors, comforts she'd never had on Bayou Deception Island. And she loved not having to cook dinner for her husband or having to mind her child.

Dancy didn't miss Adelaide on those trips. By the time she was eight years old, she'd already decided that she would *not* be like her mother when she grew up. She wouldn't ever yank on her daughter's arm, or call her stupid, or take away her dinner as punishment.

All throughout her childhood, Dancy fantasized that Adelaide would run off for New York City. Then it would be just Dancy and her daddy, who never said he wished she was prettier and never called her disgusting. Never.

This dislike of her mother remained as Dancy grew up. She supposed she had some feeling for Adelaide, in a detached sort of way and only because of their blood tie. But that was all. Any hints of warmth or trust were missing from their relationship.

If you'd asked for advice on raising a daughter, Adelaide Roman's response would have been to fall to your knees and pray for the strength to know the devil when you saw him. Although she'd never outright proclaimed that a demon had hold of Dancy, there'd been plenty of times when Adelaide had said, "Get thee behind me, Satan," the minute the girl walked out of the room. As a congregant of the International Church of the Elevated Forthright Gospel, Adelaide Roman was an expert on Satan.

She'd had a reason for joining the Forthright, but that reason had nothing to do with God. It was a reason that had come to her at her place of employment. Adelaide worked at the Bayou Cymbaline Branch of the United States Post Office on Pepperdine Street in Bayou Cymbaline. It was there, in August of 1946, that a handsome stranger with the most gorgeous blue eyes she'd ever seen walked in to stand directly in front of her. The man introduced himself as Brother Harley John Eacomb and asked if he might post a notice on the corkboard that hung in the post office vestibule. Adelaide said she didn't see why not.

The handsome stranger tipped his head in a graceful bow before going out the way he'd come in. When he was gone, Adelaide just about fell over herself getting out to the corkboard to see what he'd posted. She believed it was the first time in her life she actually felt blessed by God to be in the right place at the right time. The notice stated that a special Meeting of the Righteous was to be held down by the river the following Sunday at six in the evening. Presiding over the meeting would be Brother Harley John Eacomb, pastor of the International Church of the Elevated Forthright Gospel.

Adelaide spent all of Saturday getting herself ready. She bought a new dress, and shoes to go with it, and splurged on a white silk hat with peek-a-boo netting that came down over her eyes, and white gloves with a mother-of-pearl button at the wrist bone. Dancy was only sixteen at the time and not yet a cosmetologist, so Adelaide went to the beauty parlor for a professional wash and set, and had her nails painted in a color called Happy Heart Red.

When her husband asked her where she was going, she said, "Some of us care about the welfare of our eternal souls, Theo. So if you don't mind, I'm going to church like I always do."

"In the evening? And dressed like that? You don't usually get so dolled up. I thought maybe you were headed for Bourbon Street," he teased.

To which Adelaide insisted on knowing if she was entitled to look her best when she praised God Almighty or not.

The Meeting that night was still going on past nine. Brother Eacomb called down God and called out Satan in a voice that no one in those parts had ever heard the like of. He would teach them to praise God, he said. He would cure their ills and wash the sins from those who genuinely wished to be saved. Brother Eacomb promised to cast out demons and to purify hearts. After that, he promised to lead his flock up the holy mountain, because they were surely a righteous people, the chosen ones of God.

If his blue eyes hadn't gotten to Adelaide, his mellifluous voice surely would have. Adelaide Roman had never in her life heard such a voice come out of a man. But oh my Lord, those eyes.

On the Thursday after that first Meeting of the Righteous, Theo Roman complained of feeling ill and stayed home from work for the first time in his life. Adelaide left early for her job at the post office, but Dancy stayed home from school because she was worried. At a quarter past ten, she heard a thump and a strangling sound coming from her parents' room. She found Theo on the floor, called for an ambulance, and rode along with him to a hospital in New Orleans, where she had to borrow money for the pay phone to call her mother. Adelaide said she would be there after work. This situation aggravated her; she wouldn't be able to go shopping, and she needed to find another new dress to wear for her personal savior, Brother Eacomb.

Theo was in the hospital for a week. When he was discharged, the doctor handed Adelaide a small glass bottle with nitroglycerin tablets in it and explained to them both that Theo should place one under his tongue if he felt another heart attack coming on. He said the instructions were on the label. Adelaide put the bottle in the drawer of the bedside table when they got back home.

It wasn't but a month later that another heart attack came to call. Adelaide and Theo had just sat down to dinner when he felt the first pain. Dancy wasn't home.

"Nitro . . ." he gasped.

"What's that, Theo? What are you saying? I don't know what you're saying."

"Nitro . . ." He was turning a bluish white.

"What are you trying to say, Theo? I can't understand you."

A raspy, whispered "Nitro . . ."

"I still can't understand you, Theo." She was shouting by now. "Are you saying nitro? Do you need one of those pills?"

Theo managed to nod his head, and Adelaide folded her napkin, put it back on the table, and walked to the bedroom to get the medication. When, nearly two full minutes later, Theo fell to the floor stone-cold dead, Adelaide was straightening a throw pillow and smoothing a wrinkle in the bedspread.

The next time Brother Harley John Eacomb came to Bayou Cymbaline to conduct a Meeting of the Righteous, Adelaide showed up in a snug-fitting, black sheath dress. After the service she approached him and proclaimed that now she understood Mark 9:43–48. Her husband had been like a hand or a foot or an eye that offended, and he had been cast off.

"He was a drinker and a smoker and he played poker every Friday night, Brother Eacomb. And though he was always clean-shaven and shined his shoes on Saturdays, he was a godless man. I am convinced he will be playing cards with the devil for all eternity."

And Brother Harley John Eacomb said, "Praise Jesus, sister, praise Jesus."

Adelaide took to wearing fancy lingerie to every Meeting of the Righteous. She told herself it had nothing to do with the fact that she drove to a motel over in Chalmette and had sex with the married Brother Eacomb after services. That wasn't it at all; she had simply wanted to look her best for God, as any good Christian woman would do.

Having become Brother Eacomb's truest disciple, Adelaide believed it was her duty to save others by any means available, and she carried this out at her post office job by intercepting and opening mail that was not addressed to her, all in the name of the Lord. She reasoned that doing so would allow her to identify any works of the devil that tried to disguise themselves as United States mail. It was a practice well suited to Adelaide Roman, a woman who understood the ways of the devil.

ARRIVAL

AT no time after William's death had it been suggested that pregnant Dancy move in with Adelaide rather than Letice. She couldn't have stood Adelaide anyway—all the gossip mixed in with Bible quoting, Praise-be-to-Godding, and unceasing holier-than-thou judgments. Nor did she wish to feel unwanted, or to listen to the snide insinuations that her father had been a failure.

Most days Dancy just sat very still and stared into nothing. She nibbled at her food and sipped at her drink. Dancy couldn't place herself back in the world because her world had gone missing, completely erased by some cold, cruel void. She had lost every manner of feeling, from the sensation of touch to the experience of emotion. She could have plucked an egg from boiling water and never felt a thing. Dancy was like a sieve; the only thing she could hold were the boiled-down husks of cooked-away happiness, leftovers from a life that had drained through the wires.

If she wanted for anything she had only to ring a silver bell, which she did for the first time on the night her water broke. And she only rang it then because she was too big to bend over and clean up the mess. It was the last day of January 1950, and it was two weeks too soon for Bonaventure to happen.

· · · ·

Bonaventure heard the water break and felt something give way beneath him. Then he heard the sounds of the little bell's clapper, and of footsteps, and of questions formed from rushing words. The voice that belonged to Letice had a bit of something in it that hadn't been there before. His mother's voice was different too, stretched out and brittle at the edges, and her breathing had become erratic.

Letice marshaled an outer calm while frantically and surreptitiously looking for any sign of late-term miscarriage. She telephoned the doctor and Dancy's mother and took the suitcase that had been packed some three weeks before from where it stood beside the tall old walnut chiffonier. Mrs. Silvey sat Dancy down and cleaned her up a bit, while Mr. Silvey brought the car around and mentally rehearsed the route to the hospital.

Sensation and emotion returned to Dancy in a rush, and she began to feel two different fears, one far greater than the other. The lesser was the fear of pain; the greater was the fear of losing her connection to William. As long as the baby was inside her body, so too was a part of her husband, and she felt close to him, and warm and safe and loved and touched. She didn't want to lose him again.

Bonaventure heard sharp yelps of pain when the womb where he lived began to contract. So many sounds were raging around him that he couldn't separate happiness from fright, and his own heart started to race. He could hear the whimpering of his mother's fears but didn't know what to do with them. Her heart was telling him to stay, while her body urged him to go. He pulled on his ears in complete desperation and listened as hard as he could.

· · · ·

"Don't be afraid," said a familiar deep voice. "Everything's going to be fine."

Trinidad Prefontaine could not find sleep. Her room was bathed in a ghostly light, for the moon was nearing full. A winter rain fell against her windowpane, its rivulets turned silver by that waxing moon. She'd been restless inside her own skin for three days, as if some strange and invisible imp were blowing its breath against her neck. That scamp had been following her in the daytime too, from stove to cupboard and from inside to out, like a playful, excitable secret. The rascal would ceaselessly sing a wordless song and escape from the corner of Trinidad's eye when she turned. It was a supernatural being; she was certain of that.

Of late Trinidad had been noting signs of a coming alteration, some event of momentous consequence: there was the slightest tremble way down in the earth and the smell of birth blood riding on the wind—it was a scent that always troubled Trinidad, coming as it did from a deep dark curve in the backbone of her past.

Mam Judith sprang to Trinidad's mind, and the memory of the first time the Knowing had come. It had happened not long after her visit with the tea reader. She'd been hanging wash on the line when knowledge of the death of a certain three-year-old child came into Trinidad's head. Two months later that child's body was found facedown in a ditch. He had drowned in six inches of water.

Now all those years later she tossed and turned as she recalled other times and other Knowings: 1927, when the Mississippi River broke out of its levees, flooding the land for a hundred miles and killing 246 people in seven different states; 1940, when a hurricane made landfall across southwest Louisiana, flooding Acadiana and killing 75,000 muskrat and six human beings; 1947, when a storm put Jefferson Parish under six feet of water and claimed over fifty lives; the tornado that same year that touched down north of Shreveport, killing eighteen folks and leaving next to nothing standing in the town of Cotton Valley. Trinidad had foreknown all of those things.

But this imp was new to her. This imp knew something she did not.

Each minute became a new eternity for Dancy. When she was weak from agony and whimpering from hurt, anesthesia was administered and she fell far away. As the ether entered her body, all sensation left and she returned to those hundreds of moments she'd spent in the shelter of William's warm arms, surrounded by his familiar scent and steeped in a happiness she could not even describe.

The ether passed into the narrow confines of her body, and Bonaventure became groggy as he tried to escape the womb he'd outgrown. He could still hear his mother's heartbeat, slower now than it had been a while ago when the fastness of it had distressed him.

William was there, and he recalled how Bonaventure had turned in a circle at the sound of his voice once before, so he spoke to him again.

"Almost over," he said to his frightened child.

Bonaventure took comfort in that familiar deep voice, and then other voices came, voices he did not know.

"Hang on, Dancy, we'll get you through this," said one of those strange new voices.

"Here comes the baby," another chimed in.

And then the smothering darkness vanished as a whooshing wind came up in Bonaventure's lungs that blew him clean out of his mother's body and into a much larger world. It was two minutes after three o'clock in the morning on February 1, 1950, and someone was telling Dancy that she'd been a real champ.

Bonaventure looked like any other newborn, all scrunched up and red and mottled with afterbirth. But he did not make the usual sounds. With his eyes wide open and his little lips parted, he let out the silent cry of a mime.

"It's a boy!" whispered ghostly William into his wife's exhausted ear, and then fell to his knees, rendered humble and low by a terrible, terrible longing.

In the middle of her sleepless night, Trinidad experienced a vision. A scavenging raven circled the room, its beady eyes questing after death. The bird spread its wings to swoop and glide, its feathers sounding like rustling silk. From the bird's shaggy throat came a *prruk-prruk* call and a *toc-toc* click and a dry, rasping *kraa-kraa* cry. After the raven came a pure white dove, and after the dove, a sparrow.

Up in the sky a beautiful spiral in a pinwheel galaxy northwest of Ursa Major shone particularly vivid and unusually bright, brighter even than the stars of Cassiopeia, Orion, Pegasus, and Andromeda.

In the waiting room, the two grandmothers sat facing the American Standard clock that hung above the swinging doors leading to the maternity ward. Both of them glanced several times a minute to monitor the progress of the sweep-second hand. One of them flipped through the pages of a magazine and the other kept trying to pray.

Bonaventure would know the praying one as Grand-mère Letice, who, whether she admitted it or not, was reaching back through the years to a time when she had been called Miss Letice, when she was still deserving of proper respect, before she had committed her most grievous sin. He would know the magazine reader as Grandma Roman, a woman who was purely in love with anything that made her sound biblical. To her way of thinking, every upright Christian on the face of the earth could open a King James Bible to the Book of Romans if so inclined. She had never actually read that part and didn't know a thing about Saint Paul, but as far as she was concerned, the only thing she needed to know was that the Romans had ruled the world. That's as far as it went with Adelaide; she didn't consider the fact that, for all their might and grandeur, it was the Romans who'd made fun of the Son of God right before they killed him. She blamed the Jews for that. Adelaide tended to skim the Bible the same way she skimmed the magazine in her hands, looking at the pictures and drawing whatever conclusion she fancied at the moment.

Forrest and Martha Silvey sat off in a corner. It had been a very long time since they'd been this close to childbirth, and they didn't quite know what to think, say, or do; however, they agreed it was probably best to keep quiet or to speak in whispers if the need should arise. Mrs. Silvey wasn't sure if Dancy would be nursing the baby—given that the birth had happened prematurely, these things hadn't yet been discussed. In Mrs. Silvey's heart of hearts, she hoped there would be bottles, and that maybe she would be asked to give one now and then.

While those thoughts tiptoed through Martha Silvey's head, her husband rotated his hat brim in his hands and hoped the baby would turn out to be a boy, one who might like to putter with tools and learn how to fix things, and maybe go fishing on Saturday afternoons.

Adelaide Roman crossed one knee over the other and sat there swinging her foot. She was so irritated by the presence of the Silveys she could hardly sit still. She'd never had help in her life, but Dancy did. It wasn't fair.

When the nurse came through the swinging doors, the grandmothers and the Silveys flew up as if they'd been shot from the mouths of cannons. Knowing there was only one patient in delivery at the time, the nurse reasoned that all four of them were waiting for the same announcement.

"Congratulations!" she said. "You must be the family of Baby Boy Arrow."

There was a collective intake of breath and a spreading of smiles and a chorus of "A boy! A boy! A boy!"

Letice was the first to regain composure. She thanked the nurse and said with a distinct note of pride in her voice, "He's to be named Bonaventure."

To which the nurse responded, "You don't say. Well, now, that's different, isn't it?"

"You got that right," Adelaide said with a roll of her eyes, while the Silveys were truly delighted.

William stayed in the hospital with his wife and his child, walking through the walls of the nursery or of Dancy's private room. The first time the nurse brought Bonaventure in, William saw Dancy as he never had before: she'd turned from a girl to a woman. And then he couldn't take his eyes from Bonaventure's features: his nostrils, his eyelids, his perfect little chin. In all of his twenty-three years, William had never known such wonder and pride. He sat on the bed next to his widow, awestruck by the heels of their baby's feet, the half moons on his fingernails, and the little pink lines that crossed the skin of his knuckles.

William sang to his child during the night, and Bonaventure was lulled to sleep.

Dancy was still caught between mourning her husband and welcoming her child and seemed perplexed by the whole situation. But the barest hint of maternal instinct struggled into her consciousness on the second day after giving birth, causing her to lay Bonaventure before her on the bed, touch each tiny shoulder, and lean down to kiss the tip of his nose. After caressing his little bowed legs with her thumbs, she unpinned his diaper to see things for herself, as new mothers will sometimes do.

"It's a boy!" shouted ghostly William again, but only Bonaventure heard.

William kept a mighty vigilance during the early days of Bonaventure's life and wished there was some way to tell his wife and child just how much he loved them. Those visits brought him immeasurable joy, but they also brought him suffering. Unfortunately, they were the only salve he had for his loneliness, and for the dawning realization that eavesdropping was as close as he would ever get to being included in the family. And even that was temporary.

William was very aware of his circumstances. He knew there were three things he was supposed to do, each of them a challenge. The first was to forgive his killer, and the second to remove something Dancy was keeping. William knew he would need Bonaventure's help for that one and it bothered him. He didn't like to think about a little boy finding out violent things, but there was really no other way.

"We've got time, little man. You don't have to find any

secrets yet," William whispered as night settled in around them. He continued to push the third challenge away, not even forming it into a thought.

When mother and child were both sound asleep, William walked to the morgue to see if he could find Dancy again, as he had on the night he'd been killed, the night he had held her all the way until morning.

It didn't happen. But how could it, he thought. That had been a once-in-a-lifetime thing.

THE charge nurse at the asylum made a note in The Wanderer's chart that the patient had cried all day. It irritated her that he didn't even have the presence of mind to wipe his own runny nose, so she had to do it.

The librarian, Eugenia Babbitt, had seen the killer's picture in the newspaper. She looked for more information about him every single day.

THE MEANING OF A NAME

NEITHER grandmother ever endowed Bonaventure with a nickname, preferring instead to call him by his Christian name, one that he shared with a thirteenth-century mystic turned saint, although such sharing was said to be coincidence; he was, after all, only half-Catholic, and casual half-Catholic at that. Before long his mother was calling him Adventure Arrow, or Venture Forth Arrow, or any number of pet names like Sweetie-pie or Whirly-bird, depending on her mood.

When asked where she'd come up with a name like Bonaventure, Dancy couldn't explain it, and so insisted that she'd plucked it out of the Greater New Orleans telephone directory without even thinking twice. The truth was that one morning she'd opened her eyes from a dreamless sleep and there it was inside her head, an irresistible suggestion. Dancy spoke the name out loud several times a day after that. She wrote it on paper in a lavish hand. She kissed it onto a penny and threw the coin into a fountain as if to wish good luck upon her little unborn child.

Once Adelaide Roman got used to it, she began to like the name; she thought it sounded like something rich people would come up with.

"What's his middle name going to be?" she asked, and suggested that Bonaventure Roman Arrow had a real nice ring to it.

Dancy said she would have to think about it, though she had no intention of doing anything of the kind. In the end, when Adelaide realized that his initials would be B.R.A., she called Dancy up at eleven o'clock at night to tell her to forget it, since someone was sure to tease him by calling him *brassiere*.

Grand-mère Letice did not think the name a coincidence, but that was a sentiment she kept to herself. Upon learning of it, she looked up Saint Bonaventure in *The Lives of the Saints* and read about the son of Giovanni di Fidanza and Maria Ritella, a child who'd been born at Bagnorea in the environs of Viterbo in 1221, and who had originally been called Giovanni. She learned that when this certain Giovanni had fallen grievously ill in childhood, his mother had sought the intercession of Saint Francis of Assisi, and the dying child was healed. The boy grew up and devoted his life to God. He joined the Franciscan order and changed his name to Bonaventure.

Letice Arrow's heart beat fast as she read those things and nearly pounded out of her chest when she found that in 1257, the pope conferred the title of Seraphic Doctor upon Bonaventure di Fidanza. This was exactly what she had hoped to find, for Letice was a believer in angels—she looked for them; she listened for them; she turned to them for help. She knew that in the realms of heaven, the seraphim angels stand nearest to God.

Letice read on about Saint Bonaventure's love of learning. She read of his belief that reason and intellect can find many answers, but they can never know God as can the humblest hearts and souls. No one would ever be able to convince her that her grandson had been carelessly named from the telephone directory for Greater New Orleans. No one. Not ever. She believed he'd been born to great purpose, though she did not know what that purpose would be.

Letice brought up baptism, but received no response from Dancy. Days came and went with no further talk of it, and Letice grew deeply concerned. She was anxious about the original sin that stained Bonaventure's new soul and would do so until the waters of baptism washed it away. She nearly worried herself sick about this matter until one day as she was watering a trailing philodendron, she experienced a revelation. At the very same moment the water pooled atop the sphagnum, inspiration came to her like a wave at high tide, and an idea pooled inside her head. As the water seeped deeper into the soil, just so did that idea leak deeper into Letice. There was a duty, a moral imperative to carry out, and she was the only one who could do it. In the days that followed, she designed a strategy and counted the days until Holy Week.

Bonaventure took in his Grand-mère's excitement, and it made him feel big and strong. He was lying on his tummy the first time he heard her plans, facedown on one little fist, which wasn't all that comfortable. When he heard her anxious anticipation—*tzing, tzing, tzing*—Bonaventure was able to move his arm from beneath his head, inspired by the sound, even though he was no more than a few weeks old.

He stared at his hand and wiggled his fingers until he was plumb tuckered out.

MARDI GRAS SENTIMENTAL

LETICE Arrow's life revolved around Catholicism. She loved its ritual, its music, and its belief in a loving God. She also loved the mystery of it: the transubstantiation of bread and wine into the body and blood of Christ. She loved the idea that suffering brought one closer to God, and that forgiveness could be found through confession, even though she felt she'd never attained absolution for her sins because she'd never received proper penance.

Mardi Gras is French for Fat Tuesday and is the last day of revelry before the fasting ritual that begins on Ash Wednesday, the first day of Lent. Fat Tuesday fell on the twenty-first of February in 1950, arriving on the arm of a steady light rain. The grayness of the day made an undetectable turn toward dusk as the dark of blue became a bruise on the sky.

Letice Arrow drew the drawing room drapes against the cries of *"Laissez les bons temps rouler!"* ringing though the streets of Bayou Cymbaline.

"Go ahead and let the good times roll," she whispered. "The hours for your sinning are numbered. Your bodies will take your souls straight to hell. Your flesh will rot and you will stink for eternity. What good will your lust do you then?"

She could hardly wait for midnight, when the reveling would cease in accordance with laws of church and state; when purple and green would be returned to holy vestments; when spangles and beads would be swept from the gutters; and when pleasure and excess would be sealed tight away. Letice hated Fat Tuesday. To her, Mardi Gras belonged to Satan. It was unadulterated wanting come to life, adorned in beads and feathers and arousal. Letice was forty-five years old and had, for the most part, turned her back on sexual desire before she'd turned twenty, though not before she'd known it. There'd been a time when she had loved Mardi Gras and the wildness it brought to her body.

Letice was restless that night, feverish and disturbed. When sleep did come, it brought dreams of her youth: a ballroom, a hallway, a clandestine rendezvous. She tossed and turned as she lived out her dreams, and she woke up disturbed all the more.

Letice Molyneaux had met Remington Arrow at a sailing party in 1921, during a boat outing planned for Bogue Falaya and the Tchefuncte River and sponsored by the Jupitala Yacht Club. After that first meeting, they didn't see each other again until Mardi Gras on February 8, 1922, at the Goddess of the Rainbow ball held at the Athenaeum. Remington had never forgotten her. When Lent was over that year, he began to call upon Letice, seeing her only in the presence of her parents, with whom the couple sat in the Molyneaux parlor on Sunday afternoons.

Remington attributed Letice's demure manner and downcast eyes to ladylike behavior, when in fact she was trying to hide her impatience. Her quiet manner was not about shyness; she simply had nothing to say. Letice's thoughts were far away. It wasn't that she didn't care about Remington; he was a very good man, though she thought him too proper. All she could do was hope that he would tire of her feigned bashfulness. She did not realize her shyness made him love her all the more, for Remington Arrow thought he'd found his soul mate.

Week after week, Horatio and Emmaline Molyneaux welcomed him heartily, and they were only too happy to grant him permission to marry their only child. The wedding would take place the following year. The two were allowed to be alone after that, and though a fondness had formed in Letice's heart, she spent her love on someone else.

The Mystic Club held the Arabian Nights Ball on February 10, 1923, during the Mardi Gras of their engagement. Letice was costumed as Scheherazade, an elaborate masque covering her face. It had been a well thought-out choice—she knew there would be many Scheherazades at the ball. Remington was in her company nearly the whole evening, but somewhere around nine o'clock she excused herself for the ladies' lounge, saying she had a slight headache. A quarter hour passed, then a half. Remington scanned the crowd and every corner of the ballroom, finding many Scheherazades but none that was Letice. Nearly an hour had gone by before he saw a flash of color near the doors leading into the ballroom.

And there was Letice.

He crossed the room and executed a perfect courtier's bow, taking her hand and asking her for the pleasure of a dance. It was a complete quadrille: *le pantalon, l'été, la poule, la pastourelle,* and finale. The quadrille is not a close dance; there was no opportunity to ask if she'd been in the ladies' lounge all that time. But then again, it wouldn't do to seem possessive. For Remington, it was enough to hold this slip of a girl in his arms and feel her softness, smell her sweetness, and know their wedding would soon take place. Just once that evening he allowed himself the pleasure of brushing back a wisp of her hair that had somehow come loose from its comb.

More than six hundred people attended the mass at which twenty-eight-year-old Remington Arrow and eighteen-year-old Letice Molyneaux were joined in holy matrimony. It was June 21, 1923, and the sun shone brightly through the stained glass windows of Our Lady of the Rosary, the Molyneaux family parish church, on Hamilton Square in Bayou Cymbaline. The groom was striking and the bride was lovely, if just a wee bit pale. It was said she'd suffered an illness in the springtime soon after Mardi Gras, a fever of some kind or other, which was no doubt the reason she was so painfully thin. Nonetheless, Letice was a vision in her ivory silk charmeuse gown.

A reception was held at the Roosevelt in New Orleans. Every florist within a hundred miles had worked to fill the grand hotel's lobby, as well as the ballroom in which the reception took place, this wedding being the social event of the season in the entire state of Louisiana and in those parts of Texas and Mississippi that mattered.

Remington hardly took his eyes off Letice through the ceremony and reception, and he pinched himself more than once to make certain it was real. That night, when they were alone in the bridal suite, he asked if she would require the help of a maid in unbuttoning her wedding dress and brushing out her hair.

"No, sir, I shall not," she said. "I was hoping that you would help me." She offered him a shy smile and blushing cheeks, and he loved her all the more.

His fingers fumbled over the satin buttons and hooks-

and-eyes of her bodice, but he was better with the brushing of her long, wavy hair. The motion of it calmed him and excited him at the same time. After Letice had retired to the bedroom, Remington remained in the sitting room with a snifter of brandy. He was determined to be a gentleman, and so was giving her the opportunity to plead exhaustion. He got into bed without making a sound and then tried to lie very still.

Remington Arrow could not have been more shocked when his bride reached for him that night. Never in his wildest dreams had he hoped things would happen this way. When he noticed the bloodstain on the sheets in the morning, a quick look at his wife's face showed it burning bright red, and Remington looked away.

As time went on, Remington and Letice brought out the best in each other. His shyness let in some *joie de vivre*, and he bought her a Victrola and every 78 record he could find. On Sundays they listened to opera, but every single Saturday night the two of them danced to ragtime music: King Oliver's muted cornet, or Sidney Bechet's clarinet, or the romping style of Jelly Roll Morton and the New Orleans Rhythm Kings. And once in a while they danced in an easy slow sway as Bessie Smith sang about loving someone when that someone don't love you. For that song Remington held Letice a little tighter, and her eyes filled with tears every time.

On every Mardi Gras evening of their married life, Remington Arrow executed a perfect courtier's bow and took his wife's hand for the pleasure of a dance. He never did know the truth about that certain Mardi Gras, or of what transpired after it on St. Philip Street in New Orleans.

SACRAMENT

NOW all these years later, on Ash Wednesday in 1950, Letice felt the joy of deprivation and the comforts of sackcloth. She fasted and prayed and went to church to pray more. She closed her eyes as the priest marked her forehead with a black cross derived from the ash of burnt palms, and reminded her that from dust she was made and unto dust she would return. She fancied that she felt the mark penetrate her skin and cut itself deep into the bone of her skull. She breathed deeply, as if to fill her lungs with incense and its sacred, misty wish. She chose to kneel on the cold stone floor rather than the padded kneeler. With head bowed and hands clasped together, Letice recited the Penitential Prayer of Saint Augustine:

> O Lord,
> The house of my soul is narrow;
> enlarge it that you may enter in.
> It is ruinous, O repair it!
> It displeases your sight.
> I confess it, I know.
> But who shall cleanse it,
> to whom shall I cry but to you?

Cleanse me from my secret faults, O Lord,
and spare your servant from strange sins.

She repeated those last words many times over as if
trying to show God her desolation . . . *Cleanse me from my secret*
faults, O Lord, and spare your servant from strange sins. Prayer
was the only way Letice knew to keep herself together.

On April 2, Letice joined her fellow faithful in remembrance
of Christ's entry into the city of Jerusalem by taking part
in a procession and carrying branches and singing Hosanna
before Palm Sunday mass. Holy Week had come.

On Monday, Tuesday, and Wednesday, she meditated
on Christ's last days on this earth. After bathing and dressing on the morning of Maundy Thursday, Letice prayed
for two hours, after which she rose from her knees, went
into her *en suite* bathroom, and poured all but a small
amount of Chanel No. 5 down the sink. Then she went to
the kitchen and removed a cruet of olive oil from the cupboard nearest the stove. As she poured a modicum of the
oil in with the drops of perfume, she watched the heavy
green-gold liquid mingle with the scented water to form
a substance she believed destined for blessedness. Holding the bottle in both of her hands, she clasped it to her
chest and asked God to consider it a chrismatory. She then
wrapped it in a white handkerchief and placed it inside her
purse.

Letice left for Our Lady of the Rosary to commemorate
the agony of Christ in the Garden and to attend the Mass
of the Chrism that was held every Holy Thursday morning before the Easter Triduum. Upon returning home, she
placed the secretly sanctified oil beneath the crucifix that
hung in her private chapel. She remained there in solitude,

down on her knees and lost in a spell. It wasn't until early evening when Mrs. Silvey knocked softly on the chapel door that Letice realized she hadn't eaten all day.

Bonaventure heard a new sound coming from his grand-mère when she came to kiss him goodnight. It was a sort of constant low vibration and he didn't know quite how to feel about it. When he was all grown up, he would hear that sound again in the song of a somber cello.

On Good Friday, Letice returned to Our Lady of the Rosary to make a spiritual pilgrimage through Christ's final hours. She wished to take personal responsibility for what had happened to Jesus, and to apologize to him from noon until three, when Stations of the Cross would begin. Letice had gone to the stations every Lent of her life but had never felt such nervousness as she did on that night; she shook as if chilled to the bone. Tremors quivered through her mind, shaking her thoughts down close to her heart.

As she moved with the priest from station to station, she looked upon Jesus and saw William instead. And Letice tormented herself with all that she did not know, asking question upon question for which no answers came.

Jesus is condemned to death . . . How had the crazy man chosen his victim? Had he looked at William and said, "Him. He's the one"?

Jesus is given his cross . . . Had William realized what was about to happen? Did he think for a moment that it was all just a joke?

Jesus falls the first time . . . Did their eyes meet in those last seconds? Did the gunman blink when he pulled the trigger? Did he smile? Did he shout?

Jesus meets his mother . . . At the Cross her station keeping, stood the mournful Mother weeping, close to Jesus to the last. Letice could only sob.

Simon of Cyrene carries the cross . . . Had the first bullet entered William's heart or his stomach?

Veronica wipes the face of Jesus . . . Had death come keening out his mouth?

Jesus falls the second time . . . Had he hung on to life as he fell to the floor?

Jesus meets the daughters of Jerusalem . . . Did anyone take his hand?

Jesus falls the third time . . . Which of the bullets was the one that had killed him?

Jesus is stripped of his garments . . . What had become of the clothes he had died in?

Jesus is nailed to the cross . . . Why had he stopped on his way home from work? Why couldn't he have been in the back of the store or have left just five seconds sooner? Please God, please God, can you please tell me why? I ask this of you, yet in my heart, I know.

Letice formed her right hand into a fist and whispered, *"Mea culpa, mea culpa, mea maxima culpa"*—my fault, my fault, my most grievous fault—as she pounded her fist to her chest three times as if pounding shut a door to keep her guilt from escaping.

Jesus dies on the cross . . . Had he gone beyond pain?

Jesus's body is removed from the cross . . . Was William still warm when they took him away?

Jesus is laid in the tomb . . . Was the undertaker gentle when he closed the wounds and sewed up the terrible, torn-flesh holes?

By the fourteenth station Letice could no longer separate her own child from the Virgin Mary's, and for a few hallowed moments experienced a rapture in which William came back to her as whole as he ever was. The devotion ended and the church emptied out, yet Letice remained caught in enchantment. She stayed that way for one hour more, transfixed by the vision made real by her piety. Still on her knees, she stared at the crucifix covered as it was in the purple cloth of Lent. She imagined the face of the only begotten son who had died that she might be absolved of her sins. And then she imagined the face of her own son, who she feared had died for the very same reason.

On Holy Saturday morning, Letice went back to Our Lady of the Rosary to reach for a state of grace. "Bless me, Father, for I have sinned." And then she confessed to keeping secrets and to impure thoughts of long ago, and to the deed she wished she had never done, the one she'd confessed so many times before. The priest spoke the words of absolution, and Letice returned to the pew to recite her penance. When she arrived back home, she felt clean enough to carry out her plan.

In the very early hours of Easter morning, when she was the only one up and about, Letice took a sleeping Bonaventure into her chapel, where beeswax votives burned bright in red glass. Holding the child of her child in the crook of her arm, she knelt on the prie-dieu that stood before the crucifix and asked God to bless her intentions. After that, she rose and anointed the baby's forehead with a drop of the oil-cum-chrism; then she dipped her hand into the small font that held the holy water she'd brought back from Lourdes. Letice let the water dribble over Bonaventure's forehead, baptizing him in the name of the Father and of the Son and of the Holy Spirit.

The baptismal water trickled into Bonaventure's ears and music flooded his sleep, flowing around and through him with a soothing, fluid grace. It was a melody made in heaven and meant for the ears of God's smallest darlings.

Trinidad Prefontaine took laundry from the line, for it had begun to rain. An unknown music reached her ears, soothing and soft as the raindrops.

From an alcove off to the side, a carved Virgin Mary looked out upon the garden where Louisiana iris and bird-foot violet blossomed silent and lovely in deep Lenten purple, interspersed among periwinkle and angels made of stone. It was an interesting parallel to what had taken root inside that house: secrets growing in boxes, choking guilt-ridden hearts with their vines.

At Easter Sunday mass, Letice celebrated the Resurrection of Jesus Christ and the fact that she had cleansed her little grandson's soul, which was more than she could do for her own.

Sometimes, when Bonaventure was all alone in the quiet, there came a new heartbeat, constant as his mother's but with the character of a stranger, that walked in through his ears and rolled to his chest to swoosh through his atria, ventricles, and valves. The beat of that unnamed visitor tumbled through him from head to toe. It stayed but a minute, swirling like a whirligig powered by a spirit wind, dancing about on the fertile ground of his innocent infant heart.

Something was beginning.

A VOICELESS BABY
AND HIS LONELY MOTHER

Letice kept Bonaventure's baptism a secret. While the sacrament had brought her a great deal of comfort, her conversations with Sergeant Turcotte brought none. Her anxiety over knowing the name of William's killer was eating at her insides now. She wracked her brain for a practical explanation. Part of her wanted to believe the killer was connected to William through a lawsuit at his firm; in that case it would be nothing to do with her. But another part of her felt William had died in order for her to gain God's forgiveness, and she didn't want to believe God would do such a thing. Letice Arrow was a conflicted woman.

After a time, the police informed her that they'd found no traceable connection to William's law firm, so Letice cast about for another explanation and began to wonder if the killer had a grudge against the Arrow family. They were bankers, after all. She could remember one case in particular, that of a young man desperate to save his family's farm, though his name did not come to mind. She remembered how much it had upset Remington to refuse that young man a loan. She supposed there were any number of bank customers who'd been foreclosed on and lost everything. Any one of them could be the killer. She would bring it up with Turcotte.

But what if it didn't have to do with the bank? The thought of voodoo sparked in her mind, and the blasphemy made her feel ill. But what if? What if William's death had to do with the fact that she'd married into the Arrow family under false pretenses? The words of that woman in the house on St. Philip Street came back: *The mirror done broke and your life looking back at you from them sharp glass pieces.*

Letice Arrow was a conflicted woman, indeed.

"Believe me, Mrs. Arrow, I would like nothing more than to give you some new information, but there is none," Turcotte told her.

"I just can't believe that no one saw the man at any time or in any place," Letice said.

"Oh, he was seen. A couple of people came down to the station and reported seeing him at the public library," the sergeant said.

"And?"

"The librarians remembered seeing him. They said he didn't bother anyone, just kept to himself. It's not unusual for vagrants to try to get comfortable at the library. In fact, it's a problem the librarians deal with all the time."

"Did you check with restaurants and grocery stores? He had to eat, didn't he?"

"We checked those places, but they didn't pan out." The sergeant paused before adding, "They remembered him at a liquor store in the Quarter. He was in there buying Jack Daniel's."

"And where did he go to drink it, Sergeant?"

"We're looking into that. He wasn't staying anywhere near the library or the A&P."

"Surely he was sleeping somewhere. You've said yourself how noticeable he was; didn't anyone see him on a park bench or perhaps loitering around? Do you think he had a car? Is that where he was sleeping?" Letice was like a dog with a bone.

"There was an abandoned vehicle about a half mile from the A&P, but it turned out to be part of some college kid's prank. No taxi drivers or streetcar drivers remembered him either."

"Did you check the bus and train depots?" Letice asked.

"Yes, ma'am. But you've got to remember that he would have been arriving here, no reason to talk to a ticket seller. He could have been coming from anywhere and walked through the station unnoticed."

"I want you to go to First Regent's Bank, Sergeant; it's been owned and operated by the Arrow family for generations. Examine the records of foreclosures and disputes. Maybe the man was seeking revenge for some financial loss that happened years ago. And when he realized that no one would recognize him, he decided to act."

"Sure, Mrs. Arrow. We'll follow up on that."

Letice felt the police officer was patronizing her. She could tell by the tone of his voice that he believed the pieces were falling into place, and the picture they formed was of a man angered by his deformity and driven senseless by drink.

She couldn't help but wonder what had turned the man into a killer. How had he become disfigured? Why had he been walking around with a gun? There were a lot of people in the A&P that day, so why had he chosen William? She knew Dancy would agree with the sergeant, because the policeman's reasoning gave her an anonymous target for her hate.

Letice was right; Dancy believed that knowing the killer's past, or finding some reason for what he had done, just might relieve her of her guilt, and Dancy wanted to keep her guilt.

One of William's challenges was to do with Dancy's thinking: he needed to relieve his wife of her self-imposed guilt. William understood very well that he could remove it. He knew where she kept her guilt and what must be done to take it away. As for forgiving his killer, William felt that time would take care of it and that one day he would be able to say with ease, "I forgive you." However, William had yet to understand what it is to forgive.

Those challenges didn't worry William. The one that had him worried was the last one, the one that involved doing something to Dancy that he never thought he would.

After her surreptitious baptizing of Bonaventure, Letice had begun to see a difference in her daughter-in-law. Dancy had come out of her stupor and slipped into motherhood. Since her milk had not come in as it should have, Dancy hadn't been able to nurse, and bottle feedings had mostly been attended to by Letice or Mrs. Silvey. But now the young mother was up by six o'clock, rinsing out the nighttime bottles while the morning bottle warmed. It was as if she'd been lost in a kind of half-coma and finally had snapped out of it. She spent hours and hours just looking at Bonaventure's face and watching him sleep. Dancy had become entirely captivated by her child, and his silence only served to charm her more. She was awed by the softness of his skin and found comfort in the rhythm of his breathing. She held him. She bathed him. She rocked him to sleep. He brought her joy. He kept her sane. He gave her back a missing part.

But sometimes motherhood wasn't enough. There were nights Dancy lay in bed, longing for William. Some nights she took a swallow or two from a jelly jar she'd filled with gin and kept in the back of her closet. The gin seemed to help her get to sleep and so escape her torment. But sleep was just another kind of torture when William inhabited her dreams. She knew he was there, always in the next room or on the other side of a wall with no door. She could hear him call to her, could smell his skin; every part of her yearned for his body, his smile, his masculine voice. A thrilling hunger overtook her while she dreamed, pulling her blood flow deep and down low. She craved his touch. She wanted to take him in her young woman's body.

Dancy woke from those dreams in the grip of frustration; her wounds cut open, her grief bleeding out.

Ghostly William had to look away.

Bonaventure was really the only one who could intrude on his mother's grief. She kept him near her always, even put him in a Moses basket next to the tub when she took her nightly bath. William would perch on the edge of the tub, just as Dancy had done when they were newlyweds. He watched as she soaped her beautiful arms and raised each lovely leg, and when she rose up out of the water, he felt a longing he could no longer satisfy. *This is what bittersweet means*, he would think, as he sat there loving his child and missing his wife and holding on to them both as hard as he could. His need was enough to put a touch on Dancy's shoulder and make her turn around.

One morning, when he was not quite four months old, Bonaventure was lying on his back, waving his hands in front of his face and noting that he could move his fingers (though he wasn't at all sure how), when he heard his mother whistling. The sound of it was enough to make him turn his head, flap his arms, stiffen his legs, and spread his toes in sheer and complete delight. Dancy took him from the crib, laid him on the floor, pulled him up to a sitting position, and said, "Oh my goodness! What a big boy you are!"

And he gave her the brightest smile he could muster in lieu of an audible giggle.

By the time he was six months old, Bonaventure was holding his head steady when he heard his mother laugh, and it wasn't long before he could follow the motions of her hand for the itsy-bitsy spider.

Save his muteness, Bonaventure Arrow was just like any other child: He put everything in his mouth and he drooled when cutting teeth, such babyhood things as that. But he was also purely himself. He developed particular habits as he grew, like taking his right shoe off but leaving the sock alone; he opened wide for oatmeal but didn't care for spinach; and sooner than most he was dexterous at putting shapes into holes and stacking alphabet blocks one upon the other.

There was, of course, one considerable difference: Bonaventure could hear things from all around the world and from another world as well, but only William knew that. Ghostly William knew a lot of things. He knew guilt was locked up in the Arrow house, and he knew that everyone would remain locked up with it until he met his challenges. It was going to take a long time.

William didn't mind.

He could wait.

He didn't much want to leave anyway.

TIME WENT ON WITH
NO NEW FINDINGS

H OLD on to me," the couch cushion offered in a jacquard silk voice, while Bonaventure took his first steps.

"Try to fall on your bottom," said the floor when he made it to the end of the sofa.

"Oh, be very careful," said the dining room chair. "I might tip over and you might too, then we'd both get bumps on our heads!"

"Take your time, little guy," said the deep voice he'd been hearing all along, the one that belonged to William.

Such perceptible counsel came to the curious boy, who was figuring his legs out in those early-walking days of toddlerhood.

On his first birthday, Dancy strung balloons across the dining room, and though Bonaventure didn't understand what all the fuss was about, he most definitely could hear blue and green and red and yellow ringing themselves into the monotone of a dreary February day.

Those color sounds intrigued him and brought with them that anonymous beat he'd heard before, the one that rolled around alongside his own heartbeat every now and again. The beat that meant something was happening.

. . . . .

Every day brought a heightened anticipation to Dancy and Letice, as they waited for Bonaventure to speak. Perhaps he would be one of those children who began talking in lengthy and meaningful sentences to the astonishment of family and friends. They loved him just the way he was; they truly did. Even so, both women had begun to move as if caught in a hesitation waltz, paused and quiet and still, one step suspended before taking another. They were listening for a word, a cry, or a bubbling giggle to come from their dear little boy who, at a year and a half, still hadn't found his voice.

Dancy started to take note of the sounds Bonaventure did make: His little hands slapped against the floor when he crawled, and the bells she'd put on his shoes jingled when he kicked his legs while sitting in his high chair. He pounded his toy hammer against wooden pegs and a toy mallet on a one-octave toy xylophone. When he was being silly, he would force air out through his lips to make that raspberry sound that children love. Dancy was greatly encouraged by his silliness because it showed that he was being expressive, even if he didn't use his voice to do it. Her favorite Bonaventure sound was the smacking one he made with his mouth when he put what passed for a kiss on her cheek. But even in the thick of her enthusiasm Dancy still listened for signs of vocals. Often when she watched him nap she could tell a difference in his sleeping silence, the naturalness of it, and then she felt bad for noticing. She couldn't possibly understand that Bonaventure's silence would serve a purpose to do with the family.

Sometimes their pausing and listening had nothing to do with Bonaventure and everything to do with a split-second, quick-flashing vision of William, or the ricochet of a word he'd said, or maybe the sudden scent of him on a zephyr that seemed an exhalation. This pattern of stopping to catch a sound or sight or smell became their normal way, and so Dancy and Letice moved through the house on Christopher Street keeping interrupted time with an uncertain metronome, day after expectant day.

Sometimes when she entered a room, Letice sensed that William had just been there but had hurried out because he didn't wish to stay. This rejection upset and mystified her. She couldn't fit it in with her memories: how he'd carried around an old nightgown of hers until he was almost three; all the dandelion bouquets he'd pulled from behind his back; the year he glued macaronis to a coffee can and painted it red for Valentine's Day. Memory led to more memory: the sight of two-year-old William standing on a kitchen chair stirring dish suds in the sink; how he clomped around in cowboy boots that were sometimes on the wrong feet; how he fell asleep with his hand in his catcher's mitt. The smell of boy. His big brown eyes. Nowhere in these memories could she find a place for blood or bullets.

Letice prayed for the repose of William's soul, she prayed for Dancy, and she prayed that the police would find out the killer's name.

William didn't want her to pray for the repose of his soul. It felt as if she was praying him away.

Time went on with no new findings. Letice went to the police station for another face-to-face with Sergeant Turcotte.

"I've been to see the director of the asylum," he said.

Letice braced herself.

"There's no change, Mrs. Arrow, no change at all. The guy just stares most of the time. The nurses say he shuffles around some and likes to sit outside."

"Have you been checking records at the bank? Following up on people who might have wanted revenge?"

"Yes, ma'am, we did that. If anything, your bank
extended more loans than they called in. There were some
that got foreclosed, but we could account for all those folks
and their descendants. Of course, there would have been
situations where people came in to ask for a loan but were
never even considered. We didn't find any records of denied
applications, so there'd be no way to trace any of those
people. I'm sorry, Mrs. Arrow."

"Thank you, Sergeant. Please continue to check with
the doctors and nurses and keep me informed."

"I surely will, ma'am."

Letice wondered how it was that she hadn't gone mad.

Sergeant Turcotte was not the only one to visit the asylum
in regard to The Wanderer; Eugenia Babbitt went there
too. So did William Arrow. William was trying to figure
out the connection between him and his murderer, or at
least try to understand his killer's state of mind. It was
becoming clear to him that the man had no constant state
of mind, that most of the time his killer's mind was utterly
and completely blank.

TAKING UP THE PROPHECY

TRINIDAD Prefontaine was alone in this world. She'd never known her father, and her mother was dead from the bite of a poisonous thing, as best anyone could figure out. When she was eleven years old, Trinidad had ended up in an orphanage for Negro children, and at seventeen she'd become the wife of Jackson Prefontaine, a hardworking young fellow she'd met there. The two of them found work over in Mississippi, where they never had children and Jackson died fairly young.

She had no brothers or sisters; however, until recently there'd been a relative on her mother's side, an old maiden aunt by the name of Henriette Dimontere. Henriette had died in her sleep, lying flat on her back atop ironed white sheets. On her last day on earth, this Henriette enjoyed several moments of prescience that had inspired her to take a bath, don her best nightgown and purple turban, and lie down on those freshly washed-and-ironed white sheets. Then she closed her eyes and died.

The prescience had actually come to Henriette the week before, when she'd been inspired to leave a last will and testament (which bore the seal of a notary public), a copy of which was recorded at the courthouse by the Register of

Deeds. Another copy was mailed to her niece, Trinidad Prefontaine, care of the Virgil B. Hortons.

Henriette had been given her house and land by the judge who'd employed her for most of her life and who had also been her lover. Though the judge had been good to Henriette, he would not allow her to take her niece in when the child had been left an orphan. Henriette had kept in touch with her only living relative and now was leaving the property to her. She'd always felt sorry for the girl, surmising that she'd had a miserable childhood.

Trinidad received this news some three weeks later in June of 1952, and she took it as a sign. She'd begun to feel an itching on the soles of her feet, and she took that as a sign too; mixed in with all that itching was her own intuition and Mam Judith's prophecy, and Trinidad decided it was time to move on. She'd been serving the Dalton family for quite some time and something was telling her it was just about enough. In fact, there was more than one something. There was the imp that still skipped around at the edge of her eyesight, and there was the memory of that vision she'd once had of the circling raven, the dove, and the sparrow on a night when certain stars shone bright through holes in rain-filled clouds.

All of those things pulled on Trinidad, but what pulled on her most was a fluttering that came to her reversed heart sometimes. Good Lord, how that fluttering could get her attention!

And so at the age of thirty-nine, Trinidad began to detach from the Pascagoula Hortons, point her toes westward, and scan the horizon, sniffing at the air like a hound on a scent. The Hortons were devastated at her departure, but the best she could do to comfort them was to say she would remember them fondly and might return for a visit.

All of her belongings fit into an old leather satchel she'd

bought at a secondhand store: three cotton dresses and a sweater, as well as an assortment of objects she treasured because she believed they held spiritual powers. She carried her kitchen around on her back, rolled up in a handmade quilt—a pot, a pan, a knife and spoon, a rolling pin, and a coffee pot made of white-speckled, slightly chipped enamel over steel.

On the day she set out, Trinidad took one last look eastward and went the other way. She made it to Louisiana by means of a ferryboat that ran across Bay St. Louis, and once there walked the shoulder of Highway 90.

She entered Bayou Cymbaline on her own two feet, and not one of its citizens noticed her arrival. She reached the center of town at two o'clock in the afternoon on the very hot next-to-the-last day of June. Ten minutes after she'd crossed the city limits, she stood before the entrance of the courthouse on Lafayette Street, the one in which William and Dancy had married. She went around back in search of a hose or a water pump with a sign that would designate it "for colored." She always looked for such a sign above doorways, at hospitals, schools, churches, cemeteries, beaches, lunch counters, and most of all public restrooms.

Trinidad wanted to wash the travel dust from her face, hands, and feet. She found a fountain but no designation. This made her very nervous. She knew the boundaries. She knew the story of Homer Plessy, a man who was seven-eighths white and one-eighth black who had boarded a car of the East Louisiana Railroad in New Orleans bound for Covington and intentionally sat in a white-only car and refused to move when asked. Plessy was arrested and remanded for trial in Orleans Parish, where he was convicted of breaking the law and fined. Trinidad also knew that the United States Supreme Court supported the State of Louisiana with regard to Homer Plessy in a ruling it called "separate but equal." Trinidad believed the law would not be on her side if she mistakenly washed herself at an unmarked fountain, so she nervously washed before going to settle the business matter that had brought her all this way. She did not know that Bayou Cymbalinians in general had never embraced Jim Crow, no matter how well received he was in New Orleans.

The back door to the building was locked, and her only option was to go through the front. Trinidad began to worry about exactly where this prophecy was going; just as she wasn't used to drinking out of unmarked fountains, she wasn't in the practice of entering through unmarked front doors. Once inside the vestibule, she felt coolness settle on her head and move down her body, diminishing the sun scorch of the open road and the burning it had put on her skin. She consulted the directory posted on the wall and proceeded on through the mezzanine and up a grand staircase to Room 205, the office of the Register of Deeds. She removed a document of identification and a folded paper from a pouch that hung around her neck and presented it to the woman behind the counter, keeping her head down and being sure to address the woman as ma'am and not look directly into her eyes. The clerk checked the document's authenticity and gave directions to the property Trinidad had inherited from her dear and dead old aunt Henriette. Trinidad thanked the woman and wondered when the other shoe would drop.

The directions took her to the outskirts of town, and she ended up at a two-room house with a wraparound porch, a mansard roof, and a cupola sheathed in copper. A small barn and a chicken coop completed the estate, and a red-painted water pump stood in the yard, directly in line with the door. Trinidad liked the feel of the place, the unmistakable rightness of it. She entered the house and began removing dust-covers from what furnishings there were: a good, sturdy table with two straight-backed chairs, an ornate pump organ with a green velvet bench, a rocking chair with a seat made of cane, and a neat and narrow bed in a room off the kitchen. It was absolutely more than enough.

Opening the door of the woodstove showed that it was all cleaned out and ready for fire; there was even a box of strike-anywhere matches that had been put inside an empty can to keep the damp away. She went outside, primed the pump, and filled the bucket she'd found by the door. Putting the big tin ladle to her lips, Trinidad drank her fill of cool, clear water before setting off for the barn, where she bowed her head and expressed her thanks for the lantern oil, the ladder, the axe, and the spade that she found within it.

She spent the rest of that first afternoon giving the property a more thorough going-over than her initial inspection had allowed. She noticed a dark spot on the floorboards in the kitchen and looked up to find a watermark on the ceiling, for which she went to the woods to collect some pine pitch and make herself a patch.

Night fell, and her stomach was complaining about how she'd forgotten lunch, and so she set a big pot of water to boiling. She filled it with the onions and carrots she'd found growing among a bunch of bergamot and overgrown brambles out back, near a sagging old rope clothesline. Trinidad was thankful for her earthy dinner.

Over the next few days she made several trips into Bayou Cymbaline, where she spent her saved-up coins on such things as four balls of twine, some stone-ground flour, and a piece of fine white linen. People were friendly, and to anyone who asked she confided that she'd inherited the small house out on the Neff Switch road. Yes, that's right, the one that had belonged to Henriette Dimontere, who'd been her mother's only sister. She said she was originally from over near Bayou Cane but had spent several years in Pascagoula. She had always heard good things about Bayou Cymbaline, she would say, and everyone liked her just fine.

Bayou Cymbaline had started a generation before the Civil War and quickly became the pet project of a couple of competing women, wives of the two biggest millionaires ever made by sugarcane and old King Cotton. The women tried to out-do each other in building monuments to themselves, and as a result the town suffered no shortage of grandeur. Its fine old library was built of the very best brick and sported a portico and Doric columns and a pair of two-ton doors that swung so smoothly they seemed to be weightless. "Even a two-year-old can open those doors," is what the old ladies would say. A museum of local heritage occupied the library's second floor and was staffed by the local chapter of the Civil War Society, a group comprised entirely of sweet-smelling women who met for tea and delicate pastries on the third Thursday of every month, wearing girdles and hats and snow-white gloves, no matter the heat or humidity.

Bayou Cymbaline was home to fishermen, shopkeepers, and makers of barrels; to poets, musicians, and philosopher types, and to every sort in between. To the casual observer, it might have seemed an odd mix of folk; however, such diversity infused the place with enough character to circle the earth twice at the equator. It was not unusual to find a person skilled in the cleaning of shrimp playing chess in the park with a reader of Shakespeare. Some folks said "ain't" and "I don't got no," while others spoke with cultured refinement, each word enunciated and grammatically correct; still others fell somewhere in between. There were those who ate from homely tin dishes all bumpy with dents, and those who took their meals off bone china plates so thin at the edge you could see right through them. Bayou Cymbaline is probably best described as a municipal jambalaya—a slow-simmered stew with a hot, tangy flavor from the blending of mixed bloods and Caribbean spice. The population stood somewhere in the neighborhood of 9,000 souls, most of European descent, though some had made their way from Acadia in Canada or from African jungles by way of slave ships that had stopped in Saint-Domingue.

There was a healthy respect for individuality in Bayou Cymbaline as well as for the eccentric and the avant-garde. The fact was that the town was accepting of strangers, no matter their color, which made things easy for Trinidad Prefontaine.

She opened her heart and her home to her Purpose, and waited for it to come in.

AN ELOQUENCE OF FACE
AND HANDS

WHILE Trinidad Prefontaine settled into her new home out on the Neff Switch road, toddler Bonaventure was learning to produce all manner of clicks and occasionally tied a small breath to a *t* or an *h* or an *s*, but that was the extent of it. On an early summer evening when he was two years old, Dancy held him in her lap as she moved the porch swing with the toes of one foot and said, "Red skies at night, sailors delight," then sang a song about shrimp boats.

When Bonaventure felt her voice vibrate against the back of his head, he squirmed around to press his ear against her chest and to reach up a hand to touch her throat. He felt the rising of her sternum as it let the air in and set her vocal cords vibrating and sending forth oscillations. He could hear the muscles of her larynx move and grab hold of the air and turn it into the song.

Touching throats as people spoke became a habit of Bonaventure's. Before he went to sleep at night, when he was all alone, he would call up the words of the day and place a hand against his own throat and invite his own tongue and teeth and palate and lips to form the words that he remembered. And then he didn't do that anymore. Little by little and one day at a time even his clicks and bits of alphabet disappeared as Bonaventure put all effort into developing an eloquence of face and hands. He found it pleasing to keep unnecessary noise from cluttering up the silence. He seemed to know it was the better choice.

Dancy and Letice loved Bonaventure's expressive ways. Grandma Roman was another story; she felt that Bonaventure's gesturing made him look spastic. After every visit to Christopher Street, the same tirade stomped through her mind: How is that child ever going to learn to speak like a human being if he doesn't even have to try? His mother should make him work harder at it. What does she suppose people think when they see him behave like that, wiggling his fingers around and rolling his eyes and smiling like a chimpanzee? Yes, it was the same tirade every time.

Bonaventure was an affectionate child, but not with his Grandma Roman. He could hear her coming from miles away and it always made him fretful. At the sound of her voice he would curl himself into a tight little ball, just as he had *in utero*. And about the only time he really pitched a fit was when she tried to pick him up.

"Sorry, Mama," Dancy would say, "it looks like somebody needs a nap."

"You know something, Dancy? I don't believe I've ever been around that child when you don't speak those very same words," Adelaide Roman would say, and she was right.

It seemed to Dancy that after one of these recoiling episodes, her mother would start a casual-seeming conversation about the worries of parenthood. It sounded innocent enough, but it was vengeful through and through.

"You sure have to feel sorry for mothers who lose their babies, don't you think, Dancy? Just look at those Silveys, isn't that what happened to them?" Adelaide Roman might say. "Well, sometimes it's just in God's plan, I suppose. A fitting punishment for having sinful sex, or something along those lines. Lordy, I can't even imagine what it must be like to find your baby dead. Can you?"

Dancy never took Bonaventure to Père Anastase. She thought that a cemetery was no place for a two-year old. And she superstitiously thought that maybe Death would take a look at her wonderful child and grab him for its own. It wasn't easy having the bayou and New Orleans and voodoo hovering around at the edges of her mind, trying to insinuate themselves into her way of thinking. And even if she managed to put all of that noise out of her head, there were her mother's words and the International Church of the Elevated Forthright Gospel and that horrid preacher. What if losing William was simply a punishment for having sex before she was married, and not only having it but enjoying it and getting pregnant? What if there truly was a God and he was the sort to take her baby from her? Or what if he was the sort to take a voice from a baby because of a mother's sins, as if to give a warning?

Dancy wasn't taking any chances.

Letice had volunteered to babysit on Sunday afternoons so Dancy could go alone to the cemetery. One Sunday, after she'd put Bonaventure down for a nap and was getting ready to leave for Père Anastase, Dancy couldn't find her favorite sweater. It was in Bonaventure's room. Then she couldn't find her watch and found it in Bonaventure's room, and then she couldn't find her shoes and found them in Bonaventure's room. She was so caught up in all this losing and looking and finding that she didn't pay much attention to the fact that Bonaventure was sitting up in his bed, watching her come and go. He was also blinking his eyes and grinning when his hair mysteriously ruffled off his forehead. William was playing with his little boy.

To Bonaventure, these interactions were natural; that bodiless voice had always been there, talking to him or maybe playing the soft breeze game. He didn't question this presence; small children don't think about death and haunting and the oddness of disembodied voices. Small children believe in magic.

Dancy knew nothing of William's frequent presence or the connection he had with his son. But she thought she knew a warning when she saw one. There was a reason she kept finding things in Bonaventure's room. What if Death was waiting to take him in his sleep, which had happened to the Silveys? A nervous chill came over her, causing her to reach for Bonaventure and his little-boy warmth. She scooped him up, put him in a new set of clothes, and took him with her to Père Anastase.

She saw William standing at the door of the tomb, big as life and smiling like crazy. But then she blinked and he was gone, and she marveled at what imagination could do.

The sighting was for Dancy alone; Bonaventure wouldn't have recognized William anyway. But Bonaventure certainly could hear him, and the baby picked out the sound of William's smile and separated it from the sounds of snails moving and grass growing and ladybugs flying away home. Bonaventure Arrow did love the sound of the big, bright smile that belonged to the gentle deep voice.

As she lay awake that night, Dancy Arrow felt uneasy. She couldn't forget the chill she'd felt in Bonaventure's room, and she couldn't shake that vision of William. She got out of bed and walked through the sleeping house to the kitchen, where she sat smoking cigarettes in the dark and sipping gin from Waterford crystal. Dancy felt the crystal brought dignity to her drinking, though all it really did was let her overlook the fact that she was drinking alone. It wasn't the first time. As she flipped open the Zippo to light her seventh Pall Mall, she stared into the flame and made her mind go blank.

William was in the kitchen too, and he didn't like seeing Dancy drink. He turned away and walked through walls until he stood over Bonaventure, watching him breathe and sleep. William figured he still had quite a long time before things had to change. He'd been thinking more and more about the challenges facing him, and now as he looked at his child's innocent face, he began to question the fairness of using Bonaventure's help. Would it be so wrong to forget the challenges and just stay where he was? Almost Heaven wasn't such a bad place; he could walk the shore of its beautiful sea, and he could come to Christopher Street whenever he wanted. Dancy needed him, he reasoned, and his killer was well taken care of. Maybe he really should let things be.

William and Dancy stayed where they were for several hours more that night, two restless beings trying to cope.

MISSION

BROTHER Harley John Eacomb was preaching a sermon in the Resurrection Tent by the side of the river: "Brothers and sisters, it is your mission, your sacred purpose as stewards of Almighty God, to go out amongst the sinners and heal them. For, indeed, you are healers, brothers and sisters. And healing, like charity, begins at home, for the devil loves nothing more than to slither into the homes of the righteous. Know this, brothers and sisters: Your way will not be easy! The Lord's work is never easy! I promise that you will be tested. The spiritually ailing, the afflicted, the devil-possessed move among you, and the worst of them masquerade as the innocent! Do not be fooled by them, brothers and sisters! Do not be fooled! You must find those who are flawed and bring perfection to them."

Adelaide Roman was engorged with inspiration. She would do anything for Brother Harley John. She had felt cheated out of everything all her life, and now finally here was someone she deserved, someone who was special in the eyes of God, someone her body constantly hungered for. She took it as her personal mission to please Brother Eacomb in all things.

Adelaide made a telephone call. "Dancy," she said,

"it's high time I got to make friends with my one and only grandchild."

Dancy responded with "Well, no one's stopping you, Mama."

"Don't be hateful, Dancy. He's growing up so fast; I mean, goodness' sakes, he's more than two years old already and his Grandma Roman hardly knows him! Do you know why that is?"

"No, but I'm sure you'll tell me."

"It's because I never get to have him all to myself, that's why. He's never even been over to my house; I always have to come to yours."

Dancy had to admit there was some truth in her mother's words, and she felt a twinge of pity. She didn't for a moment think her mother would be snappish with a baby.

"Okay, tell you what," she said. "You name the day and I'll bring Bonaventure over to spend some one-on-one time with you."

"Next Saturday at one would work just fine," Adelaide said.

On the appointed Saturday, Dancy loaded Bonaventure and his constant companion, a small stuffed pink elephant, into the car and told him he was off to make a friend out of Grandma Roman. Bonaventure didn't know what that meant.

"Alrighty, then, everything you'll need is in this bag, Mama: fresh clothes, a storybook, and a snack. He ate a good lunch, so I don't think he'll be hungry, but I figured just in case. Oh, and there's some diapers too. We've been working on the potty training, but you may not understand if he tries to tell you."

"I managed to raise you, Dancy. It's like riding a bicycle; you never forget." Adelaide Roman had no intention of changing a diaper. She may have kicked up a fuss about wanting to have Bonaventure to herself, but that was for the sake of her mission. The fact was, she was perfectly happy to keep her distance; children were messy things.

"You be a good boy for Grandma Roman, Whirly-bird. I'll see you in a little bit; I'm just gonna do a little shopping." Then Dancy told Adelaide she would be back by three.

Bonaventure didn't know about this situation. He hadn't expected to be left with his Grandma Roman, but it happened so fast he couldn't even protest. When Dancy was gone, he sat down near the door and held his pink elephant next to his neck with one hand while he sucked the thumb of the other. That's what Bonaventure always did when he felt apprehensive. He'd never been comfortable with the sound of Grandma Roman, though by now he could easily muffle her voice. But that didn't mean he was happy being alone with her.

Adelaide sat down on the sofa, stared at Bonaventure, and congratulated herself on having been inspired to get him alone. Just wait until she told Brother Eacomb! She hadn't even finished her self-congratulations when a new idea struck. She got up, walked over to Bonaventure, and took the pink elephant out of his hand. He immediately reached for it, but she made no move to give it back. Instead, she went into the kitchen and waited for him to follow. When he toddled into the room, she opened the oven, put his precious pink elephant inside, and slammed the door shut. Bonaventure's apprehension tingled into anticipation.

A game! he thought. He stopped in the doorway and gave her a grin as if to say, —What next?

Grandma Roman stood still and didn't do a thing.

Bonaventure touched one hand to his mouth and then extended his arm toward her as if he was blowing a kiss. It's what he did to engage.

No response.

He did this gesture over and over, but Grandma Roman did not react. Apprehension returned.

"Do you want your elephant back?"

A certain nod.

"Say please."

Hand to mouth, arm outstretched.

"Say please."

Hand to mouth, arm outstretched.

Still nothing.

Bonaventure was beside himself. He went to the stove and reached for the door handle, but Grandma Roman slapped his hand away. When he tried again, she lowered herself so she could grab his shoulders and look him in the eye.

"I am doing this for your own good, young man. It is my sacred mission. I'll give you your elephant back; all you have to do is say please. I know you can do it; the devil's got your tongue and nobody is helping you get it back."

Hand to mouth, arm outstretched.

Adelaide Roman was irritated and she shook him. "You can be as stubborn as you want, little boy. I am trying to heal you as I've been directed to do."

By now Bonaventure was flapping his hands in the air, his bottom lip and little chin quivering.

She scooped him up and took him back to the sofa, where he curled up and listened for his elephant and his mother. His little face crumpled, and tears flowed from his eyes as he cried in his silent way. Adelaide sat down on the couch too and worked on a piece of embroidery.

Bonaventure made four attempts to go back to the kitchen. The last time, she threatened to turn the stove on and burn up his elephant if he did it again.

So he didn't.

At five minutes to three, she took the pink elephant out of the oven and gave it back.

"How'd it go?" Dancy asked when she walked in the house. "Mama, he looks like he's been crying."

"Oh, he was. Only a little bit, though. I think he was missing you. We got on just fine; no trouble at all."

"And he's soaked right through to his trousers! Honestly, Mama!"

"Well, he must've just done that. How was I supposed to know? It's not like he could've told me. Is there a wet spot on my sofa?"

Dancy didn't answer.

As she watched them drive away, Adelaide Roman reckoned that Brother Eacomb was right. Being a healer wasn't easy. She would pray about it. And why did Dancy allow the kid to have a pink toy anyway? Weren't things bad enough without him being a sissy? She guessed she would have to pray about that too.

THE Wanderer could still walk and dress himself and manage his hygiene. But he could not remember his name, or how old he was, or where he'd been born, or how such a thing had happened to his face. A tree stood in the courtyard of the place he was in; The Wanderer watched it carefully. There were birds nesting in its branches.

Sometimes when The Wanderer was watching those birds, Bonaventure could hear the breeze in their feathers.

More than two years after the crime, no one had figured out anything.

Letice continued to pray and Miss Babbitt continued to visit, as did ghostly William.

RARER SECRETS

SMALL secrets have always existed in the form of bits of information or private habits kept within personal darkness. For instance, in Bayou Cymbaline, teenage boys hid pinup-girl magazines to look at in the nighttime, and housewives skimmed a few cents off the grocery money to buy a new lipstick or a bright chiffon scarf.

But there were rarer secrets in town that had more to do with fear and shame, like those of women who claimed their bruises were caused when they walked into a door or slipped and fell down the stairs, or those of men who lost money shooting craps and hid when the insurance man came to collect the premium.

These bigger secrets came to Trinidad Prefontaine as an atmospheric change, a thickening of the air lasting no more than a second or two. Sometimes this change came as a sudden coolness, at other times as a rise in humidity, or as a crack in the sky like a flash of lightning, or as a cascade of unleashed electricity in a shower storm of sparks. After the atmospheric change, she would get the feeling that something had been altered, and then a secret would call to her, and she would try to work with it.

Not far from Trinidad's small inherited estate she found

a swamp with palmetto flats thick as a jungle and laced at the edges with cardinal flowers and bald cypress. In the nearby bottoms, clumps of sphagnum moss languished among spiderworts and Christmas fern, and bayou violets were spectacularly showcased. Low growing partridge berry and piney woods lily filled up the swamp's slopes, thriving among false foxglove and Carolina jessamine. It was her private paradise.

Due to her upbringing, Trinidad was a believer in the powers of herbs and roots and every local species of growing-in-the-wild plants. She had discovered on her own that every single thing that grew in the swampland and forest bore something of the circle within it, whether in the shape of a leaf, or the bulb of a root, or a perfectly round grain of pollen. Trinidad regarded circles as symbols of God's eternal love. Her favorite circle was that which is found in the small dark eye of a sparrow.

This respect for sparrows was something she held in common with none other than Letice. The two had something else in common: a long-ago experience in a quiet room, where a breeze had fluttered in after the blood was cleaned away.

But the memory of that common experience hadn't come to Trinidad yet, or even to Letice. It was one of those rarer secrets.

THE WAYS OF A SILENT BOY

BONAVENTURE began to notice that interesting things happened when he took risks, and so he became a swashbuckler child, venturing farther, and climbing higher, and reaching for strange, new things. It sometimes left Dancy in a quandary as to whether she should offer him praise or a scolding, since she did admire his daring. The only time he clung to her, to Letice, or to one of the Silveys was when his grandma Roman came by, and nothing and nobody was going to make him let loose his hold. It did not escape Dancy that this aversion to Grandma Roman had grown stronger since the day Adelaide had him all to herself.

Adelaide knew better than to force the issue; she could sense Dancy's suspicion. She continued her weekly visits to Christopher Street and demonstrated sweetness every chance she got. Adelaide reminded herself that patience is a virtue, and fell into the habit of biding her time.

By the time he was three and a half, Bonaventure could've melted a rock with one look, but he remained unaware of his charm. When he witnessed something particularly winsome, he would point an index finger and raise his eyebrows and take in air through his wide-open mouth to express, —Did you see? Did you see? His hands would flutter and his face would light up and his whole body would wear his wonder.

He'd have been a real chatterbox, had he been given to talking.

In fact, Bonaventure did talk to someone when he was all alone. He'd found a voice inside his head but could use it only with the very deep voice he'd always known—William's. Bonaventure's speech at these times came naturally and complete, containing every part of speech and following proper grammar. Bonaventure accepted this situation without question; very young children do not doubt the supernatural. And since he had no way to tell anyone about these conversations, they remained a confidential connection.

One such exchange went like this:

"Hey, there, Bonaventure!" William's deep voice said.

—I got a squirt gun today!

"You did? What color is it?"

—It's green and I can take it in the bath.

"Can I come see later on?"

—Sure.

"But don't you squirt me!"

Giggle, giggle. —I won't.

Bonaventure was getting older, and he would go to school one day, so William wanted to prepare him for being different. William also knew that he really did have to face his challenges and so had to ease Bonaventure into helping him fix the wreckage of the past. But, of course, it would take time.

For more than three years William had enjoyed his anonymous fatherhood; Bonaventure did not even know who he was. William could be playful and protective and special, though he was nothing more than a voice. But he knew it couldn't last forever. The time had come to set things in motion, and the first step was to make his child aware of his very special hearing.

"Your squirt gun is green, huh? I think you can hear green. Am I right?"

Bonaventure smiled and said, —Yes! I can hear every color!

"What does green sound like?"

It wasn't always easy to describe the sounds, so this time Bonaventure just said, —I like green.

"I like green too. I like green Jell-O."

—Me too. But I like red Jell-O better.

"What does red sound like?"

—It sounds like fireworks. Do you like fireworks?

"Yup. I can hear fireworks, but I can't hear red. You're the only one who can do that. You're the only one who can hear a lot of things. You're the only one who can hear me."

—I am?

This was how one challenge was set in motion.

Dancy Arrow had been traveling the road of her son's missing speech for quite a while, and her feelings on the matter ran in circles. Her main concern was for his safety, since without a voice he couldn't call for help. And it was a source of sadness to her that Bonaventure would never be able to sing. She also felt sorry for herself because of all that she missed out on: no baby cooing, no cries of delight, no laughter, no questioning why, and no hearing him call her Mama. She felt selfish for those feelings, and ashamed, and so forced herself to call to mind all that she did receive from Bonaventure's silence: the need to look into each other's eyes, his busy little hands, the language of his face.

But still.

The idea surfaced that maybe it wasn't that he could not speak, but more that he did not speak, though Dancy couldn't imagine why. She went to the library and read about aphasia and aphonia and brain damage and emotional disorders. She wondered why he could cough but not put sounds into words. She consoled herself that he hadn't had a forceps birth. She tried to remember a pregnancy trauma and could only come up with one.

Eventually she came to the realization that Bonaventure communicated better without a voice than did most people who had one, and that his silence complemented everything else about him. He was small for his age, with a round face, a pointed chin, eyes brown as chocolate, and his father's straight dark hair. His ears stuck out a bit, and the tip of a crooked smile placed a dimple on the left side of his face. The back of his neck rose with a fragile kind of grace from a delicate spine between slightly sloped shoulders. The sight of the back of that little neck could bring Dancy Arrow to tears.

Grand-mère Letice had continued to pay for every test imaginable in a tireless effort to find out what was wrong with her grandson, and why, and to determine what might be done. Or so it would appear. What Letice was really doing was seeking to remove medical science from the presence of mystery. She tirelessly looked for evidence of such mystery and believed she found it in Saint Anthony's prayer for Wisdom, a prayer that Saint Bonaventure favored and in which she found these words:

> . . . *put forth Thy hand and touch my mouth, and make it a sharp sword to utter eloquently Thy words. Make my tongue, O Lord, as a chosen arrow, to declare faithfully Thy wonders. . .*

. . . .

Touch my mouth? A chosen arrow? *Arrow?* To Letice, there was no mistaking that the words of that prayer were a portent. The doctors could test Bonaventure all they wanted.

Although there were no definitive answers, the latest test showed that voice or no voice, Bonaventure's hearing was exceptionally acute. However, the test did not quantify his ability. Everyone would have been shocked to know that he could hear such things as the blink of an eye from across the room, or the sound of a falling flower petal before it hit the floor. They would never have been able to fathom that the scope of his hearing wasn't even accurately gauged by the sounds of blinking eyes and falling petals, or even by the sounds of shooting stars. For how can such a glorious gift be measured? Surely its value is tied to the giver's intentions, which in the case of Bonaventure Arrow had to do with bringing peace to the living and the dead.

Whenever he talked to Bonaventure, William always brought up the super hearing and encouraged the boy to listen as hard as he could. This lesson presented William's heart with a paradox and placed him at war with himself.

THE Wanderer continued to live his life unmarked by the clock or the calendar. For the longest time, he did not think of the past and he did not imagine the future. He simply ate and slept and breathed. And then he began to look at magazines and catalogs. Once, he found a magazine that was all about cars and the thought of steel slammed into his brain. That night he dreamed that he sat on a stool and looked into a mirror in a place that was blue with the smoke of cigarettes. He sat there in that dream, lighting matches, one after the other, and letting them burn to his fingertips. He sort of liked the pain. There was music in the background, but the only dancers were those little flames.

The Wanderer had been in the asylum for nearly four years, although he couldn't have told anyone that. And still he remained a John Doe.

THE ABUNDANT GOOD
GRACES OF HIS SILENCE

DANCY read to Bonaventure constantly: newspapers, billboards, and his father's childhood books. He had a sharp knack for fitting print to voice, and by the time Bonaventure was four years old, tests involving written instructions showed that he could read some words. He'd begun by associating words with pictures, as children always do, but in Bonaventure's case, something more happened: the sounds of the stories came to him too, even if they existed in another place or time. He could hear whooshing lassos on the American plains, and the colors of rainbows in Ireland; he could detect Eskimos fishing through holes in the ice, and kites in the skies over Norway. Bonaventure Arrow could travel the world through the abundant good graces of his silence.

William liked to be in the room at story time; it made him feel included. He loved to see Bonaventure snuggle as close to Dancy as he could get, his little head resting against her arm. William watched his son's eyes move from side to side as he followed the words, and he noticed how Dancy would wait for him to finish looking at the pictures and then let him turn the page. William loved the sounds of Bonaventure's breathing and Dancy's voice. Sometimes he would sit on her other side, and she would wonder how it was that she felt some pressure there.

One rainy afternoon, Bonaventure brought a different book for Dancy to read, one he'd found in a drawer in the front room. It was a photo album. He set the book in his mother's lap and climbed up next to her. Dancy felt as though she'd been hit hard in the stomach. The room started spinning and suddenly became airless. When she made no move to open the album, Bonaventure opened it for her. When she still didn't say anything, he took her hand and placed it atop the first picture. Dancy managed to take a deep breath, and equilibrium returned. She had never been able to talk to Bonaventure about his father. And they certainly had never looked at pictures of him; Dancy simply couldn't bear it.

William had been taken by surprise as well, and he wondered what Dancy would say.

"Do you want me to tell you who that is?"
    Nod, nod.
    "It's your father. It says William Arrow right there, see?"

To hear her speak his name made William ecstatic.

Head tilted; puzzled look. To Bonaventure, fathers were storybook people; some families had one and others didn't, and some people called their father Dad or Daddy.
    Dancy realized that Bonaventure might not understand exactly what she was talking about, so she said, "It's like Mr. Jarrett across the street. He's the dad to John and Rosie, right? And Mrs. Jarrett is the mom, like I'm your mom."

Look of pondering.

Dancy didn't know what more she could say. She thought that maybe the pieces would fall into place as they looked at the pictures. "The writing under this one says it was taken on his birthday in 1930, so he would have been four years old, like you are now. See his party hat and the crepe paper streamers?"

A look as if to say, —I love birthday streamers!

Dancy turned toward the back of the album. "Here's one when he was older."

Bonaventure pulled the book onto his own lap and lowered his head to study the photo. She put her arm around him and said, "Your father was a wonderful man, Bonaventure. He loved me and I loved him, and one day our love made you!"

William punched at the air in his joy.

Tap on photo, questioning look as if to ask, —Where is he now?

"He died before you were born. It was an accident. He's not here anymore. He went to live in heaven. It's a place where everything is always nice, but you can't see heaven from here, or drive to it or anything like that." Though Dancy did not believe in God or his heaven, she could not bring herself to take those ideas from her child.

Knitted brow, hands palm up as if to ask, —What do you mean?

"Do you remember the time we saw that cat in the street and you thought it was sleeping, but Grand-mère said it must've gotten hit by a car by accident and that it died and went to heaven?"

Nod, nod.

"Well, it was kind of like that with your dad. He wasn't hit by a car, but there was another kind of accident and his body went still and then he went to live in heaven."

Bonaventure turned his attention back to the photo album, examining each picture carefully and turning the pages slowly and listening to the story of his father's brief life. He was so absorbed in the photos that he did not even notice when Dancy left the room.

When he visited Bonaventure that night, an anxious William asked, "What did you do today?"

—Me and Mom looked at pictures of my dad. He died by an accident, but it wasn't from a car like the cat in the street. His body went still and he went to live in heaven. It's a place where everything is always nice, but you can't see it from here or drive to it.

"I know," William said.

—How do you know?

"Because I'm him. I'm your dad." William had to choke back emotion. He had wanted to tell Bonaventure the truth for so long but hadn't known how to go about it without confusing or scaring him. He desperately wanted to be real to Bonaventure, to be alive in some way. "There really was an accident and my body really did go still. But I'm still me and I still have my voice and that's how I can talk to you."

A surprised yet very happy look came to Bonaventure's face; he had always loved the voice. —Mom thinks you stay in heaven.

"Well, I do. Sort of. I'm in Almost Heaven. It's a different special place. I can leave Almost Heaven and visit you. You can't see me, but we can still talk."

—Can you see me?

"I sure can."

—Will Almost Heaven ever let me see you?

"No, it doesn't work like that."

—Why?

"Because it's more special this way."

—Why?

"I don't know."

—Maybe God knows. Grand-mère says God lives in heaven and he knows everything. You should ask God.

"If I see him, I will."

—I'm glad you're my dad. I love your sound.

William took that to mean "I love you," for sound was all he was to Bonaventure.

"I love you too," he said.

Within a year, Bonaventure Arrow could hear flowers grow, a thousand shades of blue, and the miniature tempests that rage inside raindrops. He'd built up a great store of words, every one of them left unspoken, save for those telepathic talks with his father.

Bonaventure had begun to collect mementos of his favorite sounds and put them in a box that he kept beneath his bed. It wasn't just any box; it was one that Mr. Silvey had helped him make from a wooden shipping crate he'd found in the attic over the carriage house. Bonaventure dearly loved that box. His great-grandfather, Alphonse Arrow, had brought that crate home from Europe a long time ago. It had "PORT OF NEW ORLEANS" painted in big letters on its top, its bottom, and all four sides, which made it very special. That box always brought the sound of steamships to Bonaventure's ears.

One of the first things in Bonaventure's collection was a jar of sand from the sandbox. The sand let him hear the water and rocks and seaweed from where it used to live.

He'd also put in an India-rubber ball that held the sounds of tigers and wild parrots, a stub of chalk that offered up the sounds of tiny creatures building seashells out of lime, and a piece of twine that spoke to him of banana stalks in a place called Papua, New Guinea.

Sometimes his silence let new sounds in, sounds with no physical memento to keep. Once, when he was playing outside, he looked up and translated the white of the clouds into the joyful noise of possibility. Then he looked at the grass and turned the sound of green into the molecular chatter of growing things. In the pink and orange of a sunset, he heard the measured beats of earthbound time.

Bonaventure was getting ever closer to the day he would hear festering sounds that were locked up with secrets in the house on Christopher Street, for his mother and his grand-mère kept mementos of their own, closed up in special boxes. One of those boxes was kept in a closet and the other in a niche in the chapel.

UP NEXT TO A
EUCALYPTUS TREE

TRINIDAD Prefontaine was sitting with her mending when all of a sudden the bottoms of her feet itched fiercely, as they had right before she'd walked away from the Hortons of Pascagoula. Once again, she let her feet have their way, and they took her into Bayou Cymbaline up next to a eucalyptus tree that stood amongst cypress and live oak with their cloaks of Spanish moss. Oil melted out of the silver-green leaves, flowing down the tree's trunk and through the cool, cool grass until it worked its way to her itching feet bottoms and made Trinidad all kinds of grateful.

She stared hard at the Spanish moss with its curved and curly scale-covered foliage that hung like living chains. She knew about Spanish moss and how it sheltered all manner of creatures—rat snakes and bats and a breed of jumping spider. She also knew that it had been planted by God and brought to the trees on the hand of the wind or by birds that were trying to nest.

Trinidad stayed there till night came on, when lights from a house across the way twinkled their way through the lacy Spanish moss and were reflected in her eyes. She could sense the house's inhabitants: two women, one little boy, and a presence. She could not at that moment define the presence, for her gift of Knowing brought nothing to mind. One of those women had the feel of the past about her, along with tears and begging.

The Knowing trembled in the veins of Trinidad's legs then, and made its way past her navel to waft along the conglomeration of her vertebrae before coming to rest on her opposite heart. So that is to be the place, she thought.

Inside the house, Letice had just hung up the phone after having a conversation with Sergeant Turcotte in which he told her he was officially closing the investigation. He promised to let her know if anything turned up in the future. He also said, "The fact that the man didn't even give a thought as to how he would get away from the scene points to the fact that he wasn't rational, Mrs. Arrow. He didn't have any bus or train ticket with him. Would a sane man think he could kill someone in broad daylight in a public place and then just walk to the depot and buy a ticket out of town? He didn't have any car keys either. He didn't think that far ahead, ma'am. He didn't make any plans. Do yourself a favor and accept that your son was killed in a random shooting that had nothing to do with anyone or anything except a crazy man with a torn-up face and a grudge against the world."

Letice Arrow could do no such thing. She did not believe in random. God does not deal in random.

ACCUSATION

BONAVENTURE cheated, Miss Wells!"
Frightened headshake. —No!

"Yes he did! He peeked when we weren't supposed to! He cheated!"

Frightened headshake!

"Yes you did too, Bonaventure Arrow! You cheated and now you're a liar!"

Frantic tapping on his ears as if to say, —I could hear the color orange, couldn't you?

This accusation came from a little girl named Theodosia in late September of 1955, during a game of Find the Pumpkin being played by Bonaventure's kindergarten class as they celebrated the coming of autumn. Each child took a turn hiding a paper pumpkin somewhere in the classroom while all the other children closed their eyes and put their heads down on the tabletops. After hiding the pumpkin, the hider was to sit back down and the others could get up to search for the hidden thing.

Jeffrey Coulter was a clever little fellow. He stomped over to the sand table and took off his shoes before tiptoeing over to the bookcase. It was there that he hid the pumpkin. Then he tiptoed over to the cubbies, put his shoes back

on, and stomped around the room a bit before returning
to his chair.

The children dashed to the sand table, but the pumpkin
wasn't there. They looked and looked but could not figure
out Jeffrey Coulter's cunning ruse. The only one not looking
was Bonaventure. He didn't have to. The color orange had
called to him, and he went right to it.

And then the accusation.

"Bonaventure had his head down, Theodosia. I was
watching," Miss Wells said. But the other kids kept whispering, and no one sat by him in story circle.

He wet the bed that night. No other children sat by him
again the next day. His shoulders sloped lower and lower,
and he wet the bed again. Bonaventure Arrow didn't know
what to do. The kids in his neighborhood were all older and
had always been very nice, and so he had no past experience
to draw on. He had never been ostracized.

That visiting beat, that unknown companion, came to
Bonaventure's heart. Anonymous as ever, it walked very
softly with respect for his misery and didn't even try to
tumble and twirl. It just wanted him to know it was there.

After two more wettings and refusals to eat, Dancy was
determined to get to the bottom of whatever was going on.
"Did something happen at school, buddy?" she asked.

Very solemn nod.

"Okay, sugar. You can stay home today. We'll get it
straightened out. Don't you worry." She went to see his
teacher that afternoon.

"I'm so sorry, Mrs. Arrow," Miss Wells said, and
explained what had happened. "I'll have a talk with Theodosia's parents. Bonaventure did nothing wrong. I won't allow

him to be mistreated, but I'll do it in such a way that no one will call him a teacher's pet."

Dancy was relieved and grateful.

Bonaventure went back to school on Monday, but things were not the same. It broke Dancy's heart and Letice's too; he'd been so excited about kindergarten. Up until then they'd sheltered him in the world they'd created, where everyone understood him and thought him brilliant and knew exactly what he meant to say. In that regard, they were just like any mother who understands her child's gibberish. Dancy and Letice could keenly read the way he asked —Why? with a tilt of his chin; the excitement of his fluttering fingers; the way his nose would scrunch up to say, —Yuck; his smiling happiness; his curious eyes; the bounce in his step; his contented breathing. They'd been able to control what happened to him, and they'd had a tendency to allow only the pleasant. And now this, the sharpest side of meanness.

"We should have known," each was heard to say. "We really should have known." What bothered Dancy and Letice most was that their beloved boy couldn't defend himself or even tell them what exactly had happened, or how he felt.

What bothered Bonaventure was that no one else even said they'd heard the color orange. Why was he the only one? On the first day of kindergarten when he'd seen all the other children, he'd felt himself part of something, a child the same as the others. He'd hoped that maybe his way of hearing would spread itself around, but now he knew that it didn't, and he wasn't really part of something at all. Bonaventure had no idea how to be so different. William was always telling him that he was the only one with super hearing, but sometimes he forgot. Bonaventure didn't like being different. Different was lonely. He wished he could put his ears in the coat closet at school, underneath the jump ropes and kick balls, where they couldn't get him into any more trouble.

Dancy and Letice put their heads together and decided there was one thing they might do to empower him, and that was to employ a sign language teacher. The irony of it was not lost on them—a child with very keen hearing learning the ways of the deaf—but what Bonaventure needed was a solid means of communication, one that would tide him over until he learned to write. Sign language fit the bill. They were giddy with relief when they came to this conclusion, and set about finding a teacher who would understand their situation. Dancy suggested they start with the Yellow Pages, but Letice told her not to worry, that she sat on several committees for one cause or another and surely someone could make a recommendation. It was true, she did sit on several committees, but it wasn't to them that she turned. Letice Arrow did as she always did; she turned to God.

She began by saying the Prayer to Saint Thérèse de Lisieux, which was a plea for guidance. Then she turned to Saint Anthony of Padua, who could restore lost things, even speech to the mute. But her prayers did not ask that her grandson find a voice; rather, she asked Saint Anthony to help them find whatever means of speech God meant for Bonaventure to have. Letice did her praying at all times of day and in all kinds of places: in her garden, or at her dressing table, or in the rear seat of her new Cadillac while Mr. Silvey drove her where she needed to go. Sometimes she even woke up in the night and went to her chapel, as if a saintly messenger waited there to take her prayer to heaven. And then it occurred to her to beseech Saint Bonaventure for help, for wouldn't a mystic understand their dilemma? Forever after, she would credit Bonaventure di Fidanza with leading her to

Saint Gerard, patron saint of motherhood, who in turn led her to the Saint Gerard Community for the Deaf. And that is how she found Gabe Riley, a very nice fellow who came to the house on Mondays, Wednesdays, and Fridays at four in the afternoon to teach the hearing Arrow family how to speak in sign.

Gabe Riley was of average height and slender. He had fine, light brown hair, a smooth, calm voice, and very kind hazel-colored, near-sighted eyes. He was the son of a hearing father and a deaf mother, and he'd learned to sign before he'd learned to speak. Gabe actually preferred sign over speech; he felt it was more honest, since no trick of tone or modulation could work to bend the truth. He firmly believed that hands and faces were more expressive than voices could ever be. Gabe didn't view his new pupil as handicapped at all.

He explained to Dancy and Letice that sign language has its own grammar and vocabulary, and that words could be spelled out letter by letter or communicated through a distinct motion. He told them it involves not just the hands but the face and the rest of the body as well. As an example, he hung his head and let his shoulders slope in dejection to show how loud a posture could be. He told them to imagine words being acted out, but in consistent, specific ways.

It so happened that Bonaventure was a natural at signing, helped along by the fact that he could indeed hear. Dancy and Letice were good at it too. Grandma Roman had been offered the opportunity to learn but declined. Her exact words were "I won't have any part of it, and I don't think you should either. You might just as well stick some big sign on him that says: 'There's something wrong with me.'"

Both Dancy and Letice were secretly glad to be free of her. They were also secretly glad that Gabe was the same age as William would have been, with Bonaventure being short a father. Both women admired Gabe and thought him an ideal teacher. He was patient yet demanding, and he knew how to strike a fair balance between the two. Inside of two weeks, members of the Arrow family were trying to sign to one another every time they spoke, in consideration of the fact that practice makes perfect. Their signed conversations were uncluttered and meaningful and right to the point.

All the while, the telepathic conversations Bonaventure had with his father went deeper.

—Last night before I fell asleep I heard someone toasting marshmallows, he said to William in one of their talks.

"Which is louder, the marshmallow or the fire?" William asked.

—They're the same kind of loud. The fire sings to the marshmallow, and the song turns the marshmallow brown because that's what marshmallows do when they're happy.

"You should listen real hard inside the house. You might hear some interesting things."

—Like what?

"Oh, I don't know, like things that might help somebody. Maybe you'll be a hero someday. Come to think of it, you sort of look like a hero."

—Are heroes different from regular people?

"Nope. Heroes are regular people who do something special."

—Are you a hero?

"I don't think so. Why?"

—Because you can still be here like regular, but you're not regular; you got dead.

"Well, I don't think that makes me a hero."

A thoughtful expression came over Bonaventure's face as he changed the subject. —How exactly did you get dead?

"Did you forget? I died in an accident."

—But what kind of accident?

"It's hard to explain," William said.

Sometimes they talked about very ordinary things. For instance, William might ask, "What's new?"

And Bonaventure might say, —I heard a caterpillar out in the garden, and when I went there, it crawled over my hand. But more often than not his reply was along the lines of:

—I watched some kids play ball in the park.

or

—I watched some kids play tag on the playground.

or

—I watched some kids play jacks on the sidewalk.

And William could see how it was for his boy.

Up until the sign language came along, William never had to worry about Bonaventure telling anyone about him. Because Bonaventure couldn't speak and wasn't writing things out, there hadn't been a problem. But now all that was changing, and William wasn't ready. He felt some anger toward Gabe Riley, because what really bothered him was the bond that was forming between the Arrows and the tutor. It also bothered him that Gabe could talk to Bonaventure in a private, special way. William wanted to be the only one who could do that. He began to attend the tutoring sessions so that he could learn sign too. Even though no one would ever see him do it, he would see them and know what they said.

"We need to talk about keeping secrets, Bonaventure," William said one day.

—What's a secret?

"It's something you don't tell anyone else."

—Are secrets bad?

"Some are bad and some are good. For instance, I don't want you to tell anyone that we talk to each other. That's a good secret."

—Why can't I tell?

"Well, it might hurt their feelings, because they can't hear me."

—And then they would wish they had super hearing like me, wouldn't they?

"Exactly."

There was a pause in conversation before Bonaventure returned to what he was most curious about. —Do you remember *anything* about your accident?

"I remember that it happened on my birthday."

—Did it hurt?

"Not really. I think it happened too fast to hurt."

—Oh. That's good.

William didn't say that there are many kinds of hurt.

THE Wanderer came down with a cold. It went from his head to his chest, enflaming and infecting his bronchi and lungs. He coughed as if to die from it.

A feeling came to Trinidad Prefontaine that she must will away the suffering of one unknown to her. She did this by handling herbs and roots as she prayed for that nameless soul.

The Wanderer began to get better, and he started to read again. He tended toward the classics, especially the books of Alexandre Dumas. When Eugenia Babbitt became aware of this preference, she made sure he had them all.

THE WAGON

JUST as he was short one father, Bonaventure was short a couple of grandfathers too, but that void was nicely filled by Mr. Silvey, who conducted himself with a grace born of gratitude. He felt he'd been given another child to love, so long after the death of his own.

Bonaventure had designated certain hallmarks of the workshop experience: the heft of the tools, the cold smell of iron, and the handmade solidity of the old hemlock bench. He and Mr. Silvey spent entire afternoons examining the contents of cast-off sewing machine drawers and rusty coffee cans, while Mr. Silvey provided a history of purpose for such things as ball-peen hammers and square cut nails, planes and chisels and a brass plumb bob. But Bonaventure's hands-down favorite was the hawk's bill snips that could cut a circle in a pipe if the need for such arose.

February 1, 1956, was Bonaventure's sixth birthday. It was a school day, and when he got home, he chose to spend the rest of it out in the workshop with Mr. Silvey. He was writing in complete sentences by then, so in addition to keeping up his side of a conversation through the likes of gestures, facial expressions, and sign, Bonaventure often wrote things out on a small notepad. One such conversation with Mr. Silvey marked a significant turn of events.

—What is this? Bonaventure asked with the point of a finger and the raising of his brow.

Forrest Silvey reached for the article in question and said, "Why, that's a nail puller. It's used to remove horseshoes. Yup, that's what it is all right. Don't know why I've kept it though; there hasn't been a horse around here since I don't know when."

—Did my dad have a horse? Bonaventure wrote the question out because he wanted to be very clear. One thing about school was that most kids talked about their dads. He desperately wanted to join in but wanted to get the facts from a person anyone could talk to, just in case they wanted proof, which meant someone other than his father, who had to be a secret because he was dead.

Bonaventure's reading and writing skills surpassed those of his classmates, but he was aware of that fact and would make adjustments if it meant he could somehow join in. Ever since the hidden pumpkin incident in kindergarten, Bonaventure had remained on the outer edge of acceptance, a place assigned to those who are different. It was the reason he never tried to tell anyone, in any way, about the sounds he heard.

Mr. Silvey reached up and scratched the place on his head he referred to as his thinking spot and replied, "No, I know for a fact that he didn't have a horse. But I'll tell you what he did have is that wagon over there," and he pointed toward the corner to the left of the window where a wooden wagon stood still in the shadows.

—Did he get it for Christmas?

"Nope, not for Christmas. There was a young fella knew

your grandpa Arrow, and it was him that made it and brought it around one night after supper. I remember it like it was yesterday. He made the handle from an old plow blade, and you won't find a better one."

—Does he still make things?

"Now, that I couldn't say. He left town not long after he brought that wagon over. Nobody ever heard from him again. There was talk that he joined up to fight in the war, but I can't say for sure that he did."

—What was his name?

"By golly, I sure can't think of it right now, but I'll let you know if it comes to me."

Bonaventure went over to the corner and took hold of that very fine handle, and when he did, he felt the warmth of his own father's hand the same as he would feel it in a handshake. It was the first time something like that had happened.

"Happy Birthday, buddy," he heard his father say.

—Hey, Dad! Could you feel my hand? Because I think I felt yours!

William chuckled and said, "That was my birthday present to you. It's something I've been working on for a while."

—It was great!

"Can you come back later, pal? I'd like to talk when it's just you and me."

—I'll come back. I just have to eat dinner.

After his birthday meal, Bonaventure gulped down his milk and wolfed down his cake.

"Did I miss something?" Dancy asked.

A stop in mid-chew, eyebrows raised, eyes shifting side to side as if to say, —Miss something? I don't know what you mean.

"Did somebody forget to mention that we're supposed to be in a race here?"

Shoulder shrug, casual reach for milk as if to say, —I'm just eating like I always do.

Bonaventure knew he had to slow things down, but it was difficult. When he finished eating, he wiped his mouth with the back of his hand, cleared his plate, pushed in his chair, and gave his mother a quick kiss on the cheek before he took off for the workshop.

Everything looked the same. All the tools still hung in their places or rested in metal boxes or in wooden ones if they were very old, and they gave off all their special smells of sawn wood and oiled steel, which was very reassuring. The silence had opened up like it always did to let Bonaventure and his father use their thoughts for conversation.

—Hi, Dad. I'm back.

"I see that."

—Can I ask you something?

"Sure."

—Are you part alive or are you all the way dead?

"I'm all the way dead."

—Do you sleep in our house with us?

"No. I sleep different now."

—Do you have a cape that makes you invisible?

"Where are all these questions coming from? No, I don't have a cape. I'm just invisible."

—I sure wish I could see you.

"I wish you could, too."

—Hey, Dad?

"Yes?"

—Will I *ever* be able to tell Mom our secret?

"No, buddy. Not ever."

—Why not?

"We've talked about this. She can't hear me like you can; it might hurt her feelings."

—Would it hurt Grand-mère's feelings, too?

"Yes, it would."

—Okay. I won't tell her either.

"You can't tell anyone, Bonaventure, just like we said. Got it?"

Bonaventure gave a disappointed nod.

"Okay, then. I have to go now. I just wanted to tell you that I love you and to say Happy Birthday one more time."

—I love you too, Dad.

"It makes me happy to talk with you, son."

—It makes me happy to talk with you, too. Bye, Dad.

"G'night, buddy. Go ahead and get back to your birthday now. Your mom is probably waiting for you. Maybe she'll let you have another piece of cake."

—Maybe she will!

"See ya soon."

—See ya. Oh, hey, Dad! I almost forgot! I've been listening real hard around the house like you said I should. Guess what I heard today!

"I can't guess; you'll have to tell me."

—I heard some powder come off a moth's wing, and he was way up in the attic and I was way down in the kitchen.

"That's my boy!" William praised Bonaventure's listening the way another father might praise a home run. Then he went to the sea in Almost Heaven and sat there staring at the waves, trying to remember what birthday cake tasted like.

Bonaventure went back to the house, and Dancy gave him that extra piece of cake. But he would have traded the cake and everything else he had if his father could be a real live dad and stay with him forever.

Bonaventure often knew when his father was entering or leaving a room because the air made a sound like it was zipping its pocket: open for hello, closed for goodbye. He knew when Gabe Riley was coming into a room too because Gabe had his own particular sound. It was the note of an eagle soaring. Eagles had a special place in Bonaventure's silence; he liked the steadiness of their sound. He wished he could be an eagle, one that could unzip the air and soar behind the sky. He liked everything about eagles, and he liked everything about Gabe Riley too.

He wasn't the only one.

"I think hiring Gabe was one of the best things we've ever done," Letice said to Dancy one Friday afternoon before the teacher arrived for lessons.

"You can say that again. He sure is in the right line of work," Dancy responded.

"He has high standards. I like that," Letice said.

"To tell you the truth, I was worried about being able to learn sign, but having a teacher like Gabe has made all the difference. And he's so good with Bonaventure! He's patient, but he pushes him in an easy kind of way," Dancy said.

"I know Bonaventure looks forward to sign lesson days. So do I. It's like we're all getting a different kind of voice, isn't it?"

Neither of them mentioned that Bonaventure was able to write things out and could probably get along with the notepad alone. Gabe Riley was giving them a silent voice to have in common, one that engaged the eyes, took the mind to the hands, and gave life to unspoken, unprinted, deeply felt words. The Arrows didn't want to give that up.

Both Dancy and Letice had come to accept that Bonaventure was never going to speak, but neither of them mentioned it, just in case the other one still held out hope.

Gabe also looked forward to Mondays, Wednesdays, and Fridays. Bonaventure grasped things more quickly than any child Gabe had ever taught. He initially chalked this up to the fact that Bonaventure could hear, but soon realized there was more to it than that: the boy was incredibly observant and curious and had the mind of a poet. Sometimes he would come out with something touching and rather personal in their concise, signed conversations.

—My mom willow.

"Do you mean widow?" Gabe asked.

—No. My mom willow. Tree, beautiful, cries.

Gabe let it go.

In spite of the fact that he felt he had no right to any personal information about Dancy, Gabe sometimes tried to steer conversations with Bonaventure along those lines. He thought about her all the time and had from the moment they'd met. He got into the habit of talking with Dancy after the lessons on the pretense of giving an update, but what he really wanted was to get to know her. He wanted to smell her perfume; he wanted to make her smile. He dreamed about her sometimes, and as the months went on, he began to fantasize that Bonaventure was his son and that Dancy was his wife. Then he would catch himself and remember that Dancy Arrow had never given even the slightest hint that she saw him as anything other than the sign language teacher who came to her house three times a week and was paid to help her son. But that didn't stop Gabe's feelings.

The Dancy he'd fallen in love with wasn't the same Dancy William had known; she was more worn down now, like the side of a seawall that faces the breakers. One thing Gabe loved about her was how she stood solid in her life and did her best to keep things right. But strong as she appeared to be, he sensed that she was fragile at the same time, and so he admired her even more. He loved her dry sense of humor and the way she enjoyed learning. But he kept those things to himself because he was afraid that if he told her how he felt, the worn-down, widowed part of her would rise up and demand to know how he could say such a thing. She would be filled with disgust and send him away. So he did what he could to maintain an easy friendship in the hope that, if nothing else, a certain kind of love might find its way to her heart—most likely the kind that was one part attraction and nine parts appreciation. But one part would be enough. For now he clung to the memory of the last time he'd addressed her as Mrs. Arrow, and she'd said to call her Dancy.

Dancy did not know of Gabe's feelings, but Bonaventure could hear them and he thought they sounded like a pearl that forms in concentric layers of kindness to protect a helpless oyster from a hurtful grain of sand.

POWERFUL WANGAS
AND THE LOUP-GAROU

DANCY had spent her childhood summers with the Cormiers on Bayou Deception Island. She took to the bayou like a duck to water; even the outhouses didn't bother her and she wasn't afraid of bugs or the dark or the swamp or even voodoo stories. There were Creole and Cajun folk thereabouts who could sing and dance and play music on washboards and cook crawdads that melted in the mouth. Never in her life had Dancy heard anybody tell stories the way the Bayou Deception Islanders could, tales about spells and charms and the loup-garou and gris-gris, which was pronounced "gree-gree," even though it wasn't spelled that way.

Old Miz Antonet told the best stories of all, especially about the loup-garou. The loup-garou was said to look like a wolf; he could catch you in the woods and take your blood and make you crazy if you told anyone that you'd seen him. Miz Antonet had lived on the island her whole entire life and claimed to have firsthand knowledge of the loup-garou. When she talked about the creature, her voice was a rasp that started in the hollow of her neck and came out through lips that curled over toothless gums. She said she'd met up with the loup-garou when she was "nine yeah ole, ya ya. Right here on 'Ception Island." She could describe how its eyes glowed red and how it took three drops of her blood before it got scared off by a hoot owl that was her familiar, ya ya, and how she lived to tell about it because she never said a word for "nigh on ten yeah." Miz Antonet knew how to survive the loup-garou: "You just has to keep shut you mouth and the loup-garou leave you alone."

Dancy had started hearing those stories when she was only six, and in the years to follow she learned that the loup-garou wasn't nearly as powerful as voodoo and gris-gris.

Right before she turned thirteen, Dancy had thought she was dying. She was positive she suffered from some dreadful disease that came and went on a regular basis. These certain symptoms would appear and disappear, and she figured that every time they came around she was dying a little bit more. Summer couldn't come fast enough for Dancy, because if she was going to die, she wanted to die on Bayou Deception Island and be buried in a tomb erected and whitewashed by her grandfather and decorated by her grandmother with fresh chrysanthemums and colored glass beads. Someone would sing the old Cajun waltz, *"J'ai passé devant ta porte,"* and there would be a sad, slow procession, and everyone would cry and say how she had had her whole life ahead of her and how she was such a sweet, pretty girl and how only the good die young. Adelaide would fall to the ground and cry out how she really did love her daughter, and beg Dancy to forgive her mother for not paying attention when she tried to tell her how sick she was. Dancy's almost-thirteen-year-old eyes filled with tears at the mere thought of her imagined passing.

The symptoms always came on the same way: a terrible headache and a sleepiness that came over her no matter the time of day. And as if that wasn't enough, her face would break out in spots and her stomach would bloat up, and when that happened she knew the worst was about to come: blood would start to drain out of her body and keep draining for at least four days, sometimes more. By the third time this happened, Dancy confided in her father, who was still alive back then, but Theo got all tongue-tied and kept clearing his throat and finally croaked out that she should go tell her mother about it.

"I thought as much, moody as you've been," Adelaide said, and showed Dancy an advertisement for Kotex in a magazine and sent her off to Charbonneau's Drug Store to figure things out for herself. But she needed something more than a magazine ad and some sanitary napkins. She needed to know why this was happening and she needed someone to tell her that it was going to be all right. When she and Theo made their annual pilgrimage to Bayou Deception Island, Grandma Cormier gave the answer in her earthy, bayou way.

It was early evening and they were sitting on the porch shucking peas for supper when Dancy dove in with, "I been getting my monthly since March," and then it was woman-to-woman. Grandma talked about the pull of the moon and the making of new life. She hugged Dancy to her in her warm, strong arms and said the bleeding was a magical thing, an initiation into the mysteries of the body and the first step toward becoming a woman.

Eventually the conversation led to the use of a woman's bloody flux by hoodoo women in the making of powerful love potions, which were a favorite topic in some circles.

"Hoodoo? Don't you mean voodoo?" Dancy asked.

"No, I mean hoodoo. Hoodoo is about conjuring, you know, bringing magic. The hoodoo maker puts together what's called an amulet—that's a little cloth bag—and they put things inside it and that's the gris-gris."

"It sounds like voodoo," Dancy said.

"Voodoo uses gris-gris too, but voodoo is more of a reli-gion that has gods and such. They say it come here from the west part of Africa after it passed through the Carib-bean Islands. Voodoo tampers with evil. Voodoo gris-gris can look like a charm, or some kind of doll, but it usually comes in small cloth bags with herbs or oils or even bits of fingernails or small bones inside. Sometimes they hold some personal possessions, or even a piece of cloth that still holds a body's sweat.

"Hoodoo come from Africa too, but maybe from the deeper part. Hoodoo wants to set magic on a problem. Although now that I think on it, there's hoodoo that's called root work, and root work be the using of roots and herbs and oils and such for curing. Ain't no fooling with charms or curses or spells in root work.

"When I was a child, there was a colored woman name of Big Angeline lived down the road from us, and she was a root worker. Big Angeline always say voodoo was about sacred things. Course, I didn't know the meaning of *sacred* since my mama and daddy didn't hold much with any kind of churching, so Big Angeline she explains it to me, and she says that sometimes voodoo charms got voodoo-sacred stuff in them, stuff to do with one god or another, but some had powders that were supposed to be medicines. I can still hear that Big Angeline just like it was yesterday: 'Doze be de ones possessed by de spirits,' she would say. 'Holy spirits dat make de medicine work, sometime good, sometime bad. Some-time dey bring money to your pocket, or love to your heart. Sometime dey stop a tongue dat gossip.' Ya, ya, that's what Big Angeline would say." Grandma Cormier laughed at the memory.

"How do the charms work?" Dancy asked.

"Well, they get put on a person, throwed on them, or maybe set in the doorway where they live. Big Angeline used to tell about a voodoo queen lived in N'awlins name of Marie Laveau who wrote somebody's name on a balloon and then tied it to a statue of Saint Expedite. She did it so when the balloon broke free and flew away, the person whose name was on that balloon went away in the same direction. I always did love to hear about Marie Laveau. Big Angeline said Marie Laveau made some real powerful gris-gris. She liked to put in little bits of bones or stuff from animals: bird nests or horsehair. Sometimes she put in dust from the graveyard, called goofer dust. Sometimes she used gunpowder or salt or red pepper."

At that point in the conversation, Mama Isabeau, a Creole woman of color who lived just down the road, came ambling up the Cormiers' path. Mama Isabeau couldn't have done much more than amble even if she'd wanted to because she weighed close to three hundred pounds and Mama Isabeau weighed that much because Mama Isabeau loved to eat.

"Do I hear you talk about Marie Laveau?" she panted as she climbed up the steps real slow.

"Ya, Mama, ya, you know all about Marie Laveau, don't you?" Grandma Cormier answered back.

"My auntie, she used to caution all us about the voodoo. She talk about Marie Laveau all the time. She say Marie's most powerful bad luck gris-gris be called wangas. She say Marie like to tell about her worst one. It seem she make a gris-gris bag from the shroud of somebody been dead nine days. She put in a dried-up lizard what have only one eye, the little finger off a black man who killed hisself, a dried toad, the wings from a bat, the eyes from a possum, a owl's beak and a rooster's heart. That gris-gris meant to kill somebody."

"Can anyone make gris-gris bags?" Dancy asked.

"Well now, gris-gris bags they take some planning, ya, ya," Mama Isabeau said. "You has to have a altar with something of the earth and the air and the water and the fire. And you has to put in the ingredients by the numbers. You has to be able to count them ingredients by odd numbers, but never more than thirteen, ya, ya. You can't never have a even number of things in the gris-gris bag."

"Did you ever know of anybody who got good gris-gris put on them?" Dancy asked.

"Oh, ya, ya! I know a gambling man once who swore he got good luck from a gris-gris charm he kep in his left shoe. The gris-gris maker mixed pine-tree sap with some blood from a dove and use it for ink to write an amount of money on a little piece of cowhide. She wrap the cowhide in a piece of green silk and put a snake's tongue in between the layers. Then she sew it together with cat's gut. The gambling man swear that charm give him real good luck!"

Now Dancy was remembering the loup-garou and gris-gris, and she came to the realization that the loup-garou was any fear that had taken a form and intended to drive someone crazy.

But she had no idea there were makings of gris-gris right there in the house on Christopher Street, or that root work was happening not far away in Trinidad Prefontaine's garden.

IN A PIECE OF TIME
TOO SMALL FOR A CLOCK

WINTER passed, spring came, and life was uneventful until the end of March in 1956. On a Saturday afternoon, Bonaventure was in the kitchen with Mrs. Silvey, who stood at the butcher-block table humming a song and rolling out dough. She was making fresh-baked bread and cinnamon rolls, and putting together something she called *blitzkuchen* that came from a recipe she knew by heart.

Bonaventure was drawing on a roll of white shelf paper that Mrs. Silvey kept in the pantry just for him; he loved that he could keep going and going, the paper was so long. He'd drawn a wagon train and some cowboys and Indians, and the swans that lived in the pond in the park, and now he was drawing the tools that hung on the workshop walls. While he drew, he listened to the dough's *pfff-pfff* breathing, and to the hiss of melting butter, and to the grit-sandy voice of light brown sugar. He was a one-boy audience for objects that liked to tell stories. On this day, a saucepan was telling him about heating his bottles when he was a baby, and how one time Dancy almost caught the sleeve of her bathrobe on fire because it was two in the morning and she was still half asleep.

Then right in the middle of the story, a notable noise

grabbed Bonaventure's attention. He banished all other sounds and listened, trying to liken it to something he might have heard before. He couldn't place it, but it reminded him of the tip of the root of the penultimate sound of a train whistle, the one made in the instant before it releases a roaring scream that comes from a long way off and reaches its highest intensity in seconds. He was certain of two things about that sound: It was something to be worried about, and it was coming from inside Mrs. Silvey's head. And then Mrs. Silvey collapsed. Bonaventure instantly searched for the sound of grand-mère, then ran to where she was and pulled her all the way back to the kitchen.

Letice grabbed the telephone and dialed the operator and begged for an ambulance. It was too late. In a piece of time too small for a clock, Martha Silvey had lost all sensibility and was dead before she hit the floor, killed by an aneurysm she'd carried for years without even knowing it.

The noise made by the ambulance siren turned all other sound to whiteness and felt like acid being splashed onto the cochlea whorls inside Bonaventure's ears. Even after her body had been taken away, he could still hear an echo of the frightened screech of tearing that had come from inside Mrs. Silvey's head. In the days that followed, he signed and wrote and drew pictures: He used the black and gray crayons to draw a speeding train; he drew yellow and orange sparks coming off the track; he mixed every color to draw the explosion of sound; he drew her face with empty eyes. He drew her fallen to the floor and himself standing off to the side, a stick person pressing his hands to his ears and opening his mouth in a silent scream. And he took those drawings to his mother. It was the first time he had tried to tell anyone about the extraordinary things he could hear, but Dancy just thought he was blaming himself for what had happened. She hugged him and said, "Oh, Bonaventure, it wasn't your fault. No one can know when a stroke is coming. You did the right thing and you did it as fast as you could."

The funeral was held in Baton Rouge. It was a small affair, but the flower arrangements were enormous; the Arrows felt it was the least they could do. Plans were made for burial to take place in Baton Rouge, where the Silveys had started their life together. Mr. Silvey turned into a very old man overnight and had to carry around an extra hand-kerchief to keep up with the tears that still traveled down his face a full three weeks after the funeral. His shoulders were more stooped, and the skin of his face sagged down farther over his collar. His walk had wound down to a shuffle, and he grew forgetful of the tools and the workshop and Let-ice's automobile a little bit more every day. He didn't always remember to bathe or to change his clothes, and he started to smell kind of sour.

The Arrows were considerate of Mr. Silvey and his loss. They did for themselves things that he used to do and they wove conversation around what he remembered. Hours became days and days became weeks, and Mr. Silvey never got any better. The part of him that remained aware approached Letice, hat in hand, and told her he just couldn't bear to be where his wife would never be again. He was off to live with his sister in Baton Rouge, what with Martha being buried there and all. Miss Dancy knew how to drive, he said, and he would talk to the fellows at Lemke's Auto about maintenance on the car.

Letice responded that she had always thought of him and Mrs. Silvey as family and would certainly never wish him to suffer unhappiness. She completely understood, she said, and told him the door would be open if he ever changed his mind, but even if he didn't, she hoped that he would visit.

This new death distracted Letice and Dancy from their usual grief and bitterness. Their sympathy for Mr. Silvey covered them like the Bible's balm of Gilead. But the respite was temporary. Dancy headed back inside her private loneliness, and Letice took up her worries once again. Six years had gone by, but she could not forget that the assassin was still alive in the asylum for the criminally insane. What if he escaped? What if he did have a grudge against the Arrows? What if killing William wasn't enough and he came after Bonaventure? What if he was still that crazy? What if God had allowed a curse to fall down on their family? And all because of her.

STARING INTO LIQUID

EVEN with Mr. Silvey gone, there was more than enough bereavement left in the house. Letice's thoughts often turned backward when she looked at Dancy; she knew what it was like to be left with a little boy and no husband and a big gaping hole in place of a marriage.

Letice had been the perfect wife to Remington; she'd run his house and planned his meals and soothed his brow at the end of the day. She'd been an interesting conversationalist during business dinners too, for Letice was intelligent and charming. He'd bought her flowers and all kinds of jewelry and loved her with all of the strength that he had. Sex didn't happen frequently in their marriage, but there was sweetness when it did, as though they were both very grateful. Remington Arrow always thought himself an unremarkable man, and he never could figure out how it was that his beautiful wife had settled for him.

Letice was clearly aware of what she didn't have in her marriage, but she chose to dwell instead on what she did. One of her most cherished memories was the night she'd whispered to Remington that she was pregnant, causing him to get as close to delirious as he ever would. Pregnancy brought a sudden and brilliant passion to their bed, and Remington pampered her more than ever. There was a steady parade of jewelers and florists through the house, and once a furrier brought a long coat made from the pelts of silver foxes, even though it was never very cold in New Orleans for any length of time.

On December 16, 1926, Letice gave birth to a son. If ever a baby brought a husband and wife closer, William Everest Arrow was certainly the one. Here was a child who'd inherited every good quality his ancestry had to offer. The best Molyneaux traits came to him from Letice: good looks, dignity, and a passionate heart. From the Arrows he'd inherited charm, though not the cunning, humor, kindness, and a penchant for daring that reached all the way back to County Armagh in his great-grandfather Cormack's Ireland.

Though Remington Arrow did not possess the larger-than-life personality of Cormack, he was a caring and patient father to William, one who tirelessly tossed a baseball and sat him on his lap to pore over the sports section; one who bought the boy his first bat and explained that it should be held with the fingers because they're stronger than the palm. Remington showed William how to line up his knuckles so that his wrists could roll properly after he hit the ball, and cautioned him to keep his fingers loose, maybe even wiggle them while he waited for the pitch, and not to worry because they would tighten up when he swung. The two of them carefully cut out box scores for William to paste in a notebook to worship George Herman Ruth—the Babe, the Bambino, the Sultan of Swat.

In the end it was too good to last. Remington came down with congestion of the lungs in November of 1934. The illness started with a feeling of being bone-tired, followed by a tickle in his throat that grew into a fiend and traveled to his chest, where it rumbled and pounded and took his breath violently, leaving him gasping and writhing in pain. The doctor made a house call and prescribed bed rest, camphor vapor, and a liquid containing a dose of belladonna to act as a sedative and hopefully bring some relief from the coughing.

When she felt him burning up with fever even as he shook with chills, Letice called an ambulance. She left eight-year-old William in the care of the Silveys so that she could go along with her husband. She kept vigil at the side of his hospital bed, telling him not to worry, that the doctor was a specialist, that they would go to some warmer place after the holidays, a place where they could sit in the sun, so he could recover and come home stronger. She watched his mouth open and close, open and close, as he pulled and pulled for air. And then his mouth stopped opening and closing, and his eyes stared straight ahead without focusing at all.

Letice's stomach dropped to her feet and her mouth went dry. She squeezed his hand, put her face close to his, and whispered his name as a desperate question: "Remington? Remington?" She hoped he might open his eyes or let out a breath. He did neither. Again she whispered frantically, and again he stayed silent and still.

Hospitals are very quiet at night. But when Letice bolted out into the hall, she sliced that hospital's quietness right down the middle with a scream. Two people came running, and one stethoscope explained things.

"I'm sorry, Mrs. Arrow," the doctor said. "I'm sorry, but he is gone."

Remington Arrow had died of pneumonia. It was four days before Christmas; he was thirty-nine years old. It was decided that his body should repose in the morgue until further plans could be made. There was no one around who could even imagine a funeral at Christmastime, least of all the heavily sedated Letice, who could no longer imagine anything.

Just as he had died four days before Christmas, Remington Arrow was entombed four days after, as if some fateful pendulum had swung in an unfeeling and perfect mathematical arc, finishing Remington's time on this earth. With no more moments to measure, the pendulum dropped to the middle and remained there unmoving, keeping Letice there with it.

Like his father and grandfather before him, Remington Arrow had been president of the family-owned First Regent's Bank, and in her heart of hearts Letice believed it was the bank that had killed her husband by pulverizing his good man's soul. First Regent's had survived the crash of 1929, and Remington had continued to keep the doors open by working from early in the morning until late at night six days a week, doing all he could to resist foreclosing on homes or turning down requests for loans that came from hardworking people who'd given up pride in favor of begging. But sometimes he had no choice.

That had been the case with the Heckert family. Mr. Heckert was a long-standing customer at the bank, a farmer the Arrows knew well. But his farm had more than a few failed crops and had fallen into serious disrepair. His eldest son, George, tried to help out by doing odd jobs and selling items he'd made by hand, such as a child's wagon with a handle he'd fashioned from a plow blade. Ostensibly, that is what brought him to the Arrows' back door. He knew they had a little boy, but his real purpose was to speak with Remington of a matter to do with business. No one knew about his plan, for George Heckert was trying to be a hero.

When Remington Arrow came to the door, George asked what his family's chances of getting a bank loan might be. They needed to pay some debts and buy some seed and get medical attention for the animals. They'd already had to sell some milk cows and two of their horses because they couldn't feed them, he'd said, unable to keep the begging out of his voice.

"I'm sorry, George," Remington Arrow told him. "Times are tough and your family's farm needs too many repairs. The bank can't accept it as security against a loan."

The young man hung his head; he'd hoped maybe his family's reputation for honesty and hard work would have tipped the scales in their favor. But he could see that Remington Arrow thought like a banker and put no value on honesty and hard work.

Remington tried to help in the only way he could; he bought the handmade wagon.

George Heckert returned home, his back bent under the weight of his failure. He told his folks that the farm was going to kill them all, and he for one was not willing to die. But they were people who believed that hard work would right things; they did not perceive the mortal wound to George's pride. He left that night, and his family never saw him again.

It was cases like the Heckerts' that aided in Remington Arrow's decline. Pneumonia had an easy time of it with Remington; he was already broken when the sickness got there.

The depth of her grief astounded Letice. Her husband had been, after all, a man she'd had to learn to love after having given her heart and passion to someone else. Widowhood did not put her in dire financial straits; Remington had been a cautious investor with a grave mistrust of buying on margin. But money didn't do much for her loneliness, and so she looked for something that would. Letice searched for respite from all the vacancy around her: Remington's place at the table, the left-hand side of the bed, her empty arms when Bessie Smith sang. She found relief from her sorrow in bottles of liquor that had accumulated in the cellar even during Prohibition, a residual effect of Cormack Arrow's immortal influence and charm.

At first it was an evening glass of sherry. Before long it was Dewar's White Label several times a day, but only after she'd styled her hair, put on a fine set of clothes, and applied perfume, powder, and lipstick, because that's what a lady would do. Letice could not admit that liquor was the only thing that helped her carry the regret. She would never have the chance to tell Remington how undeserving she was. She would never have the chance to make love to him and think only of him, or to tell him she was sorry. Letice had fallen in love with her husband after all, and now it was too late. She found that if she drank enough, she could manage a dreamless sleep.

At her Garden Club's Annual Spring Tea, Letice excused herself from the table and walked as steadily as she could to the powder room. She believed she was doing quite well— left foot, right foot, left foot, right foot, keeping her eyes fixed on the powder room door. "Almost there," she said to herself, and thought of the delicate flask inside her purse, and of how she would go into a stall and relieve her craving instead of her bladder.

Cora Davis, a Garden Club member Letice had known all her life, followed her into the powder room. When Letice came out of the stall, Cora caught her arm and turned her around.

"Look at me, Letice. You're drunk, aren't you?"

"I most certainly am not! How dare you say such a thing?" Letice spat.

"Oh, Letice. I know you're in pain; we all know you're in pain. Let us help you."

"Do you want to help me, Cora? Do you really want to help me? Because if you do, then leave me alone."

After that, Letice stayed home from Garden Club events and from all other social activities. Six months later she found herself staring into amber liquid and planning to end her life. That's when she turned to God and asked him to take her back. What followed were two weeks of anguish. And then, during the evening hours of a difficult day, tortured in mind and body, Letice determined that God did not care. She could almost hear the sounds of a bottleneck touching a glass rim, and of blended scotch whisky pouring into it, and she could smell that liquor's mellowness, and savor its pain-easing taste. In those moments there was nothing else in Letice's world, not even her eight-year-old son. The craving for whisky simply took hold of her. All she wanted was to feel it wash down her throat and flow through her veins. And then the craving battled with self-loathing, and finally self-loathing won. In an act of desperate determination, Letice walked into Remington's study, a room in which she knew there was a small pearl-handled gun. The door closed behind her with a quiet catch.

Standing on the brink of destruction and staring into the icy waters of despair, Letice jumped in and got caught in a roiling current that rushed her, body and soul, over punishing rocks and through the jutting, deadly arms of fractured sorrows. She ached with coldness, and when she couldn't take it anymore, she surrendered to the desire to finally drown. She let her body go limp and felt it crash into boulders.

She opened the door of a cherrywood cabinet, reached into its darkest recesses, and closed her hand around the gun. Determined though she was, Letice's hand shook.

Then just as she tightened her grip on the revolver, it dropped from her hand and was replaced by a root that grew out of the bank of her frigid, roaring misery. It took her a moment to realize her hand was not wrapped around an imagined tree root or a real revolver but curved instead around a leather-bound book. She pulled the Book of Hours from the cabinet, and the book fell from her hand to lie open and bright upon her lap. Chilled to the bone and dripping with a death wish, Letice looked down upon the words of evening vespers:

O God, come to my aid. O Lord, make haste to help me.

And she knew then that God had not left her and that he never would.

The very next day she called on an architect and ordered plans for a private chapel to be drawn. Letice lost her taste for blended scotch whisky as she pored over sketches, and imagined Cipollino marble and long velvet drapes. She considered her chapel to the last detail, from the wood of the crucifix to the scoop of the holy water font. She favored sparseness in her design, reminiscent of the cells inhabited by prayerful monks. But that is not to say she kept her costs down. Quite the contrary, in fact; no expense was too great, and so the building materials were the best to be found in several corners of the world. It was the lines and shape of the place that mattered to Letice, the expanses of flatness where nothing could hide within the blank, smooth planes of ceiling and floor. She wished her chapel to represent the ideal of her soul—hollowed-out and filled with purity, with nothing for sin to hold on to.

There were two straight-backed pews and a stand for the votives. The only other furnishings were a small prie-dieu upon which she could kneel, and a crucifix that bore the figure of Christ. The Christ figure was an interesting one. Letice had commissioned it to show the muscular form of a hardworking carpenter, his body slumped forward and collapsed in suffocation, every rib countable, arms pulled from shoulder sockets, head hung to chest, blood and water flowing from his sword-pierced side. It was Sacrifice rendered in plaster, and it made Letice wonder how she'd ever dared despair.

Light was provided by the votive candles and through the clear-glass window that looked out upon a garden. And rendered in mosaic with the promise of life in her glittering glass eyes was the face of the Angel Lailah, guardian of babies from conception to birth. Letice had her reasons for that. And beneath the angel there was a niche in the wall in which rested a carved wooden box. Letice had her reasons for that too. She needed to take responsibility for what she'd done, she needed to be penitent, and she needed to hope that what was inside that box was held in safekeeping. It was a difficult thing that she tried to do, this holding on to something while giving it back to God.

Every time she went to her chapel, Letice looked at that box and told the relic how sorry she was. Then she would turn to the Gospel of Luke for comfort:

> *Are not five sparrows sold for two pennies? Yet not one of them is forgotten by God.*

AS FOR DANCY

GENTLY, and with subtlety, Letice taught her daughter-in-law the finer ways of living: how to determine quality, how to dress, how to eat. But she didn't want to change that which made Dancy who she was: an unmistakable honesty that Letice knew was one of the reasons William had loved her.

The relationship between the two women is best described as strength surrounding hollowness, like a steel pipe. The steel had to do with shared loss, the hollowness with unshared belief in God. But despite that considerable philosophical difference, the two women enjoyed a peaceful coexistence. For the most part. Sometimes the years of stifled grief and self-imposed guilt found a way to escape Dancy's control and turn her into someone she wasn't. A red-hot rage could come up from nowhere and sweep through her without a breath of warning, gathering up the hatred she felt for William's killer and the anger she felt at a God she ignored. When that happened, she yearned to tear every page from her mother-in-law's missal, to throw her holy water, and to smash her religious statues with an axe, sparing not even the bust of a thorn-crowned Jesus or the small green marble Pietà. She wanted to destroy them all, especially the Pietà.

She knew that the sculpture of a grieving Mary holding the body of her crucified son was Letice's favorite, knew that her mother-in-law drew consolation from the statue, even identified with it, and Dancy wanted to smash it until it was reduced to little more than a powder that could be swept up with a broom and tossed into the trash to be mixed in with eggshells and old coffee grounds.

At the start of one of these rages, Dancy was always able to summon the self-control necessary to manage it, but the control never lasted and she would become snappish with Letice and short-tempered with Bonaventure. The slightest thing would irritate her and she would stomp through rooms and slam cupboard doors.

More and more often, when she felt herself burning from the inside out, she would go to her room, open that jelly jar she kept in the darkness of her closet, and pour liquor over the lump in her throat. Then she would light a Pall Mall cigarette and smile grimly over the fact that gin looked just like water.

And William would push against the thought that love looked just like pain.

Letice was on to Dancy, having been down that road herself. She knew to tread carefully so as not to offend the girl or make her defensive. Letice prayed for the wisdom to know what to do to cauterize the young woman's nerves. She suspected that when Dancy lost William she had also lost God, and the thought of it caused Letice agony, for she was more certain than ever that it was she who'd brought this tragedy upon them. Yet she could not confide her secret, could not risk being seen as a hypocrite.

. . . .

Dancy was like an amputee who'd been left with a bloody stump in the place where her life had been, and she was wracked by phantom pains. She knew that people thought it had been long enough, that she should let go and move on. But they didn't know what it had been like to love and be loved by William. They didn't know that he had been proud of her, or that he had chosen her over prettier, wealthier, better-educated girls who knew the right way of speaking, and which fork to use, and how to arrange cut flowers in a vase. They didn't know that he had begged her to meet his mother, that she, not William, was the one who felt she didn't measure up. They didn't know that he had sung to her and taught her to drive and let her cut his hair for practice when she was studying at the beauty school above Slocum Brothers Furniture. They didn't know that her heart still turned over at the thought of him and brought her a few seconds' worth of remembered happiness. They didn't know he was her once-in-a-lifetime. But most of all, they didn't know that she owed him.

William knew very well why Dancy felt she owed a debt. But he chose not to think about it, dwelling instead on those seconds of happiness she felt when her heart still turned over at the thought of him. He was sorry for those times when she went to her closet and drank booze from a jar and smoked cigarettes. William knew that closet was a harmful place because that's where she kept her guilt.

MAN TO MAN

BY June of 1956, six-year-old Bonaventure's hearing went beyond vibrations and out and away from frequencies and wavelengths. It sliced through pressure. It defeated time and space. He liked to curl up in his favorite chair on the sunporch and listen to exploding sunspots, and sometimes on nights he just couldn't fall asleep, he listened to stars being born. A long time ago his dad had told him that everybody couldn't hear the things he heard, and Bonaventure always wished that they could, or at least that he could wrap up the sounds and make them into gifts. But he couldn't, and it caused him to feel a crushing isolation.

In the best sound times, the world became a womb expanded, its open folds filled with an amniotic sea of brilliant, irresistible sound. Day after day, he sailed that sea both wakeful and dreaming, and he made wandering explorations of Bayou Cymbaline, at least those parts he was allowed to travel. Bonaventure wasn't always alone on these excursions. Sometimes William was with him.

"I used to play baseball over there."

—What was the name of your team?

"The Bayou Cymbaline Blue Gators."

—Why were you called that? Gators are green. I never

saw a blue gator. There's no such thing as a blue gator.

"I dunno. Somebody just thought it up, I guess."

—Who?

"Don't know that either."

Bonaventure scratched his nose, which was something he did when he was trying to solve a problem.

—Was it the coach?

"Coulda been, I guess."

—Hey, Dad!

"What?"

—Where does a baseball bat eat its dinner?

"I dunno. Where does a baseball bat eat its dinner?

—On home plate.

"Ha. That's funny."

—I know. It's a joke. Hey, Dad: Knock-knock.

"Who's there?"

—Broccoli.

"Broccoli who?"

—Broccoli doesn't have a last name. Hey, Dad.

"Hey, what?"

—Where do babies come from?

"Is that a joke question?"

—No. It's a real one. We're done joking.

"Oh. Sorry. What did you ask me? Where do day-bees come from? What are day-bees? I never even heard of day-bees." This was a stalling tactic on William's part.

—*Babies*. I asked where *babies* come from.

"Oooohhhh. *Babies*. Ask your mom. She might know."

—I asked her already; well, really I asked her where I came from, but I think she just made up the answer.

"What did she say?"

—She said I came from Rubenstein's. It's a department store on Canal Street in New Orleans.

William had to smile at Dancy's sort-of-true answer. "Well, we did get you in New Orleans, but I think it was somewhere on Washington Avenue right around Coliseum. Or maybe it was Rubenstein's. I was too happy at the time to notice the details."

—Okay. But I don't think that's where all babies come from.

"Yeah, you're probably right. I'll bet only special ones come from Rubenstein's." Then William pointed out where the best climbing trees were and took Bonaventure to the place two yards over where a family of rabbits lived. He was killing time, trying to figure out how to broach an important subject, when Bonaventure unintentionally did it for him.

—Did you ever find out why I'm the only one who can hear you?

"As a matter of fact, I did. I heard it was something God decided. He has a job for us, and you have to be able to hear a lot of things and we have to be able to talk to each other so we can get it done."

—But how can we do a job together? I'm here and you're in Almost Heaven.

"Well, it's like this: I have to do a few things to get to Real Heaven, and I'm going to need your help with one of those things. That's what the job is about."

—Okay. So what's the job?

"It has to do with your mom. She's keeping something she shouldn't, something that makes her sad. It's in her closet."

—Why does she keep it if it makes her sad?

"It's a mistake is all. My part of the job is to tell you about it, and your part of the job is to go get it."

—There's lots of stuff in her closet. How will I know what it is?

"You'll have to listen for it."

—What do I do after I get it?

"Well, first you take it all the way out of the house. After that, you'll have an idea. That's all I know right now."

—When am I supposed to get it?

"Not yet. I don't think it's time just yet. I'll let you know when."

Bonaventure winked and said, —Gotcha.

Then they knocked around the backyards some more before going to count dragonflies over at the park. William was treading carefully.

THEY offered The Wanderer pencil and paper at the asylum, but he never wrote anything sensible.

One time Bonaventure heard the graphite of a pencil rasp across a piece of paper and leave a slight and quivered mark behind. He listened so hard he heard the graphite's history, when it was still a part of metamorphic rock that didn't know it would one day almost capture what was almost a thought from the mind of an insane man.

Wondering who The Wanderer was and why he'd murdered her son ate away at Letice as much as it ever had. She began to make inquiries regarding private detectives.

Eugenia Babbitt continued to fill the emptiness in her life with regular visits to the asylum.

THE BLUEBOTTLE FLY

BONAVENTURE sat in the kitchen all by himself, which was not unusual given the fact that he favored the kitchen above all other rooms in the house, especially in the mornings when he could swirl up dust motes and pretend they were miniature snowflakes, a phenomenon he'd read about but had never actually seen. Some mornings he pushed a chair over to the east-facing window and pulled the ring on the string that lowered the shade until it blocked out the sunlight except for one single beam that shot through a pinpoint hole in the canvas. On this day he was in the mood for daylight, and so he didn't lower that shade but let sunshine fill the room and find the cat's eye marble he'd pulled from the depths of his pocket. He shut one eye and held the marble to the other, concentrating on how his kitchen might look through the eye of a cat; then he put the glass ball on the table and set it in motion with a flick of finger and thumb, relishing the sound of rolling glass. He watched the swirl of purple in the marble's middle turn and turn, and at the very last second he moved to save it from a fall.

Just as he scooped the marble up, the border of his concentration was touched by the buzzing of a bluebottle fly. The sound ceased when the insect lit on the marmalade spoon and scuttled around its edge twice, even walked upside down where the convex side of the tip curved up from the surface of the table. Gradually, the creature returned topside and descended the spoon's shallow bowl as if walking down a slide. It flew away just when the swinging door opened and Dancy entered the room. Bonaventure thought it took a lot of courage for something as small as a fly to come anywhere near human beings.

"Hey there, cutie-pie! You're in luck if you're here for breakfast, because I'm in the mood to cook," she said, and tweaked his nose on her way to the refrigerator. Within seconds she brought a bowl from the cupboard, cracked four eggs into it, took a whisk from the drawer, and slid bread into the toaster, all the while humming "Hark the Herald Angels Sing," even though she wasn't religious, and even though it was the last week in June.

Bonaventure scooped out some marmalade with the spoon so recently visited by the bluebottle fly, put it into his mouth, and rolled it around a time or two before swallowing. He tucked the spoon into his trouser pocket then, because he thought that it really belonged in his memento box. No sooner had he tucked that spoon away than his stomach growled, so loud his mother heard it way over by the sink.

Putting emphasis on the first syllable of her favorite nickname for him, Dancy asked, "Adventure Arrow, is there a lion in this house?" To which Bonaventure gleefully nodded as his stomach growled again.

"Adventure Arrow, are *you* that lion?"

Another vigorous nod.

This was a game they played. Sometimes he was a spider, sometimes a snake or a fox or a shiny brown beetle; one time he'd been an albino squirrel, and yesterday he'd been a one-eyed, hook-beaked screech owl. His mother didn't know that now he really was part fly because he had fly footprints inside him from the walked-upon spoon.

"I beg your pardon, but you most certainly are not a lion," she said. "You are well and truly Bonaventure Arrow and you live on Christopher Street in Bayou Cymbaline, and I'm your mama and don't you forget it!"

For someone who claimed to have chosen her child's name with a haphazard peek at the phone book, Dancy Arrow spent a lot of time singing its praises. On a recent visit to Père Anastase, Bonaventure had noticed his father's full name on the graveyard plaque. He'd tugged on Dancy's sleeve, pointed to the name in the center, and raised his eyebrows to pose a question. She explained that Everest had been his father's middle name.

Bonaventure signed, —Middle name you?

"My whole given name is Danita Celine; pretty fancy, huh?"

—Middle name me?

"Well, some names don't need any help because they're strong enough to stand on their own, and Bonaventure is one such name. Your Grandma Roman wanted me to give you Roman as a middle name, but that would have made you Bonaventure Roman Arrow, which I didn't care for at all. People would hear it as roamin', as in wandering aimlessly, so no thank you very much."

Dancy placed their eggs and toast on the table, sat down, and reached for the marmalade spoon. When her hand came up empty, she wondered out loud where in blue blazes it could have gone to. Bonaventure let her wonder. Some things he kept to himself.

A happy breakfast in a sunny kitchen did not hold any guarantees. After supper on the third of July, just four days after

Dancy had joked with Bonaventure about a lion in the room, another rage got hold of her. When it felt as if she would jump right out of her skin if Letice so much as looked at her, Dancy went to her room and doused her rage with the entire contents of the jelly jar, which on that day held enough liquor for at least five rages, possibly six, maybe more.

It was dusk when Bonaventure heard something come to him clear out in the yard where he was trying to catch fireflies in a mayonnaise jar that had holes poked in its lid. What he heard was the sound of Dancy peeing herself because she was too drunk to know any better. But he heard something more than urine streaming out of her body—he heard anguish, and it sounded like someone gulping for air and choking when it got some. Bonaventure followed the sounds to his mother's room, where he found her passed out on the floor with her mouth gaping open and drool running out one side. He listened intently for the sound of her breathing but could barely hear it for the loudness of that anguish, which was drowning out everything.

The anguish was coming from inside the closet. Maybe it was that thing his dad had talked about that he was supposed to get, that thing inside a box.

Bonaventure grasped one of his mother's hands in both of his and signed the letters W-A-K-E U-P into her palm, and when that didn't work, he patted her cheeks; and when that didn't work, he pounded on the floor. Even though he had no voice, his lips moved around *Mama, Mama*, over and over, and his face wrinkled up into pitiful, soundless crying.

The visiting beat came to Bonaventure's heart then, adding strength and helping him shake his mother hard enough to wake her.

. . . .

Dancy stayed all gin-drowsy and stupid, though she did manage to turn herself over and crawl to the bathroom on her hands and knees. Her long blond hair fell into the toilet as she retched up bile and vomit. It wasn't until the next afternoon that she realized her little boy had seen her be sick, after he'd found her sour-breathed and passed out and stinking of piss. What she didn't know was that her dead husband had seen the whole thing too.

William hadn't meant for anything like that to happen. The sight had caused him to feel great pain, as if he had suffered a shower of blows to a body he no longer had.

Bonaventure was never the same. In the time it took to go from catching fireflies in the yard to finding his mother unconscious from pain, he'd got caught up in constant worry. He began to break down the sounds that came into his silence, checking their structure for harmful details. Such concentration took a lot of work, and sometimes he needed to sift through the sounds to find one that was pleasant and restful.

It was during one of these sifting times that he picked up on the Spanish moss whispering about a lady who felt itching on the bottoms of her feet.

ON THE LATE AFTERNOON
OF A FINE SUMMER DAY

TRINIDAD Prefontaine had been scouting her land and finding its medicines ever since she'd come to Bayou Cymbaline. She harvested trees of their apples and plums, and a small vineyard of its grapes, and then she turned the bounty into pies and tarts and bottles of juice. She pulled wild plants from the base of tree trunks and from under the feathery fronds of wild ferns. She plucked them and dried them and boiled them into tinctures or ground them into powders to be used as curatives.

She'd set up a stand at the edge of the Neff Switch road, selling her pies and tarts and juices, and giving the cures away for free, some for illnesses and some for secrets. For example, Enoch Willets and Tabula Cristy held hurtful secrets inside them. Enoch, a clerk at Graber's Hardware, never told anyone that he liked to knit. He was trying to weave himself into someone a woman would let close enough for him to talk to and court and hopefully marry her. He'd been told too many times that he was ugly, and the knowledge had made him painfully shy.

Tabula, a nurse's aide at the hospital, loved to unravel tablecloths in the evenings, carefully transforming them into tight balls of thread. She was a nervous young woman with no self-esteem, who liked to think she could unravel herself until she disappeared.

Vida van Demming's secret was a good deal riskier. Vida did not consider herself an official kleptomaniac, although she really did steal. She took things regularly from Claymore's Candy & Gift Emporium or from F. W. Woolworth's Five & Dime, but they were always small things that fit up her sleeve or in the pocket of her skirt or in her cleavage inside her brassiere; and she never took anything that cost more than seventy-five cents. Also, she did her stealing in the morning and was sure to put everything back in the stores before they closed at five p.m. What stood in the shadows of Vida's stealing was the fact that there wasn't one single thing that made her feel alive. There were precious few thrills in Bayou Cymbaline, so Vida made do with the stealing.

Enoch, Tabula, and Vida all found their way to Trinidad's stand out on the Neff Switch road. When Trinidad handed Enoch his bottle of grape juice in a paper sack, she slipped in an envelope containing dried sage. On the front of the envelope were the instructions: *Put some under your tongue before you talk to a special lady.*

When Tabula returned home, she found a small pouch that was gathered closed at the top with a drawstring. The pouch was filled with lavender flowers, rosemary leaves, mint, comfrey root, and thyme. A note attached to the end of the string said: *Put in your bath and think good things.*

When Enoch saw Tabula in Graber's Hardware, he slipped some of that sage beneath his tongue and asked if he might take her to hear the concert band on Sunday at the gazebo in the park. Tabula Cristy said yes.

Vida van Demming, the semi-kleptomaniac, noticed

that the apple pie she'd bought was wrapped in a page from the *Times-Picayune*. She smoothed the paper out and got to reading it and ended up in a letter-writing relationship with a man from Port Arthur, Texas, who had placed an ad for a pen pal in the second column of the personals. It was enough to help Vida quit the stealing.

Things changed in Bayou Cymbaline. The bullied took charge of their lives, gamblers turned their backs on dice, and folks in general were happier. Everyone knew where to find Trinidad. They came to her for baked goods, and for the powders and potions that cured corruptions of the flesh and abscesses of the soul and the mind.

Trinidad was interested in every customer, but none so much as the two women and the silent little boy who drove up to her stand in the late afternoon of a fine summer day in 1956. Letice was on her third driving lesson that day. She felt her life was more than half over and it was high time she learned to get around on her own. Dancy chose the Neff Switch road to practice on because it was good and straight and not heavily traveled.

Bonaventure was sitting in the backseat, listening to the swishing tail of a cat that was watching a goldfinch balance on a twig in Texarkana, when from nowhere that never-seen companion came to run though the various parts of his heart and sail all through his veins. *Bup-bup, bup-bup*, it swirled through his body and out through his ears and filled up the car and the road and the land. It grabbed his heartbeat up into the sky to join with a perfect twin rhythm.

"There are an awful lot of people out here for a road that isn't used much," Letice said.

"Sure seems like it," Dancy replied. "I've never seen it

this busy, but then again I haven't been out this way in a while. Do you want to keep driving, or would you feel better if I took over?"

"Well, it is making me a little nervous. What's that up ahead there? Can you tell?"

"It looks like a stand of some kind—somebody selling stuff," Dancy said. "It must be pretty good—looks like there's a sizable crowd. Maybe we should check it out."

"Yes, let's. My neck is getting stiff; I've had enough for one day. We'll see what's for sale and then you can drive us home."

They had to wait while a black woman who was wearing a dress made of bright blue cotton and a hat made of tall fescue grass took care of her customers, all of whom were praising her wares.

Trinidad's transposed heart was pounding against the right side of her rib cage, pumping blood through her veins, swelling them up and making them joyous. And floating upon her fast river blood was that delicate quivering feather.

Bonaventure heard that switched-around pounding and it sounded to him like a drum that could sing.

"Hello, there, my name Trinidad Prefontaine. How you all be on this beautiful day?"

"We're just fine, thanks," Dancy replied. "I'm Dancy Arrow, and this is my mother-in-law, Mrs. Arrow, Senior, and that handsome young man over there is my son, Bonaventure. We were out for a drive and stumbled onto your stand here. Everything sure does look good!"

Trinidad smiled and took a good long look. She didn't think there'd been any stumbling about it, not with that pounding taking place in her heart. She knew the older woman, perhaps not by the name of Arrow, but she'd seen her someplace before. And the child's eyes were dearly familiar. If she had ever doubted that her Purpose had brought her to Bayou Cymbaline, she doubted it no more. She didn't know the details yet, only knew that fate had something to do with these two women and their little boy. Of that she had no doubt. Not even the faintest shadow of a doubt.

While his mother and grand-mère talked with the lady in the fescue-grass hat, Bonaventure listened to the syncopated rhythm of her work-worn but beautiful, sturdy black hands.

Letice was thoughtful on the way home. "Did she look familiar to you, Dancy?"

"The lady at the stand? No. I'm sure I've never seen her before. Why? Do you think we should know her?"

"There's something about her, but I can't think what." This bothered Letice, though she couldn't imagine why.

For the rest of that day and every day to follow, Trinidad Prefontaine waited for the recollection to come to her of how she knew the woman called Mrs. Arrow, Senior, and for the memory of where she might have seen that little boy's eyes. It would come to her as a Knowing. In the meantime, she would go about her business as best she could, bringing cures to the citizenry of Bayou Cymbaline as their fixed-in secrets presented themselves.

Trinidad spent the rest of the summer cleaning out the root cellar she'd discovered while clearing the wild cucumber that had spread all over its hatchway doors. Evening was taken up with the carding and spinning of wool that she'd bartered for, and then dyed with colors she'd pulled from the land. She gathered seeds from sunflowers and pine trees. She sorted them and boiled them and extracted their oil. She thought about that little boy and how he had not said one solitary word on that day when the Arrows had come to her stand.

She baked.

She sang.

She waited.

SASSAFRAS AND
SPANISH MOSS

AFTER recovering from her low moment of grief drowned by drink, Dancy Arrow went to the bank and withdrew the insurance benefits paid her all those years ago by the Greater Louisiana Life & Casualty Company in compensation for the loss of her husband. She used the sum to purchase a neat little shop on Seminole Street, which she filled with potted palms and wicker furniture and equipment such as a beautician would use: an aqua-blue sink, three sizes of curlers, five hundred bobby pins, four pair of special scissors, and some strong-smelling liquids in dark brown bottles. Added to all that were two Halliwell Advantage hair dryers and the cosmetology certificate she'd earned about a million years ago. She opened Glamour by Dancy and commenced doing hair, plucking eyebrows, and painting nails in hues of Passion Fruit Red and Sweetheart Pink.

There was no denying that Dancy possessed a superb talent when it came to administering the professional's equivalent of the Lilt Home Permanent Wave. She could bring out the best in eyebrows and make dishpan hands look pretty darned smooth. Her clientele grew in no time. She worked from nine until five, six days a week, and slept in on Sundays instead of going to church.

Dancy Arrow had found her calling. She knew it wasn't as if she was curing disease or feeding the poor, but she liked having somewhere to go, and she liked that she could make other women feel a little better about themselves. Something new had come into her life, and a small part of Dancy started to heal. The jelly jar of gin began to go dry—a state in which it remained.

Letice told her that she did not need to worry about money, but she did not discourage her business pursuit, even though running the household suffered some because of it. They still hadn't found Mrs. Silvey's replacement. In fact, there hadn't been a single response to the ad Letice was running in the *Daily Presse*. The house was haphazard and their meals were paltry. Letice never had been much of a cook, and even though Dancy could have done better, she'd lost interest in cooking after William was killed. They were eating a lot of peanut butter sandwiches, or baloney, or toasted cheese and tomato. On a good day they might have spaghetti.

Dancy felt bad about all those slapped-together meals and about spending so much time away from home. On a lazy Sunday she came up with a surprise. "Adventure Arrow," she said. "I did some shopping yesterday. How's about we go to the kitchen and whip us up some of that filé gumbo you like?"

Bonaventure didn't know his mother could make filé gumbo; Mrs. Silvey had always made it. Nor did he know that Dancy had once read cookbooks and would practice a recipe until she got it just right, back when she was trying to be the best wife ever.

In no time at all, they were dancing together as Dancy tried to sound like Hank Williams singing to good lookin' about what she had cookin'.

That little bit of healing that had begun inside her

allowed the filé gumbo to bring a good memory to Dancy instead of that horrible night when the police had come to the door. This good memory had to do with her Cormier relations and how they were fond of eating crayfish and calling them mudbugs, a name she found a tad off-putting. She shared the memory with Bonaventure, who loved the word mudbugs.

While Dancy washed her hands, Bonaventure crawled halfway into a bottom cupboard to come up with some crockery bowls, a black Dutch oven, and a well-used cast iron skillet that was so heavy he could barely lift it. Dancy went to the Kelvinator fridge and took out the sausage she'd bought, along with the holy trinity of Louisiana cooking: bell peppers, onions, and celery. Bonaventure climbed up on a stool to watch his mother chop the vegetables while the sausage turned brown and the kitchen filled up with a pow-pow sizzle and a mouth-watering smell.

William sat on the kitchen counter, thoroughly enjoying being with his wife and his son. He'd never stopped missing Cajun cooking, and this was going to be good. But then he remembered that he could not eat.

Dancy took flour and butter and commenced making the roux, setting the butter to melting in the Dutch oven over a low blue flame and sprinkling flour in while she stirred it with a whisk. "Never forget, Bonaventure, that a good roux has to be stirred real fast and cooked real slow," she said.

An okeydokey nod that said, —Yes ma'am. I will never forget about the roux.

She sautéed the vegetables right in with the roux and then put the sausage in the skillet. The last thing she started was the filé powder made from dried sassafras, which would be used to thicken the gumbo. Grandma Cormier had used okra to thicken, but Dancy preferred her okra deep-fried and served on the side.

When she opened the sassafras jar, a story escaped and found its way into Bonaventure's silence and began to tell him how Dancy had made filé gumbo a long time ago, how happy she'd been and how worried she'd become as she watched the clock and waited, and how she went to the door when someone rang the bell and how there were policemen on the other side who asked if she was Mrs. William Arrow . . . And then his mother put the lid back on the sassafras and returned it to the cupboard.

Bonaventure was subdued through dinner and he still wasn't saying much by bedtime.

"Everything okay, Mr. Venture Forth Arrow?" Dancy asked.

—How did my dad die? (He wished she would finally tell him because his father kept saying he didn't remember much about the accident.)

There was a noticeable pause before Dancy said, "Oh, Bonaventure, not again," and she let out a tired sigh. He could tell that she still didn't want to talk about it, and he decided that there was another way to find out.

The next day when everyone else was busy, he went to the kitchen, pushed a chair over to the counter, and reached for the sassafras jar. He put it in his pocket, got down, and quietly moved the chair back where it belonged.

The voice came from his mother's closet then, beckoning to him and telling him to bring the sassafras along. When he got to the closet door, he began to twist the jar's lid slowly, lefty-loosey, and then the sassafras picked up with its story about the policemen at the door:

"There's been an accident, ma'am. We need you to come

along to the hospital with us," and then Bonaventure heard
his mother saying the same things over and over . . .

"What's happened to William? Where is he? Oh, please,
please tell me. Why won't you tell me? I'm begging you!
Please!" And then he heard a terrible sound like nothing he'd
ever heard before. It was coming from the box way up on the
top shelf.

Bonaventure began to feel dizzy and sick to his stomach,
and he was afraid that maybe being sneaky was making him
feel that way. He put the lid back on the spice and returned it
to the kitchen. His curiosity was gone. He no longer wanted
to know the secret that was hiding inside the word *accident*.

As he did on so many nights, William came to Bonaventure's room; he knew what had happened in the closet and
he wanted to see for himself that everything was all right.

Bonaventure heard that stir in the air and looked up
from his book about airplanes.

—Dad?

"How ya doing, buddy?"

—I didn't have a very good day. I think I found that bad
thing in Mom's closet and it made me feel sick.

"Are you feeling better now?"

—Yeah, but it was pretty scary.

"I promise it won't hurt you, son. Let's forget about it
for now."

—Yeah. Let's forget about it and talk about something
else.

So they talked about how to build a really good go-kart,
until Bonaventure nodded off.

William had a look around the room while Bonaventure
slept. It was obvious from the book and the balsa-wood model

planes hanging by strings from the ceiling that Bonaventure was fascinated by flight. William wondered how he hadn't known this before. Gabe Riley had known it for a while.

Bonaventure felt fine in the morning. After breakfast, he went to wait outside Grand-mère's chapel; they were going to look at stuff in her library after she finished her prayers and had something to eat. Bonaventure couldn't understand how Grand-mère could wait so long to have breakfast. He listened for the morning sounds to finish their quiet concerto: the click of rosary beads, the whispers that went in search of God, and the windy little breath that put out the candle. He heard all of that, and then he heard something else. It was a new sound that was small and sad and was coming from the chapel. He wasn't scared by it. He just felt sorry.

Bonaventure started signing with Grand-mère the minute she stepped from her chapel:

Roll of eyes, blowing breath out loudly. —You, no food?

"Man does not live by bread alone, Bonaventure," she said to him in reply.

—I know. We eat gumbo two days. Remember?

Letice pulled him into a hug and told him that she loved him and that she had her work cut out for her. Once in the kitchen, she made herself some tea and attempted to poach an egg but gave up on it and had toast instead.

—Find new Mrs. Silvey today?

"Oh, Bonaventure, don't I wish! I think the only thing that has stood between us and starvation has been the grace of God," which was pretty much what he would have expected her to say.

Grand-mère finished her breakfast, and they went into the library. Waiting there for Bonaventure was the newest sound yet: drums low-whispering in an unbroken rhythm.

Grand-mère talked about Saint Bonaventure and his special prayer, which she had on the back of a holy card. While she read it out loud, the whispering drums put a good solid tempo to the peaceable words of the prayer:

> *Be Thou alone ever my hope; my entire confidence,*
> *my riches, my delight;*
> *my pleasure, my joy*

When she finished reading the prayer, Bonaventure signed, —Okay, ask God for something?

"Like what?"

—New Mrs. Silvey. You remember lady, grass hat, pie, when you drive?

"Yes I do. What about her?"

Eyebrows raised, palms turned up as if to say, —Maybe she can cook.

"You might be onto something, Bonaventure. You just might be onto something. What made you think of her?"

Bonaventure shrugged his shoulders as if to reply, —I don't know.

Actually, he did know. The Spanish moss had been speaking to him again, and it mentioned that the lady with the itching feet was the pie lady, and that she was magical. Bonaventure didn't care much about food, but he did want to be with someone magical.

He returned to the library later that day to find out if the drums were still there. They were. He tracked them down to a book by Henry Wadsworth Longfellow, and since he was all by himself, he could give them his full attention.

Books are generally considered to be soundless things, but Bonaventure knew better. He pulled Longfellow from where he stood between Oliver Wendell Holmes and Herman Melville, carefully, as Grand-mère had taught him to do, relishing first the unsticking and then the sliding sounds the book's cover made when it broke ranks from its place on the shelf. When he opened the volume, its binding made a pleasant cracking noise. There was a wonderful peeling-away sound when he grasped the corner of the first page and turned it, and the gold leaf on the page's edge let out a snapping salute. A picture appeared on the frontispiece that showed a young Indian girl wearing beautiful beads and a fringe-sleeved dress. The caption said "Minnehaha, Laughing Water," and Bonaventure heard that lovely name flow across the page.

A fine piece of leather with a ribbon on one end marked a place in the pages of the book. When Bonaventure went to it, the whispering drums became louder and louder until they filled the room with trochaic tetrameter and steady rumbling voices:

> *Forth then issued Hiawatha,*
> *Wandered eastward, wandered westward,*
> *Teaching men the use of simples*
> *And the antidotes for poisons,*
> *And the cure of all diseases.*
> *Thus was first made known to mortals*
> *All the mystery of Medamin,*
> *All the sacred art of healing*

While Bonaventure was listening to the voices of drums, Trinidad Prefontaine was in her root cellar putting the twelfth Mason jar into a wire basket. That's when the itching returned to her feet. She took the jars to the kitchen, set them in the sink, put on her fescue-grass hat, and walked to Christopher Street in town to find that certain eucalyptus tree where she'd found cooling for that itching before.

Once there, she fixed her feet on the ground and found that hole in the Spanish moss that let her look upon the house across the way.

Then she started to Know.

She knew who lived in that house. She knew Bonaventure had put a book back in its place and was right at the moment scavenging the pantry, as if maybe he was starving. She knew he'd reached for a jar of peanut butter and a sleeve of saltine crackers. She knew Dancy had tossed aside a magazine and was pacing back and forth. She knew Letice had gone into an unused bedroom and plumped up the pillows as if such a thing was necessary. She knew Bonaventure was keeping still every now and again, as if maybe he was listening.

And then an important thing happened: the beat that was Bonaventure's once-in-a-while visitor, and the gentle quivering feather that floated through Trinidad every now and then, found each other and got pressed between two hearts that fit together, one of them right-sided and one of them left.

And the Spirit's task was done.

THE Wanderer was allowed to dig holes at the far end of the garden. It was a large garden, a half acre at least, used for therapeutic purposes. The staff kept an eye on him, after it had been suggested that what he was digging looked like a grave. In his personal actuality, The Wanderer was digging a tunnel in the Château d'If, trying to reach the Abbé Faria. He had become Edmond Dantès once again, locked away in a lonely place.

There are many kinds of prisons. The Wanderer's was brick and mortar, while William Arrow's was an ethereal place somewhere between physical death and eternity. As he watched The Wanderer digging a hole to nowhere, back bent, arms trembling, William realized the man suffered greatly inside his own mind, and he wanted the man's suffering to end. It was then that William forgave his killer.

The first challenge had been met.

LIKE RIPPLES ON THE
SURFACE OF A POND

TRINIDAD Prefontaine was not surprised to see Letice Arrow come driving up the Neff Switch road. She'd been expecting her.

Letice couldn't seem to talk fast enough. "We've been looking to fill the position for months but haven't even come close to finding anyone . . . we so greatly admired your baked goods . . . I know you've built up a very fine business, and I will certainly compensate you for it if you'll be so kind as to hear me out . . ."

Trinidad knew she would take the job. The only requirement subject to negotiation was the assumption that she would live in the carriage house lately occupied by the Silveys. No, she said; she would continue to live in her own house, but they didn't need to pick her up or take her home because she liked to walk. She promised to be there by seven in the morning, six days a week, but she would not work on Sundays. She volunteered the name and address of the Virgil B. Hortons for reference. Letice said the offer spoke well for her, but she just had a feeling about things, and would August 1 be a good day to start? It was a Wednesday, but of course she would be paid for the whole week.

Trinidad accepted.

"By the way," Letice said, "I would swear that you and I have met before. Do you get that same feeling?"

"It occur to me, yes," Trinidad replied. "I think maybe a long time ago. You ever been to Pascagoula?"

"No. Never. It must have been someplace else," Letice said.

"Okay, then, but I do believe it was a long time ago."

"Hmmm. Well, I'm sure it'll come to me. Oh, I almost forgot! Our address is 918 Christopher Street."

But Trinidad knew that already. The address had been visible through the Spanish moss that hung from the eucalyptus tree.

All the way home Letice tried to think of places she might have met the woman, and Trinidad wondered when further Knowing would come. She was certain she and Letice had been bound together briefly before they were thrust apart. Perhaps if they saw each other nearly every day, she would remember the first time they'd met, and why.

It was Bonaventure who answered the door when Trinidad reported for work on August 1. He'd heard her coming long before she got there; in fact, he'd heard her wash her face that morning all the way out on the Neff Switch road. Her eyes went to his, and neither of them blinked as each looked into the soul of the other.

Letice walked briskly into the kitchen. "Why, Trinidad, I was listening for you at the front door. Come in. Come in. I see you've met Bonaventure."

"Yes, ma'am. I remember him from when you come by my stand that first time."

"Oh, that's right. Well, I don't think I mentioned it when we spoke, but Bonaventure here is the best boy you'll ever meet. He's smart and he's friendly and he's funny. But even more than that, Bonaventure is unique; he has special ways of talking that have nothing to do with a voice."

Trinidad smiled and said, "Hello, there, special-talking boy."

Bonaventure gave her a smile that lit up his beautiful eyes.

"Are you thirsty after your walk?" Letice asked.

"No, ma'am. I be just fine."

"All right, then, in that case let's get started. Come along with me and I'll explain things, get you situated a bit and familiar with the house."

Letice turned for the door and Bonaventure took Trinidad by the hand. They followed the *tip-tap-tip* of Letice's high-heeled shoes as she passed over the hardwood floor of the dining room and down the hall that led to her office. Letice laid out the details of the job: "Groceries are ordered by telephone on Mondays. Can you read, Trinidad? Yes? Wonderful. A list of foodstuffs we like to keep in stock is posted inside the pantry; laundry can be done at any time, but bed linens are always changed on Fridays. The Hoover is used on the big rugs weekly, but the small ones get shaken out or beaten; the hard-surface floors are dry-mopped, except for the kitchen, which is also washed once a week. The baths are scrubbed weekly as well. Oh, yes, and dinner is served at six. Naturally, no one expects everything to fall into place at once; there needs to be a period of adjustment. If you have any questions, please don't hesitate to ask."

Trinidad felt closer to the unnamed with every step she took. The air in the house seemed to curdle at times. It was cooler here and warmer there and sticky with dried-up tears in places. She had no concerns about the job; she knew she could do it. It was the sense of suffocation and the smell of noxious secrets that made her ill at ease. They skimmed around beneath the surface, and in some rooms pressed in on her from every side. But more than that was the constant haunting. She knew as surely as she knew her own name that the folk in this house did not dwell here alone. A spirit moved among them and watched them and loved them.

It was the love that disquieted her, for it was the kind of love that doesn't know when to leave itself to memory.

Bonaventure tried to concentrate on the sounds at hand. He was able to tune everything else out with two exceptions: that sinister sound from his mother's closet and the one that was small and sad in the chapel.

On Trinidad's second day, Bonaventure heard Grandma Roman a full ten minutes before she drove past the house. The first sound of her was always the same: a lip stretching into a sneer.

Adelaide saw Trinidad sweeping the front steps and wasted no time in getting over to Dancy's shop. "My baby girl sure has come up in the world. Had them Silveys working for you and now you got a nigger woman."

"Don't talk like that, Mama."

"I saw her sweeping your porch steps. Isn't she the one who sells pies and stuff out there on the Neff Switch road? I swear I'm sick to death of hearing about her and her miracle pies or whatever it is she fools people with. What's she doing sweeping your porch?"

"She's our new employee, and outside of being a lovely lady, she may very well be the best damn cook and housekeeper in Dixie."

"Don't curse, Dancy, it's low class," Adelaide said, and then continued, "Eustace Hommerding told me she gave him some treatment for the gout. You just go ahead and tell me what curing feet has got to do with cooking."

"I don't have time for this, Mama. Do you want your hair done or what?"

"How about if I bring my ironing over and slip it in with yours?" Adelaide Roman loved the idea of a black woman ironing her clothes on a hot and humid Louisiana day. It was the life she should have had.

As the days passed, Bonaventure became more and more enthralled by the look and the sound of Trinidad Prefontaine. He thought she was just the right colors: the golden brown-ness of her skin reminded him of maple syrup, and when she laughed, her pink tongue and very white teeth made him think of a cake Mrs. Silvey had made for Easter once. He also liked the way Trinidad moved, fluid and graceful, like ripples on the surface of a pond. He could hear the contralto voice of her gracefulness, thick as butter and smooth as satin.

Bonaventure took pride in providing Trinidad with the information she needed to make the most of the kitchen and to keep the house running up to snuff, since Grand-mère's instructions hadn't gone much beyond, "You'll find every-thing you need in the cupboards, the pantry, or the mud-room." Grand-mère didn't know much about housekeeping. Sometimes common sense just wasn't enough to take you right to the something you needed to find. Anybody would know that the measuring cup should be in the cupboard, but which one? And what about the Hoover, the rug beater, the broom, and the dustpan? Those things weren't kept in the cupboards or the pantry or the mudroom at all; they were kept in a closet under the back stairs. Bonaventure excelled at helping Trinidad out, and in no time the house was running smoothly.

Bonaventure loved that it never bothered her when he sat on a kitchen stool and watched her work. His note writing didn't bother her either; nor did the fact that some of the notes posed questions of a personal nature.

—Where do you live?

"Off the Neff Switch road, just a little ways from my stand where you bought a pie that time your mama say you all stumbled up to me."

—Are you married?

"Not anymore."

—Were you married before?

"Yes."

—What was your husband's name?

"He be named Jackson."

—Jackson was his first name?

"That's right."

—That was a president's name, but it was his last name.

"I know."

—Did your husband die?

"Yes."

—When?

"A long time ago."

—How did he die?

"He got too close to a horse that be scared by a storm. That horse reared up and knock him to the ground and then come back down on him. His chest be crushed by that poor scared animal, and that's why my man died. And him never sick a day in his life."

Head hung down, shoulders sloped. —An accident, Bonaventure wrote. (It was just as he'd suspected: people who died before they got old probably all died in accidents.)

"I don't know if it be a accident, Mr. Bonaventure. I just think it be his time."

Well, there was something new. Bonaventure didn't know what to say. He decided to come back to it later, and so took the conversation in a different direction.

—Do you have kids?

"No, I am sad to say I never be so blessed."

—Do you have a cat?

"No, sir, I surely do not."

—A dog?

"Nope. No dog neither."

—Do you wish you did?

"I don't believe I do."

—Do you have a bird?

"Oh, I got plenty of birds. They out in the woods and they sing to me every day. And a little old hoot-owl sing to me at night."

—I like birdsongs and owl hoots.

"Me too, Mr. Bonaventure, me too."

When the day was done and dusk had gone to bed, Trinidad sat in the rocking chair left to her by her old maiden aunt and thought of little Bonaventure Arrow. She knew the purity of his heart and the completeness of his innocence, for she'd felt them the first time she'd ever laid eyes on him, back on that day at her roadside stand when she looked at his beautiful eyes. She also knew that while she had certain gifts that let her know of secrets, little Mr. Bonaventure had something very much more than that. She knew that was why he did not speak, and she knew he was part of her Purpose.

FRIENDS

D ANCY Arrow's social life was confined to haircuts and manicures. She had put on widowhood the day William died and had not once taken it off since. In all those years, she'd never felt that anyone really understood her aloneness, as there were no widows among her friends. But maybe that had changed.

"Hey, Venture Forth, is Trinidad married? Do you know?"

Headshake. —Nope.

"Is that, no, she isn't married, or no, you don't know?"

Signed response. —Husband dead.

"How did he die? Was it an accident?"

—No. Trinidad say time to die.

He watched for a reaction from his mother, but she didn't show one.

Dancy had planned to take the day off to shop for clothes for Bonaventure, since he'd outgrown everything he owned overnight. But first she went to the kitchen and made a pot of coffee and invited Trinidad to sit and have a cup with her.

"Oh, I don't know, Miss Dancy, I got a lot of work to do."

"Aw, come on, Trinidad, it doesn't take more than fifteen minutes to drink a cup of coffee. Besides, you do enough work around here for five people."

So Dancy poured and Trinidad sat.

"I asked Bonaventure if you were married, and he told me your husband died."

"That's right, he surely did. His name be Jackson and he the finest looking man I ever did see," Trinidad said, and closed her eyes as she called up the memory of him. "He got kicked by a horse what be scared of a storm. That how he died."

Dancy didn't need to tell how William had died. Letice had informed Trinidad of it right after she'd come to work for them, but Trinidad offered her condolences nonetheless.

The minutes ticked by, the coffee pot emptied, and a friendship began to form. Dancy changed her hours on Wednesdays, postponing opening the shop until eleven. Without any formal announcement, she showed up in the kitchen on those mornings, made a fresh pot of coffee, and set out two cups. Before long, she and Trinidad began to share life stories, which brought them around to love.

"My Jackson, he the best man I ever did know. And hard-workin'? Lordy, you had to tell Jackson Prefontaine when to stop and come in to supper. That man would work by the light of the moon if I let him. I swear he would."

"William was a lawyer, a brand-new one. I think he would have been one of the best and most honest lawyers ever if he hadn't gotten killed. Mr. Robillard and Mr. Broome—they were the bosses where he worked—they came to the funeral and said it was a terrible shame what happened; they said William had a real bright future."

Trinidad, a woman with spiritual leanings, and Dancy, a woman with none, enjoyed sympathy and empathy and mutual solace over coffee and conversation. Until now, neither had spoken much to anyone about how it felt to go from wife to widow when still in the early years of desire. The bond they were forming allowed them to admit that even when they were among people, they still felt all alone.

"I'm real glad to have you for a friend, Trinidad," Dancy said on one of those mornings, "and I hope you're glad to have me."

"Well, now, you be easy to get on with. Just like Mr. Riley."

Trinidad noticed a flicker in her friend's eyes. Dancy had taken to watching the clock on Mondays, Wednesdays, and Fridays, and she'd started talking to Gabe less about Bonaventure and more about songs she liked or books she'd read or something she'd seen in the paper.

"Do you have a favorite book?" she'd asked him.

"I have several," he had replied.

"You can't have several favorites. There can only be one favorite," she said.

"Not for me. I have two: Steinbeck's *Cannery Row* and Hemingway's *For Whom the Bell Tolls*. I like them both the same."

"I'm going to allow you to have a favorite and a favorite favorite, but just this once," she said.

"What about you? What's your favorite book?" he asked her.

"Well, since we seem to be able to change the meaning of favorite, I'm gonna say that my favorite book is anything by William Faulkner," she said.

"What do you like so much about Faulkner?"

"The first time I read the words Yoknapatawpha County, the gentleman had my heart."

Gabe Riley lay awake nights trying to think of a set of words that would do the same for him.

Their conversations continued, and one day she gave him a playful touch on the arm and said, "Sorry, you go ahead," when they both started to speak at the same time.

The touch surprised them both, and they became self-conscious. Dancy began to withdraw after that.

Subtle changes came to her behavior, and they were not lost on Trinidad. For a time she'd thought about certain herbs and certain potions, but had rejected the idea in the end, believing that love should happen on its own. Trinidad knew the problem was nothing to do with Gabe or Dancy. It was to do with the phantom presence in the Arrow house; the one that put a mixed-up, bittersweet ache into the air; the presence of one departed.

During one of those coffee times, Dancy was a million miles away.

"Don't you try to tell me there be nothing wrong, Miss Dancy, cuz I know there is."

Dancy looked up, took a deep breath, let it out, and slumped her shoulders.

"Oh, I don't know, Trinidad. I've just been feeling kind of bad lately."

"About what?"

"Just things, I guess."

"Might it be one thing in particular?"

Dancy looked into her coffee cup as though she'd find an answer there. She seemed unsure and not at all like herself. "I think maybe I should let Gabe go."

Trinidad reached over and took both of Dancy's hands in her own. "You could do that," she said, "but your William still be dead."

"There's more to it than that," Dancy said. "It's hard to explain." Then she added, "I gotta get going. I'll see you later."

After Dancy had gone, and their coffee cups had been washed, dried, and put away, Trinidad fetched the broom and began to sweep the floor. She could feel the gaze of the half-departed; she'd felt that gaze before. Sometimes she would step to the side to move around its shadow by way of showing respect for the dead. But not this time.

"I know you be there, Mr. William. I knowed it the whole time. I knowed it from the day I come into this house. And I gots to wonder why you still here."

THE VOICES OF CRAYONS

D ANCY noticed that she was not the only one to have a friend in Trinidad; Bonaventure had one too. When Dancy got to thinking about it, she realized he probably made friends out of adults because he'd always been surrounded by them. She wondered if she'd done him wrong by keeping him too close to the family. Perhaps she should have given him more of a chance to be with other kids. There were children in the neighborhood, but they were all older and Dancy hadn't even tried to find other options for Bonaventure. She resolved to raise the matter with Mrs. Humphrey when parent-teacher conferences rolled around.

The teacher began with, "If I had a classroom full of Bonaventures, I would be a very happy woman."

"I'm glad to hear that," Dancy said.

"Of course, that's not to say his attention doesn't wander at times, but that's the way of all children, isn't it? Even then, it's not that he completely abandons what he should be doing and starts to do something else. It's more like he gets very still and then all of a sudden he'll pick up with what he was about."

Dancy had noticed the same thing and always thought it unusual. "Do you know what sorts of things distract him?" she asked.

"Well, if I had to guess, I'd say it's something he hears."

Dancy had experienced the same thought so many times, but always pushed it to that place in the back of her mind where she'd put it years before when he was only a baby and she realized there was something more to his silence. She set the idea aside this time too and brought up her concern about Bonaventure having friends. She asked how he got along with other kids.

Mrs. Humphrey paused before saying, "Mrs. Arrow, I can honestly say that I see no difference between Bonaventure's social interactions and those of the other children. They all have their ups and downs, and I'd say he's doing very well, considering."

"Considering that he doesn't speak?"

"Considering that he's so very bright," the teacher said. "This is an age when jealousies rise to the surface, and that has definitely come into play. Bonaventure is reading, writing, and spelling years ahead of his grade level, and he has no difficulties that I can see in any other area. His printing is absolutely beautiful, though I suppose he gets more practice than most, what with all that writing he does on his notepad. Given all of these factors, it's not unusual that he faces some resentment, but it's an occasional thing. He's formed some friendships, though if I'm being honest I'd have to say that he does seem to hold back a little bit. I think that's due more to shyness than anything else."

"I worry about him getting his feelings hurt," Dancy said.

"That's something all parents worry about. Acceptance is a problem every child faces, Mrs. Arrow, not just Bonaventure. The best we can do is to take it one day at a time," the teacher offered. "And don't forget that he's caring and helpful, which the other children definitely pick up on. For example, when we have art, I put out two shoe boxes full of crayons and the children are to find the crayon they need and put it back when they're finished. It's a good way to teach the importance of sharing and being considerate of others. Of course, it always seems that someone is digging for a red or a black and becoming quite frustrated in the process. Well, it's the darnedest thing, but Bonaventure will go to the child and comfort him or her. And then he reaches right in and finds that specific crayon. I've seen him do it time and again."

Bonaventure could have told her that the red crayon sounded like the trombones in the brass band that played in the gazebo in the park on summer Saturdays; it started out low and then slid around your ears. The black crayon was different; it made a sound like a pancake dropped off a spatula and landed on a plate with nothing more than a puffed-up thud.

Mrs. Humphrey assured Dancy that she would continue to keep an eye on social interactions, and that for the most part Bonaventure was blending in well with the other children. To which Dancy responded, "But he's not really like the other children, is he?"

"No, Mrs. Arrow, he's not. Your son is definitely the kindest child I've ever seen, and in twenty years of teaching, let's just say I've seen a few."

The session ended, but Dancy's worst fear remained—that Bonaventure's muteness made him vulnerable to tragedy. Her maternal instincts worked overtime imagining terrible things that might happen to a child who could never cry out for help. She could remember every story she'd ever heard about children who fell down abandoned wells or got locked in discarded iceboxes or died in a fire because no one knew where to look for them.

Dancy didn't need to worry so. Her gifted boy lived in a silence that brought him the sound of danger whether it lurked down in a hole or in an icebox left for junk, and he most definitely could hear the change that takes place in the air right before a flame is lit.

Bonaventure was waiting on the front porch for his mother. He was waiting as hard as he could, which involved not moving even one single muscle. He kept both feet stuck flat to the step; knees pressed together, hands over kneecaps. He'd been sitting so long in one spot that his little behind had started to hurt. It was how Bonaventure conducted himself when hoping for the best.

He didn't think he'd messed up in school, but he wanted to know for sure. Mostly he loved school; it was recess that was the problem. For one thing, there were too many sounds to keep up with, and for another, there were two boys in his class who would trip him sometimes or shove him on the playground, calling him teacher's pet. But he'd never told on them because he wasn't a tattletale.

Dancy saw her son sitting rigid on the bottom step and correctly assumed it meant he was anxious to know how things had gone.

"Hey, there, Sunshine. I sure am glad to see ya. I was afraid you mighta run off and got married while I was gone."

Bonaventure flapped one hand at her and rolled his eyes. —You and your jokes, he was saying.

She put an end to his anxiety then and started to go on about how Mrs. Humphrey could hardly find enough words to sing his praises, what with him being such a good student and very, very kind, not to mention easy to get along with. Bonaventure blushed and beamed all at the same time, the recess bullies forgotten.

MARKING TIME

EVEN though Dancy had become strong in the ways that an independent businesswoman needs to be, she had no desire to move herself and Bonaventure out of Letice's house, and Letice had no desire to see them to go. It could be said that love held them together, but that would not be the entire truth, for there was another reason neither one of them could define. In fact, an existential gravity held them in orbit in that house, revolving around secrets and existing within a darkness that held the dust of long-dead stars.

This gravity had no pull on Trinidad, but she could sense its heaviness, and she could feel the infinitesimal wind caused by the dust of those dead stars as they skimmed around Bonaventure and came to rest on Dancy and Letice.

Even though Letice regularly invited Trinidad to move into the apartment once occupied by the Silveys, she continued to politely decline, choosing to stay in her house on the Neff Switch road. It was there that she kept those things she believed sacred on an altar she'd set up in a corner of the front room. It was there that she harvested healing and contemplated that odd kind of gravity.

Trinidad knew that Dancy kept on paying a debt she didn't owe. She also knew that Letice worried all the time and was looking to hire a detective to make the anxiety go. And she knew that Adelaide Roman bore the guilt of the Pharisees. The very sight of Adelaide always brought conjuring to Trinidad's mind, and that was an idea she didn't want much to do with because it brought her own mother's beliefs up to her stomach, like a case of indigestion.

Life on Christopher Street went on. Autumn came and Bonaventure dressed up as Captain America for Halloween because that's who he wanted to be every day of his life. Thanksgiving that year was somewhat subdued, it being the first major holiday without the Silveys. The Arrows invited Trinidad for the meal, but strictly as a guest, even though Letice was hopeless in the kitchen and turkey was one thing Dancy had never made; she had some serious reservations about pulling the giblets out of the bird. In the end they bought a turkey breast and some mashing potatoes, opened a can of jellied cranberries, boiled some yams with marsh-mallows and brown sugar, and had store-bought pumpkin pie with whip cream from a can and maraschino cherries from a jar.

Bonaventure made pilgrim hats out of folded-up news-papers and insisted on having popcorn instead of regular corn in remembrance of the Wampanoag Indians who'd brought it to the first Thanksgiving. Mrs. Humphrey had read that story out loud in school, and it was one of his favorites because it held the sound of friendship.

Grandma Roman showed up in time for the meal; she said she'd been dishing up dinner to the homeless at the Resurrection Tent, and doggone it if she didn't have to rush right back over there and wouldn't get the chance to help them clean up. No one believed her, outfitted as she was in a new black dress and stylish satin pumps.

PEACE ON EARTH
AND MERCY MILD

CHRISTMAS was different that year too, mainly because Bonaventure had gone to the trouble of examining the fireplace; of late he had formed some suspicions. He didn't know why they even had a fireplace; it wasn't like they ever used it much. He bent over and stuck his head in to get a good look, and one good look was all he needed. He straightened up and determined his suspicions had been correct—a cat couldn't get down that chimney, never mind a fat man carrying a sack big enough to hold toys for all the children in the world. Bonaventure Arrow had let go of Santa Claus. Bonaventure Arrow was growing up.

Trinidad's baking talents multiplied exponentially during the holiday season. She turned out butter cookies and spritz and pfeffernüsse and gingerbread and fruitcake. She made nougat roll and peppermint bark. She baked tiny pecan pies called teatime tassies and a chocolate-covered Yule log cake. To enter the Arrow kitchen at Christmastime was to transcend this earth entirely.

Dancy invited Gabe to go along with her and Bonaventure to get a Christmas tree. The three of them gave each possibility a good looking over, turning them this way and that. They had all agreed that the best trees weren't perfect, that it was the flaws that gave them character. The ninth tree they examined was the keeper. When Dancy went to pay, she found out that Gabe had settled up with the tree man.

"I can't let you do that, Gabe."

"Of course you can," he said. "Consider it my Christmas gift."

"That's not why I wanted you to come along."

"I know that, Dancy."

"Well, I hope so."

"So why did you?" he asked.

"Why did I what?"

"Want me to come along?"

"Because it's Christmas," was what she said. But what she didn't say was that she liked to be around him. She couldn't say that even to herself.

Bonaventure got full of pine pitch when they sawed off the bottom to make sure the tree wouldn't lean off to one side.

"People who sign should be careful of pine pitch," Gabe told him, and ruffled his hair. "Their fingers could get stuck on a word."

Bonaventure loved the joke.

They had eggnog and cookies in the living room, and listened to Christmas music while the tree settled in. Later, when they were putting on the lights, Gabe got kind of warm, so he took his sweater off and rolled his shirtsleeves up to just below his elbows. It was an innocent thing, but it grabbed Dancy's attention and she felt a stirring she hadn't felt since William. She didn't know what to do with that feeling, so she fussed around with the ornament boxes.

When all the decorations were on, Bonaventure got to plug in the tree lights and turn off the lamps, and they all stood back and said "ah" in whatever way they could.

Dancy thought about Gabe for a long time that night

and decided she needed to get things back on track once and for all.

The next morning at breakfast Letice suggested they invite him for Christmas dinner.

"I thought about that and decided against it."

"You decided against it? Why?" Letice asked.

"He might feel like he should bring gifts, and he already bought the tree. And anyway, I think he said something about spending the day with his folks."

Gabe, of course, had said no such thing.

Adelaide Roman got all gussied up on Christmas Eve and sashayed over to the Resurrection Tent to get lost in a reverie about Brother Harley John. While over in her little house on the Neff Switch road, Trinidad Prefontaine sat down on the green velvet bench and played "Oh Come, All Ye Faithful" on the old pump organ. She'd taught herself to play and felt she wasn't too awful bad. She'd baked some sugar cookies that morning, decorated her door with holly at noon, tossed some seed outside for wild birds at suppertime, and lit a candle in honor of Peace on Earth and the Little Lord Jesus when starlight filled the sky.

Grand-mère, Bonaventure, and even Dancy went to Midnight Mass. It was sixty-three degrees that night, with a mist in the air like suspended rain. Bonaventure loved the sound of that mist; it made him think of angels' wings. When he mentioned this to Letice, she said it was the best present he could have given her.

The sounds of the Christmas Vigil Mass nearly carried Bonaventure from the church pew all the way to Venus. Mixed in with the beautiful music, he heard a candle sputter in Trinidad's house and it made him feel warm and good.

. . . .

William felt a pounding where a physical heart would be, as if he wasn't dead at all. He stayed away on Christmas morning to walk the shore of the Almost Heaven sea.

On New Year's Eve, the Arrow household stayed up until midnight and welcomed 1957 with a champagne toast for the grownups and root beer for anyone who was almost seven. It had been the happiest holiday season they'd known in years.

Dancy and Letice would survive the winter as the passion flower vine survives the same: their roots would sleep in the soil of the past and their stems would survive the dark and the cold while dreaming of bees and hummingbirds and being tended to lovingly by Trinidad and Gabe.

The Spirit that had brought them all together wished them the best in what was to come.

THE Wanderer thought he'd had a button once. He could remember how it felt to reach into his pocket and rub his thumb over it. Then he thought that perhaps there'd been the likeness of an eagle on the front of it. Yes, there was, and that eagle still looked big, even though it fit on such a small thing as a button. The Wanderer couldn't understand that at all.

That lady who came to see him always wore a sweater with buttons, but none of them had eagles on the front.

The Wanderer had no thoughts of Christmas.

PART II

Innermost
1957

THE PINKERTON

NOTHING had ever calmed the resentment Dancy felt toward William's killer. Her hatred, always a blister on her soul, had become a fetid ulceration, cracked and sore. She hoped he lived a long life in that prison for the insane, and she hoped he was in pain every single day.

Letice did not feel resentment or hate, but her curiosity had never lessened. Even after all these years, she still wanted desperately to know the man's name, and why, why, why. So in January of 1957 she gave up on ever receiving resolution from Sergeant Turcotte and hired a retired Pinkerton detective named Coleman Tate, a man so dedicated to his work that he'd never found time to marry.

Mr. Tate was of average height and was getting a bit round in the middle. He kept his hair cropped short and always wore a suited vest and a pocket watch affixed to the end of a fob. Tate was a quiet man, patient and thorough. He remembered reading about the murder in the paper.

Coleman Tate asked Letice to go over everything pertaining to the police investigation. She gave him Sergeant Turcotte's name and relayed the gist of their conversations. She recounted that no connection to William's law firm had been made; she spoke to Tate of her suspicions that the murderer may have been a disgruntled customer of the Arrow family bank, perhaps someone who'd been foreclosed on. She was honest with him in saying that the police believed they had accounted for all those possibilities, and there was no record of anyone who'd been denied a loan. Nonetheless, she felt it was a possibility that deserved a closer look.

"Everything is worth considering, Mrs. Arrow," he said. "But I must familiarize myself with the physical evidence first."

"Whatever you think best, Mr. Tate."

The day after being retained by Letice, Tate went to the asylum and enlightened the administrator as to his client's unending grief. He knew it was the right approach. A door was unlocked and a metal box brought out. Tate asked if he might be left to conduct a thorough inventory and maybe take some notes.

"Certainly. Take your time," the administrator said.

The box contained much more than Tate had expected. He handled each piece of evidence gingerly, examining it with a magnifying glass he'd brought along for that purpose. He asked permission to take custody of the objects for the duration of his investigation "in order to bring closure to the Arrow family." The administrator knew well the power of the Arrow name and said that while it was unusual, even unprecedented, this one time he would make an exception.

Tate thanked the man and deftly took his leave. At home in his den, he took careful notes, recording even the smallest details.

PROGRESS REPORT
IN THE MATTER OF WILLIAM EVEREST ARROW
(DECEASED)

**A visit to the asylum in which the killer is
incarcerated yielded access to the items he was
carrying at the time of the murder. In total: a
button; a *Chicago Tribune* newspaper folded
triple-wise and dated December 1,1949; a paper
napkin from a coffee shop in Memphis; a scrap
of paper bearing the notation F379.N5A182; and
a matchbook imprinted with the words "Zip's
Tavern—Melvindale, Michigan." A receipt
accompanies these possessions noting that he had
$705 in cash, which is locked in the asylum vault. I
have determined that these are enough to conduct
a thorough investigation. Further findings to
follow.**

Per his agreement with Letice, Tate was to deliver his
reports in person, during the daytime when Dancy was at
work. Letice didn't want to risk things coming in the mail.
On the day he brought the first report, Trinidad was cleaning in the front room and Bonaventure was by her side.
He was listening to the travel story of a piece of rice dust
that claimed to have journeyed from the stratosphere into
the troposphere on the foot of a bar-headed goose that had
flown over the Himalayas on its way to Pakistan. The par-
ticle had just described the delightful dryness of the tropo-
pause and was about to tell how it had ended up in the front
room, when the sound of the doorbell interfered. Trinidad
answered it with Bonaventure at her heels.

    Coleman Tate introduced himself and asked to see Mrs.

Letice Arrow if you please; she was expecting him. Trinidad stepped aside and motioned him into the foyer, where he waited while she went to announce his arrival. Tate bent down to shake hands with Bonaventure.

"How are you today, young man?"

Index finger to thumb, three fingers straight up as if to say, —I am A-OK.

"I see you're the strong, silent type," Tate said.

Nod, nod, nod.

"Well, nothing wrong with that. You know what they say: loose lips sink ships." ·

Bonaventure smiled. He liked Coleman Tate.

Trinidad returned and said, "Please follow me, sir."

As Tate walked away, Bonaventure heard a cracking, tearing, shattering noise coming from an envelope the man had tucked in his suit-coat pocket.

Not being gifted with access to Bonaventure's silence, Trinidad didn't hear that sound, but she did experience a vision when the Pinkerton passed through the door of Letice's office. She saw a ragged jawbone take wing and fly above his head. That bone-scrap phantom was still flying in a circle above the visitor when he walked through the house to leave.

"There's some very big hurt in this world, Mr. Bonaventure," Trinidad said as she closed the door behind Tate.

Boneventure placed one hand on the lower right side of his face in response, as if her vision had reached out to his hearing and let him in on something.

That night, he told his father about Mr. Tate and the scary noises he'd brought into the house.

"I know something about Mr. Tate," William said.

—Really? What?

"Well, you know how in books and movies there are good guys and bad guys?"

—Uh-huh.

"Mr. Tate is one of the good guys. You should listen really hard around him, and if you start to hear things that you don't know what they mean, you should send those sounds to him."

—Why?

"Because he's a detective."

Bonaventure took in a surprised little gasp. —Like the Hardy Boys?

"Yup. Only grown up."

THE SIGHT OF HER
BROKENNESS

B ONAVENTURE was certain he looked different when he peered into the mirror on the morning of his seventh birthday. He thought he looked taller and more grown up. There really was a difference, but it was nothing you could see. He had insisted on inviting Gabe to his birthday dinner, after which they had cake and ice cream and went to see *Lady and the Tramp*, which Bonaventure and Dancy had already been to twice.

The passing weeks were preserved in construction paper and Elmer's glue and posted on the fridge: valentines, shamrocks, and yellow-headed daffodils.

Dancy was working harder than ever. Talk with her customers was easy and light, tending to revolve around movie stars and sewing patterns and recipes found on Campbell's soup cans. But lately, their easy camaraderie had begun to intrude on Dancy's personal life.

"You're twenty-seven years old," Donna Rae Miller said. "Don't you want a man in your life? Why do you keep living like you're ninety-seven??"

"Oh, that's a huge exaggeration, Donna Rae, and you know it. I don't have the slightest inclination to look for a man, or for that matter to cook for him or take him to bed.

I've got a child to raise and a business to run. What with needing to sleep a few hours at the end of the day, that's just about all I got time for."

"Well, you're gonna get all dried up on your insides. See if you don't."

Dancy merely laughed.

"Go ahead and laugh. But you know what they say. 'Use it or lose it,' they say, and if it was me I wouldn't want to lose it. Not at twenty-seven years old, I wouldn't," Donna Rae continued.

"Well, I don't know who *they* are, but I do know that I don't want to talk about it. Not one more word, and I do mean not one," was Dancy's firm response.

Donna Rae ignored the admonition and went on. "Look, honey, I know you loved him, but you're not the one who died. I mean, this is 1957. Come December it'll be eight years. I worry about you is all, and I just wanna help."

"Let it be, Donna Rae. I'll work it out," Dancy said, in a tone that was a little bit weary.

Once in a while, someone would try to set her up on a date without her knowing what they were up to. "It's just a get-together," they'd say. "Dinner, maybe some cards."

Dancy never fell for it.

William spent a lot of time at Dancy's shop. He loved to watch her when she was concentrating on her work. But the best was when she was all alone, sitting in front of the mirror and playing around with her own hair, trying it this way and that, and experimenting with makeup, though she never really wore much. He happened to witness that conversation with Donna Rae, and it bothered him that his passionate Dancy didn't care if she dried up, and the way she'd turned cold sort of bothered him too.

William would have to do more than remove Dancy's guilt; he would have to face his hardest challenge. The mere thought of it felt like the bullets that had already killed him once. He couldn't bring himself to do it. Not yet. If only he could just talk to her . . .

And so he pulled her to the cemetery as he had always done, and stood at the door of the crypt. When she got there, she sat down on a marble bench.

"Dancy," he said.

She sat very still.

He spoke again: "I'm here. I'm right here."

She looked up in a sudden hair-rising-up-on the-back-of-the-neck kind of way and kept very still.

"Stand up if you can see me, Dancy. It's okay. Don't be afraid."

She stood up then and ran for her car, and tightened the lock on her tears. Dancy feared she might be going crazy and starting in with hallucinations.

She dreamed of William that night, and woke up with proof that she had not dried up on her insides. She threw herself into her shop after that, the better to become exhausted, too tired even to dream. Dancy lost herself in work. She spent so many hours on her feet that her back hurt at the end of the day. But it was worth it. She was too worn to feel anything.

Bonaventure could hear his mother battle with her nerves. He tried to distract her by making her sing with the radio; he thought she had the most glorious voice. He listened for that certain little catch in it that wasn't quite a yodel, the one that made her sound like Patsy Cline.

Dancy mostly listened to country music. Sometimes the radio was tuned to doo-wop or to Cajun, but never to the proudly mournful blues as sung in the bayou-filled delta of southern Louisiana.

On an evening when she felt kind of restless without knowing why, Dancy decided she needed to leave the house for a while. She made sure Bonaventure brushed his teeth and allowed that he could play in his room for another half hour. When time was up, she tucked him in and asked Letice if it would be all right if she went out for a drive. Letice knew to let her go.

Dancy drove out to Papa Jambalaya's, put a coin in the jukebox, and pushed J-17. As Hank Williams sang "I'm so Lonesome I Could Cry," Dancy Arrow became the lonesome whip-poor-will and the midnight train and the weeping robin and the leaves that had begun to die.

She had herself a couple of beers and ordered the special but didn't eat a bite, just sat there staring and smoking Pall Malls one right after the other.

William stood behind her, remembering the night they'd met. It had been nothing like this. The sight of her brokenness became too much for him, and he went outside to wait.

Back in his room on Christopher Street, Bonaventure could hear Dancy's cigarette smoke wafting up to the ceiling and hovering over the happiness at Papa Jambalaya's. He could also hear the heavy unshed tears that stung his mother behind her eyes and ran down her throat all the way to her chest.

Sometimes he hated his ears.

THE SICKNESS BROUGHT
ABOUT BY IGNORANCE

WE hafta hurry it up a little bit, Venture Forth Arrow. Grandma Roman is coming over, and since it's an every-other-Saturday, she'll be wanting her hair done before going to services at the International Church of the Big-Ass Righteous."

Bonaventure's hands flew to his mouth and his head and shoulders shook with silent laughter. Grand-mère Letice would keel right over if she heard his mother cuss like that, but he thought it was awful funny.

So did William.

Adelaide Roman was certain of her soul's perfection, and so felt comfortable pointing out iniquities committed by others. To that end, she brought her religion with her wherever she went, including to her job at the United States Post Office.

"Yoo Hoo."

"In the kitchen, Mama."

Adelaide Roman sat down and placed the newest Sears Roebuck catalog on the table, saying she was entirely mindful that it was addressed to Creathie LaRue, but seeing how Providence changes things for certain mail recipients (namely, fornicators and liars), she believed the catalog had rightfully come into her possession. She supposed that forfeiting the Sears Roebuck catalog was just one of the consequences visited upon a person who run off in the night and then had the gumption six months later to come back from where she'd run off to with not only a husband but a child too, one she claimed was prematurely born. Not that Adelaide knew anything personal about Creathie LaRue. Just sayin'.

Bonaventure would have to wait through Grandma Roman's entire wash, set, dry, and comb-out, because he had to stay clean for their standing date at Bixie's Luncheonette. These lunch dates were a fairly recent development. He hadn't been alone with his Grandma Roman much since that time when he was two and she'd threatened to cook his pink elephant in the oven. He only went along with it now because he loved Bixie's and neither his mother nor grand-mère did, so Grandma Roman was his best chance of getting there.

His shirt collar chafed from Staley's Sta-Flo laundry starch and his shoes felt way too tight, but being Bonaventure he wasn't saying a word; and anyway, the discomfort brought him welcome distraction.

Grandma Roman perused the Sears Roebuck while she sat under the hairdryer, each page making a crinkly, rustling sound that Bonaventure liked very much, although its connection to his grandmother worried him. He never kept sounds that had to do with Grandma Roman, as he'd never even heard one he wanted. But he did like that crinkly sound of those pages, and after a few anxious moments he reasoned that the catalog was only indirectly related to her because, according to the United States Post Office, it really did belong to Creathie LaRue. So twenty minutes later, when Adelaide had her eyes closed against the mists of Helene Curtis Spray Net, Bonaventure tore out a page from the middle, folded it up real small, and tucked it in his pocket, where it would reside until it joined the mementos in that box beneath his bed.

The two of them finally headed for Bixie's, where the specialty was always biscuits and gravy and where tin advertising signs decorated the walls, which is how Bonaventure came to develop a certain fondness for whiskey, billiards, and tobacco, charmed as he was by their very fine slogans: "Jack Daniel's—Charcoal Mellowed Drop by Drop" and "Don't Be Vague, Ask for a Hague—Hague Scotch Whiskey." He also loved "Easy Eight's Billiards & Pool—The Best Racks in Town!" and "Happiness Is a Cigar Called Hamlet." But his highest admiration was reserved for "L.S.M.F.T.—Lucky Strike Means Fine Tobacco." He particularly loved the pure, sparse poetry of those five initials, and the way they had of proclaiming the fineness of something in such a small confederation of alphabet letters. Bonaventure would sign those letters over and over, as if they were a little chorus in a tune about Bixie's.

Grandma Roman ordered the meatloaf and a slice of soda cracker pie. Bonaventure had a grilled cheese sandwich with a strawberry milkshake, the accompanying straw of which naturally found its way down his shirt as another piece for the memento box, qualified as it was by the unique timbre of its gurgling, slurping sound.

Claude and Opal Rondelle, twins somewhere past fifty years old, were taking lunch at Bixie's that day. Claude wore the dark green trousers and shirt of a working man because that is what he was—a fellow who cut grass, repaired radios and small appliances, and sharpened knives and scissors. Opal always had an apron on, even when she went out in public. She took in wash for a living, and once in a while she babysat.

Grandma Roman said the Rondelles always sat in a booth because they were midgets and couldn't manage the stools at the counter. "You can tell they're midgets even when they're sitting down," she was fond of saying. "They got that midget look to their features, like two little old elves who wandered off from the North Pole." She always got a kick out of herself with that one.

Every time she spotted the Rondelle twins Grandma Roman would shake her head side to side and mutter the same thing, "Now I wonder just what in the Sam Hill their normal parents done to deserve it. I mean, Good Lord, those two must hafta buy their clothes in the children's department. Don't you think so, Bonaventure?"

Bonaventure began to sign a response, moving his hands around the story of the gumball machine that stood just inside the front door of Bixie's, and the time Claude Rondelle had put two pennies in its slot and had given the gumballs to Bonaventure rather than keeping them for himself. Bonaventure still had them, one red and one yellow; he hadn't chewed them because of the wonderful rattling sound they'd made as they left the machine's glass bubble. He had barely started the story when his grandmother reached over and yanked his hands down and pressed them to his sides.

"Stop it!" she hissed. "It is not at all polite to draw attention to yourself like that. Honest to Christmas, sometimes I just don't know where your mother's head is. I positively don't. You listen to me, Bonaventure Arrow. One day you're gonna do that finger-wagging nonsense and end up arrested for being lewd and lascivious. Do you hear me?"

Bonaventure didn't know the meaning of lewd and lascivious, but he did know the sound of a woman ashamed, and it was coming real loud from Grandma Roman.

She nudged him then and motioned toward a cross-eyed girl sitting at the end of the counter. Then she looked at Bonaventure and crossed her own eyes and said, "Where you at, Bonaventure? On my left or my right?" and laughed a snorty laugh.

After that, she talked about how she'd love to take him to hear Brother Harley John Eacomb preach about the sickness brought about by ignorance. She said that every single week she could hardly wait for Sunday to hurry up and get here.

"Hey, guess what," she said. "There's plans for Brother Eacomb to hold two special ceremonies and initiations down to the river come the twentieth of July. The first one is at two o'clock in the afternoon and the second one is at seven in the evening; there has to be two separate ceremonies because of the expected multitude, and Brother Eacomb needs to rest in between because he throws his whole self into saving souls. It would kill a lesser man, but Brother Eacomb just needs to rest a bit. Any-hoo-how, I'm thinking it would be a real treat for you to go with me because you, Mr. Bonaventure Arrow, are an interesting case. But like I said it's not gonna happen until July."

Bonaventure did not encourage her to go on. He knew there was no need.

"I been thinking, see. And what I been thinking is that Brother Eacomb can speak in tongues, by which I mean in languages only God can understand. Now, what makes these meetings special is that there's gonna be the laying on of hands. Do you see where I'm going with this?"

She paused to allow Bonaventure to show some sign of eagerness, but he wouldn't so much as blink. Keeping his face motionless around Grandma Roman was something he did on principle. Sometimes he listened only to her consonants, which erased all meaning from whatever she said, and sometimes he imagined her as a big old crow, squawking away and pecking at people.

"What I'm trying to tell you is that Brother Harley John Eacomb is a healer." She paused again and threw her grandson a look meant to ask if he got her drift. When he didn't respond, she continued with, "I'd say it stands to reason that Brother Eacomb is your destiny, young man. I absolutely would say that very thing."

Bonaventure's eyes widened the tiniest bit, but enough for her to notice.

"You heard me right. He's a healer. Brother Eacomb can heal people and bring them to redemption. Why, sometimes folks don't even know they're sick. There might even be some in your very own family." Lowering her voice, she added, "Even though I could name names, I won't. You just take it from me that there's folks whose sins have harmed the innocent; they are people who did things before you were born that they had no business doing. But like I said, you won't hear any names from me. My lips are sealed and yours should be too, so don't you go wagging your fingers or writing out notes about this conversation. This is confidential business between you and me."

She dabbed the corners of her mouth with her napkin, folded it neatly, and laid it next to her plate, upon which rested one uneaten bite of rhubarb pie. Adelaide Roman happened to know that well-bred people never ate every bite.

"No, sir, you won't hear their names from me," she repeated.

She kept up her incessant chatter all the way home, complaining, among other things, about how some women wore white shoes before Memorial Day and then turned around and wore them long after Labor Day, like they didn't have the sense God gave a flea. She complained about her job at the post office and about all the junk mail she had to handle, and about how most people didn't have the manners to know they should remember their postal workers at Christmas. She insisted that not a single letter would ever get delivered in Bayou Cymbaline if it wasn't for her diligence, considering how the only help she had on her shift was in the person of Eustace Hommerding or, as she called him, Useless Hommerding.

"I'm here to tell you that that man is the laziest human being in these United States. Why, just the other day he comes back from his mail route an entire twenty minutes later than he should have and he says to me"—and she screwed up her face and did her best to sound whiney—"'I'm sorry Adelaide, it's just my gout's been acting up and it's godawful painful. I got to go back and get some more of the cure from Miz Prefontaine.'" And then in her normal tone she said, "That would be your nigger woman he was talking about."

Bonaventure heard a whip crack and the snapping of sliced-open skin.

"And you know what I says back?" I says, 'You're sorry all right, Eustace. You are the sorriest excuse for a mailman I have ever seen.' Honest to Christmas, what does that good-for-nothing take me for? But I been thinking about things, and I think I just might contact the U.S. postmaster and see to it that Mr. Eustace Hommerding gets reprimanded. There is absolutely no reason I should have to work myself to death just because he never learned how to take care of his feet. I mean, can you just imagine someone with foot trouble sticking their neck out to be a mailman?"

She lowered her voice then and said, "You know what

kind of name Hommerding is, don'tcha? It's German. And just in case nobody's ever told you, the Germans were enemies of the U.S. of A. in two big wars, and I don't think there's any of them ever got over losing twice. So what I'm wondering is how Mr. Eustace Hommerding could be a good American with him being a German and all. I'm just sayin'."

Bonaventure Arrow lost himself in his silence.

EUGENIA Babbitt read aloud to The Wanderer, and on this day she'd begun *The Count of Monte Cristo*. The Wanderer listened intently, and the headaches came back full force.

Bonaventure heard the sound of swallowing that was going on in The Wanderer's crooked throat. The man was swallowing fear, just as he'd done in the war.

HEARING EXTRA

THE hammock swayed as Bonaventure explored his silence from inside out and above and below. He heard cosmic vibrations flowing under dirt and through air, and the vivacious life of the lands and the oceans. He listened to sinuous underwater plants and the portamento movements of sea cows gone graceful as they moved through undulating sub aqua waves. He heard a river laugh as it tumbled along in the English town of Ottery St. Mary. He heard emperor penguins move atop ice as they waddled their way to the Antarctic Sea. His listening intensified day by day until he could hear the adagio movement of a nucleus inside an electron aria that floated through the operatic galaxy inside a single atom. And then he began to hear extra.

The extra was nothing to do with fishes in rivers or penguins on ice or operas that played inside atoms. The extra part had to do with what brought about a sound and what it could possibly mean. In the case of the marmalade spoon, the whir of the bluebottle fly was more than a buzzing; it also spoke of the splendor of courage. That was the extra part.

Every day brought new sounds that refracted and found

him and roused his curiosity. He heard rooster feathers and catmint and sea glass, and the sound of a rabbit's foot that whispered of running. Bonaventure Arrow was bringing his hearing homeward.

Very soon he would hear the innermost secrets that were concealed in the house on Christopher Street.

DRAWING NEAR

BEING a big C. S. Lewis fan, Grand-mère Letice had given Bonaventure *The Chronicles of Narnia* to read. The story captivated him so much that he wanted to live it. There was no question that his mother's closet was the one most like the wardrobe in Professor Digory Kirke's house, the one that was the passageway to Narnia. But there was a problem: he was still afraid of that terrible sound that came from that box on the closet's top shelf. He remembered how much it had scared him and made him feel sick to his stomach. He brought it up the next time he talked with his dad.

"I promise that box won't hurt you," William said.

And so Bonaventure went back into the closet.

His mother's clothes made the sound of curtains brushing over the sill of an open window or dancing upon a very light breeze; one sweater in particular sang a comforting little song in its wispy cashmere voice. Dancy's shoes, if listened to all at once, were a symphony of every kind of percussion from tapping and chiming to cymbals and drums. Bonaventure figured the shoes took their sounds from where they had walked, which explained why her cemetery shoes were as quiet as a saw bug rolling over moss.

The low shelves held boxes that were full of hair curlers and rattail combs and half-empty cold cream jars. When he opened those boxes up even a crack, they sounded like a bunch of different radios playing all at once, each one trying to tell its stories the loudest. Bonaventure liked to get them all going to see if he could differentiate one from the other.

Though he avoided listening to that one certain box, he couldn't help but catch a look at it every now and then. It was black and unlike the others in its size and the fact that it was cloth-covered. Bonaventure had never seen a cloth-covered box before and figured it had to be special, though he had no clue why it was living on a shelf in his mother's closet. No sound at all came out of it that day, but the next time he went to play Narnia, that box said, "Bonaventure."

How did the box know his name? What did it want? What would happen if he opened it right now? Would whatever was in it fly out? But that wasn't what was supposed to happen. He was supposed to take something out of it. Bonaventure felt cold all over, as if he really had gone to Narnia and was standing in the snow.

"Bonaventure," the voice said one more time, "come closer."

Bonaventure stood rooted to the floor.

"I'll tell you a secret," said the voice from the box.

His father had promised that the box would not hurt him, so he looked up at it and put a question on his face: —Is it a good secret or a bad one?

"It's a wrong secret," the box replied.

And then Bonaventure heard the sound of a prison door slamming shut and the bolt sliding into place. It was the sound made by savage remorse as it locked up a human being, and it frightened him worse than before.

—BE QUIET! BE QUIET! BE QUIET! he shouted with the motion of his hands. His heart started to pound and he scrambled away.

"Wait!" the box cried. "Come back. Come back!"

But Bonaventure couldn't do it. He ran to his room, took his memento box from under the bed, opened it up, took its good sounds into his ears, and sent them rushing to his thundering heart. He pulled his knees up to his chin and rocked back and forth until his mementos sang him quiet.

Trinidad found him rocking like that when she came to his room to put laundry away. He started when she reached down to touch his shoulder.

"I knocked on your door, Mr. Bonaventure. Didn't you hear me?"

He hadn't heard her, which in and of itself was alarming.

"Are those goose bumps on you, child? It gotta be more than ninety-five degrees today. Why you be so cold?" And then the Knowing told her he'd got too close to an unnatural thing that dwelled within the house. Trinidad took Bonaventure to the kitchen and made him a cup of cocoa on that sweltering summer day. She could feel that the haunt was in the kitchen with them, so she addressed it silently, saying, "Now would be a good time for you to help this child with some of that love you think you got."

William went to Bonaventure's room that night.

Bonaventure couldn't get the words out fast enough: —The box said it holds a wrong secret!

"I know."

—I didn't hear what it was, though. I got scared because I heard this other sound, like getting locked up. But I'll go back. I promise. I want to help you, Dad. I really do.

"Just go when you're ready, son. You know I would never put you in danger."

Other sounds began to beckon after that; they were ones from Grand-mère's chapel. Bonaventure couldn't name the chapel's main sound with any certainty, but it was one he heard in other places all the time, a sort of humming, and it was always good. He'd once decided to take some of that sound with him, and so had removed a sliver of wood from the crucifix that was mounted to the wall. He put it in his memento box for the nights he couldn't sleep.

And then there was that other one, that small and sad kind of smothered-up noise. Bonaventure always heard it best over by the mosaic of the angel. Unlike the humming sound, this was a sound he never heard anyplace else. If he listened too closely, it made his skin hurt as if he'd been scraped and burned. Bonaventure did not take a souvenir of that sound to put in his memento box because it was too different to fit in. The memento box was a joyful place and not a place for a smothered thing.

The small noise called to him at bedtime that night, and right along with it came the sounds of those rooster feathers he'd heard before, and of saltwater on sea glass, and of the rabbit's foot, which he was certain were coming from Trinidad's house out on the Neff Switch road.

Bonaventure decided to stock up on comforting sounds, like someone gathering up little bits of well-being. Many of them were unique to his mother. Most were little keepsakes of things he heard when he went to her shop—hair from the floor because it reminded him of the neat, shearing sound of her scissors, or an empty vitamin bottle full of water that had sounded like a tiny river when it flowed from the tap of her shampoo sink. Bonaventure could hear extra when he listened to those sounds, and the extra part was Tender Care. Those sounds told of the things his mother did to make people feel beautiful.

Bonaventure concentrated on his comforting mementos and tried to forget about the black box's noise and the smothered little whimper in the chapel.

William decided to say nothing to Bonaventure about Dancy's closet. Instead, he asked his son to tell about the things in his memento box, which Bonaventure was only too happy to do.

"Do you have a favorite?" William asked.

—I like them all the same.

"I think I like the marmalade spoon best," William said.

THE AGE OF REASON

DURING that summer of 1957, Dancy's rages had all but disappeared, and she even softened toward Letice's religion. In a burst of well-being and newfound tolerance, she told Letice that it would be okay for her to teach Bonaventure about the Catholic stuff, so long as she didn't overdo it.

Conversely, Dancy told Bonaventure that if ever he was subjected to "that cockamamie, Tower-of-Babble garbage of Grandma Roman's" he was to let her know immediately. Her scorn for her mother's beliefs had not lessened; if anything, it had grown more severe. Dancy wanted no part of an itinerant preacher or a vengeful God to come anywhere near Bonaventure. Although, if her mother was a chosen one of any God, Dancy believed that it must be a vengeful one.

Letice wasted no time in seeing to Bonaventure's religious instruction. She began by bringing up the fact that he was seven years old and that the number seven is a very important number in the Bible.

Head tilted, eyebrows raised, Bonaventure signed, —Why?

"Because of the many times it has something to do with God."

Bonaventure switched to note writing. —Like what?

"Like that he created the earth in seven days, and the seventh day was special. It's the one we call a holy day, you know, Sunday, when I go to mass."

—My mom doesn't go to mass. She sleeps in on Sunday.

"Well, for now let's just say that's your mom's way of making Sunday special."

—Tell me more about sevens.

"Heaven is filled with angels, but there are seven of them who are especially close to God. They're the archangels, and their names are Michael, Gabriel, Raphael, Uriel, Sealtiel, Jegudiel, and Barachiel."

—Gabriel is Gabe's real name!

"That's right. And that's very special because the Archangel Gabriel was the messenger of God."

Bonaventure switched from note writing to sign, thereby honoring Gabe Riley, and asked, —Angels only in heaven?

"All angels live in heaven, but they come to earth sometimes and make good things happen. Each one of us has our own angel. Did you know that?"

Headshake side to side.

"We do, and they're called guardian angels because that's exactly what they do—they guard us all the time, even though we never see them. Guardian angels . . ."

Hand brought suddenly forward, palm side out as if to halt the conversation. Furious note writing. —I know my guardian angel.

Grand-mère was taken aback. "You do? Who is it?"

Very certain signing motions. —My dad.

Letice was speechless. She felt as though Bonaventure had offered her a way to believe that William was still alive, even if he wasn't flesh and blood, and she was very touched.

Tug on sleeve as if to say, —Did you understand me, Grand-mère?

"That's a very nice thought, my love," she said.

Smile on face, very pleased nod.

Then Letice talked about seven years of plenty and seven years of famine in Egypt, and of how Jesus made seven loaves and seven fish feed five thousand men. Interestingly, she did not mention that forgiveness is given seventy times seven times.

The echo of past sevens came into her head and she recalled words spoken to her all those years ago: *Do you see all them sevens? They all in the Good Book: seven plagues, seven sorrows, seven deadly sins. Seven times seven gwine come to you.*

Letice shook off the memory and steered the conversation back in the direction she wanted it to take. "Last February first you turned seven years old," she said. "And that's when a person attains the age of reason. Do you know what that means?"

Headshake no.

"Well, that's when boys and girls can think better than they could when they were six. I'll bet you've been coming up with questions and answers ever since your birthday," she said.

This conversation, like so many he had with Grand-mère, was taking place in the library, that wonderful, hushed room that held some of the very best sounds within its walls. Inspiration and thought came together in a lovely crescendo formed by harmonious words in the library. Bonaventure had the idea that all those silent books standing tightly together on Grand-mère's shelves formed a kind of shield.

He had figured out that thoughts exist in silence and have no color or sound or shape until they are turned into words. Spoken words exist in the mind first and then go to the voice and sit temporarily inside ears, and if words are conveyed through sign language, they exist in the motion of hands. He resolved that words remain invisible unless they are put into letters and set down on a page. Bonaventure wondered what the very first word was and what language it might have been in, and if the sound of it still echoed somewhere out in space. He often tried to listen for it, and when he was in the library, he felt as though he was close to the answer; his silence catching echoes of color and light. Some of the books made the sound of flowing water and others of pebbles under footsteps in a very dry place, which made him think of someone trying to find Bayou Cymbaline. One of the books held the secrets of feathers, telling him all about hollow quills and flight, while still others knew the ways of scattered seeds or widespread spores that travel aloft on the wind.

He wondered if the age of reason was maybe connected to all the sounds he heard, but decided that it wasn't. Grandmère had said the age of reason meant that you could think better, but Bonaventure was pretty sure he was thinking the same. Hearing better was another story. Ever since his birthday he'd been hearing new kinds of sounds: melodies of anticipation or vibrating strings of suspense. When they came to him many at once, some sounds formed into a spectrum of color and merged together behind his eyes until there was only whiteness in his head, and that whiteness would take him up out of his body. It was a very heady feeling.

At their next lesson Grand-mère said, "Did you know that you have more than a guardian angel to help you?"

Raised eyebrows, tilted head, as if to say, —I do?

"Yes. You have Saint Bonaventure; he's your patron saint."

Curious hands moving in sign. —What is that?

"A patron saint is someone very special who had your name before you did. All the saints live in heaven, but at one time or another they lived here on earth, and they were very, very good and they helped people who were sick or in trouble. They still do, just from heaven."

And then she spoke to him of Saint Bonaventure and her own favorite, Saint Francis of Assisi, and she showed him pictures in a book. Bonaventure always liked pictures because even though they had no mouths they managed to speak. When his eyes fell on a picture of Saint Francis holding a very small bird in his hand, Bonaventure could actually hear that bird sing—a sound that lifted right out of the past, off the page, and into his silence's hand.

While Saint Francis's bird sang to Bonaventure, Letice got caught up in a memory of another time and place, and of another little bird.

The year was 1916, the season was spring, and the time of day was mid-morning. Eleven-year-old Letice sat on a window seat, a book in her hands. She'd been transported with Alice through the looking glass to where the White Rabbit was in a hurry and the Walrus and the Carpenter walked beside the sea. She was just to the part in the story where the Queen of Hearts says, "Off with her head!" when a thumping wild wind drew her attention away. Letice left the window seat and headed for the kitchen's back door, but the wind pushed back as she tried to open it. She pushed harder three times more before she managed to get out.

That wind swirled all around her then, strange in its coldness, coming as it did from the south. It bounded westward, rolling through the bayou where it dried up the dampness and bullied old orchids. Lilac-tree fingers snapped out a protest while the elm tree next to them groaned. Letice stood at the edge of the drive, which was made of russet-red clay, hard-packed except where tracks had worn ridges and left watery ruts still squishy in their dips, full as they were of yesterday's rain.

Letice stood under a sky that was lustrous with the patina of mother-of-pearl and filled with gray-blue gauzy clouds that hid the sun and held that wind down. This was unusual in the bayou. The earth and Letice were caught in a between-time, no longer winter but not yet summer; no longer little but not yet grown.

Her gaze moved across the drive, over the fallow garden to the fence, sliding past the eighth post from the corner where she'd lately buried a cat who had used up all nine lives. She decided to go around front, maybe play a game of hopscotch on the bumpy sidewalk that led from the front door to the culvert.

The wind made clappering noises as it slurped and gulped at shingles and clotheslines and root cellar doors while Letice set out for the east side of the house. The lone, gnarly plum tree and its wild rhubarb stepchild occupied a corner of her eye, when all of a sudden the wind called her name.

She turned to see Tristan Duvais coming toward the house from a good way off. He was the son of their hired man and was the same age as she, though unlike Letice, Tristan was allowed to wander wherever he wished. Accompanying Tristan was his dog, Storm, a black and white English springer spaniel whose name was meant to confront a fear of thunder. The dog ran in circles around the boy, keeping slightly ahead and twisting his body in a leap every ten feet or so. Letice wondered if the dog's behavior had to do with that strange, cold wind.

"Letice, come here!" It was less a command than an urgent plea; a Duvais issuing a command to a Molyneaux was not even to be considered. She ran toward him and they met at the edge of the vegetable garden.

Tristan had rescued a bird—a sparrow—and needed her help. It was a life or death situation; there was no room for indecision. She held out her hands and accepted the tiny body. Tristan slapped his leg and whistled for Storm to follow him, while Letice stood alone in that unusual wind, a faltering life in her hands.

The bird seemed no more than a wisp, nearly weightless. She believed she could feel its bones and imagined them to be made from straw, all hollowed-out and light. Letice decided the bird was a girl sparrow, a young and delicate one. The tiny creature lay on its left side, breathing very fast. Letice could feel its heart beating in sync with her own.

With all the gentleness she could summon, she used her thumb to caress the top of the little bird's head, making the sign of the cross as she sought to comfort, to somehow anoint her. Letice wondered what had caused this bird's life to fold over on itself and put her in human hands, a place no wild bird would have chosen on its own.

And then she was torn from her reverie—English springers are excellent bird dogs. Instinctively, Letice held her hands high from Storm's leaping. His nails scratched the exposed skin of her arms where her sleeves had ridden up just past her elbows. She could hear his gravel-roughened footpads snagging her dress. She could feel his warm, moist breath and hear the low growl that originated in the back of his throat. She could smell his exertion, a musty, wet-dog smell.

"No, Storm, no!" The wind pushed the words to the back of her mouth.

The dog's eyes were fixed above Letice's head. The force of his forelegs nearly pushed her down. She tried to turn, to get away. Where was Tristan?

Storm kept barking and jumping higher. He'd caught her collar, his nails raking her ear as he fell back from a leap. Her hands were going numb, and she felt a stinging all over from that strange, cold wind. The dog kept on circling, jumping, and pushing against her from every side.

Finally, Tristan came and grabbed Storm's collar, managing to drag him away so Letice could lower her arms. The bird was as nothing in her hands then. There were no more rapid breaths, and the only detectable heartbeat belonged to Letice.

They buried the sparrow under the old elm tree, and the earth accepted the gift.

Letice's past was something she'd locked up a long time ago, and she still believed it was safely shut away. But she was only fooling herself. Her past was anything but shut away.

Gentle shake. —Grand-mère?

"Oh. What is it, sweetie? I was lost in thought. Where were we?"

—Patron saint.

"Oh, that's right. Did I tell you that Saint Bonaventure was very smart?"

Eyebrows raised, eyes opened wide. —Oh?

"Yes. In fact, he said there are two ways to be smart: You can be smart with your mind and you can be smart with your heart.

—What does that mean?

"It's part of reaching the age of reason. As you get older, you figure out a lot of things with your mind, and you get better and better at it. But one day you realize that some things can't be figured out at all, no matter how old you are or how much you use your mind, and then you just have to listen to your heart. That's what Saint Bonaventure did. That's what made him a mystic."

Slow nod. —I see.

This was good news, Bonaventure thought. Maybe his patron saint would help him be smart with his mind and smart with his heart.

Letice stayed behind after Bonaventure left the library. She was thinking about the sparrow, and about Remington and William, and about her long-ago secret loss. She wrapped a request in a petition she'd made so many times before:

> *Agnus Dei, agnus Dei*
> *Qui tollis peccata mundi,*
> *Dona eis requiem, dona eis requiem,*
> *Sempiternam, sempiternam requiem.*
>
> *Lamb of God, Lamb of God*
> *You who take away the sins of the world,*
> *Grant them rest, grant them rest,*
> *Rest everlasting, everlasting.*

William stood in the rear of the room, terrified of the word *everlasting*.

When Bonaventure said his prayers that night, he asked his patron saint what to do about that sound in the closet, the one that really scared him.

GOOD AFTERNOON,
MISS BABBITT

COLEMAN Tate sat in a straight-backed chair in front of the police officer's desk. After reviewing reports and newspaper articles written about William's murder back in 1949 and 1950, he had a couple of questions for Sergeant Turcotte.

"There was a report that the perpetrator had been seen at the public library. What did you find out about that?"

"Nothing much, Mr. Tate. Just that he was seen there several days running. He didn't do anything that bothered anybody."

"Did you talk to the librarian at all?"

"We did. In fact, we talked to several. All they could remember was that he would write out a note if he wanted to see a book."

Tate seized upon the statement with the speed of a snake: The perpetrator had made specific requests.

**PROGRESS REPORT
IN THE MATTER OF WILLIAM EVEREST ARROW
(DECEASED)**

**After speaking with Sergeant Turcotte, I turned
my attention to the library in which John Doe had
been seen in the days prior to the murder. When
I returned to the asylum for further inquiry, a
review of sign-in sheets from the past six years
yielded the information that one Eugenia Babbitt
has regularly visited John Doe; she is his only
caller. Seeking to confirm that the name signed
in was genuine, I found out that all visitors must
show identification. Subsequent investigation
revealed that Miss Babbitt is a librarian at the
main branch of the New Orleans Public Library
and also that she is the only individual in the state
of Louisiana with that name. Further findings to
follow.**

Bonaventure could hear the conversations that took place
between Grand-mère and Mr. Tate, who she said was getting
some business information for her. But Mr. Tate only ever said,
"Here it is, Mrs. Arrow. I believe there is reason to continue,"
and Grand-mère would thank him and tell him Good Day.

Odd sounds began to filter into Bonaventure's silence,
ones possessed of the sharps and flats of mysterious information. When Mr. Tate delivered this latest report, Bonaventure heard the sound of an index finger sliding down a
certain page in a certain book in search of a certain word.
He knew that sound well; it was one he himself made on
a fairly regular basis. And then he heard the thump of an
arrow hitting a bull's-eye.

As Coleman Tate walked through the house to leave, Bonaventure set both those sounds to the rhythm of the man's footsteps: step, slide, thump—step, slid, thump. Those sounds went out the door with Tate and worked their way from his feet to his mind and attached themselves to the decision he'd made to visit Eugenia Babbitt.

The next day, Coleman Tate stood in front of the library's card catalog. A lidless box containing slips of scratch paper sat atop it, and near the scratch paper stood a leather cup full of short sharpened pencils. The slips of paper were of a yellowish hue, thin and fibrous. He thought them to be a good match to the one among the perpetrator's possessions.

He moved to sit at a table in the reference section, perusing a book of maps and admiring the permanence of latitude and longitude and the concept of true north. Tate enjoyed the ambience of a library—all that knowledge just waiting to be found.

From the corner of his eye he watched Eugenia Babbitt and he waited. He'd already confirmed her identity. He knew when she took lunch. And now he knew about those slips of paper. Right before her break, he went over.

"Good afternoon, Miss Babbitt," he said. "My name is Coleman Tate; I'm a private investigator. Might I trouble you with a few questions?"

Eugenia Babbitt seemed to recoil, or at least hold her guard. "I hope they are questions pertaining to library usage, sir; as you can see, I am working right now."

"They are about a particular patron's library usage. I was hoping that perhaps you were about to take your lunch. I promise it won't take long."

"Very well. Meet me outside in five minutes."

Tate took her to be late-forties and the very picture of a librarian: sensible shoes, sweater worn around her shoulders with a cardigan chain to keep it from slipping, eyeglasses, hair in a bun.

"Thank you for agreeing to speak with me, Miss Babbitt. I'll get right to the point. I have been retained by Mrs. Letice Arrow to investigate the murder of her son, William, who was shot to death over at the A&P back in December of 1949. There is no question as to who did it; the man was captured on the spot. However, he is uncommunicative and his identity has never been ascertained. Mrs. Arrow has commissioned me to find that information. You see, she has never been able to find peace since the loss of her son. Are you familiar with the incident?"

Eugenia Babbitt nodded. "I remember it, though not in detail."

"That's all right. It's not exactly details I'm after; it's more like general information." At that point he reached into his suit pocket and removed the yellowish slip of paper that the perpetrator had in his pocket at the time of his arrest, the one that bore the notation F379.N5A182. "Can you tell me what this number might be, Miss Babbitt?"

It took less than two seconds for Eugenia Babbitt to blurt, "I would say that it's a call number for a book. Every book has its own specific number, one that's placed at the bottom of the spine for ease in locating it on the shelf." She did not mention that she recognized the slip of paper; it was one of those details she claimed not to remember.

"Why, yes, now that you say it, I can see that that is exactly what it is. Can you tell me whereabouts in the library a book with this particular call number would be located, Miss Babbitt?"

"That one would be in the closed stacks," she answered.

"And what sorts of books are found in the closed stacks?"

"Reference books, mainly," the librarian said, rubbing at

a twitch that had begun beneath one eye. "Is that all then, Mr. Tate?"

"If you'll just bear with me, Miss Babbitt. The official report states that witnesses came forward placing William Arrow's killer in this library for several days running before the crime. Police interviews show that librarians said the man would write down a note if he wanted to request a book." Tate then held up that yellowish slip of paper. "I believe this might be one of those notes, Miss Babbitt."

The librarian knew that Coleman Tate would smell a lie and decided that she'd best cooperate. "Now that you bring it up, I do remember something. Normally, the patron gives the call number to a staff member and that staff member retrieves the item. I happened to be the staff member in this case, but I did not follow procedure. You see, people were staring at him—as I'm sure you know, he suffers a deformity—and I felt he might be uncomfortable. He'd expressed an interest in back issues of the newspaper, and so I let him into the back stacks. I also let him into the closed stacks by himself. I thought perhaps he was doing research. I didn't ask what specific book he was looking for."

"I see. It was kind of you to consider his discomfort."

"Have I answered all your questions, Mr. Tate?"

"Just one more thing, if you don't mind, Miss Babbitt. William Arrow's killer has been incarcerated in the state asylum for the criminally insane since December of 1949. You visit him there regularly," Tate said. A slight blush came over the librarian's face. "You had to show identification. You are the only Eugenia Babbitt in Louisiana. Had you known him before the time of the murder?"

Eugenia Babbitt looked down and then back into Coleman Tate's face. She closed her eyes and took a deep breath and stepped into her own fiction. When she opened her eyes, she was no longer a dull and plain-faced librarian but had become one half of a doomed pair of lovers.

"No, Mr. Tate, I did not know him prior to those days before the shooting. But he seemed so very alone that I felt sorry for him. Hence the visits." She did not tell Tate that she had feelings for the killer because he was lonelier than she. Nor did she speak of the night she had taken the man into her home, where she cooked him a meal and placed a soft blanket over him when he fell asleep on her sofa. She did not mention that The Wanderer had gone before she awoke the next morning or that the blanket she'd put over him was neatly folded. She'd taken such thoughtfulness as a gesture of love.

"Thank you, Miss Babbitt. I know I speak for the Arrow family when I tell you how much your cooperation is appreciated."

Eugenia Babbitt walked away from the detective. She had entered a new chapter in her personal novel, one in which she was a woman who could not warn her tragic lover that a dangerous man was after him.

Coleman Tate went back into the library, where he asked the librarian at the circulation desk to please retrieve F379. N5A182, which turned out to be the New Orleans Social Register for 1949. What could the killer have wanted with that? The book contained public information, not family secrets. Was he trying to find someone? Prove that he was related to them? What?

And then the sounds of a sliding finger and thumping arrow found their way into Coleman Tate's mind. On a hunch, he turned to a certain page and slid his finger down it. The detective stared at the entry for Arrow, but found no immediate clue. The listing that came before it was that of a family named Arndt, noteworthy as brewers who'd made a fortune in beer. The one that came after was Artemus, the founding family of Artemus, Tennessee. Tate was absorbing the Register, getting a feel for it and hoping it would share something more.

And then he saw the mark. He had not seen it at first; it was fine and faint, perhaps the breadth of a human hair. Under William's name was a very slight pencil line. Anyone at any time could have put it there, Tate thought; William himself might have done it. Or maybe Dancy Arrow had gone looking for proof of his pedigree before she made the commitment. Such a thing was not unheard of.

The detective read the complete entry and saw that it gave Letice's name as Letice Arrow (née Molyneaux). He consulted the page for Molyneaux and saw that it too had been underlined. This was no coincidence. William Arrow had been a target. Perhaps if the killer had not been apprehended, he would have gone after Letice as well. It did not pay to be newsworthy, thought Detective Coleman Tate.

In fact, The Wanderer had done just as Tate supposed: He'd read all about the Molyneaux and Arrow families, their births and deaths and club affiliations. He'd read about marriages, fêtes, and charity events. He'd traced William Arrow to Tulane, and law school, and his eventual employment at the law firm of Robillard & Broome. And then The Wanderer had firmed up his plans.

PROGRESS REPORT
IN THE MATTER OF WILLIAM EVEREST ARROW
(DECEASED)

PREVIOUS FINDING:
Miss Eugenia Babbitt, a librarian at the main
branch of the New Orleans Public Library, has at
various times over the years visited the subject of
this investigation.

FOLLOW-UP:
An interview of Miss Babbitt revealed that
said subject spent time in the back stacks where
he read stored copies of local newspapers. He
also requested an item that was stored in the
closed stacks. Under normal procedure, a request
is made and the material brought out, but in
this case that procedure was not followed. Miss
Babbitt stated that she believed he was conducting
research, and since the closed stacks contain
reference books and journals, she let him in that
locked room and left him there alone. She felt it
the courteous thing to do, since it appeared that
other patrons were staring at him.
The perpetrator had in his possession at
the time of the crime a slip of paper bearing
the notation: F379.N5A182. I have confirmed
that this is the call number assigned to the 1949
New Orleans Social Register, which is held in
the aforementioned closed stacks visited by the
perpetrator. There is a faint pencil line under the
name Arrow and one under Molyneaux as well.
Further findings to follow.

Letice looked at one particular sentence of Tate's report over and over and over: *There is a faint pencil line under the name Arrow and one under Molyneaux as well.*

Bonaventure heard the determination behind The Wanderer's library deed. It sounded like a thousand marching boots.

THE SCARY STORY CHAMPION
OF SOUTHERN LOUISIANA

DANCY had recently been thinking about Bayou Decep-tion Island. Part of her wondered if maybe the loup-garou really did exist as a claw-and-fang belief that would kill you if you talked about it. She went to the library and checked out a book about spells and charms. She read about gris-gris meant to give protection and gris-gris that brought harm and bad luck. She fantasized about seeking out Wil-liam's killer, tearing off a piece of his shirt, and making it into a gris-gris bag. And into that bag she would put a snake's rattler to cause him terror, and a poisonous leaf to make him scratch his skin raw, and salt to put in his wounds, and muddy water to fill up his lungs and make him suffocate, and mag-gots to eat into his brain. She wanted to fashion some very powerful wanga that would bring unbearable pain on the man, as he had done to her. She would call it a justice wanga.

Bonaventure found Dancy lost in one such gris-gris rev-erie and signed, —You angry?

"No, sugar. I'm not angry. I was just thinking."

—You look angry. What you thinking?

She didn't want to tell him the truth, so she said she was thinking about those summers she spent on Bayou Decep-tion Island.

—Can we go there?

"Someday we just might," she said.

During Adelaide's next every-other-Saturday hair appointment, Dancy brought up Bayou Deception Island, and Grandma and Grandpa Cormier and Mama Isabeau.

"I think I'm gonna take Bonaventure back there sometime so he can see where you come from. I wish he could have known Grandma and Grandpa. He would've loved them to bits. I did," Dancy said, knowing this would irritate the bejesus out of her mother.

Adelaide Roman couldn't believe her ears. "Now why would you go and do a thing like that? As God is my witness, I have no idea what gets into you sometimes, Dancy. It's bad enough you don't praise the Lord and seek salvation, but why you want to fill Bonaventure's head with all that pagan stuff is beyond my understanding, just as sure as it is beyond the understanding of every God-fearing man, woman, and child on the face of this earth. I haven't thought about those people in years, and I'm not gonna start up now."

"Who are you calling 'those people'? They were your family, Mama."

"They were heathens. And if you ask me, that mother-in-law of yours isn't far off from one, with her statues and candles, her foreign incantations, and those damn rosary beads she's got stashed all over the house."

"You don't need to curse, Mama. It's low class." Dancy couldn't resist the dig.

"You're right. She'll curse herself. She don't need any help from me."

Adelaide Roman held that the righteous would be saved by memorizing the Bible, chapter and verse, and being able to spout it at will. Letice Arrow's Catholicism, with its statues and holy water, was just as bad as the omens and caution-ary tales of voodoo as far as Adelaide was concerned.

"Hey, Adventure Arrow, did I ever tell you about the loup-garou?" This was Dancy making conversation on a Friday night after dinner when they were too full even to move.

Headshake side to side. —Nope.

"Well, there's this creature, see, and he looks like a wolf and he's got red eyes and he skulks around in the woods . . ."

Written note: —Like Little Red Riding Hood?

"Oh, the loup-garou is much more serious than that. The loup-garou would eat the big bad wolf for breakfast and use his bones for toothpicks."

And so began a sort of contest in which Dancy and Bonaventure tried to out-do each other with the telling of gruesome tales. Every Friday night, they would make a tent out of bedsheets, use the stub of a candle for a flickering light, and then they were ready to go.

When Dancy had dug up her entire repertoire of scary bayou stories, she said her brain had gone and shriveled up like a raisin, and she was throwing in the towel. She then declared the competition over and Bonaventure to be the Scary Story Champion of Southern Louisiana.

—Now what we do Friday nights? he signed.

"Well, let's see. I suppose we could talk about gris-gris and work out what we would use to make some."

—What is that?

"It's a kind of lucky charm. You put it on somebody or put it in their house. Some gris-gris looks like a doll, but the kind I'm thinking about would be in a little bag people could wear on a string around their necks or carry in their pockets. You can make the bags out of anything, but the best thing is to make it out of something that belongs to the person you're making the gris-gris for."

Quick sign: —What is in bag?

"Stuff you gather up, usually small things. My Grandma Cormier said people used to put in things like herbs or stones or maybe even bits of hair or bones."

Open-mouthed look of total surprise. —Bones?

"You heard me. But that was in the olden days. You don't really have to use stuff like that. You can use ordinary things. Like if you wanted someone to never be hungry, you might put in a peanut or something that's connected to food. Or if you wanted a person to be happy and laugh a lot, you would put in a tickling feather. Get it?"

Nod.

"Well, all right, then, that's what we'll do instead of tell scary stories. We're not really going to make gris-gris, though; we're just going to think it up."

One solid handclap and two thumbs up.

When Friday night came around again, Dancy suggested they should first think up gris-gris for each other. She said she would make a pouch out of one of Bonaventure's baby booties and fill it with the feather of a hummingbird so he could hover wherever he wanted to, a bee's wings so he would always find something sweet, a lead pencil that would never wear down, a scrap of paper so he would be able to talk if he had a broken arm and couldn't sign, and a real strong magnet so if he ever got lost he would be pulled back home to Bayou Cymbaline.

Bonaventure said he would make Dancy's gris-gris out of the pocket of one of the smocks she wore in her shop. He would soak it in shampoo first and then put the tooth of a comb in it and three different sizes of curlers so hair would do itself and she wouldn't have to work too hard. And he would put in the Indian Head nickel Mr. Silvey had given him so she would always have money, the knob off the radio so she could hear Hank Williams sing, and the wishbone and heart from the Thanksgiving turkey so she would always have good luck and lots of love.

They both wrinkled up their noses at the mention of the turkey heart, but they had to admit that gris-gris was like that.

William waited until Dancy left the room and Bonaventure was working on a new airplane model.

"Hey, buddy. Whatcha doing?"

Bonaventure smiled and said, —Hey, Dad. I'm going to paint this airplane.

"What color?" William asked.

—Gray, with red and white stripes on the tail and a big white star inside a black circle on the wings and the sides. The star will have a red circle in its middle. It's an F4F Wildcat.

"Wow."

—What are you doing?

"Oh, nothing much; I was just wondering about those gris-gris bags you and your mom talk about."

—Gris-gris bags are fun.

"I'll bet they are. I wouldn't mind having one myself."

—Really?

"Yeah, really. Hey, you better not let your paint dry up."

—Oops.

"Okay, then, I'll let you get back to it."

—Dad?

"What, son?"

—I'm glad you came by.

"Me too. Sleep tight, pal. Don't let the bedbugs bite."

—Will you come again tomorrow?

"I'll sure try."

Bonaventure slumped his shoulders and bowed his head. "Okay. I'll be here for sure and we'll talk some more."

—Want to talk some more right now?

"Nice try, Bonaventure, but I know it's time for bed."

Over the next weeks, Dancy and Bonaventure came up with gris-gris for Grand-mère, Trinidad, and Mr. Silvey; for Dancy's customers at the beauty parlor; and for Gabe Riley and Miss Wells and Mrs. Humphrey. They collaborated on one big one for all the kids in Bonaventure's class and on another big one for the regulars at Bixie's Luncheonette. They'd had to be especially careful with Grand-mère Letice's because she could be a little funny about things like gris-gris.

One conspicuously absent from the gris-gris endeavors was Grandma Adelaide Roman.

"Oh, let's not worry about it, Adventure Arrow. She would just say it was devil stuff anyway."

A you've-got-a-point-there nod.

"Who else should we make one for?" Dancy asked.

—My dad.

"He doesn't need one," Dancy said.

—He wants one.

"You shouldn't make up stuff like that, mister. Let's talk about something else."

William was in the room for this conversation. He watched while Dancy and Bonaventure shined a flashlight on the wall and used their hands to make shadow-bunnies that danced around until they got in a shadow-fight and got their ears all tangled up. Then he listened to them summarize the day and tuck in all its edges.

Dancy plumped up Bonaventure's pillow and said, "It's

not like I don't know you've got a book and a flashlight under the covers. Just don't read for too long. You need your beauty sleep."

—*Mom!* Bonaventure said in sign shout, —*Boys don't beauty-sleep!*

Dancy chuckled and smoothed his hair from his forehead. "You're right," she said as she moved toward the door. "You're beautiful enough already. I love you, Sweetie-pie. Good night."

—Good night. I love you and you are beautiful too.

William waited a minute or so after she left before he said, "Hey, there, buddy."

—Hey, Dad.

"So how's the gris-gris business treating you?"

—Mom doesn't think you need one.

"Maybe she'll change her mind."

—Yeah. Maybe.

"Well, don't worry about it," William said, and then he did something he hadn't done since Bonaventure was in the newborn nursery: he sang a song to him, making it up as he went. As Bonaventure listened to that song, he heard a shower of comets go sweeping across the galaxy and raise a sparkling, whooshing, dazzling wind that blew stardust around in a swirl.

Dancy took a long soak in the tub and then polished the nails of her fingers and toes. She fussed with her hair and flipped through a magazine before going to the kitchen for a glass of warm milk.

Then she began to collect.

She opened a bottle of root beer, poured it down the sink, and kept the cap. She took a sugar cube. She tore the recipe for chicken etouffée from a cookbook. She went out to Mr. Silvey's old workshop, where she found a compass and a piece of steel and she took those too. Then she went into William's old room, where Letice had insisted that everything be left as it was when William lived. Dancy took a sock out of a drawer and took it back to her room, where she sprayed it with the same perfume she'd worn so long ago. She put one of her own earrings in with all that she'd gathered and slipped everything into the sock.

The recipe was to keep away hunger, and the bottle cap was to keep away thirst; the sugar was for William's sweet tooth, the steel was to protect him from bullets, and the compass was to bring him home. The earring and the perfume weren't part of the gris-gris; they were just to remind him of her.

William spent the rest of that night in Dancy's room, watching her toss and turn, for sleep did not bring her rest. He was still there the next morning when Trinidad came in to change the sheets. She went about her business just as calm as could be.

"You should get some rest, Mr. William," she said.

THE HANDSHAKE

EVEN though Bonaventure thought Trinidad was wonderful, he still missed the Silveys sometimes. He missed keeping company with Mrs. Silvey in the kitchen, and how she always smelled like talcum powder, and how if he happened to break one of Grand-mère's knickknacks accidentally when he was running through the house or maybe got some dirt on something that he wasn't supposed to touch, he could go to her and she would say, "Well, now, let's just see what we can do about that."

And he missed Mr. Silvey something terrible. He went out to the workshop almost every day in search of the sounds left behind in the coffee cans and sewing machine drawers and the jars full of nuts and bolts and screws. Though he and Mr. Silvey had often worked side by side without saying anything, the workshop had never been quiet. The tools, every last one of them, spoke in pings and taps and catch-toothed ratchets about stair treads or railings or holes they had fixed. But now there were only breathing sounds for him to hear because no one ever used the tools or the hardware anymore, and so they just slept all the time. Bonaventure could hear them snore.

Sometimes he went to the workshop just to feel close to

Mr. Silvey again. It was during one of these visits that he heard some whistling coming from the wagon by the window. He walked over to it and wrapped his fingers around the handle and was overjoyed that it felt warm once again.

"Hiya, pal."

—Hiya, Dad!

"Hey, I wonder if you could do me a favor. It's not as hard as going after that sound in your mom's closet."

—Sure.

"I'd like to meet that fellow who teaches you to sign, the one who comes during the week. What's his name? Mr. Riley?"

—Yeah.

"I think he's about my same age, and I was wondering if maybe I might know him from somewhere."

—Gabe isn't from here. He's from New Orleans.

"Well, there you go. I lived in New Orleans for a while."

—I thought I wasn't supposed to tell anybody about you. How can I help you meet Gabe if I can't tell him about you?

"You don't have to tell him anything. All he has to do is touch the wagon handle here and it'll be like a handshake, just like you and I do. You can tell a lot about a man by his handshake. I think he might be a pretty good guy, but I'd like to know for sure. Do you think you can arrange it for me? I sure would appreciate it, son."

Bonaventure jumped at the chance to be helpful by doing something that wasn't scary. —I'll help you shake Gabe's hand, Dad! You can count on me!

"Thanks, buddy. We'll talk again soon. I promise." And then William was gone.

Most of the paint had disappeared from the wagon, worn away by humidity and the passage of time, but Bonaventure spotted one small scab that had survived, which he peeled away and put in his pocket before going back into the house. The smile still beamed across his face, as his father's words echoed and echoed in his head, *I think he might be a pretty good guy.* He wanted his father to like Gabe Riley.

He took an envelope from Grand-mère's desk in her office and put the paint chip from the wagon in it; then he went to his room and carefully placed it in his memento box.

The following day, after finishing the part of his lesson that included Dancy and Letice, Bonaventure had a sign conversation with Gabe.

—You know square-cut nail?

"I don't think so."

—You know tool cuts hole in pipes?

"No. Do you?"

Spelling out letters of —Hawk's bill snips.

"You are smart about tools."

—I will show you.

"Okay."

A waving motion as if to say, —Come this way.

Boneventure led Gabe out to Mr. Silvey's workshop, where he showed him the square-cut nails and the hawk's bill snips.

Holding up the wagon handle, —You know what is?

"It's a wagon handle."

—Come from plow blade.

Bonaventure placed the wagon handle in Gabe Riley's hand.

"This was made from a plow blade?"

—Yes. I love.

Gabe stood motionless, as if maybe he was under a spell, and then he signed, "Heavy. Warm. Nice."

. . . . .

Sometimes Gabe was mystified by Bonaventure, as teachers often are by gifted children. It was obvious that the boy had a high IQ, and it was getting more and more difficult to present him with something challenging enough to keep him from getting bored. Gabe did some thinking on the matter. One idea led to another, and eventually he saw no reason that Bonaventure Arrow could not be multilingual. And so it came to pass that a flashlight, a set of bongos, and the naval flag semaphore system found their way into the tutoring that took place on Mondays, Wednesdays, and Fridays. It wasn't that Bonaventure really needed to know Morse code or how to communicate with flags—it was just for fun.

Bonaventure was crazy about the idea. It was something he could talk about when other kids talked about stuff they did with their dads. His happiness was not lost on Dancy. She wanted to do something special by way of thanking Gabe for going above and beyond, so she invited him to come to supper on a Saturday night.

He showed up early, flowers in one hand and a comic book in the other. It was just the three of them having pork roast and dirty rice at the table in the kitchen. They would have eaten in the dining room if Letice had been there, but she was at a meeting of the Altar Society over at Our Lady of the Rosary. That was one thing about Letice: she was a dining room person. It was just how she'd been raised. Adelaide Roman, on the other hand, had never even seen a dining room until she was almost twenty-five years old and taking a tour of historic homes that were decorated for Christmas, after which Theo Roman didn't get a moment's peace until he'd added on to the back of their house.

There were only a few awkward moments in an evening that was more than a tutoring session but definitely not a date. They signed and talked and laughed, and Bonaventure joined in at first, but then he seemed to draw back some, and when the table was cleared, he asked to be excused. He said he wanted to read the *Captain America* that Gabe had brought him.

Dancy let Bonaventure go, which left her and Gabe to linger over coffee for a while before doing the dishes together, just like a regular couple. He washed and she dried, since he didn't know where to put things away. Their hands never touched at all.

Bonaventure could hear his mom and Gabe talking, and he wished that Gabe could be there every night. He started to feel bad about that wish and sent a thought out to his father, but William didn't answer.

William was out in the kitchen. Dancy had laughed quite a few times during the evening, but he thought it sounded different, at least from the way it had sounded back when it was for him. And he wouldn't have thought Gabe was her type; he didn't seem to be as athletic as William had been, but more bookish.

The next day William started to pull Dancy to Père Anastase, but then he changed his mind.

A PROMISE MADE OF CHAINS

Aweek after Gabe had come to dinner, Bonaventure brought something up with his dad.

—Did you like Gabe that time you shook his hand?

"Yes, I did. He has the grip of an honest man. You like him too, don't you?"

—I like him a whole bunch. He knows a lot of jokes and he makes me laugh.

There was emptiness in the conversation then, just for five seconds or so, before Bonaventure, looking away, hands in pockets, said, —He makes Mom laugh too.

The emptiness sagged between them again until William said, "Laughing is good," but then the emptiness came back.

—Yeah. Gabe knows a lot of stories too. And he lets me practice reading and signing with comic books. Did you read comic books when you were a kid?

"Not much. I mostly liked baseball. My dad used to read baseball stuff to me. He helped me keep a real good scrapbook too. But he died when I was eight."

—You were lucky.

"How was I lucky?"

—He didn't die until you were eight.

There was a pause before William said, "I've always wanted to talk to you about that, but I didn't know what to say. I'm sorry I never got a chance to meet you, Bonaventure." He had to stop then. It took two more attempts before he could clear his throat and get the words out. "I always wanted to have a son to hug and play with, to teach things to. I guess that's why it felt so good to teach you about your special hearing. I'm so glad we have this way of talking together. I wouldn't trade it for anything."

—I like having a voice with you.

When his dad had gone, Bonaventure thought that William had sounded sad, and he decided to try again to help with that favor they hadn't talked about in a while.

The very next day, he set about his task. It was going to be harder than he thought. He was still afraid, but William had promised that it wouldn't hurt him, and Bonaventure trusted his father.

Bonaventure headed for his mother's closet, taking the sassafras jar with him because it had helped him through scary times before, like hearing the echo of police coming to the door. He sat down on the closet floor and carefully opened the spice jar to let the dry voice out.

"I've already told you all that I know," the sassafras said. "I was there the night your mother waited for your father to come home, a long time ago, before you were born. I heard the police come to the door. I don't know anything more than that. But the box does. Open the box if you want to know more."

Bonaventure looked up expecting something to happen. But no sound came from the box. He set the jar down and pulled out the small ladder used to help reach that top shelf. He unfolded it and set first his right foot then his left on the lowest step. Still no sound. He set his right foot on the second step and followed it with his left. Still no sound. He moved up to the third step and finally to the top of the ladder. Still no sound.

It should have been warmer up near the ceiling, especially on a hot July day, but it wasn't. Bonaventure put a hand on either side of the cloth-covered box and was surprised at how cool it felt. Although there was no sound, several scents had swirled themselves into a smell-print and embossed the box with their combined characteristics. Unfortunately for Bonaventure, the extraordinary silence that let him hear extra did nothing at all for his sense of smell. He could identify only one of the odors: it was cologne like a man would wear. He did not recognize the cold, metallic scent of dried blood; he knew nothing of the smoke left behind by a bullet.

The box remained quiet, holding its breath because it was desperate to keep the boy there and not frighten him again.

Bonaventure stuck his fingers under the lip of the lid in order to pull the box toward him. He was surprised he had to tug so hard; the box was heavier than he'd expected. He managed to inch it forward and scoot it over the shelf's edge enough to place a hand against either side and pull it toward him. He was breathing hard from the struggle and had to rest a minute. That's when he got the idea to rest the box on top of his head before slowly making his way down the ladder.

He knelt down to set it on the closet floor and sat back on his heels beside it. Bonaventure noticed the lid was hinged on one side and held closed by a pin-and-hasp lock. He used his thumb to move the pin, but stopped at the edge of discovery. He took in a breath and held it, and he felt a little like he had to go to the bathroom, which is what happened whenever he got nervous.

The voice of doubt snuck into his silence then, warning him that the box belonged to his mother, that it was hers to open or to keep locked up. And then Bonaventure heard something besides that doubt—the crunching ruffle of tissue paper. He let out his breath and lifted back the lid. The wrinkly tissue crackled and creaked, and said to him, "Keep going."

Bonaventure pulled back the tissue to find a man's neck-tie lying crosswise over a neatly folded white shirt. Beneath the tie and shirt were the suit and the belt they'd been worn with. And beneath the suit and the belt were a pair of under-wear, a pair of men's socks, and a pair of black shoes. They were the clothes William had on when he died.

Bonaventure removed the garments one by one. The tie was silk and seemed to be solid blue until he looked closer and found a pattern of tiny diamonds. The white cotton shirt was expensive, but something had put holes in it and left a rusty stain. He couldn't identify the mark, and the shirt offered no explanation. The coat and pants were of dark gray wool, and the coat had holes and rust stains too. The belt was black and made of very soft leather and was fitted with an engraved silver buckle. The shoes were made of leather too, and shiny as a brand-new penny.

He laid the shirt out on the floor and undid every button before picking it up to slip his arms through the sleeves. It took a long time to re-button because he had to keep slid-ing the sleeves back up his arm. He managed to loop the tie around his neck and tie it in the same kind of bow he tied his shoelaces in; it was the only way he knew to tie anything. He pulled off his own shoes and stepped his small feet into the black leather ones that shone like a brand-new penny.

Bonaventure examined himself in the mirror that hung on the closet door and was amazed at how different he looked. Though the sleeves kept sliding down, and he'd gotten off track with the buttons so the shirt hung sort of crooked, and the tie didn't look like it should, Bonaventure still thought he looked very fine. The last thing he put on was the soft leather belt, which wrapped around him twice. It was then that the clothes spoke to Bonaventure, telling him they belonged to William.

Bonaventure reluctantly took each article off, folded it as best he could, and returned it to the box. It was then that a good and tender silence took over, extinguishing every sound except one. From inside the pocket of the torn and rust-marked shirt came the whisper of a promise made of chains.

After what sounded like a clearing of the throat, the cloth-covered box found its voice. "Look in the pocket," it said. "Your mother thinks it was all her fault."

Bonaventure reached into the shirt pocket and pulled out a piece of paper. It was a little note that wept, and it was written in his mother's hand:

> *Sweet William,*
> *If you'll stop at the A&P on your way home and get*
> *some butternut squash, I will love you forever and ever*
> *and ever.*
> *XoXo*
> *Dancy*
>
> *P.S. I would love you forever even without the squash.*

And that is when Bonaventure heard the bullets, loud and fast, coming from those rusty holes in the clothing. There were four of them. He counted.

Bonaventure returned the box to its place on the shelf. But he had not put the note back in, for he knew it was the thing he was supposed to take away. He also knew that he couldn't put it in the memento box that lived under his bed, full as that box was of happiness. To put it there might make the note even sadder, which didn't seem fair at all. And anyway, he was supposed to take it out of the house.

He talked to William about the dilemma that night.

—Is this what Mom is keeping that she shouldn't keep anymore?

"Yes, Bonaventure, it surely is."

—It makes a real sad sound. Can you hear it?

"No, but I know you can."

—Does Mom hear it?

"She hears it all the time."

—Those are your clothes in the box, aren't they?

"Yes."

—You and Mom say you died in an accident, but I think somebody shot you with a gun. I heard gun sounds like in the movies.

"That's right. Somebody did. I used to think he did it on purpose, but then I realized he couldn't help it."

—Why couldn't he help it?

"Because his mind got hurt and it never got better."

—His mind must have been hurt pretty bad."

"It was. Broken just like his heart."

—The box told me something.

"What did it say?"

—It said Mom thinks it was all her fault.

"Your mom blames herself because she asked me to stop at the A&P that day, and that's where I got shot. But it wasn't her fault at all. We need to take the note away so it can't blame her anymore."

The second challenge was met.

—What should we do with it?

"I don't know, but you will. Wait and see."

—I've been wondering about something, Dad.

"What's that?"

—Will you be leaving for Real Heaven now because our job is done?

"Not yet, but soon."

—How soon?

"I don't know."

—Will you still be able to talk to me from there?

"I don't know that either."

Bonaventure lowered his head and said, —I've been wondering about something else.

"Oh?"

—After you go to Real Heaven, will I get a voice?

The question took William by surprise. "Do you want one?"

Nothing at first and then, —Maybe. It might be nice to be like everybody else.

"No, Bonaventure, always be you. And anyway, maybe you're supposed to be the only super-hearing guy in the world. Like there's only one Captain America."

Bonaventure's head lowered once again, and he gave a pretty big shrug, —I don't know about that.

"Well, it sure would explain why none of the other kids at school can hear like you can."

Even that didn't cheer Bonaventure up. Ever since kindergarten, when he'd heard the color orange and been accused of cheating, Bonaventure had held himself apart, not wanting to get hurt again because of his super hearing.

Later that evening, after he'd said good night to everyone, Bonaventure reached under his pillow and pulled out his mother's note. He knelt down, closed his eyes tight, pressed the paper between his hands and said every prayer he'd ever learned. He kept his eyes shut for a few minutes even after the prayers were done, and listened for his father.

He called to him, —Dad?

But William wasn't there. He'd gone back to the shore in Almost Heaven to think about what was left to do. He'd forgiven his killer and removed the reminder of Dancy's misplaced guilt, but he hadn't met the third challenge yet: he had to let go of Dancy, and there was no help for that one. And then something opened up inside William, some small perforation on the dark side of his soul that let in a cosmic light. He admitted then what he'd known for a while, that he'd held them both captive far too long, and it was time for him to go.

Bonaventure listened for maybe ten minutes more, which is a very long time to a seven-year-old boy, and then he figured that maybe his father was tired. He opened his hands and told the note he was sorry, but he would take it out back to Mr. Silvey's shop until he could think of what to do. His last thought of the day was that maybe a gris-gris idea would come along and mix in with all the prayers.

THE Wanderer recalled the white light of welding and the sound of flying sparks. He could feel the wetness of his own sweat and the soreness that entered his muscles at the end of a day that had been filled with grueling work. He could summon the taste of an ice-cold beer, and how it felt to drink when he still had a jaw. But The Wanderer didn't know when any of those things had happened.

Bonaventure heard the echoes of that white light and those sparks and the cries of those worn-out muscles. The biting sound of hatred accompanied those sounds, as if the welder was taking things out on the steel. Bonaventure conveyed those clues to Coleman Tate the next time the investigator came around, just as his father had told him to do.

VOODOO AND HOODOO
AND THE SWEET BY-AND-BY

BONAVENTURE had grown to love Trinidad like a second mother. She smiled and sang more than most people do, and everything she baked tasted better even than the stuff from TouTou's Patisserie. Trinidad had a smell like soap, sunshine, and sweet, moist earth. Bonaventure liked to breathe her scent until it filled up his lungs and went to his ears and mixed in with the sounds of his silence.

He wanted to ask her something and he wanted to be very specific, so he used the note system for the conversation.

—Did you ever put the gris-gris on somebody?

Trinidad turned from the kitchen island where she was frosting a cake and acted like she hadn't read his note. Bonaventure waited for a minute, and when it looked like she had gotten busy with washing the cake pan, he went over to the sink and tugged on her arm and held the notepaper closer to her face.

She sighed. "Well, now, there's gris-gris and then there's gris-gris. If you mean the voodoo sort that brings all kind of bad down on people, then no, I haven't done that. But if you mean the hoodoo kind, well, then, maybe I have."

—What's the difference?

"One's spelt with a *V* and one's spelt with a *H*."

Hands on hips, exasperated look.

"Oh, go on with that face. You know Trinidad only joking with you," she said. "Voodoo be a religion. It got its own spirits. Voodoo folks make gris-gris out of all kinds of things. Voodoo folks have a lot of superstitions and charms and such. And some believes things like if you lay a broom across your doorway at night a witch can't come in; or if you sweep trash out the house after dark, you'll sweep away your luck; or that you can bring harm down on people by burning some of their hair.

"Hoodoo, now, at least the hoodoo I know, be different than that. Some hoodoo be about conjure, you know, calling up magic. My kind of hoodoo comes from root work. It bring about God's healing. That's the hoodoo I know. Now, here be a example of the difference between hoodoo and voodoo: There be a voodoo cure-all recipe that say to mix jimson weed with sulfur and honey in a jar, but then that recipe say that you gots to rub that jar against a black cat before you sip the mix down real slow.

"Well, now, I might use what God put in the soil of this earth to make a cure, but I don't ever tell nobody they gots to rub it on a black cat. I just go ahead and make a medicine out of growing things that I know will help a body make it through they troubles. I don't hold with no fetishes like voodoo folk do. If I keep a thing and look at it when I pray, it because it remind me of the God of Abraham and Moses who deliver the Hebrews away from the Pharaoh and take them to the Promised Land. Now, lets us talk about something else."

—Where's your family?

"They all be gone."

—Where did they go?

"They gone on before me to the Sweet By-and-By.

—Is that in Louisiana?

"What you mean, 'Is that in Louisiana?' Mercy sakes, chile, who been teaching you geography? The Sweet By-and-By be in heaven!"

Bonaventure made a mental note to ask his dad about the Sweet By-and-By.

—Did you ever see anybody do voodoo?

"Are we back on that old stuff? Yes, I did. But she gone now."

—Did she go to the Sweet By-and-By?

"That depends."

—On what?

"On whether she be sorry or even understand the bad she done."

Trinidad busied herself at the sink and stove then. She didn't like to dwell on certain memories.

Bonaventure had this feeling that Trinidad knew things other people didn't. Not stuff like if somebody happened to eat a cookie before supper or if somebody maybe forgot to wipe his shoes on the mat and maybe tracked some dirt in the house. It was more like he thought she could tell when folks were feeling bad, like when they were sick or sad or worried.

The next time he met with Grand-mère Letice for what she'd begun to call his catechism lessons, the story of the Ten Commandments was the topic of the day. After their lesson, Bonaventure signed, —Trinidad knows Ten Commandments.

"Oh? What makes you say that?"

—She knows about God.

"That's good."

Nod, nod.

"What does Trinidad say about God?"

—She keeps things for him.

"I see."

—And Trinidad can make hoodoo medicine. Not voodoo.

Even though Grand-mère was superb at understanding sign by this time, Bonaventure used the notepad to write out the stuff about hoodoo and voodoo, just to make sure she knew what he said.

Letice tried not to give her thoughts away. She didn't speak; she didn't blink; she didn't breathe. She looked at her watch and said, "Well, I think that's all we have time for right now, Bonaventure," and kissed him and sent him out to play. She couldn't stop shaking for the rest of the day.

Letice had a dream that night in which William was alive, locked inside his tomb. He flailed and gasped for air, spending his breath in anguished screams. The door was solid brass, heavy. William scraped at it until his fingers bled. Then the vault transformed around him: its cement walls and iron braces softened into human flesh, and he was trapped inside a grasping membrane within a hollow, gray-tissued, scarred-up womb. William peeled and tore and rubbed at the membrane, and as he did, the cord wrapped tighter and tighter around his neck, leaving it covered in welts and bruises.

Letice awoke sick to her stomach. That afternoon, when Gabe came for the tutoring session, she excused herself, saying she had something to take care of, and headed for the kitchen.

"How are you today, Trinidad?" she asked.

"Well, I'm just fine, Miz Arrow, just fine. And you?" Trinidad wondered how it was that Miz Arrow was in the kitchen with her instead of at the lesson with everyone else.

"I guess you could say I'm mostly fine."

As determined as she was to find out about Trinidad's connection to hoodoo, Letice was nervous and was having a hard time getting started at it. She busied herself rear-ranging the apples and bananas that sat in a wooden bowl. Finally, she spoke.

"Bonaventure tells me you're familiar with hoodoo."

Trinidad felt the presence of suspicion in the room. "Yes, ma'am."

"In that case, I would like to ask a favor of you."

Trinidad supposed it was possible that Miz Arrow was about to ask for an herbal remedy for some slight malady or other, but Trinidad didn't really believe that was the case.

"You're more than just familiar with hoodoo, aren't you, Trinidad? In fact, you are a hoodoo practitioner. Am I right?"

"Yes, ma'am."

"Please don't be offended by what I'm about to say, but I would appreciate it if you would not discuss hoodoo or voodoo with Bonaventure. I'm trying very hard to educate him in the Catholic faith and I don't want him to become confused. Can I count on you?"

"Yes, ma'am, you can. I know you be Catholic. I have Catholic in my soul too."

"You're Catholic, Trinidad?"

"I say I have Catholic in my soul, Miz Arrow. I hold with the notion that it not enough to preach, that you got to do good too. And I hold with Blessed Mary."

"How did you come by your faith?"

"When my mother pass on, I got put in a orphanage that be run by Catholic Sisters; the Sisters of the Holy Family they be," Trinidad answered. "Well, one of them, Sister Sulpice, she tell me about how we got to show God our goodness, not just brag on ourselves like the Pharisees do, and she told me about that good Saint Francis and how he love all God's crea-tures and all God's earth, and she told me about Mary too. And it felt real good to hear what Sister Sulpice have to say."

Letice asked to hear more of what Sister Sulpice had said.

"She say Mary never have one sin on her soul because she be the mother of Jesus. And she tell me that Mary's heart big enough to be mother to everybody. She say Mary all good and all kind and will lead a soul to Jesus if they ask her to."

Letice reached into her pocket, pulled out a rosary, and handed it to Trinidad. "I want you to have this. If you like, I'll teach you the proper prayers and the joyful and sorrowful mysteries."

"Well, now, I thank you for that, Miz Arrow, but there no need to teach me the prayers; I already know them," she said. "But I always did suspect there be mysteries. Lord knows, nobody understand where love come from if not from inside a mystery. Maybe you could teach me about the mysteries at the same time as you teach Mr. Bonaventure."

"I would like that," Letice said. "I would like that very much."

Trinidad put the rosary into her apron pocket. She intended to place it on her altar when she got home, along with the other sacred objects she kept there. Wanting to make sure things were all right with Miz Arrow, Trinidad offered a further explanation.

"If you don't mind, Miz Arrow, I'd like to say something more. But like I said, that be if you don't mind."

"Well, if it's important to you, then please go ahead."

"It be about the hoodoo, ma'am. See, I don't mix with conjuring or voodoo charms. I only deal with root work. It be the healing of the body with herbs and such. Root work be all I do with the hoodoo."

Letice hadn't heard the words *root work* in nearly thirty-five years, and hearing them now caused her mind to fly back to April of 1923, to a whitewashed room on St. Philip Street, where voodoo and hoodoo leached through the bricks like a creeping scum and crawled down her throat and into her belly and out from the place between her legs. She remembered the fever and the terror and the pain. It was the night she had become haunted, made anxious and devout by the fragile apparition of a torn and bloodied infant.

MÉMOIRE D'ARCHIVE

ETICE Molyneaux had kissed Tristan Duvais for the first time on a Thursday in 1921 when they were both sixteen years old. She'd been watching him clean saddles in the tack room. He looked different to her on that day. She suddenly noticed his hair curled at his collar, and she was awed by the breadth of his shoulders. Letice hadn't planned the kiss; she simply walked up behind him, stood on her tiptoes, and touched her lips to the back of his neck.

"Miss Letice, please don't do that," he'd said.

"Mr. Tristan, why not?" There was laughter between her words.

Tristan looked a long look at her before saying, "Don't make fun of me, Letice. You know why not."

"Because you're the help?"

"Right the first time."

"I don't care, Tristan."

"I do. We're not children anymore, Letice. We're too old to play together."

Tristan Duvais left the tack room and went out into the stable yard so as not to be alone with the boss's daughter.

Three days later she kissed him twice, and the second time he kissed her back. A third kiss came through open lips, and a fourth with seeking tongues. The two of them lived with desire after that; a desire they satisfied on a cot in the tack room, or in a hidden place by the riverbank, or on a blanket in a far corner of a pine tree woods. They risked everything to feel each other skin to skin.

Letice sought out her father, saying she wanted to become a better equestrian. Sportsman that he was, Horatio Molyneaux was only too happy to oblige. Arrangements were made for Tristan to give Letice advanced instruction, and no one questioned how much time she spent in the stables.

Tristan and Letice fell in love, in the way only the very young can. What had begun as a sexual awakening became so much more in their eyes. At first, they worried about Letice becoming pregnant, but the longer they were together, the deeper the spell became, until neither of them thought about that at all. They went on sharing their bodies and their dreams, not noticing that more than a year had gone by.

Letice made her debut into New Orleans society at the ball before Lent in 1922, when she was seventeen. She had dressed in white, as debutantes most always will. Tristan had dressed for the evening too, in crisp dark livery, as chauffeurs most always do. Being so close on the night of her debut, but not being able to touch, had put them in a frenzy.

Everyone noticed Letice Molyneaux on Fat Tuesday at the Goddess of the Rainbow Ball. She was presented with a "call-out" card and given a seat in a select area until she was "called out" early in the evening by Remington Arrow, a Rex Krewe member and sender of the card. Remington was older than Letice by ten years.

"Have we met before?" she asked as they danced, trying to make conversation.

"Indeed we have, a year or so ago, on a boat outing."

Letice did not remember.

"It was a sail down the Bogue Falaya and the Tchefuncte River put on by your daddy's yacht club.

"Oh, yes, now I recall."

The evening passed pleasantly enough. Remington took Letice's quietness for shyness, when in fact she was consumed with thoughts of Tristan.

When the Lenten season ended, Remington Arrow came to call, and by summer they were engaged to be married the following year. But in stolen moments the bride-to-be cried in her secret lover's arms and begged him to run away with her, though she knew Tristan needed time to save money.

From the moment the engagement became official, Letice's mother, Emmaline Molyneaux, kept Letice relentlessly busy with wedding preparations: invitations had been die-cut and printed in Paris, and dressmakers and florists were always underfoot. As a result, she and Tristan had not been together for a very long time.

The year went by. For Mardi Gras in 1923, Letice told Remington she would like to meet him at the Athenaeum rather than arrive together. She said she wanted to surprise him with her costume. Remington agreed and Tristan was once again her chauffeur.

When Remington looked at his fiancée that night, he marveled at the thought that soon she would be his wife. She seemed distracted and a little curt, but he attributed her behavior to a case of stretched nerves due to the wedding plans. Letice was anything but nervous; she was anxious, sexually excited, and watching the clock. At nine, she was to rendezvous with Tristan in an anteroom she knew off a little-used ballroom corridor.

Minutes passed slower than days. At last there was a break in the dancing, though the musicians continued to play for the pleasure of those couples who chose to step through the doors that were open to the terrace. Letice complained of a headache and told Remington that she needed to lie down for a while in the ladies' lounge.

Over her Scheherazade costume, Letice had deliberately chosen to wear a shawl that was pale pink on one side and sea-mist green on the other. She left the ballroom wearing the pink side out, but when she turned a corner in the outer hall she ducked behind a decorative Oriental screen. Anyone who happened to be looking when she emerged would have seen a young woman in a green shawl walking briskly down the corridor. She passed love seats and paintings and lush, potted palms until she came to a door marked *Mémoire d'Archive*. Behind that door were *objets d'art* and also her *objet d'amour*. Tristan had been pacing behind that door, too anxious to concentrate on the book he'd brought to read while he waited for Letice.

Their first embrace was full of the violence born of want. They grabbed on to each other like starving people grab for bread. Both hearts pounded and ached.

"How does this thing come off?" he whispered as he tried to remove her gown.

She turned around and said, "I had them make it with a zipper."

"Ah, she is not only beautiful but smart," said Tristan.

"He is not only handsome, he is mine," said Letice as her costume and masque fell to the floor. She turned back to face him, and he helped with her underthings until all she wore were her hair combs and jewelry. She pressed her body to his. He placed one hand on the back of her head and the other on her waist as he brushed his lips along her neck from her ear to the base of her throat. The rhythm came easily, as it did every time, and their lovemaking left them gasping. Passion had robbed them of physical strength.

Now Passion had robbed them of their luck, as well.

Letice reentered the ballroom wearing her shawl pink side out once again. Remington found her when she returned and asked if she felt well enough to dance. She remarked that she was feeling much better. She wondered if he could smell the scent of love on her skin, a fragrance she wished would never wash away.

In the weeks that followed, Letice kept looking for a menstrual flow that did not come. And she knew.

Emmaline Molyneaux noticed how tired her daughter was, napping during the day and sleeping all night as well. Emmaline also noticed that Letice had gone off her food. Waiting in a corner of the upstairs hall, Emmaline heard retching and feeble spitting and the running of water in the sink. When Letice came out of the bathroom, Emmaline followed behind.

"Letice."

Letice fell to her bed and throwing her arm over her eyes moaned something about not wanting any breakfast. Emmaline shut the door, yanked her daughter up off the bed, and slapped her as hard as she could.

"It's that stable boy, isn't it?" she demanded to know. "Don't think I haven't seen how you two look at each other, how you let him keep his hands around your waist a little too long when he helps you down from your horse. You have the look of a tramp when you're around him, Letice. And now you're throwing up. You're pregnant by Tristan Duvais, aren't you?" Emmaline snarled and grabbed Letice's arm, giving her a shake that almost snapped the girl's neck.

Terrified, Letice kept silent.

"Answer me!"

"Yes, but he doesn't know yet," Letice admitted and began to cry.

"And you're not telling him; in fact, I forbid you to leave this house. Pack a bag. We're going on a little trip. We leave tomorrow."

"Where are we going?" Letice asked.

"To a place I know. You're going to get rid of that stable boy's leavings," Emmaline spat.

"No, Mama, no. I love Tristan! We're going to get married!"

"Married? To the stable boy? Don't be ridiculous and don't be stupid. You're going to get rid of that baby and you're going to keep your mouth shut about it or your precious Tristan will be accused of stealing. I'm not afraid to press charges and have him put in jail for a good long time."

"Mama! You wouldn't do such a thing!"

"Oh, but I would, Letice. You are marrying Remington Arrow in June. Even if this baby was Remington's, and we both know he's too much of a gentleman to put you in this predicament, the scandal would be bad enough. You will not ruin this match for me, Letice."

Emmaline Molyneaux belonged to an unnamed sorority of women whose members knew things—like where to procure an abortion for oneself or a reckless daughter. Emmaline joined her husband at breakfast and announced that she and Letice would be spending some time in New Orleans. The Phelan Beales were in residence at Le Pavillon Hotel, she said, and were looking to purchase property in Pass Christian.

"Letice and I have been invited to join Mrs. Beale for teas, shopping, and luncheons; and we will be going. These are desirable people, Horatio, very desirable people."

Emmaline liked to cloak her lies in verifiable truths. It amused her.

Mother and daughter left the next morning, and once in New Orleans took a room at Le Pavillon, where Emmaline bribed a waiter into seating them near the Phelan Beales at breakfast the following day. Emmaline ordered eggs, toast, and tea for both of them but forbade Letice to eat. Emmaline knew how to cover her tracks.

After breakfast, she asked the concierge for a jitney, which they took from Poydras Street to Rampart to Canal. They left the cab to walk the streets of the Quarter, following a circuitous route and stopping to browse in the shops. Emmaline wanted it to appear as though they were on a mother-daughter outing, just in case they should run into someone they knew. It seemed to Letice they'd walked for miles before they passed through a wrought-iron gate and into a lush garden, where they followed a stone path until they came to a dark green door.

Emmaline tapped the knocker four times, waited, and tapped it four times more. It was opened by a coffee-colored woman who stepped aside to let them in. A coffee-colored girl no more than a child stood at a table folding bright white cloths. The child looked up but did not stop her folding.

And then from the shadows came Suville Jean-Baptiste.

THE DREAMS OF A BRIGHT
AND AMBITIOUS GIRL

To understand the mind of Suville Jean-Baptiste, it is important to know of her ancestry and of a social system that once flourished in the American South, most openly in the city of New Orleans. This system, *plaçage* it was called, enjoyed society's unspoken yet unmistakable approval. And so with its nose in the air and a flip of its fan, plaçage shrugged its lovely shoulders and turned its backside toward the law.

Plaçage had originated in the heart of the Caribbean, in the French colonies of Saint-Domingue, Martinique, and Guadalupe; places where there were not enough French women to go around. To compensate for this shortage, French men took enslaved women as their concubines and fathered children on them.

From this system there arose *gens de couleur libres*—free people of color, a phrase possessed of a certain irony, for though they were not slaves, neither were they considered equal to whites. They were a people trapped within a third class, and that third class was associated with slave society despite the fact that free people of color formed a culture in which refinement was paramount and education and wealth were achieved.

Suville was a Creole woman of color, descended from a past full of assorted blood. Her ancestors had been so lovely as to appear angelic, each of them able to cast a spell. Suville's mother was truly beautiful and moved with grace; she was also extremely intelligent. Her name was Clémence, and she had been mistress to a white Creole doctor since she was eighteen years old. His name was David Gaudet, and he kept her in a house on Dauphine Street, a respectable distance from the Garden District where he lived with his wife and children. Dr. Gaudet fathered Suville in the year 1900 and allowed the child and her mother to use his surname in all things unofficial. He visited Suville and Clémence every Sunday, unless of course it was the day of the week upon which Christmas fell or the birthday of one of his legal family members.

David Gaudet had graduated from the Académie Impériale de Médecine on Rue Bonaparte in Paris, a school that followed an edict stating that among the Académie's endeavors would be the evaluation of natural medications. David Gaudet had a fascination for the origin, production, and efficacy of medicines found in nature. His was a classical education, and he was a devotee of the ancient Greek, Pedanius Dioscurides, studying Dioscurides's *De Materia Medica Libri Quinque* every single day. The book listed over five hundred plants possessed of medicinal properties.

From the age of ten, Suville Gaudet accompanied her father to his laboratory, where she sat upon a high stool and beheld bacteria jitter this way and that, and the mating dance of sperm in frenzied search of ovum. She saw all this through the microscope's unerring, non-judging, magnificent clear glass eye.

"Come along, *mon bébé*," the doctor would say. "Let us go to the laboratory to see what we see."

In this manner, Suville received an education worthy of the finest medical school, the small back room of Dr. Gaudet's clinic becoming a private lecture hall. Suville soaked the information up and reached for more. Her father introduced her to the works of another famous Greek, Pliny the Elder, most especially those to do with the medicinal properties of trees and herbs, Gaudet's own particular fascination.

Dr. Gaudet marveled at his daughter's aptitude and trained her to work beside him. Year after year she traced abracadabra to the capillary passageways in the veins of leaves and to tinctures made of roots. Year after year she learned of nature's own abortifacients and of their leafy and flowered and rooted disguises. She accompanied her father to patients' homes, and to Charity Hospital in the Faubourg St. Marie, and to Touro Infirmary at Louisiana Avenue and Prytania Street. She was always assumed to be his serving girl, but this cultural error, this mistaken identity, escaped Suville's notice, driven as she was by the soothing of suffering and bringing cure to the poor and diseased. She was caught up in healing like a Christian caught in the Rapture, so caught up that she did not detect the social code, though it was plainly there.

It became obvious to Gaudet that Suville had a mind better even than his own, and that she had the makings of a truly brilliant physician.

Unfortunately, none of that mattered. Dr. Gaudet could not look at Suville when he said that no university would ever accept her. Rarely did young women become doctors, never mind illegitimate young women of color.

"But, Papa," she cried, "I would make a fine doctor! You have said it yourself many times!"

"Yes, *ma petite fille*, I said so because it is true."

"You are well respected, Papa. You can open this door for me."

"Ah, *mon trésor*, but I cannot."

"Why not, Papa? You are a powerful man in New Orleans. You sit on the board at the university. They listen to you."

"But, Suville," said Dr. Gaudet, "what of my family? It would be a disgrace. Although it puts a deep cut on my heart to hurt you, I cannot do them such harm."

The betrayal put a deep cut on Suville's heart too, which she healed with a thick-muscled bloodlust.

Suville severed herself from her father and kept to her room, coming out only to get food from the kitchen or to use the toilet. She did not play the piano or dine with her mother or go to the shops or spend afternoons among friends. Rather, she stayed in her room and read those texts precious to the man who had destroyed her dream. She reread Dioscorides's *De Materia Medica Libri Quinque* and made note of the ingredients in "abortion wine"—hellebor, squirting cucumber, and scammony. She read from Pliny the Elder and learned of the killing powers of common rue. She read of the deadliness of birthwort and pepper and myrrh. Then she took all that knowledge and opened her own clinic in which she performed abortions, free for her own people and at an exorbitant price for whites. Suville changed her surname from Gaudet to Jean-Baptiste in imitation of the saint who had baptized souls to new life.

She performed abortions in a sanitary environment and made a handsome living at it. Her surgical skills were undeniably precise, and her small hands were deft and delicate as she scraped the wages of womanliness out of fruitful wombs and fed them to her bitterness, one baby at a time.

. . . .

Suville stood tall and dignified and looked straight into the face of Emmaline Molyneaux, savoring for a moment the power she held over this white woman of position and means.

"Follow me," she said, leading the mother and daughter into a small room that held a bed draped in very white sheets and a small table that was draped in its own white cloth. Upon the table there rested a tray, and upon the tray there rested what looked at first glance like a piece of shiny cutlery. That is not what it was at all. It was a curette, a small thing described in the field of medicine as a spoon-shaped instrument for cleansing a surface. That is the definition Suville offered to her clients if they asked; personally, she thought of it as a blade and loved how nicely it fit in her hand. Whenever she held it or even just caught a glimpse of it from the corner of her eye, Suville always thought the same thing: how feminine, how powerful, how elegant and deadly.

THE SINS OF THE MOTHER

EMMALINE Molyneaux was surprised at the abortion-ist's elegance. She was not, however, surprised by the woman's barely concealed hatred. It crossed Emmaline's mind that the woman could harm Letice. But what did it matter? Letice had brought this on herself; she would have to live with the consequences. Emmaline withdrew an envelope from her handbag and laid it on a small black-lacquered table. "Would you like to count it?" she asked.

"That is not necessary. You may go now, Madame," Suville told her. "Leave your daughter here. Come back at nine tomorrow morning. Don't worry. She will be safe. I need to watch her to make sure that no products of conception remained inside. They could poison her blood."

Suville did not need to offer such aftercare. Accountability was an option for her, not a requirement; if a well-to-do white girl died from an abortion, no accusations were made.

Letice began to entreat her mother with gasping, half-choked words:

"Mama, no! Don't leave me here! Please, Mama! I love Tristan; I want this baby, Mama!" Letice was screaming by then. "Please, Mama! I'm begging you!"

"Go, Madame. I will take care of her." Though Suville's voice was soft, the command was clear.

When Emmaline had gone, Suville put her hands on Letice's shoulders and said, "Calm down, girl. I won't hurt you like some might do. Or would you rather die?"

"I want my baby," Letice whimpered.

"Your mama won't let you have this baby. If I don't take it out, she'll find someone who will, maybe someone who would not be so careful. There are those who might ruin your pretty body. What would you do then, eh? There's plenty of white girls die from dull knives and dirty water. I'll take this baby out cleanly. Do you understand?"

Letice could not stop crying.

"Calypso," Suville called out. "Bring the tea."

The woman who had answered the door to this place entered the room bearing a tea tray with a steaming pot and a white china cup. The woman's back was as straight as a rod and her face was as unreadable as a Mardi Gras *déguisement*. She had been trained by Suville Jean-Baptiste in diction and procedure and, in the few months she had worked for the abortionist, had put her training into practice at least twice a day, sometimes more, and had served the tea every time. What no one, not even Suville, knew was that Calypso had not been sane for years.

"Help her undress," said Suville, and Calypso did as commanded.

"May I have your hat, miss?" Calypso asked. And then, "Your gloves, miss? Your coat, miss? Your shoes, if you please?" as if this was nothing more than a visit to the dressmaker.

"How will you do it?" Letice asked Suville.

"I am trained in surgical techniques and versed in natural medicine," Suville replied, "and Calypso here practices hoodoo root work. I assure you we both know what we are about. I have supplied her with what she needs to brew a medicinal tea. She will boil the water and measure out a combination of snakeroot, cohosh, tansy, and seneca. Those things will cause your uterus to contract and your cervix to open just as if it were your body's own idea. After that, I will do some surgery."

"What do you mean? What kind of surgery?"

"A surgery that lets you go back to the way you were before," though no one knew better than Suville that no woman ever goes back to the way she was before.

Letice grabbed Suville's hand. "Please don't do this. I want my baby. Doesn't the medicine fail sometimes? Can't you please leave my baby be and just say you did the surgery?"

"You have to be quiet now, miss. Drink Calypso's tea. It will send you to sleep." Suville was not willing to compromise her reputation for the sake of this stupid, sniveling, lovesick white girl. "I'll come back when you are ready," she said.

Calypso poured hot water into the cup and let it steep for a moment before holding it out to Letice. She began to speak then in the Creole patois that she used on such occasions. It was a way she had of hypnotizing as she slipped into voodoo ways.

"Drink it, miss. It take you away from here. You know your spirits then, and the angels gwine come to help you."

Her words encouraged Letice, coaxing her to finish the tea. When she had drunk it all, Calypso took the cup and began to read the bits of herbs that had settled on the bottom, and then in a mesmerizing rhythm, she spoke of what the voodoo kind of hoodoo had conjured:

"Look at them writings over on that wall. Even though you got your back turned, them writings, they looking at you. You listen to Calypso and I tell you about the eyes and the teeth in them writings. Fearful, monstrous things they is. Listen good now. Them writings, they you. And they mean something. Something bad. They quiet right now, but they gonna scream one day. Fearful things. Too much fear. Fear of numbers. Everything be numbered. The days till you bleed at your moon time be numbered. The days you carry a child be numbered. You number for that done come up with this baby, eh? And seven. A body got to fear the oddness of a seven. One too many for half a dozen. Two too many to count on one hand. Three too many for the corners of the earth. Seven years a long time. In seven years your childhood pass. In seventeen years your girlhood pass. Do you see all them sevens over on that wall? They all in the Good Book: seven plagues, seven sorrows, seven deadly sins. Seven times seven gwine come to you, girl. You listen to Calypso now. The devil, he coming. I know it in my bones. I know it like I know my own hand. Too much gone wrong now. Mercy, Lord, too much gone wrong now. The mirror done broke and your life looking back at you from all them sharp glass pieces. There is words left here in the bottom of your cup. They say that all the good you do be buried under bad luck. Look out for the numbers. Look out for them sevens."

This soliloquy on the written word, this waxing poetic in Bayou patois, was remarkable for one thing: Calypso could not read. She was an émigré from the deep country, raised away from schooling and the influence of science; a frightened and gullible believer, a conjurer who gathered what drained from superstition and then attached it to numbers and meaningless words. Calypso was not a bad woman. She simply inhabited the dark side of her mind, a mind choked by a painful past endured in the dampness back of the swamp, for it was in that part of her mind where she felt empowered, in that part of her mind where she felt safe. And that was where she took all of the girls who came to Suville Jean-Baptiste.

"*Seven times seven . . . the devil, he coming . . . seven times seven*" wound around Letice's mind, hypnotizing her fears. Calypso's words became drawn out and distorted as the walls began to expand and contract like the smooth yellow skin on a bullfrog's throat. The words became a lullaby then, and Letice gave in to sleep.

Suville came to the room and began to bathe her patient, pouring water over Letice's outer womb. Suville had entered a trance of her own, one in which she saw herself as the reincarnated John the Baptist. But Suville was nothing of the kind. Suville Jean-Baptiste brought no babies into life; Suville Jean-Baptiste took babies to death.

A cramping came to Letice then, and a sweet-smelling cloth came down over her face. Suville took the curette into her right hand and began.

The infant never saw that small special knife, but the infant felt the scraping. With care and precision, Suville placed torn placenta and tattered baby into a basin being held by the insane Calypso.

The past and the future descended upon Letice, sweeping her deep into hallucination and bizarre phantasmagoria:

Tristan stands before her, hand outstretched. The two of them dance over treetops. They are covered by the past they share and the love they were born with. Then they are dancing at Bal Masque until she finds herself alone beneath a tree and it becomes a pew and she is in the church of her childhood. She holds a book but cannot decipher the words on its pages. Two doors are painted on the ceiling of the church, and she believes that one of them leads to heaven, but she does not know which one. Saint Anne and her daughter, the Virgin Mary, stand frozen in statue serenity on the side altars, but Letice knows that they can see her.

"You were baptized right there," the Virgin says. Letice cups her hand in the baptismal font and brings the water to her mouth. She drinks it down in hopes that it will wash away her sins. And in her dream her innocence is restored; she can feel the tightness of virginity between her legs once again, and Letice knows the innocence of the newly born.

And then she steps into the confessional, but no priest is there to hear her sins. Next, she is walking up the center aisle, dressed in white, a miniature bride on her way to First Communion, clutching a book of prayer. A circlet of flowers rests on the communion rail. She cradles it in both hands and floats up to place it on the Holy Mother's head, a crown for the church's Queen.

And then Letice is a bride, placing a flower at the Virgin's feet. But she is simultaneously in the back of the church, attending her own wedding as both bride and guest. She moves to take a seat, but an usher tells her that she must sit at the front. She gets only as far as the middle pew when she is startled by a disruption at the altar. She watches her bride-self cry, for the groom is not Tristan. Letice is to marry a stranger.

And then she is a mother, and the bells ring out at her baby's baptism. She holds her baby in her arms and begins to feel a spreading wetness. Letice screams when she sees that blood is soaking through the blanket the baby is wrapped in. She folds the cloth back to find the source of the bleeding and sees that her child has been torn to pieces as if chewed by a wild beast. And then that baby is gone and a little boy holds her hand.

A casket rises up before the altar then, solid and sealed

and still. Someone recites the joyful mysteries as the casket is covered in stained-glass light, and Letice cannot find her little boy. She can hear something a far way off. It is the sound of mad laughter known as *un fou rire* and it is coming from the fearful monstrous writings on the wall, the ones Calypso spoke of. And then the laughter melts away and all that she hears is the cry of a baby.

Suville laid the knife down, pleased with her work.

Calypso washed and dried Letice and packed a dressing between her legs. The abortionist was busy washing her own hands, and Letice continued to sleep. No one saw Calypso take a bit of the dead fetus's bloodied tissue from the porcelain basin and smear it between two glass prisms as she imagined the voodoo queen Marie Laveau would have done in the making of a powerful wanga.

"Have you finished cleaning her, Calypso?"

"Yes, Miss Suville."

"Then call your daughter in to sit with her. Another patient will be here soon."

"Trinidad," Calypso called. "Come in here and sit with this girl."

Ten-year-old Trinidad came into the room and perched on a stool near the foot of the bed. Calypso took satisfaction in the fact that her daughter had on a very clean head cloth. She didn't want this white girl to take Trinidad for a sharecropper's child or for white trash either. She wanted this white girl to know that Trinidad be a Fontenaise.

Trinidad thought the young woman looked as white as the sheets; even her lips had lost their color. The only sign that she was alive was the slight rise and fall of her chest as she breathed. She looked so very young.

A breeze whispered through the room, bringing with

it the sound of a newborn's cry. Trinidad could feel the air on her own skin and could see it quiver through the long brown hair that surrounded the sleeping girl's face. Trinidad stared at the girl in the bed, watching for some sign of stirring. She looked hard enough to see a bruised and bloodied angel place a kiss on its mother's face. The tiny thing looked at Trinidad then, with the most beautiful eyes she had ever seen, so beautiful they could only have come from God, and she felt for that angel baby and for its bleeding young mama every kind of compassion.

The following morning Calypso helped Letice to dress. When they finished, Calypso handed her a carved wooden box. Inside it were the prisms that held the relic of Letice's dead baby between them like so many drops of martyr's blood.

Calypso slipped back into that thick Creole patois and whispered, "You keep this with you. This be you baby. You let it know you be sorry. You still be its mama. You has to keep this baby safe now. I gwine put your baby in this bag with the bandages you need. Don't you tell you mama, now. She mean this baby harm."

When Emmaline came to collect her, Letice was sitting up in a chair, fully dressed, with several folded rags packed between her legs to soak up the blood that wept from her uterus like sticky, dark red syrup.

"She did well," Suville assured Emmaline Molyneaux. "Keep a clean dressing on her. There are several in that bag. No baths until the bleeding stops. And no sex. Do you have any questions?"

Emmaline blushed and cleared her throat before voicing what was on her mind. "Will she be able to have other children? Will her future husband be able to tell anything?"

"There is no physical reason she cannot have more children," Suville said, and turned around to remove something from a chest of drawers behind her. She held a small pouch out to Emmaline. "As for a future husband, brew this as you would a tea and give it to her before the wedding night. It will bring about a bloody show that will make her seem a virgin."

"Is there any chance that this has disfigured her somehow?" Emmaline persisted.

Suville was enraged by the woman's impudence. How dare she question her expertise? But her face remained composed. "She has not been harmed," Suville said.

But Suville Jean-Baptiste was wrong about that. Letice's heart and soul had been scraped to a bloody pulp by the sharp and gleaming, delicate curette.

They remained in New Orleans for five more days, during which time Emmaline alternately browbeat, comforted, and threatened Letice until she'd convinced the girl of what had to be done.

"We'll put you out, Letice. No one will help you"—and then—"I love you, sweetheart. You're my own sweet girl. I only want what's best for you"—and then—"I'll ruin them, Letice. Tristan's father works for us. I'll ruin the entire family. Is that what you want?"

Emmaline was relentless. She finally broke her daughter, and they began to rehearse what Letice would say and how she would say it.

The day after returning home, Letice found Tristan in the tack room.

"God, I missed you," he said, reaching for her, but Letice pulled away.

Tristan looked stunned. "What's wrong?"

"Tristan, I'm going to marry Remington Arrow." Letice brushed some lint from her sleeve in an effort to appear very casual. "Don't look so shocked. You knew this was going to happen."

Tristan shook his head as if to clear it and said, "You said you wouldn't go through with that wedding. You wanted to marry me, remember?" He reached for her again, and again she pulled away.

"Oh, honestly, Tristan, you never really believed that, did you?"

The hurt on his face was unmistakable. "Letice, what are you saying? We love each other. I only need a little more time; I almost have enough money saved . . ."

"Tristan, you'll never have enough money."

She may as well have thrown ice water over him. When he was able to speak, he stammered, "This is about money?"

"Not just money," Letice answered in a voice that seemed slightly amused. "Did you really think I would marry a stable hand?"

"Letice, why are you talking like this? What's happened?"

"You almost ruined my life is what's happened, Tristan. You got me pregnant." Letice slipped the tone of bitterness into her charade.

"Pregnant?" Tristan was momentarily speechless. "We'll get married right away!"

"Don't be ridiculous. I got rid of it."

Tristan looked her in the eye and said, "You're lying."

"No. I'm not. You were fun, Tristan. But that's all. My mother knows everything." Letice went on, "She wants you to leave; as I do. If you breathe one word about this, she'll bring your father into it. Mother will accuse him of stealing and he'll never find work again, not to mention the shame." And then she echoed Emmaline's words: "Is that what you want?"

Tristan turned away from her and simply said, "I'll go."

Letice reported back to her mother, then took to her bed and slipped fully into numbness. Her only consolation was that she had loved him enough to let him go.

Emmaline went to her husband to tell him that Tristan Duvais would be leaving their employ. Horatio Molyneaux was distressed and suggested they raise his pay.

"No dear. Let the boy go. I don't like the way he looks at Letice."

Emmaline's threat had done the trick. Tristan told his parents he wanted to do something else with his life. They said they didn't understand. He could hardly look at their faces when he said he wanted a better life than the one that they had managed.

Remington Arrow came to call on the following Sunday, and the elder Molyneauxs regretted to say that Letice was ill but should be fine in a week or so. Hardly two months after her abortion, Letice stood at the altar as Remington's bride. She went through the motions, she spoke the vows, but her heart was not in attendance.

During the reception, Emmaline made certain that Letice drank the tea as advised by Suville, all the while assuring her that everything had worked out for the best.

Letice played out her part. It was she who reached for Remington that night, and in the morning the sheets were stained with false virginity, just as Suville had said they would be.

The carved wooden box was kept in a locked drawer of her letter-writing desk for years, though she took it out and looked at it all the time. When her chapel had been completed, after Remington died, Letice placed that box in the niche she'd had built into the wall beneath the mosaic of the

Angel Lailah, guardian of babies from conception to birth. But the ache of regret stayed with her.

Trinidad never forgot the beautiful eyes of the baby she'd seen cross over in that room on St. Philip Street. It was those eyes she saw so many years later in the face of Bonaventure Arrow, who'd inherited them from his paternal grandmother on the old-moneyed Molyneaux side.

A REASONABLE SUPPOSITION

COLEMAN Tate laid out The Wanderer's possessions on his desk in an effort to determine some sort of hierarchy, some meaningful strategy, some line of dominoes ready to fall. Had he been less inclined toward cold, hard facts, he might have seen them as a kind of gris-gris.

Since the man's cash was still held in a vault at the asylum, Tate used a dollar bill of his own as stand-in. Given the amount the man had carried, he assumed he had closed a bank account. Tate figured that one did such a thing when one did not intend to return to that bank, either out of dissatisfaction or because one is moving on. In this case, he favored the moving-on theory. Tate also believed the absence of a wallet to be deliberate. The man did not want to carry proof of who he was, or perhaps he wished to forget his identity altogether.

The matchbook bearing the inscription *Zip's Tavern—Melvindale, Michigan* seemed like half a clue, since there had been no package of cigarettes or even a cigar to go with it. And then of course there was the fact that none of the matchsticks had been burned. A souvenir perhaps? Tate consulted an atlas. Melvindale was near Detroit.

The newspaper was a common enough thing—people

bought newspapers every day. The clue this one provided was the date. It placed the perpetrator in Chicago on December 1, 1949. It had been neatly folded as if to fit in an inner coat pocket and be taken out later to read.

The detective believed the killer had considered the button to be the most valuable of the objects he carried with him; it seemed a sentimental thing. The button was made of brass, had a shank inset into holes, and bore the Great Seal of the United States on its front and, on its back, the words Scovill Manufacturing Company, along with two stars. Coleman Tate had served in the army himself and knew it to be the button of an enlisted man. He deduced that the man had fought in World War II; perhaps that was where he'd suffered the injury to his face. Perhaps not.

The paper napkin struck Tate as a whimsical thing. The only characteristic that set it apart from any other paper napkin was the slogan printed on it: *Memphis—Home of the Blues*. It seemed to Tate that the man might have identified with the notion and general mindset of the blues. Maybe he was a killer with a soft spot for the sad side of romantic. Maybe he'd been jilted a time or two. Maybe he felt no one could love his ruined face.

It occurred to the detective that the objects had all come from different locations, and on the heels of that idea he began to arrange them geographically. He situated the dollar bill and the matchbook toward the top of the desk as if to place them near Detroit; he then placed the newspaper slightly lower and to the left as if sitting west of Detroit in Chicago. The napkin he placed southerly, where Memphis would be. He believed it likely that more trains or buses bound for New Orleans left from Chicago rather than Detroit, which didn't explain the Michigan connection; he would have to come back to that. He deemed it a reasonable supposition that William Arrow's killer had traveled from Chicago, thence to Memphis, which would have been a likely stop, and wound up in New Orleans, where he started to use the public library with a specific purpose in mind.

The next day Tate went to Union Station to check a schedule and see if there was such a route. There was.

**PROGRESS REPORT
IN THE MATTER OF WILLIAM EVEREST ARROW
(DECEASED)**

Upon careful review and consideration of the items found in the possession of John Doe, I have determined that the perpetrator most likely took a train from Chicago to New Orleans on or shortly after December 1, 1949. I will continue pursuing this line of inquiry. Further findings to follow.

A couple of sounds had come to Bonaventure, and he'd saved them up for Tate: they were a motor sound and the sizzle of a match. While the investigator met with Letice to discuss his report, Bonaventure raced a small die-cast metal car on the floor of the foyer, sending it flying across the marble tiles until it spun out and crashed and flipped over on its top. When the detective reached for the doorknob upon leaving, Bonaventure placed the tiny car within Tate's hand and wrapped his fingers around it as if to say, —Here. Take this. You can keep it.

That toy car had an official name: Matchbox. Bonaventure had given Tate a double clue.

That night, Coleman Tate turned the toy over and over in his hand while he ruminated about the case. He determined that Michigan, not Chicago, was the place to look; Melvindale, specifically, Zip's Tavern to be exact, and he began to assemble a plan. The first thing he did was obtain the police photograph taken of John Doe at the time of the murder. Coleman Tate didn't need to prove the man's guilt; he merely needed to find out his name.

REMAINS OF A SHARED PAST

SOMETIMES the remains of a shared past unearth themselves; memories emerge from the crust that covers them and they are newly discovered by the mind. So it was for Letice and Trinidad when they were the only ones home, working out menus for the upcoming week.

The kindness on Trinidad's face took Letice back to the quiet child who'd sat at her bedside while she'd cramped and bled and dreamed a bad dream. At the very same moment, Trinidad once again saw the frightened young woman who was white as the sheets, and the bloody little ghost with the beautiful eyes. Each woman suspected then that they had met in a room on St. Philip Street in New Orleans a long time ago. They recalled the how and the why of it, but a sense of politesse prevented either one from voicing the memory of what had gone on behind the dark green door.

Secret memories have the power to isolate, and even an unspoken sharing is soothing. Letice steered the conversation in a direction meant to uncover the past without bringing it up directly, and Trinidad followed her lead.

"Where are you from, Trinidad? Originally, I mean."

"Well, I be born in Terrebonne Parish, but we call it by the Cajun, Paroisse Terrebonne. My mama and me we live about an hour's walk outside Bayou Cane. There wasn't no streets or anything like that where we lived; just a bunch of Negro families in cabins. We all work the fields for the man who own the land. Mama and me, we live there until right after my birthday when I turn nine years old."

"You mention only your mother," Letice said.

"Yes, ma'am. That because I don't ever know my daddy. My mama say he die when I be a baby too young to remember. She say he be a fine man who had some education. His family name was Fontenaise."

"How did your mother support you?"

"Well, like I say, we work in the fields outside Bayou Cane until Mama found us work in New Orleans. We worked for a woman on St. Philip Street."

There it was. The first implied evidence.

"She found work for you too?" Letice asked.

"Yes, ma'am. We work together for a Creole lady. I did the washing and Mama help the lady with her work. Mama be in charge of the tea. See, this lady used certain teas in her work."

Letice did not miss the second offering. As if propelled toward a full confrontation with her past, she asked, "What was it the lady did?"

"She doctored females is all I know; she say she put them back together. Some of them that come to her, they all excited to be there, and they fall all over theyselves thanking the Creole lady. But there be a terrible sadness on others. I feel real bad for the sad ones. Always when one of the sad ones go back out the door I think to myself, 'Lord, that girl look like she still need help.' Of course, I be only ten years old at the time, but I surely did feel bad for them what had come the Creole lady and left all covered in sadness."

Confirmation came over them all of a piece, and both

were sure of the memory. Their eyes met long enough to acknowledge the truth, and then, as if by unspoken agreement, they wrapped that memory back up in quiet.

Letice was the first to reach for idle conversation. "You mentioned once that you spent time in an orphanage, but you didn't say how you got there. What happened?"

"My mama die when I be eleven. Don't nobody know for sure what it was killed her, though. Bibelot was the one saw it come on. Bibelot shared a room with us, and as I look back on it, I think Bibelot maybe a prostitute, cuz sometimes there be a man the other side of the curtain with her, and it not always the same man. And Bibelot, she make sweet talk to whatever man be with her, and she wear a plain dress when one of them not there, and nothing but her chemise when one of them was. That's when Mama would grab my arm and rush us out the door.

"Anyway, Bibelot say Mama die from a spider bite on the soft side of her ankle. I remember she got a blister there, and then a rash come and her whole foot swell up real big and her skin split open and her foot and leg turn real, real dark. I begged her to show the Creole lady cuz the Creole lady know about medicines, but Mama say no. She say she got a curse on her and she hide that swelling. I think she afraid we lose our jobs if the Creole lady think Mama been cursed. So Mama wrap her foot and leg in a bandage and go to a voodoo woman name of Pleasance who give her a amulet. That amulet don't do no good. The fever come on and an awful terrible sickness. Three days later, she die."

"How did you get to the orphanage?"

"Well, don't nobody know exactly what to do with a colored girl who got no mama or daddy left, so Bibelot take me to the Creole lady and ask her what to do, and the Creole lady say to take me to Charity Hospital. Bibelot take me there and tell me to sit nice and quiet until somebody ask me my name and then I supposed to tell how I never know my daddy and how my mama be dead from a poison bite. It seem like most of the day go by, and my stomach just about turn inside out I be so hungry, when this woman come up and ask me who I waiting for. I tell her just like I supposed to, and before I knew what was what them folks send me to the Providence Asylum. But I be too old for there, so somebody from that place take me up to Lafayette Parish where the Sisters of the Holy Family look out for colored children who got nobody else. I remember then about my Auntie Henriette here in Bayou Cymbaline—she the one to leave me the house out on the Neff Switch road. The Sisters send her a letter, but she couldn't find a way to take me in, so they kept me at the orphanage and it all work out for the good because that's where I met the boy I married; his name be Jackson Prefontaine."

"Ah, and that's where you learned about Mary," Letice said.

"Yes, ma'am. That be where I learn about Mary. And where I learn how to sew, and how to read, and how to write with a pencil. The only thing I didn't learn real good be how to talk like a white girl."

And so the two spoke of things long past, but not of the bloody little baby with the beautiful brown eyes.

YOU NEED TO GIVE ME A
LITTLE MORE TO GO ON

W HAT'LL it be, mister?" the bartender asked.
"Scotch, neat," was Coleman Tate's response.

It was four o'clock in the afternoon, early yet for the rush. Tate took in the details of the working man's bar: dishes of peanuts, metal ashtrays, and memorabilia tied to baseball glories. It was a shrine to the Detroit Tigers and that team's anointed: Ty Cobb, Goose Goslin, Bobo Newsom, and Schoolboy Rowe. A 1945 World Series pennant graced the mirror behind the cash register. The place reeked of cigars and cigarettes and beer as well as the unmistakable smell of danger. People ran out of luck in places like Zip's; they got roughed up and rolled in the alley or worse—Zip's was a little too close to a river, a little too easy to disappear from.

Tate raised one hand up off the bar to signal for another drink. "How's business?" he asked the bartender.

"Seen better, seen worse," was the reply.

"I was wondering if you might help me out with something," Tate said.

"Yeah?"

"I'm trying to find out about a guy who was a patron at your bar a while back. I believe he might have been coming around here sometime after the war, probably up until late 1949."

The bartender said, "That's a long time ago. I might be able to help, but then again I might not."

Tate inched a twenty-dollar bill in the man's direction.

"What's his name?" the barkeep asked.

"Well, now, that's the problem. I don't have a name. I was hoping you might remember the guy by his looks." Tate pulled the photograph from his suit pocket. "As you can see, he was missing part of his face—the jaw on the right side."

"I don't know; there's lots of men got their faces messed up."

Another twenty left the detective's wallet. "I have reason to believe this fellow was a veteran. Do you remember him now?"

"There's lots of vets around here, mister. You need to give me a little more to go on."

A third twenty slid across the bar. "He doesn't look familiar to me. If I was you, I'd try over to the Rouge," the barman said. "There's guys over there that got hurt in the war, and guys that got hurt when they first tried to bring in the union, and there's guys been hurt by dynamite too."

Tate made a visit to the auto plant, where he had another costly conversation, this time with a personnel worker who gave him the names of four disfigured men who'd served in the military and ended up at the Rouge after returning home from the war.

JULY 14, 1957
THE SOUNDS OF SORROW
AND OF ANGEL BLOOD

IN the moment between dreaming and waking, it came to Bonaventure that the mournful slip of paper he'd taken from his mother's closet and the small smothered sound that lived in the chapel might comfort one another.

Grand-mère was at Sunday mass and his mother was sleeping in. He skipped breakfast altogether, retrieved the note from Mr. Silvey's shop, and took it to the chapel. Bonaventure looked at the carved wooden box for a while and listened to that sad, soft weeping. When he pulled the box from its niche, the weeping quieted down to the little hiccup breaths that trail after sobbing. He bent his knees, lowered himself to the floor, and sat there Indian fashion. Then he opened the lid as gently as he could.

All that was inside was a small rectangle made of two pieces of glass that were stuck to each other by a reddish-brown smear. He pulled the note out of his pocket and put it inside the box, on top of those pieces of stuck-together glass, and then he closed it up. There was nothing but quiet. Bonaventure smiled, and on the heels of his happiness the inspiration came that the note and the glass pieces should be buried in the garden, where they would be away from the house and could console each other forever and be surrounded by flowers.

Bonaventure went back to Mr. Silvey's shed and removed a small spade from where it hung on a hook between a long-handled hoe and a three-pronged cultivator. He took the spade to a spot in the garden and began to dig.

It had rained the day before, leaving the soil dark as wet coffee grounds and soft as butter that's been left to sit out. Bonaventure listened to the earthworms in their tunnels and tried to be very careful. It was slow going when such care was taken, but he would never want to bring harm to the earthworms and so he didn't mind. He didn't fling the dirt up and scatter it but rather placed each scoop gently down one upon the other. Bonaventure maintained concentration on the grave until the spade's point hit upon something that had managed to get past his uncommon hearing. He immediately stopped digging and acknowledged the surprise.

He put the spade down and dug in the cool moist soil with his hands, probing with his fingertips until he recognized roundness. He used the spade to loosen the shape until he could pry it free. At the end of his efforts, Bonaventure held in one grimy hand a cool and hefty, dirt-covered stone that gave off the finest silence he had ever had the pleasure to encounter.

That stone was immediately precious to him. He took it over to the old brass tap beneath the chapel window in order to wash it. He held the stone under the running water, rubbing it gently until it was smooth as a pearl and cleaner than rain. Then he took it to the garden bench and set it to dry in the sun.

The stone maintained a constant stillness, which

Bonaventure took to mean that it was always listening, for in his experience you could hear a lot more if you kept real still. And then too there was the idea that the stone made no sound of its own; Bonaventure could only imagine how much it must be able to hear, what with not having to listen to its own breathing or its own footsteps or its own chewing, and he began to feel a reverence and a solid admiration. Now that the stone was clean, he could see that it was speckled, black and white.

He listened to that stone harder than he'd ever listened to anything, and indeed the stone did speak, sharing its knowledge of how earth and time and all other things had been brought out of darkness and into great light by the Source of all there is.

And then the marvelous sounds began, and Bonaventure heard that good and steady *bup-bup, bup-bup,* the same as he'd heard inside Dancy's womb.

The stone's knowledge carried him through a wind that caused the cosmos to fall inward and then burst open.

Bup-bup, bup-bup.

Bonaventure could feel the rushing of waters blown over by that wind, and then he himself was swept into the sky.

Bup-bup, bup-bup.

His whole body filled with stars being born, with the spinning of atoms, with the pull of the planets, and with suns and moons and constellations.

Bup-bup, bup-bup.

He saw fishes and creatures and trees. He saw people living and loving and dying.

Bup-bup, bup-bup.

And then the stone brought forth echoes of its own birth and how it had tumbled from oceans and rivers and streams to come to rest in the garden. The stone took joy in the warmth of the light now, having known the coldness of the dark.

Bup-bup, bup-bup.

Bonaventure knew then for certain what to do with those sounds of sorrow and of angel blood he had been about to bury.

Dancy still wasn't up when he went back in the house. Bonaventure didn't want to wake her, so he wrote a note that said *Gone walking* and propped it up against the coffee can where he knew she would see it. Then he went to get the wagon. He took hold of its handle in hopes of feeling his father's warmth or perhaps hearing the sound of his voice, but none of that happened. What did happen was a gravitational tug, much like the one that had brought Trinidad Prefontaine to Bayou Cymbaline. Bonaventure did not fight that tug, but leaned back to feel it pull him all the more.

He walked alone save for the company of the carved wooden box that was perched in the wagon and the speckled stone tucked in his pocket. The stone bumped against his leg with every left step, all the while blending its silence with his, just as a soul mate would do. The narrow trail of hard-packed sand felt solid and warm beneath his bare feet, and its dusty surface sent the softest powder sifting up between his toes. He passed by blue gentians, purple trilliums, and pink yarrow. The day was so wonderful that Bonaventure thought it would taste like cherry pie if he took a bite of it. Feathery clouds streaked the sky, and even though the sun was out, he could still see the moon.

By the time he'd walked long enough to get thirsty, he'd come to the Neff Switch road. He kept right on walking, and in five minutes' time found himself in a clearing where stood the two-room house with a wraparound porch and a mansard roof and a cupola sheathed in copper.

Bonaventure stood as still as he possibly could, feeling the gladness that always accompanied the sound of Trinidad's smile, a sound nearly identical to that of sun sparkle on water. He wished he could capture it to put in his memento box.

Birds and insects pierced the stillness with their songs and beckoning buzzing, while a light breeze whispered through the weeds and wild grasses. Bonaventure considered the scene wildly pleasing and so plucked a blade of grass to keep. A lark stood in the rainwater pond that was growing warm in the old birdbath, and a dragonfly hovered close by, iridescent and splendid.

Inside her house, Trinidad felt Bonaventure's approach with her right-sided heart. She pulled the big crockery bowl down from its shelf, set it on the wooden block table, and filled it with ingredients whose amounts she knew by feel, sifting flour and brushing it between her hands. She reached into the bowl to knead the smooth, cool dough before plopping it onto the cloth and working the rolling pin, performing the everyday miracle that would turn the mixture into beautiful, thick, round golden biscuits.

She sent a shout through the open window—"Who you are out there?"—even though she knew perfectly well who had come.

Bonaventure sent his silent answer.

"Does that be you, Bonaventure Arrow? Come on, okay, move yourself and get up here then. I can't be waiting on you all the day." Then she wiped her hands on her apron and stepped out onto the porch.

Bonaventure approached the house, parked his wagon, and threw his arms around Trinidad's waist. When the hug was done, she brought him in and set him to work scrubbing the crockery bowl as if he'd done it every day of his life, while she busied herself with the biscuits. When the baking was done, they sat down to partake of not only the biscuits but the juice of ripened muscadine grapes that grew wild on Trinidad's land. When they finished eating and cleared their plates, she took a small spade from a hook and motioned for him to follow.

"I'm glad you bring your wagon. It going to come in handy."

Bonaventure listened to the wind singing through the sweetgum and sassafras, the prickly ash and hickory, and tried to absorb their tree-songs through his skin. And just to make sure he wouldn't lose that music, he plucked a leaf from each one to put in his wagon and carry back to Christopher Street.

Trinidad began to dig.

"This be a whole lot of healing we digging up today, Mr. Bonaventure. A whole lot of healing," she said.

—Okay! Bonaventure said, by way of making a circle with the thumb and index finger of his right hand and giving her a wink.

Thready roots snapped as they were tugged from the earth, and bits of loamy soil pattered to the ground. One by one, and with the greatest of tender motions, Trinidad placed plants in the bottom of Bonaventure's wagon very close to the carved wooden box. The two of them worked in quiet companionship until the sun had moved beyond its greatest height.

"That be enough now," Trinidad said, and led the way to the small barn back of the house.

As his eyes adjusted to the shadowy interior, Bonaventure noticed thin lines of sunlight filtering through the boards of the walls and imagined he could feel them touch him and fracture apart as he walked into dusky dimness. Their splintering sounded like the pinging of raindrops, which pleased him through and through.

Trinidad began to shake out the harvest and hang it from twine strung diagonally for that purpose.

"These here be what called simples," she told Bonaventure. "They get they start in the dark of the earth, and then they reach for the light."

This trajectory reminded Bonaventure of his black and white stone and how he'd found it buried in the garden.

"The simples be wild herbs, and they be for tea and poultice and chew." She touched the brown leaves and went on. "Some folks, they use the simples like poisons, but that not what God intended at all. The simples is supposed to be used for good. Take this one here now; it be witch hazel and good for the skin. And this one here with the tiny pink buds on it, that comfrey. It be used to knit up flesh and bones."

Bonaventure reached toward another plant, a question in his eyes.

"Don't touch that one, child; it be stinging nettle. Stinging nettle good for the gout."

Finger point, raised brows. —And this one?

"Yarrow. It for the toothache."

—How do you know all these things? Bonaventure communicated this question by sweeping his arm to encompass the hanging herbs, then holding his hands out palms up and shrugging.

"I knows some of it from my mama, but only some. She didn't fix on the notion that simples be meant for healing. She had a fear in her that made her think they only be used for harm."

Index fingers pulled down the sides of his mouth in a sad face.

"Don't I know it, Mr. Bonaventure. Don't I know it. All's we can do now is ask the Lord to forgive her."

A very solemn nod.

With their bounty hung to dry, they returned to the house to wash the dirt from their hands and eat one more biscuit with butter and jam. When it was time to go, Bonaventure took the carved wooden box from the wagon and regarded it solemnly. He opened it gently, removed Dancy's note and Grand-mère's pieces of stuck-together glass and set them on the table. Then he removed the speckled stone from his pocket and set it down alongside them. He felt he'd best leave the stone with Trinidad, a woman he associated with the seraphim angels, the ones Grand-mère liked to talk about, the ones that were closest to God.

Trinidad accepted the offering entrusted her, in silence, as was appropriate.

Bonaventure set off then, the empty carved box and the sounds of simples filling his father's childhood wagon all the way up to the brim.

THOSE THINGS
SHE FOUND SPIRITUAL

WHEN she could no longer see Bonaventure's small back heading down the Neff Switch road, Trinidad picked up the note, the prisms, and the stone and went into her front room to kneel before a small altar upon which rested those things she found spiritual: a plaster-of-Paris Virgin Mary, three red feathers of a Shanghai rooster, and pieces of sea glass worn smooth as silk by lapping waves of salty water. There was also a rabbit's foot, a pouch filled with catmint, and the rosary of fine wooden beads so recently given her by Miz Arrow, senior.

From the time she'd awakened that morning, Trinidad Prefontaine knew one thing for sure: this day held a promise in its hands. She laid the note and the prisms on her homemade altar amidst those symbols and souvenirs of her deity's Spirit, the Blessed Mother who loved every single child: the sea glass, like pieces of broken lives made lustrous and baptized by the ocean's healing waters; the feathers of a bird that can fly precious little yet proclaims the new hope of every day's dawn; and those odd little bits of nature's bounty. From her pocket she pulled a holy card, one given to her in the orphanage by Sister Sulpice. The card was soft as a piece of old leather, made so by the oils in the skin of Trinidad's hands. The front bore a picture of Francis of Assisi, and printed on the back were the words to his Canticle of Brother Sun and Sister Moon. Her lips moved silently over the words of the prayer until the very end, when she spoke them loud and sincerely:

> *Praised be You my Lord through our Sister, Mother Earth,*
> *who sustains and governs us,*
> *producing varied fruits with colored flowers and herbs.*

Then she returned the card to her pocket.

Like Mam Judith, Sister Sulpice had been a kind of prophet. Mam Judith had spoken of Trinidad's Purpose and Knowing, and Sister Sulpice had seen by what means they would be made manifest.

Trinidad placed the note and the prisms upon her altar and then she placed there one thing more: the silence of Bonaventure Arrow, contained as it was in the smooth, round, black and white speckled stone. The stone was heavier than she'd expected it to be, maybe because it carried the weight of so much more. Indeed, that stone carried the secret sorrows so recently removed from Letice's chapel and Dancy's closet. And it held too William's undead longing, the weight of Calypso's fearful superstitions, the vengeful anger of Suville Jean-Baptiste, the rancorous madness of The Wanderer, and the lonely delusions of Eugenia Babbitt.

Trinidad pulled her hand away, closed her eyes, and bowed her head in an attitude of prayer until a warming came over her. Then she opened her eyes to see a ribbon of light rise up from the speckled stone. It shimmered and spread itself over the Canticle and across the note and the prisms as well. The light covered the fear; it brightened the longing; it whitened the anger, bleaching it to nothingness.

All sorrow was soothed until there was only a small whimpered crying that softened to sighing, that floated forever and ever away, fading along with the speckled stone's light.

Several other things happened in that instant: Bonaventure heard *bup-bup, bup-bup*; Dancy found herself thinking about Gabe Riley; and Letice felt the smallest brush on her cheek like the feel of a baby's kiss.

Once back home, Bonaventure put the box back in its niche and pressed the simples between the pages of a book.

At supper that night, Grand-mère invited everyone to go to mass with her the next day. "It's the Feast of Saint Bonaventure," she said.

THE Wanderer stopped eating and drinking, for all he could do was think. He thought until his sanity returned, and with it the memory of what he had done. The recollection torched him everywhere; he could hardly breathe through the pain. The muscles of his face stayed twisted into knots, tight and painful and full of remorse.

Bonaventure could hear The Wanderer's regret. It made the sound of burned skin that cannot scab over because it is too far gone.

ONE OF US HERE
KNOWS THE RULES
JULY 19, 1957

VENTURE Forth Arrow, we gotta get going. It's gonna be a busy day; I got two perms and a bleach job and nobody should have to sit through all that, least of all you, since you'll be stuck with Grandma Roman tomorrow."

Bonaventure winced.

"And speaking of Grandma Roman, pretty soon we'll all be suffering the great misfortune of having to hear about those Meetings of the Big-Ass Righteous. Unfortunately, there's two gonna be going on tomorrow, and she'll be screaming her head off, hounding God for what she wants. She keeps looking for a miracle even though we don't need one. That woman could send me right off the deep end, I swear. Anyway, you better go outside and play while you still got the chance."

And that right there was one of the many reasons Bonaventure loved his mother so much: she was plain downright considerate.

"Be back by eleven," she hollered as the screen door slammed. "Sooner if ya miss me."

. . . .

Over at the post office, the air around Adelaide Roman was fairly charged with a crackling static that radiated from her fingertips and gathered in a nimbus that glowed around her head. Something big was going to happen tomorrow, something really big, and it would all be thanks to her. She loved the sensation of power that was rushing through her body; sometimes she just wanted to squeal, she was so wound up.

Near the end of the workday, when Adelaide was lost in this mental ecstasy, Trinidad walked through the door of the post office, stepped up to where Adelaide stood behind the counter, and set a letter down. It was quarter to five.

Adelaide acted as if she was busy, fiddling with this set of keys and that rubber stamp, picking through paper clips, and sorting out pens until Mrs. Louella Stempley came through the door.

Adelaide craned her neck enough to look behind Trinidad and say, "Hey, there, Louella, what can I do for you today?"

Louella Stempley said, "Go on and finish there, Adelaide. I'm not in any hurry."

"That's fine. I'm done here. Come on, now, step up and let me see whatcha got."

Mrs. Stempley looked questioningly toward Trinidad, who gave a gracious nod and stepped a bit to the side. "All's I got is this one letter, but I couldn't find my stamps. I'da swore I had some in my purse, but I guess not—must be getting old and senile."

"Well, that's what I'm here for, Louella, to sell stamps to the feeble-minded," said Adelaide, laughing at her joke.

Louella Stempley bought her stamps and left. It was so quiet in the post office that Trinidad could hear the soft tick of the clock's second hand every time it moved. It was now seven minutes before five. Adelaide ambled about, organizing her cash drawer, bending to tie her shoe, and straightening up to put some hand lotion on.

"Good Afternoon, Mrs. Roman," Trinidad said. "I would like to buy a stamp, please."

"Is that right?" Adelaide sneered.

Trinidad froze. Had she missed the sign that said for whites only? No, there wasn't one. Bayou Cymbaline was a peculiarity in the South, never adhering to Jim Crow laws.

"I'll need to see some identification," Adelaide said.

"I'm sorry? Identification? What kind do you need, and why?"

"I'll need to see a valid driver's license or a social security card, either one—or a birth certificate, that'll work too."

"But I don't drive and I don't have those other things with me."

Three minutes to five.

Adelaide turned Trinidad's letter around to look at the addressee. "Who's Mrs. Virgil B. Horton?" she asked.

"She was my employer back in Pascagoula," Trinidad responded.

"What is it you're sending her?"

"I don't believe that is any of your business, Mrs. Roman."

Adelaide Roman's lips pressed into a thin line. She took a breath and hissed, "One of us here works for the United States Post Office and knows the rules. I think it's me. What do you think? Now I'm gonna ask you one more time. What are you sending to this Mrs. Virgil B. Horton?"

Trinidad did not answer.

"Must be something you think you gotta hide."

And then when the clock struck five Trinidad experienced the Knowing. She picked up her letter; there was no urgency to mailing it. Next week would be just fine. She stepped away from the counter, turned, and made her way to the door.

"You wash your hands real good when you touch my family's food," Adelaide hollered after her. "And don't be drinking from their cups or putting their forks in your mouth. You hear me?"

Trinidad heard most clearly.

At 5:02 Adelaide stuffed a letter into her pocket. She felt more strongly than ever that it was her duty to monitor the mail and intercept anything she felt was suspicious. She could do no less for the Lord her God or for Harley John. She had never forgotten Pastor Eacomb's sermon in which he'd preached to his flock that the downright possessed moved among them. Why, she could even remember his exact words: "You must find those who are flawed and bring God's perfection to them."

She snapped closed her purse, turned off the light, and locked the post office door. She could hardly stand having to wait for the Meeting of the Righteous, but she had to get through one more night. Adelaide had plans for passing the evening.

Once home, she threw the deadbolt and lowered the shades. Then she took out that letter she had stuffed in her pocket; it was addressed to a man in Port Arthur, Texas. She didn't open the letter right away; she just ran her fingers over it and occasionally touched a corner of it to her lips, as if engaging in an odd kind of foreplay. She didn't want the titillation to be over too soon, so she put the envelope down and forced her thoughts over to Mr. Donald Tipton, the pharmacist at Charbonneau's Drug Store.

Adelaide had been monitoring his mail, and she thought she was onto something: Mr. Tipton had been receiving parcels at his P.O. Box; one such parcel had arrived that day. Adelaide sat musing for a while and then struck up a one-sided conversation with the African violet that sat on a plastic doily in the middle of her dinette table.

"Miss Vi," she began. "It certainly was a day at the Bayou Cymbaline Post Office, let me tell you. Mercy sakes alive I would venture to say that I believe there has never been one like it. No, sir, I truly do not. For one thing, that nigger woman who works for Mrs. Rich Bitch Letice Arrow had the gall to come into the post office and step right up to my window; then she sets a letter down and acts like I should drop everything and get her a stamp just like she was white. That's nerve, Miss Vi. That is some uppity nerve. I showed her, though. I run out the clock and there wasn't a blue-bellied thing she could do about it. You can just bet I showed her.

"But that's enough about Miss High and Mighty Field Hand. Just what do you suppose it could be that comes through the United States mail every now and again addressed to Mr. Donald Tipton?"

She paused then, letting suspense tingle up her arms.

"What could it possibly be that arrives in a brown paper wrapper? If I had to guess, I'd say it had to be a book, which doesn't seem like much, but a body has to wonder why anyone has to order a book through the United States mail when there's a public library over on Cavalier Street that is busting at the seams. But here's the real thing I got to wonder about, Miss Vi: this parcel for Mr. Donald Tipton that arrived today come exactly thirty days after the first one. I know it's been thirty days cuz that first one come the day after Miss Slattery died from whatever was eating up her insides.

"I have to ask myself if maybe there's something illegal

going on, something Mr. Donald Tipton doesn't want anybody to know about. He's an odd bird, you know. Never been married, no relatives hereabout. I think I better keep an eye on Mr. Donald Tipton is what I think.

"I know that it's suppertime and we should be enjoying some cold chicken and three-bean salad and lemonade and strawberry pie, but there's something else happened today that we should talk about, Miss Vi, something else that has to do with said Mr. Donald Tipton. See, this strange man comes sauntering through the door about noon. I remember it was noon because my stomach was yowling louder than the church bells over to that heathen Catholic Church. Anyway, here comes this man, all fancied up with shiny hair combed back like William Powell. You know, Mr. Powell from the movies? And bold as you please, this fellow with the pomaded hair swaggers right up to my window and asks me, do I know where he might find Charbonneau's Drug Store. Now, what do you make of that, Miss Vi? I'll tell you what I make of it. I think our pharmacist, Mr. Donald Tipton, is one of those homosexuals. And I think he's got himself in some homo book club and this man with the hair pomade is a homo, too, and they've managed to make a connection. Well, we'll just see, won't we, Miss Vi? We'll just see."

But Donald Tipton wasn't the only subject of Adelaide Roman's scrutiny. She had been following the correspondence that was going on between that snippy Vida van Demming, who thought she was better than anybody else, and her pen pal from Port Arthur, Texas, a Mr. Harold Hopkins. Vida's letters had been coming and going every week for quite some time. Adelaide found them boring at first, kind of flat, just a lot of stuff about the weather, weekend plans, and bits and pieces of local news. But lately the man's letters had a taken on a distinctly romantic tone: "What color are your eyes?" he'd asked, and "Do you think you could send a picture of yourself? You must be lovely." After that, Adelaide started to keep an eye peeled for Vida, who always came into the post office to drop her letters to Port Arthur in the outgoing slot. More often than not, they hardly made it to the pile before Adelaide snatched them up.

Adelaide had got around to that letter she'd stuffed in her pocket. "Now what I got here, Miss Vi, is a piece of correspondence," and she carefully opened the purloined letter. "Oh, Lordy, Vi, this is what you might say is something of a serious nature," and she kept licking her lips as she read. "Just listen to what Vida van Demming writes to her Romeo over in Port Arthur. You're not going to believe this, Miss Vi." She read the letter aloud:

> Dear Harold,
>
> You say that you are starting to have feelings for me, and I think it's time you know that I am starting to have feelings for you too, but before things get even more serious, I have a confession to make. Before we started our correspondence, my life felt empty all the time, like there was nothing to look forward to and every day was just like the one before. I always thought that if I could forgo Bayou Cymbaline for some place more exciting, I would be a happy person. But I couldn't leave. I was afraid to. Then one day I went into Claymore's Gift & Candy Emporium and I stuck a pack of Necco Wafers up my sleeve and left the store. I am ashamed to say it now, but it was the most exciting thing I had ever done. I went back to the store later and returned them, but the truth is that I continued stealing and returning things. I only just stopped when I found you. I hope you can understand that I know what I did was wrong and that I am sorry

from the bottom of my heart. I also hope with all my heart that your feelings for me have not changed, but if they have, I would understand.

    Yours always,

    Vida

"Well, well, well, Miss Vi, now what do you suppose we should do about this? I'll tell you what I think: I think that, first of all, this letter definitely needs to reach Mr. Harold Hopkins in Port Arthur, Texas. And second of all, I think there's quite a few folks right here in Bayou Cymbaline who would be interested to know about this."

She folded the letter back up, resealed the envelope with Elmer's glue, and stuck it in her purse. "I got to get going now, Miss Vi; I got to take a bath and lay out my clothes for tomorrow. It's gonna be a special Meeting of the Righteous, and I got plans."

CAN I GET A WITNESS?
JULY 20, 1957

THE next morning, Adelaide headed over to Dancy's shop for her usual wash and set. It happened to be one of those every-other-Saturdays that she took Bonaventure out to lunch.

"Hey, Dancy, I been thinking about doing something special for Bonaventure," she said.

"Oh, yeah, like what?"

"*Gunfight at the O.K. Corral* is playing over to the Palace Theater, and I thought I'd take him for lunch at Bixie's and then to a matinee."

"Well, you'll just have to take him another time. He's supposed to clean his room and weed the flowerbeds after you bring him back from lunch."

"Oh, now, don't be that way, Dancy. I heard this is the last day that picture is showing and then it'll be gone."

Dancy knew that Bonaventure wanted to see the movie about Wyatt Earp and Doc Holliday, but she didn't want to be the one to take him because she had no desire to see anyone get shot, even if they were only actors.

"I guess his chores can wait. Okay. I'll allow it. But I don't want you taking him anywhere near that church meeting of yours; you bring him straight home after the movie."

"You don't need to worry, Dancy. You've made it perfectly clear that you want to raise your child a pagan. I'm not going to the afternoon meeting, anyway; I'm going to the seven o'clock."

When Bonaventure got back, Dancy said, "Get yourself cleaned up, Venture Forth Arrow. Grandma Roman talked me into something."

Bonaventure couldn't figure out what was up with Grandma Roman. She'd rushed him through lunch and now she was gripping the steering wheel until her knuckles turned white, and she had her eyes squinted and her mouth puckered. She blew right through the Stop sign on Dooley Avenue because she was driving like she was in a super big race. He thought it was kind of fun until she drove them past the movie theater, which was where he'd hoped they were headed, and then she kept right on racing.

Tug on her arm, —Slow down, Grandma!

"Oh, hush up your hands, Bonaventure Arrow. I know exactly how fast we need to go. I want seats close to the stage, and I'm gonna make sure we get them."

She stopped the car in a field that had been commandeered as a parking lot and told him to hurry it up.

In his wildest dreams, Bonaventure Arrow would not have imagined that his mother had given permission for him to attend the two p.m. Meeting of the Righteous, but it looked as if that was exactly what happened. That must be why she had used the words "talked me into something."

Anticipation filled the air that surrounded the meeting. Grandma Roman said she'd heard there were folks coming from as far away as Little Rock! At 1:30, one of the church elders mounted the stage and beseeched the crowd for quiet. Noise rippled away only to explode again upon the introduction of Brother Harley John. The preacher clutched his Bible

and raised his fist in the air and hollered about sin and salvation until he'd worked himself up to speaking in tongues,
which was the whole entire point of the International Church
of the Elevated Forthright Gospel. It was the speaking in
tongues part of things that Adelaide Roman had pinned her
hopes on, praying with all her might that her only grandchild
might speak. She'd been waiting for years to bring glory to her
blue-eyed lover, and this was the day it would happen.

In short order, Brother Eacomb made a crippled woman
walk, made a blind man see, and brought stillness to a young
girl who suffered from palsy. Adelaide figured they must've
all been some of those Little Rock people, because she
couldn't remember ever seeing any of them before.

The sound of the preacher's voice had become like knife
cuts in Bonaventure's ears, which is why he muffled all sounds
of the meeting and was not listening when the announcement was made at three that one among the crowd would be
allowed to mount the stage and receive the gift of speaking in
tongues. But Grandma Roman heard it, and she grabbed his
arm and rushed the stage, agile as a deer. Before the congre-
gation had a chance to choose anybody else, she had hauled
Bonaventure up the steps to stand before Brother Eacomb.

"Brother Eacomb, I am begging you to call on God to
heal this boy. He cannot speak because the devil's got his
tongue, Brother Eacomb! The devil's got his tongue!" Adelaide was gasping for breath.

The atmosphere became thick, more like water than
air. Lightning flashed all around, casting white shadows and
turning the world ghostly for an instant. For miles around,
birds and bugs fled to their hiding places deep in the pine
woods, chickens huddled in the corners of coops, and barn
cats were nowhere to be seen; or so it was later said, when
the event had turned to legend.

Harley John Eacomb did not appreciate the spontane-
ity of Adelaide Roman's actions, but did the only thing he
could: he took the boy by the shoulders and commanded
him to kneel. Bonaventure would not do it. Brother Eacomb
commanded him a second time and still the boy remained
standing. When Bonaventure refused a third time, Brother
Eacomb pressed down hard on the boy's shoulders, forcing
him to his knees. Grandma Roman stood behind him, a
hand on each shoulder lest he try to get up.

With fire in his eyes and ice in his soul, the preacher
raised his arms to heaven and began to shout:

"Lord, remove the devil from the sinful soul here before
me! Do I hear Amen?"

AMEN!

"Lord, bring about the gift of tongues! Do I hear Amen?"

AMEN

"I feel the Lord coming down, brothers and sisters! The
Lord is among us! Can I get a witness?

AMEN! AMEN!

"I feel the Lord! I feel the Lord! O brothers and sisters, I
feel the Lord! Can I get a witness? I feel the Lord!"

AMEN! AMEN! YES, BROTHER! AMEN!

The preacher himself began speaking in tongues and
swaying side to side. Adelaide let loose of Bonaventure and
joined him, and eventually she and the preacher collapsed.

Bonaventure got up from his knees and stood completely still.

Silence covered the crowd like a blanket. Adelaide
Roman got to her feet and spread them wide. Eyes bright
with fevered zeal, chin shiny with drool, she lifted her arms
to heaven, threw back her head, opened her mouth, and
spoke in more languages than Harley John Eacomb could
ever have imagined. The woman had been prayed into

nonsense, cleansed of iniquity, and gifted with tongues.

Harley John Eacomb proclaimed to the multitude that his was not to question the Lord.

A ways off from the crowd, where the riverbank met the forest, Trinidad Prefontaine stood all by herself, hidden by the loblolly pines. Unlike the crowd of the Forthright, she was completely composed.

Dancy was in the kitchen trying to scare up some dinner out of leftovers, since Trinidad had put in the unusual request to be given the afternoon off. "Come on in here and tell me all about the movie," she shouted when she heard the front door open.

Bonaventure and Grandma Roman made it to the kitchen by then; however, Dancy had her back to them because she was staring into the refrigerator sizing up her options.

"Did you get the seats you wanted? Did you see anybody we know? Did you get a root beer or a cherry Coke?"

No answers.

"What's the matter? Cat got your . . . ," but she didn't finish the question because she'd turned around by then and gotten a good look at her mother.

"Mama, what is wrong with you?" she asked. "Did you get sick at the movie? You didn't eat too much popcorn, did you? You sure don't look right."

To which Adelaide burbled out blithering nonsense.

"That's enough now, Mama. Come on, stop fooling."

To which there was only more burbling.

Dancy became alarmed. "Bonaventure, what in the heck is going on? What is wrong with your Grandma Roman?"

To which he replied, —She got healed.

LADIES' CHOICE

WILLIAM stood barefoot on the wave-wet sand, looking out at the horizon in Almost Heaven and at the narrow strip of land that seemed closer than it used to be. A generous sun touched his face and scattered gleaming bits of itself over the neap tide that signaled a third-quarter moon.

William knew what he had to do.

In her house on the Neff Switch road, a breeze came up inside Trinidad's chest and swelled her turned-around heart. She felt herself rise right up off the floor and she knew a weightless joy.

William Arrow had told her goodbye.

Then William went to his mother's chapel and waited for her there. Letice came through the door and immediately sensed him there, as she had sensed him so many times in so many rooms in the years since he'd been killed. Letice looked all around, hoping to find some proof of his presence. She waited, still and quiet, but no apparition came. Five minutes passed, then ten, then fifteen, and Letice conceded that it must have been her imagination. That is when she heard William's voice tell her that he loved her, and when she sensed he was already gone.

William left the house on Christopher Street to stand in the back room of Dancy's shop, where she was busy putting away an order of beauty supplies she'd received the week before. He looked at her breasts when she bent to take bottles from the box, and he let his gaze linger on the shapeliness of her legs before moving to trace her face in profile from her forehead to her neck. He noticed that she'd changed her hair-style since the week before. She usually wore her hair up, but now it hung below her shoulders, the way he'd always pre-ferred. Even though he'd watched Dancy nearly every day since his death all those years ago and had even touched her lightly, this time he planned to actually hold her.

He concentrated and put a thought inside her head. She walked over to the radio as if responding to an invitation to pick the song for the ladies' choice dance. She began to turn the dial, stopping at the sound of Karen Chandler singing "Hold Me, Thrill Me, Kiss Me" and recognizing the feeling of walking into water until it gets chest deep and takes your breath away. She closed her eyes as she listened to the music, and then she was in his arms. For the length of a song, Dancy let herself believe that William had never died.

Caught in the embrace of what might have been, she rested her head against his shoulder, and her right hand lay in his left. She could feel the warmth of him and each beat of his heart. She felt his five o'clock shadow brush against her forehead. She could even feel the tremor of unmistakable passion in every one of his breaths.

So many of the days and nights they'd had together went through her head: She took that first order for chicken etouffée, and they walked hand-in-hand through the loblolly pines. He talked to her about second gear, and she showed him how to whistle real loud through his teeth. They rode the St. Charles streetcar. They drank a glass of fine red wine. They made real love for the first time. They stood, all dressed up, before the justice of the peace upstairs at the courthouse on Lafayette Street.

William felt her delicate ribs when he pulled her close, and the softness of her made him tremble and gasp; then he got caught up in reminiscence, too. As snapshots of memory passed before him, they dissolved into mist and soaked him with want: He got one more look at the tip of her tongue as she touched it to her pencil. Once again, her cheekbone transfixed him, her jaw threw him down, and her ear lobe ran off with his heart. He held her on his lap and let her steer his car across a parking lot. He breathed in the scent of her, just as he used to when he came home from work and she met him at the door. He could see her in his bathrobe, tousle-haired, barefoot, and fresh from sleep. He watched a pregnant Dancy smother corn-bread in molasses, lick the spoon when she finished eating it, and then give him a lop-sided grin. They painted the nurs-ery yellow and drank lemonade on the porch swing on a hot August night. They watched their unborn baby push against Dancy's stomach, and they sang to him about shoo-fly pie.

The song faded away, and William went with it, never to return.

The third challenge had been met.

Dancy looked around at where she was and cried a flood of pent-up grief. They were tears she'd kept locked deep inside her as a way of keeping William alive. And now, in the after-math of the sweet, slow dance and the absence of gentle haunting, she began to let the tears flow.

That night she dreamed she walked barefoot along

a shore, the wet sand warm beneath her feet. Her legs felt good and strong, and she could leap great leaps if she chose to. The sun was a bright lemon yellow in the sky, the water a deep blue-green. The tide was coming in, and she could feel the pull of the waves as they caused her to sway where she stood. She had a hat but let it be carried off by the wind, as if letting go of her cares.

Dancy walked along the shore of her dream, basking in the wind, the water, and the sun. Sometimes she danced a made-up dance, running in circles with her arms out wide. She ran out to meet the tide and danced away as it reached her. She kept running and laughing, and then the tide grew stronger. She was engulfed by the waves and felt the water wash into her body, where it grew warm inside her, making her feel an elation she loved. She was weightless as the waves carried her out and back, out and back, and then returned her to the shore and laid her down on the sand.

Dancy felt a pleasant, sleepy weakness. She wished never to leave the reach of the ocean because she wanted to know those feelings again.

PART III

Evensong
Summer 1957

THINGS began to change in Bayou Cymbaline. Much as a wild plant changes to a cure, or a stone changes from a buried thing to a found thing; much as hate, guilt, sorrow, and vengeance become vessels of forgiveness. That is how the change happened, incrementally and from within.

Mr. Silvey excused himself from his sister's supper table in her house in Baton Rouge; a bit of indigestion, he said. He went to his room, and who should be there but Mrs. Silvey, sitting on his bed just as he remembered her. His heart gave a fluttering movement then, and his lungs filled with merry exaltation.

"Forrest," she said, "do you know how I've missed you?"

His brother-in-law found him later that night, keeled over on the bed with no pulse and no breathing, his arms opened wide in a joyful embrace.

Vida van Demming's confession had indeed reached Mr. Harold Hopkins in Port Arthur, Texas, who washed his hands and straightened his tie before opening her letter. He read it once and read it again and then promptly put it in the sink, where he set it afire and watched it burn to ash before turning on the water and letting the blackened remains of a painful admission run down his kitchen drain.

Vida answered her doorbell on a Sunday afternoon to find him standing before her wearing his very best suit, a boutonniere in his lapel, and some brand-new wingtip shoes. He made the trip from Port Arthur every weekend after that. Sometimes they looked for a roller coaster to ride, and sometimes they read the paper together over coffee and buttered toast.

Adelaide Roman learned the hard way that God cannot be manipulated. After that last Meeting of the Righteous and for the rest of her natural life she could speak in nothing but tongues, not one of which could be understood by another living soul. She couldn't even write in anything but gibberish after that day, and she'd lost the ability to read in any language whatsoever. Never again would she make fun of people who were different. Never again would she gossip. Never again would she refuse to serve a black woman who wanted nothing more than to purchase a stamp. She had, as Bonaventure said, been healed.

Adelaide was put out to pasture by the United States Post Office. They were sorry, they said, but a postal worker needed to be able to read. You understand, don't you, Mrs. Roman? At which she seethed. It wasn't that Adelaide needed the money; it was the loss of the power to bring down ruin. That's what she would miss.

One week into her gibberish life, she sought a private audience with Brother Harley John. It wasn't the first time, or even the three hundredth, that she was wearing black satin lingerie beneath her churchgoing clothes. Brother Eacomb looked at her as if she were scum from the throat of the devil.

"Get thee behind me, Satan!" was all he said before pushing her out the door.

The Forthright Gospelers shunned her altogether upon the recommendation of Reverend Eacomb. (It would not do to have her ask for healing in front of a crowd of believers.)

Adelaide consulted with specialists: neurologists, and ear, nose, and throat doctors; she even went to see a hypnotist. None of them did any good. The neurologist suggested she see a psychiatrist, but Adelaide refused. Bonaventure suggested she learn to sign. Adelaide refused that too.

Between Dancy, Letice, and Trinidad, someone checked on her every day. The only one she let through the door was Dancy. Adelaide would open the door to Letice but immediately wave her away, and she would not even answer the door to Trinidad, and so missed another chance at redemption week after week after week.

Adelaide didn't have much to do. She took to rummaging through the house and found a pair of binoculars Theo had kept in a drawer. She used them to spy on her neighbors, but couldn't even tell her African violet about the private things she saw. The frustration took over everything, and Adelaide became bitterly angry. After several months of self-imposed isolation she was found by Dancy, slumped over at the kitchen table, dead of a heart attack, just like Theo.

Trinidad Prefontaine kept that smooth and speckled stone on the altar in her front room.

When the light from the stone had gone that day, she'd put the prism relic of baby's blood and the note that had been written by Dancy into her apron pocket. The next morning she took them back to Christopher Street and placed them both inside the box that Bonaventure had returned to that niche in the chapel wall. She stayed in the chapel for a moment more and said a prayer of deep thanksgiving.

After that day, Trinidad began to look back at her past in

search of her personal prophets. There was good Sister Sulpice, who'd given her the Canticle of Brother Sun and Sister
Moon with which to bless endeavors; and of course there
was Trinidad's first prophet, Mam Judith, with her silks and
her tea kettle, who'd spoken in that snake-hissy whisper of
Purpose and of Knowing.

Those look-backs became a regular habit and always
brought new Knowing. For instance, it came to Trinidad
that her mother had been raped and left with a child she had
not known how to love. She knew that Calypso had been
hurt beyond repair and didn't know how to fix herself, and
Trinidad forgave. She withdrew enough money from her
savings to purchase a stone for her mother's grave. The arti-
san had done as she requested, engraving Calypso's name as
Mrs. Fontenaise, which happened to incorporate that bit of
punctuation that kept it from being a superstitious thirteen
characters long. In addition to marking the grave, the monu-
ment bestowed the respectable title the living Calypso had
never attained. Trinidad also placed a small bunch of chick-
weed on her mother's grave, in order that Calypso might
soothe that bite of a poisonous thing and walk without soreness to the Promised Land.

Now, one might suppose that the itching would return
and cause Trinidad to move on. It did not. Though she
remained in the employ of the Arrow family, she continued
to live in her house on the Neff Switch road, harvesting simples and turning them into cures. It was, she felt, her permanent Purpose.

Romantic love came into Trinidad's life, taking her by
surprise. Her Knowing had not foretold that love, for it had
come from inside a mystery.

Personnel records at the Rouge provided Detective Tate
with the names and last known addresses of four possibili-

ties. They all had lived in Melvindale. Pairing information gathered from the Department of Veterans Affairs with his belief that the John Doe had been an army man allowed Tate to eliminate two of the possibilities because they had been in the navy and so would have carried a different uniform button. The remaining two were army guys, and the similarities between them were striking. Both had volunteered to serve; both had been born in the New Orleans area; neither had listed any living relatives when they joined the military.

The first possibility was George Heckert, who'd lived on Maple Street in Melvindale. Tate went around to the address on record and introduced himself to the owners of the house as a private investigator who'd been hired to resolve a family situation. He promised compensation for a moment of their time. When he showed them the police photo of the John Doe, they said it was not George Heckert. They knew him well and had kept in touch after all these years; in fact, they'd had a letter from him just the other day. He'd moved to Louisville, Kentucky, a year or so ago, which meant he was not incarcerated in the asylum for the criminally insane. What Tate didn't find out was that George Heckert had been the maker of the wagon with the plow blade handle, the one who couldn't get a loan to save his family's farm.

Tate went to the remaining address, a rooming house on Taylor, stated his name and his purpose, and made the offer of compensation. The owner took one look at the photograph and said he remembered the guy all right; he'd stiffed him on the rent, just took off without notice. The man consulted an old green ledger and matched a name to the photo. It was that of the last possibility. The Wanderer had been identified.

"It was strange," the man said. "He'd never been any

trouble, kept to himself. You know the type. A lot of those war wounded were like that."

"Do you recall when he made his sudden departure?" Tate asked.

"It was winter. Let me see now—it would have been between Thanksgiving and Christmas. I think it was in 1949. Yeah, it was definitely in 1949. I remember all the talk at the time of hitting the half-century mark on New Year's. And I remember all the trouble I had finding another tenant so close to the holidays. He had the basement apartment; it's a tough one to rent out. Most people don't like living in a Michigan basement. Too dark, they say, and too cold."

Tate paid the man and tipped his hat. Upon returning home, he checked the name against bank records in Bayou Cymbaline. It was easy to establish a connection to the Molyneaux family. He reported his findings to the police, who undertook formal confirmation.

Finally, Tate set down his summation. When it was finished, he removed his glasses, closed his eyes, and pinched the bridge of his nose. It was what he always did at the end. He thought back through every step of the investigation and all he had done to bear out his conclusion.

"It's all there, Mrs. Arrow," the detective said as he handed Letice the envelope. "Would you like me to tell you or would you prefer to open it in private?"

"In private, Mr. Tate," she said, and then handed him final payment. When Coleman Tate had gone, Letice took the envelope into her chapel and stood still before the crucifix. The words fell all around her then like a kind and curing rain: *Father, forgive them; they know not what they do.* Right there and right then, Letice Arrow knew in absolute clarity that forgiveness is unconditional; it is complete in and of itself and always rises above the facts.

She went to the kitchen and put the kettle on. Then she sat down at the table, the envelope before her, and took a sip of tea. She had waited so long to finally know the man's name, and now it did not matter. The envelope remained sealed that day and the next. But on the third day, Letice decided to open it.

She went into her library and slit the envelope in one swift motion and then pulled the paper out slowly. It was folded, and for a second or two she considered leaving it that way.

Her hands shook, and she'd suddenly gone cold.

There were just a few lines on that single sheet of paper. The case was no longer in progress but closed.

FINAL REPORT
IN THE MATTER OF WILLIAM EVEREST ARROW
(DECEASED)

The man who murdered your son has been identified as one Tristan Duvais. Confirmation has been ascertained by legal authority. Details provided upon request.

Letice bent over double, her body wracked with pain. When the sobbing was through, she inhaled the present and exhaled the past. For the first time in forever she slept through the night and woke up knowing that Saint Bonaventure had been right. The mind can take in many things, but it cannot take in God.

Letice still owned the Molyneaux family home—she'd never been able to bring herself to put it up for sale. Once or twice a year she met with the caretaker to discuss maintenance issues of one sort or another, but that was the extent of her dealings. And then she got into the habit of driving out there on Sunday mornings after mass. She never did more than pull into the driveway before turning the car around and heading back home, but one day for reasons she couldn't quite make out, she left the car and went to stand in the stables where she collected what remained of the long, long ago.

With every succeeding pilgrimage, she grew closer to personal peace.

She forgave her mother.

She forgave Tristan.

She resolved that God still loved her.

On what Letice calculated would have been her first baby's birthday, she went to her chapel and removed the carved wooden box that held the relic, not knowing that it now held Dancy's note to William too. Letice did not open the box but took it out to the Molyneaux home and buried it beneath the elm tree, near about the grave of the fragile little sparrow. When her task was done, she recited from Ecclesiastes: *There is a season for everything, a time for every occupation under heaven: A time for giving birth, a time for dying.* Then she went on to her next destination.

"Someone to see you," the asylum guard said.

Tristan sat down to face his visitor, a flicker of memory passing over his ruined face, but only for an instant. Letice reached across the table and gently took his hand, telling him she was sorry. She visited him every week after that. They sat in the garden and watched the birds and finally were at peace. The visits ended when Letice Arrow died at the age of seventy-eight.

The Wanderer remained in the asylum the rest of his natural life. The memory of what he'd done left him for good. He wasn't in pain and he no longer cried. Each time Eugenia Babbitt visited him, he would press her hand to his chest by way of saying goodbye.

On a day when Letice and Bonaventure were out, Dancy Arrow sent Trinidad to the store because she wanted to be alone. She entered her bedroom closet and took down the box that held William's ruined clothes and the note. She did not know that the original note was missing—she opened the lid only enough to slip this new note in:

Dear William,
  I wish it never happened. I will always remember
our happiness. You will ever be in my heart. Rest well.
  Love,
  Dancy

Dancy removed the box from the closet and placed it on her bed. She took a bath and did her hair and took great pains with her makeup. After putting on a cotton summer dress in two shades of yellow, she slipped her feet into new espadrilles and dabbed drops of perfume behind each ear and at the pulse points on her wrists. She checked her appearance in the full-length mirror, inhaled deeply, and then blew the breath out as slowly as she could. She picked up the box and held it against her body, close to where her breath had grown thin as a wedding veil.

Dancy walked down the staircase with grace and with trembling. Her feet barely made a sound. She stopped in the kitchen and soaked a dish towel with cold water and held it to her neck to avoid becoming faint. She gave herself a moment more and then continued on.

When the darkness of the garage cooled her heat-covered skin, Dancy fell into a clammy cold sweat. But it had nothing to do with the sun or the shade. The car keys rattled in her shaking hands and her left foot missed the clutch. She was powerless even to start the car. Panic shot from her gut to her throat and exploded out her mouth. Her breathing turned into great gulps of mourning. Her whole body shook with the dread that she felt until she was finally too weak to shake more. She placed her hands on the steering wheel and laid her head against it. When her agony was spent, Dancy looked in the rearview mirror and reached for her purse. Then she took out her compact, powdered her face, and applied a touch of pink lipstick.

She clenched her jaw, turned the key in the ignition, depressed the clutch with a sure foot this time, and backed out onto Christopher Street. Dancy went to the caretaker's office at Père Anastase and asked the sexton to please open the Arrow family crypt. The man asked if she'd like him to wait outside, and Dancy said, "Thank you, but no."

She stood for a moment in the tomb's deep-bronze quiet before placing the cloth-covered box on the floor and giving her husband his shroud.

And that was the thing that allowed Dancy Arrow to let go of hatred and guilt. She no longer wanted to bring vengeance down upon a man who couldn't tell right from wrong; she understood that nothing would bring her husband back, not even loving him as if he were alive.

William had met his three challenges, and though he'd gained access to Real Heaven, he couldn't make himself go without one last goodbye.

Bonaventure heard that familiar sound of the air zipping open its pocket and letting his father's voice in.

—Hey, Dad!

"Hey, Bonaventure. What's happening with you?"

—I got a new *Captain America* comic. Oh! And I made a friend in school!

"You did?"

—Yeah. His name is William too, just like you, but everyone calls him Billy. He got polio when he was two, so he wears a brace on one of his legs and he needs crutches to walk, but he's a really good swimmer.

"He sounds like an interesting guy."

—He is. He's my best friend.

"I'm glad. Everybody needs a best friend."

—Did you have a best friend when you were a kid?"

"I did. His name was Clark."

—Clark? That was Superman's real name.

"I know. This kid's last name wasn't Kent, though. It was Andrews. He wasn't exactly Superman, but he sure was a terrific pitcher. We played on the Blue Gators together."

They were quiet for a while, and then William said, "It's time for me to go to Real Heaven."

And Bonaventure said, —I know. I can hear Almost Heaven moving away from you, but I don't want you to go.

"I have to, son, but we'll meet again. I promise."

—Do you have to go so I can get a voice? I don't want a voice. I want you to stay.

"No, I have to go because it's right. You've always had a voice, Bonaventure. It just doesn't come from your throat. Maybe someday."

Bonaventure hung his head and said, —Yeah, maybe someday.

William summoned all his strength then and spoke: "Hey, Bonaventure, look up."

Bonaventure was the only one in the family who had never seen William, and now when he raised his head, his father stood fully visible before him. William grabbed his son in a desperate deep hug and held him for a very long time. Then he kissed him goodbye and faded.

Bonaventure listened as hard as he could, but all sound of his father was gone.

William went to the shore in Almost Heaven, where he stared at that strip of land in the distance. He felt his mother's prayers spill over his feet, soothing him where he stood. He remembered the warmth and the feel of Dancy as he'd held her close and they'd moved to a song. He thought of Bonaventure's small arms around his waist, and then he began to walk.

He met up with the tide some twenty yards out, its waves so sublime he could only surrender. The waters washed over him, body and soul, cleansing him of every earthly desire. He rode on the breakers high up and away, and then on the crest of the highest great wave, William Arrow crossed over to the opposite shore, while his saltwater tears fell home to the sea in a weeping Alleluia.

The mournful sounds that had lived in Dancy's closet and Grand-mère's chapel were gone, replaced by grateful prayer. But votive candles still burned bright in red glass, and a carved Virgin Mary still looked out upon a garden that was filled with periwinkle and angels made of stone.

The wagon handle stayed warm even after William had gone. Through the years its steadfast solidity would provide Bonaventure with a sense of his father during times of indecision.

Bonaventure would come to know that life is not always made of beautiful sounds, that too many sounds make cacophony, and that every voice matters.

He would come to understand that there's a difference between the will of God and the will of man, that the acts of one person affect the lives of others, and that God reaches out when it all goes wrong.

He would come to accept that he was different, but different in a good way and for mystical reasons.

He would marry a girl he fell in love with in college—someone with a special gift of her own.

He would hear the sound of his own voice.

But before all those future things happened, while still in that summer of 1957, Bonaventure Arrow conducted a symphony as the sunset softened that place in the sky where a newborn dusk meets an elderly day. He did not plan that symphony; it happened on its own.

He'd pulled his memento box from beneath his bed to sort through the souvenirs of his favorite sounds. As he handled each precious reminder, he thought of its time and its place and its cause and tried to relive the moments from which they'd come, moments that had offered a glimpse of God's intentions. The sounds came first as a quiet sonata that grew into a composition of glorious proportion.

The symphony reached Dancy where she was walking with Gabe near Saint Anthony's Garden some fourteen miles away. And in that masterpiece of memories Dancy Arrow heard the voice of Love, singing to her of the living. She turned to look at Gabe Riley then, and she was overcome.

The music interrupted mockingbirds and cardinals and half-hour church bells. It was at times orchestral and at times a cappella, a mighty love song made of lullaby, angel chant, opera, and hymn. There were the tap water and scissor sounds of wished-for beauty; the gumball rattle of giant kindness; the crinkly-page sounds meant for Creathie

LaRue; the joyful, last-sip gurgle from Bixie's Luncheonette; the moist-earth sounds of healing; the echo of wind in trees; the pinging of broken sunlight; and the courageous buzzing of a bluebottle fly all mixed together in a wonderful, powerful, magical gris-gris.

ACKNOWLEDGMENTS

THIS book would never have been written were it not for my husband, Paul. He encouraged me to go back to school, he was patient with my endless anxieties, and he believed in me every step of the way. This book took nearly three years to write and develop; it dominated my life and conversation, yet Paul's love and support never wavered and his interest never flagged, not even a little bit. But, more important, Paul taught me about forgiveness, and constantly reminded me of the power of faith. He is ever my strength and my solace, and not only that, he makes me laugh. I have no words to express my love and gratitude.

And how do I thank my editor, the talented, funny, and darling Maya Ziv? Her editing savvy, sharp eye, and even sharper instincts well and truly brought out the best in my work. She helped me develop my manuscript in every imaginable way. Maya is dedicated and tireless. I admire her as a professional and cherish her as a friend. I'm also grateful to the staff at HarperCollins, including: Jonathan Burnham, Cal Morgan, Erica Barmash, Amy Baker, Martin Wilson, Rachel Levenberg, Kate McCune, Lillie Walsh, Samantha

Hagerbaumer, Diane Jackson, Cathy Schornstein, Mary Beth Thomas, Eric Svenson, and Kathryn Walker.

I owe a mountain of thanks to my literary agents, Wendy Sherman and Kim Perel. Wendy has been my champion from the beginning—uncommonly generous with her expertise, enthusiasm, and care. Kim put her trust in a manuscript that was too short by half. But she saw something in my writing and took me by the hand. We workshopped the manuscript together until it became so much more. Kim's encouragement helped me through those times when I felt overwhelmed. What an angel she is.

I would also like to thank the wise and delightful Jane Rosenman for helping me focus on theme, mood, and character development, specifically that of Trinidad Prefontaine.

I would be seriously remiss if I failed to acknowledge the excellent teachers who helped me hone my craft: first and foremost, Professor John Kimsey, my mentor at DePaul University's School for New Learning. John devoted endless time and attention in order that I might realize my ambition. He directed me to the likes of James Joyce and Flannery O'Connor, and I can never thank him enough. Contrary to Miss O'Connor's famous proclamation, in this case a good man was not hard to find.

Bonaventure Arrow began as a short assignment in Dan Stolar's graduate fiction-writing class at DePaul. A talented author himself, Dr. Stolar enthusiastically encouraged me to continue developing my magical realist story. Craig Sirles, professor and linguist *par excellence*, introduced me to the concept of *le mot juste* and helped me develop my own voice and style. As I struggled with working full time, going to school, and trying to progress as a novelist, I was fortunate enough to be part of Kristine Miller's Advanced Writers'

Workshop at the College of DuPage. Her instruction spurred me on at a critical point.

And now I wish to thank those near and dear, most especially my sons, Neil and Tom Gorman, for the joy and pride they inspire and express in me. I will love them eternally. My spunky mother, Ella Iris, is a constant inspiration. She and the rest of my family have always let me know how proud they are of me, and honestly, sometimes it moves me to tears. My love and thanks to Mike and Cindy Iris, Bruce and Mary Raith, Celia Amerson, and Mark and Jamie Wojcik. I also wish to thank my first readers for their helpful comments and nonstop encouragement: Alisa Waldman, dear friend and fellow writer who read this book more than anyone; Karin Vojtech; Carol Boyke; Carol Grudzinski; Amy Boschae; Amelia Orozco; and Mike and Tracey Leganski (Tracey helped me see how the story should begin). Last but not least, I really must thank Maisie and Harry for lifting my spirits ever so high.

I am indebted to the following people for the professional expertise and kindness they extended to me during my research: Mr. Charlie Farrae, historian at the Hotel Monteleone, for bringing the New Orleans of the forties and fifties to life, most especially the French Quarter; Cher Miller, manager of the New Orleans Visitor Center and wellspring of information, for steering me down every right path; Anita Kazmierczak-Hoffman, library cataloguer at the Williams Research Center on Chartres Street, a division of the Historic New Orleans Collection, for her diligence in helping me access and sift through a vast number of documents to find those pertinent to my story; and finally, Claire Henderson at the National Railroad Train Station Museum on Basin Street, for helping me envision exactly where The Wanderer would have gotten off the train.

Invaluable to my research as well were the aforementioned Williams Research Center; the Historic New Orleans digital collection at www.hnoc.org; the Louisiana Digital Library at http://louisdl.louislibraries.org; the Catholic Encyclopedia at http://www.newadvent.org/cathen; the Catholic Study Bible Second Edition (New American Bible); and the King James Bible online at http://www.kingjames bibleonline.org.

Anyone familiar with religious texts knows about the Psalms. My hope is that someday I'll be able to turn the joy in my heart into a Psalm of thanksgiving and offer it to God, for He has been good to me.

Insights,
Interviews
& More . . .

Meet Rita Leganski

RITA LEGANSKI grew up in northern
Wisconsin, and believes it was the
long and magical winters of her
childhood that cultivated her
imagination and love of books,
especially Southern literature. She
holds a BA in literary studies and
creative writing from DePaul
University's School for New Learning,
where she won the Arthur Weinberg
Memorial Prize, as well as an MA in
writing and publishing from DePaul.
She currently teaches writing courses
at the School for New Learning. She
and her husband, Paul, live in the
Chicago area with a Siamese cat
named Tiramisu and an orange
tabby named Jeebz. ∾

The Southern Side of My Heart

I GREW UP IN NORTHERN WISCONSIN, where winter makes the snow squeak under your boots and turns your breath into crystals of ice. But summer does come around, full of sunshine and the smell of earth and most usually a breeze from the west. Whatever the season, it was a wonderful place to curl up with a book; I did it all the time in a well-worn wing chair in my room, or on a makeshift couch in the sunporch.

Southern writers were my favorites—Carson McCullers, William Faulkner, Eudora Welty, Tennessee Williams, Harper Lee, and many, many others. They took me from the plains of my northern home to a landscape vined in lushness, where flora had names like magnolia, scuppernong, and trumpet creeper; where people had names like Scout, Calpurnia, and Battle Fairchild; where places had names like Yoknapatawpha; and where a streetcar was named Desire. I got lost in that place of different constellations, with its mint juleps and velvet evenings.

After high school, I left my small town for a job in a bigger city. I always intended to go to college—the best-laid plans and ▸

all—but I got married, and then the children came along. It wasn't until they were grown that I finally earned bachelor's and master's degrees at DePaul University in Chicago, and determined that I would become a writer.

This novel began to form in graduate school as an assignment to write a short story. The first thing I did was type out a title: "The Silence of Bonaventure Arrow." It had come to me with no forethought at all, and it instantly felt right. Next I began to write character sketches. The eponymous Bonaventure was a mute little boy with a gift of rarest hearing. He was quickly followed by Grandma Roman, Dancy, William, Brother Harley John Eacomb, and Trinidad Prefontaine. Last, I imagined the International Church of the Elevated Forthright Gospel.

I heard echoes of those favorite Southern writers of mine, and so I set my story in 1950s Louisiana in the fictional town of Bayou Cymbaline. A magical, haunted, and lovely place steeped in faith and superstition—the ideal home for a gifted little boy who could hear fantastic sounds.

I finished with graduate school, but not with Bonaventure Arrow; I went back into that short story, adding characters and events and weaving a larger plot. Letice and Remington joined the cast, as did Mr. and Mrs. Silvey, Tristan Duvais, Gabe Riley, Calypso Fontenaise, and that most complex of women, Suville Jean-Baptiste. The last to join the story were Eugenia Babbitt, The Wanderer, and the retired Pinkerton, Coleman Tate. As I wrote, Bayou Cymbaline became a metaphorical house of God, a place of joy and sorrow and forgiveness, with Bonaventure and Trinidad its partners in salvation.

While most of the book takes place in made-up Bayou Cymbaline, some of it happens in New Orleans. Trust me—no one could make up New Orleans. When this novel was in the later stages, I went there to verify my research. But one does not "go" to New Orleans; one experiences it. New Orleans is music and sass. It is beads and carnival and Creole spice. If it were human, New Orleans might be a society lady with holes in her stockings and her feet in dancing shoes.

Being there allowed me to walk the streets of the story I had written, going where my characters had gone, placing them squarely in the reality of the Garden District and the ▶

unforgettable French Quarter. I ate beignets at Café Du Monde and was charmed by Antoine's Restaurant. I took in the elegance of the Hotel Monteleone and checked the time on its wonderful clock. I went to the Roosevelt to see for myself where Letice's wedding reception would have been. I strolled past Saint Anthony's Garden tucked there behind Saint Louis Cathedral, that most beautiful church on Jackson Square. I looked in the windows of Rubenstein's. I found houses like those I had imagined for my characters—Consette's on Esplanade Avenue in Faubourg Marigny, Suville's on Dauphine Street in the Quarter, and William's on Washington Avenue in the Garden District. I rode the St. Charles streetcar. I saw where The Wanderer had gotten off the train. I went to cemeteries. I saw angels made of stone.

New Orleans is fiercely and justifiably proud of its uniqueness. I was fortunate enough to meet some of the extraordinary people who take pains to preserve its history; they offered me not only Southern hospitality but incredible expertise. An extensive visit to the Williams Research Center on Chartres Street led me to archivists who provided access to the Historic New Orleans Collection, which yielded artifacts from the 1920s to the 1950s—train schedules, Mardi Gras tickets, menus, and hotel bills—all things my characters would have seen or even touched. Concierges gave wonderful directions, and in one case, a gentle correction: Initially I had The Wanderer arriving in New Orleans on the Great Southern Railway. But when I mentioned that to Mr. Charles Farrae, the charming historian at the Monteleone, he said in his smooth-as-butter New Orleans accent, "Why no, dawlin'. That would have been the Panama Limited. It left Chicago at five in the evening and arrived in New Orleans 9:30 next morning. There would have been a glorious breakfast."

Of course research proved Charlie right. It was indeed the Panama Limited, a Pullman with a wonderful dining car—a fitting thing to have with a destination like New Orleans.

Though every effort was made to achieve historical accuracy in this book, it is after all a work of fiction. Though most places I mention with regard to New Orleans really do or did exist, I must ask the reader to imagine that a law firm called Robillard & ▶

The Southern Side of My Heart *(continued)*

Broome had offices on Magazine Street, and that the A&P Tea Company had a grocery store near the corner of Gravier and Tchoupitoulas.

You can't forget a name like Tchoupitoulas. Even as I write it here, I'm taken back to the Southern literature I love so much, and other unforgettable names—Atticus Finch and Boo Radley; Goodhue Coldfield and Eulalia Bon Sutpen; Berenice Sadie Brown and John Henry West. I am imagining Spanish moss dripping from trees and dogwood flowering profusely. And I am willingly lost once again in the Southern side of my heart. ∾

All-Time Favorite Books

BOOKS ARE THE STRONGEST MAGIC—they can bend reality into unexpected shapes. The best of them bend our thoughts and feelings until they, too, have taken on a new shape. My favorite books are those in which the writer's voice is unique and the language is rhythmic and lyrical—think *One Hundred Years of Solitude* by Gabriel García Márquez. I also love a strong sense of time and place.

Here are some books that have had a great influence on me:

A Gracious Plenty by Sheri Reynolds

The voice is strong from the start, and so are the characters, especially the narrator, Finch Nobles. Imagine a disfigured and sassy outcast and you've got Finch, a cemetery caretaker who talks to the dead—but the thing is, the dead talk back. Finch finds out that even the promise of acceptance can be enough to keep you going. That's something we all need to be aware of.

A Good Man is Hard to Find by Flannery O'Connor

I owe much to the short story for which this collection is named. O'Connor's very Southern voice is unforgettable, and her ►

characterizations are flawless. I'm not sure I could have come up with Adelaide Roman without having read Flannery O'Connor.

Peace Like a River by Leif Enger

Reminiscent narrator Reuben Land tells an unforgettable story of love, loss, and faith as seen through the eyes of his eleven-year-old self. Although he is plainspoken, his voice is mesmerizing as he relates the quest he went on with his father, Jeremiah, and younger sister, the feisty and memorable Swede, as they searched for their fugitive son and brother, Davy. Leif Enger makes the ordinary extraordinary as he writes of life and death and miracles.

The Member of the Wedding by Carson McCullers

This story is told by an anonymous third-person narrator possessed of a uniquely Southern way with words. It's my favorite when it comes to a character-driven story. In a short period of time, twelve-year-old tomboy Frankie Addams undergoes emotional transformation as she awkwardly tries to be accepted. She goes from Frankie to F. Jasmine and finally refers to herself as Frances in an attempt at sophistication. Frankie is mostly an irascible child, yet you can't help but be touched by her vulnerability. Carson McCullers explores hope and despair as a rite of passage in this book. Like Frankie, we all yearn to belong.

The Magician's Assistant by Ann Patchett

With masterful prose, Ann Patchett explores the human condition: the nature of love and the need for it, the complexities of trust, the lure of secrets, and the redemptive power of starting over. It's a superb story in which death is the catalyst for action.

To Kill a Mockingbird by Harper Lee

Told by the reminiscent narrator Scout Finch, this book will be forever relevant. There is nothing more to say. I've lost count of how many times I've read it, and I'll read it many times more.

Life of Pi by Yann Martel

Philosophy is twined around fantasy in this wonderful story within a story. Not only is Pi adrift on a lifeboat, he's also in the company of a hyena, a zebra, an orangutan, and a talking Bengal tiger named Richard Parker. One by one the characters are killed off until eventually just Pi and Richard Parker are left. This ▶

insightful tale brings a startling revelation about instinct, will, and survival.

As I Lay Dying by William Faulkner

As with many of Faulkner's novels, this one is set in Yoknapatawpha County, Mississippi. Addie Bundren has died, and her family sets out to honor her wish to be buried in the town of Jefferson; however, the task proves quite eventful. There are motivations at work, and therein lies the story. Chapter nineteen is just five words long: "My mother is a fish." It doesn't get much more intriguing than that.

Dubliners by James Joyce

This collection of short stories is immortal. Joyce's characters range from young to old and occupy different stations in life, but they all undergo a common experience— they come to know themselves. It's purely lovely.

The Curious Case of Benjamin Button by F. Scott Fitzgerald

Fitzgerald's simple yet elegant plot turns time backward. I love the idea of an inexplicably different child aging from old man to infant.

The Third Angel by Alice Hoffman

This is a skillfully crafted retrospective that unravels the interwoven lives of three different women, all of them looking for something to believe in. This is a story about strength, weakness, and the fascinating nature of love. ∾